A cry escaped Star's lips as she found herself in Kyle's arms, her body pressed against his lean frame, her arms about his shoulders. His mouth was only inches from hers as she gaped up at him, wide-eyed with shock from their close contact.

A slow, mischievous grin curled one corner of his shapely mouth as he smiled down at her and tightened his arms about her waist, drawing her closer to his warmth. Before she could protest, his lips claimed hers in a searing kiss.

The feeling of his mouth, combined with her earlier kind thoughts about him, made Star forget her bitterness toward Kyle. She responded to the subtle, heady caress. . . .

"Cordia Byers once again delights her readers with a charming, sassy heroine, an irresistibly sexy hero, and love scenes that make your bones melt."

Affair de Coeur on PIRATE ROYALE

PIRATE ROYALE won a Reviewer's Choice Award from
Romantic Times

STAR OF
THE WEST

Cordia Byers

FAWCETT GOLD MEDAL • NEW YORK

Chapter 1

The chorus of spring frogs and the distant rumble of a paddle wheeler upon the Mississippi were the only sounds to disturb the stillness of the night. Moonlight silvered the sleeping white blooms and waxy leaves of the magnolias that surrounded the elegant mansion known as Jasmine Hall. The sultry breeze from the river stirred the dark green foliage and caught the sweet fragrance of the jasmine for which the plantation had been named. Its gentle current moved across the landscape and floated upward to the intricately crafted wrought-iron balcony that gracefully wrapped the mansion's second story on three sides with vines of iron jasmine.

Savoring the heady aroma that scented the tranquil evening, Star Grayson lifted her thick cascade of hair off her neck to catch the cooling breeze as she stood gazing out across the moon-drenched land that had been her home since birth. As she felt the caress of the cool air against her flesh, a sigh of contentment escaped her soft, full lips. She ruffled the ebony curls before letting them fall once more down her back to her waist.

"Within the week, I'll be eighteen and the bride of Brett Tremayne," she murmured dreamily to the night as she rested her cheek against one of the twelve Doric columns that rose majestically from veranda to roof. A sense of euphoria settled about her at the thought of the handsome man who had asked her to become his wife. So much had changed since she had met Brett two months earlier. After years of loneliness, her life had suddenly seemed to right itself when Brett entered it.

It had been seven years since her world had come crashing down around her. Until she was eleven her life had been filled with love and happiness. That had abruptly changed with her father's death. She had been left in the care of her stepmother, Fiona Grayson, who, though only twenty-three herself, had made certain that her step-daughter knew who was in control of Jasmine Hall soon after Charles Grayson's funeral. She had regulated Star into the position she deemed proper for what she considered an obnoxious burden placed upon her shoulders by her husband's early demise. She had no wish to be saddled with the responsibility of a child at her young age and had left Star in the servants' care to resume her carefree life.

Fiona firmly believed in the old adage: Out of sight, out of mind. She preferred the excitement of Natchez to the gracious life of the plantation and seldom visited Jasmine Hall after her husband's death. When she did make one of her infrequent visits it was not out of concern for her stepdaughter's welfare but to entertain friends from the city. Fiona thought little of the gangly-limbed child who was growing into a beautiful, lonely young woman who desperately needed love and companionship.

Reflecting upon the past years spent virtually alone at Jasmine Hall, Star knew that her life had given her a strength that most young women her age lacked. With only the slaves to say yea or nay, she had grown independent, doing much as she pleased against all of the protests of Dulcie, her maid and constant companion through all of her exploits.

While most young ladies were learning to become efficient housewives, Star was teaching herself to shoot her father's guns. It had not been easy without someone experienced with firearms to guide her, but after many months of aching shoulders and arms, she had finally become competent enough with the rifle and pistol to hit the bull's-eye on the target. Learning to use the guns had not been the extent of her adventures. She had learned to swim by accident. It had been either swim or drown and she had chosen the former quickly enough after falling into the river while fishing. After that it had not been unusual for Dulcie to find Star stripped down to her chemise and pantalets, ready for an early morning swim in the river. Her exploits would have had the mothers of other young women pulling their hair out by the roots, but after several more of her daring feats, the slaves at Jasmine Hall had come to accept her actions as normal and had stopped worrying.

The slight smile that her memories aroused faded as her mind returned once more to Fiona. Her stepmother's neglect had made one part of her much stronger while another part of her had suffered through the years of adolescence, a time when a young girl needed a mother's love most of all. Her father had done his best to make up for the fact that she had lost her mother at birth and his love had been enough to assure her a happy childhood. However his death had come at a time in her life when she was the most vulnerable; when she was changing from a child into a young woman and needed a parent's love and understanding to see her through that volatile period. Star had been left filled with uncertainties about herself. Through the years she had managed to keep her insecurities hidden, but deep within her young heart she had grown to feel that for some unknown reason, no one could love her. She had not been able to conquer that feeling until Brett had entered her life and swept her off her feet with his blond, boyish good looks and a charming manner that made her feel beautiful and wanted.

Star frowned into the night. Of late her stepmother's actions had been totally out of character for the woman she had known over the past lonely years. Recently Fiona had begun to act as if she realized for the first time that she had a stepdaughter. She had come to Jasmine Hall more often and had begun to pay attention to Star. She had ordered Star's wardrobe refurbished and invited her to the elegant parties that she gave when her friends arrived from the city. That in itself had been unusual. In the past she had forbidden Star even to watch the dancing from the top of the stairs.

Her friendly overtures puzzled Star, but she would not question Fiona's sudden change of heart. She was too grateful to her for having invited Brett to Jasmine Hall. If only for that one thing, Fiona would always have her gratitude. Wrapped in the warm glow of her newfound love for Brett, she didn't hold any harsh feelings toward Fiona for the years of neglect. Everything was too wonderful to let past grievances mar the beauty of her approaching wedding to the man she loved.

A movement near the edge of the lawn caught Star's eye, interrupting her visions of the future she would share with Brett Tremayne. Curious as to the reason why any of the slaves would be skulking about so late at night, she watched from her vantage point on the dark balcony. All had been quiet at Jasmine Hall for well over an hour and the only reason she was not curled snuggled in her bed was the fact that she was too excited about her wedding to sleep.

She remained still and quiet as the man emerged from the deepest shadows beneath the magnolias and quickly strode along the path that led to her father's study. The shadows of the balcony hid her from his view, but she was able to see him clearly. The moonlight silvered his pale hair and wide shoulders. It was her betrothed, Brett Tremayne.

At the sight of Brett, her heart began to race wildly within her breast and she opened her mouth to call out to him, before some sixth sense warned her to remain silent. Something in the way he moved seemed to indicate his desire to keep his presence undiscovered.

Never one to deny her own natural curiosity, Star crept stealthily along the balcony to the winding stairs that led to the garden below. Her thin silk night rail molded itself to her shapely legs as she sped barefoot down the circular steps to the dew-dampened grass. The hem of the gown and her feet were quickly wet as she made her way toward the circle of light that spilled through the double french doors, still ajar after Brett's entrance. The soft sound of voices from within the study drew her forward until she could recognize that it was Fiona with whom Brett spoke. Yet something in their muffled tones made her seek the deepest shadows so that her presence would not be noticed. Instinct ruled her actions as she edged closer to the open doors so that she could hear their conversation clearly.

"Have you no sense at all in that handsome head of yours, Brett?" Fiona asked, her voice tinged with exasperation. The clink of glass against glass betrayed the fact that she was pouring two glasses of Charles Grayson's treasured stock of fine Madeira. "You could have ruined everything by coming here tonight. Whatever possessed you?"

"It's late, love. I waited until everyone had retired for the night before I ventured near. No one will ever know that I came back to Jasmine Hall before my wedding to our dear sweet Star," Brett said, and laughed. "As for what possessed me, I should venture to guess that you already know the answer to that, Fiona."

"What if one of the slaves saw you, or even Star? You could have jeopardized everything that we have worked to gain."

"Calm yourself, Fiona. No one would take a slave's word against mine and as for Star, the lamp in her chamber went out well over an hour ago. She's now dreaming of our wedding the day after tomorrow. And even if she had seen me, I could have convinced the poor, misguided child that I had come back to see her because I couldn't stay away any longer."

"Do you think she would have believed you?"

"Of course she would. She's in love with me, or haven't you noticed the cow-eyed expression she gets on her face every time I come into the room?" Brett chuckled as he took a sip of wine. "Ah, this is delicious. I have to give old Charles credit for his taste in wine as well as women.''

''I've noticed quite a few things of late and they do not please me,'' Fiona said, ignoring his last comment.

''Don't tell me you are jealous of your little stepdaughter, Fiona?'' Brett said, giving her a roguish smile and arching one sandy brow.

Fiona set her glass abruptly on the table. ''Do I have need to be jealous, Brett?''

''What do you think, my love?''

''Damn you, Brett. I had better not have a reason to be jealous of that little brat. You and I both know the reason you are marrying her and I won't put up with anything else.''

Star managed to stifle her moan of protest and pain as their cruel words assaulted her. Yet she was unable to stop herself and as if drawn by a magnet, she eased closer to the door and peered through the crack at her stepmother and the man who had stolen her heart. She flinched as Brett also set his glass down with a loud clink and pushed himself from the chair. He grabbed Fiona by the upper arms and drew her against his lean body.

''Now is not the time for your jealousy, my dear. We are too near to reaching our goals. Once the marriage is performed then we will have total control over Grayson's estate. I'll be able to clear my debts and then we'll be free to do as we want. This fit of temper does not suit you or our plans for the future, so I suggest you calm yourself. If Star should ever suspect there is anything between us, then everything we've done will have been for nothing.''

''Brett, you're hurting me.''

''I'll do more than hurt you if you jinx my marriage to Star. I need that money much more than I need you, my dear Fiona,'' Brett growled insultingly as he shoved her from him.

''Sometimes I hate you as much as I hate that little baggage upstairs,'' Fiona whimpered, her voice filling with tears as she rubbed her bruised flesh. ''I married

Charles so that I wouldn't ever have to live in poverty again and since his death I've had to rake and scrape to live off the pittance he left me in his will. That little brat of his gets everything while I have to suffer. I won't allow her to have you as well, Brett.''

''Hate me, Fiona? No, you don't hate me because I'm the only man who has learned your little quirks. I'm the only man who can please you like this,'' Brett murmured with a cruel little smile curling his lips as he recaptured her within his arms and ground his mouth down on hers, hard and brutally.

Fiona whimpered again and then wrapped her arms about his neck, pressing her body to his, her hips writhing against his. As their kiss ended, she looked up at him, panting with desire, her eyes glazed. She moistened her lips with the tip of her tongue and her voice was husky as she said, ''Brett, I'm sorry. I know you don't care for Star. It's just that my temper is always on edge when I'm at Jasmine Hall and separated from you. I want to be free of this place and my stepdaughter once and for all. I love you, Brett, you know I do.''

''I know that, love, but you have to be patient for only a few more days. Then it will all be ours,'' Brett murmured, his own voice growing husky as he gazed down into her large, pale blue eyes.

Fiona smiled seductively up at him as she ran her hand up the ruffled front of his chest, her nails digging into the white silk like a cat seeking to be petted. She moved her hips against his again as she said, ''I know you're right, but I prefer to spend our time together doing other things than discussing my stepdaughter's marriage.''

''I, too, Fiona,'' was all Brett said as he lowered his mouth to hers once more.

Star stood frozen, watching them from her hiding place as silence enveloped the room. She could taste the sweetness of her own blood where she had bitten down on her lip to keep from screaming in agony as their words split her heart asunder. All of her old insecurities rose hauntingly from the depths into which she had forced them after meeting Brett. Her stepmother and her betrothed had managed to confirm what she had suspected all along, that she was incapable of being loved.

They had taught her a cruel lesson, but she would heed it well. Never again would she be so gullible as to believe such lies. Never again would she trust anyone as she had done Brett Tremayne.

The young girl whose lonely life had made her desperate for love vanished into the still Mississippi night as Star blocked off the pain and shuttered her feelings. In her place stood a woman determined to see that Fiona and Brett would not succeed in their scheme to take her inheritance away from her.

Drawing in a deep breath, she squared her shoulders. An air of resolve that had been lacking in her demeanor only a short while before now surrounded her as she stepped from the shadows through the doorway. Her staunch vows wavered precariously for a moment as she watched the couple embrace, but she refused to give way to the urge to flee into the night, screaming in misery. She might suffer, but she would not allow herself to let anyone know of her feelings. The strength she had gained through the years now stood her in good stead. Clearing her throat loudly, she then smiled sweetly at the couple as they jerked abruptly away from each other.

"I assume this means our wedding has been canceled, Brett?" she said, forcing her voice to remain calm.

"Uh, Star," Brett stuttered, his face turning several shades of red. "This isn't what you think, my darling. I came only to clear up several matters about our wedding settlement and uh—we were—I mean I was only showing Fiona my gratitude for introducing me to one so lovely as yourself. It was nothing more, I can assure you."

Star looked from one shocked face to the other, hot anger overshadowing her hurt. Her dark blue eyes sparkled with ire as she stared them down without mercy.

"Do you honestly expect me to believe that lie, Brett? I've been a gullible fool far too long as it is, but that has now come to an end. I heard your devious plans and I can assure you both that our wedding will not take place," she said, her gaze sweeping scathingly over Fiona. "As for you, my dear devoted stepmother, I expect you to have your bags packed and be gone from Jasmine Hall by early tomorrow. I will notify the guests that the wedding has been postponed indefinitely."

"You spoiled brat," Fiona growled, and took a step toward Star, "I'll not take orders from you. This is my home."

"As of tonight, you are no longer welcome here, Fiona. This is my home, not yours. Next week I will be eighteen and by my father's request Jasmine Hall and all else he owned will come to me. If you will recall, I was present when his will was read, though as I remember it, you didn't approve of my presence at the time. I know exactly what is stated in Father's will and I also know that had I married Brett, everything I was to inherit would have gone to him automatically under the law." Seeing Fiona blanch under her direct attack, Star did not relent. "Be grateful that I don't go to Father's attorney and tell him of your schemes so you won't be cut off from your allowance."

"Star, this is all a misunderstanding. If you will only listen to me for a minute and calm down, I can explain everything. You know that I love you." Brett sought desperately to diffuse the situation before all of his plans dissolved before his eyes.

"Explain!" Star exploded as she rounded on him with her fists clenched tightly at her sides. "I'm not the simpleton you seem to believe. You can't explain what I heard. I know of your plans and there will be no wedding. You do not love me, nor did you ever. You only wanted my inheritance to pay off your debts. Get out of my home, Brett. I never want to lay eyes on you again for as long as I live."

Star clamped a mental fist around her emotions as she gazed into his boyishly handsome face. How she had adored that face less than an hour before. Brett Tremayne was magnificent to look upon with his golden, wheat-colored hair and cornflower-blue eyes that were fringed with russet lashes. His smile had often made her knees grow weak when he bestowed it upon her. Even now, knowing of his deceit, the attraction his masculine beauty had upon her was still strong.

Firmly reiterating her vows to herself and remembering all she had heard, she turned her back on him and strode from the study. She had to get away from him. Her emotions were still too raw and vulnerable where he was concerned. She had succeeded in foiling their scheme but at great expense to herself. Her resolve, no matter how firm, had not shielded her from the pain of her breaking heart. Her throat was constricted with unshed tears as she began to ascend the winding, dark walnut staircase to her chamber.

The sound of angry voices erupted from the study and floated upward as the door was jerked open and Fiona rushed out into the foyer. Her face was wild with rage as she looked up and saw Star at the top of the stairs. She did not slow her steps, but raced up, taking the stairs two at a time, and grabbed her stepdaughter by the arm, jerking her about to face her.

"You little, ungrateful bitch. You think you can order me about as if I was one of your slaves? Well, you can't. I am still your stepmother and you will do as I say until you are eighteen years of age. The wedding will take place as I have planned. Your bastard of a father didn't see fit to leave me Jasmine Hall, but I'll not be cheated out of what I deserve by his brat. You will marry Brett or you'll live to regret it."

Star's temper snapped. She jerked her arm free of Fiona's hand and glared at her. Her dark blue eyes shone like sapphires as she spat, "You can go to hell. I'm not marrying Brett so the two of you can have what is rightfully mine. Now get out of my way, Fiona. I've had enough of you during the last ten years and I won't put up with any more. I have suffered at your hand for the last time."

"Suffered! You know nothing of suffering yet, you little hussy. I'll have you stripped and whipped like one of the slaves if you disobey me again.''

''Fiona, you're mad,'' Star said, and started to turn away.

''No, you don't, bitch. You're not going to walk away from me until this is settled.'' Fiona grabbed Star's arm, jerking her backwards toward the top of the stairs.

Star spun about and her hand crashed against Fiona's cheek with the impact of a pistol shot. Fiona screeched like a mad animal and grabbed her face. Her eyes narrowed to mere slits as she launched herself at Star with a low growl, grabbing a handful of ebony curls with such force Star felt her scalp would come loose from her head. Her only thought was to protect herself as she grasped Fiona's wrist and pulled her hand free. Her stepmother staggered backwards, teetering on the stair landing before regaining her balance.

''I'll kill you,'' Fiona screamed, and again launched herself at Star.

Star ducked to avoid the talonlike fingers aimed at her face. She fell to her knees to one side as Fiona's momentum carried her to the edge of the stairs again. Star saw her stepmother's expression change from mad anger to one of fear as she frantically sought any hold that would keep her from falling. There was none. Before Star had time to move to help her, Fiona screamed in terror and tumbled backwards. She fell head over heels, her frilly petticoats tangling about her legs, and landed with a dull thud at the foot of the curving staircase. She lay with her arms and legs sprawled about her, a wound on her head tinting the blond hair a sickening shade of reddish brown.

Star stared down at her stepmother with dawning horror. She knew without having to be told that Fiona was dead. No one could have survived such a fall. She stood frozen in place, unable to make her legs carry her down the steps to confirm her belief as Brett bent over Fiona's prone form. In a haze of shock she watched as he placed his fingers against her stepmother's throat and shook his

head before removing his velvet jacket and placing it over
her pale face. That done, he rose and slowly turned to
look up at Star, his face inscrutable.

"You killed her," was all he said.

"No, it was an accident. You saw what happened. She
attacked me and then fell," Star murmured, and began
to shiver uncontrollably.

"I know that, but the officials don't," Brett said, a
small smile of victory touching his lips. Placing one
carefully manicured hand on the bannister, he started to
ascend the stairs. "It seems, my dear, that our wedding
will take place after all."

Star frowned, unable to comprehend Brett's unspoken
threat. "How can you even think of such a thing at a
time like this? The authorities must be notified at once
about Fiona's accident."

"I'll notify the authorities all right if you don't agree
to marry me, Star," Brett said as he reached the landing
and stood gazing into her ashen features.

"Are you mad? You already have my answer about
marrying you. Now, please send someone for the sheriff," Star said, her eyes resting once more on the velvet
jacket amid the ruffles and torn lace.

"Yes, you'll marry me, Star, or you'll hang for the
murder of your stepmother. Remember I saw it all and
I'm the only person who can clear your name. Either you
marry me or I'll tell the sheriff of your fight with Fiona
and that you pushed her intentionally down the stairs."
Brett ran the tip of his finger along the smooth line of
Star's pale cheek. Tipping up her chin, he looked down
into her bewildered eyes. "What is it to be? The choice
is now up to you, my dear."

The import of his threat registered through her shock
and made her feel as if she would faint for the first time
in her life. She had always had a strong constitution, but
the events of the last hours had sapped her strength. Unbidden tears brimmed in her eyes as she gazed up at the
man she had thought she loved. At that moment she won-

dered how she could have been so blind as not to see the evil that he seemed to exude from every pore.

She squeezed her eyes tightly closed in an effort to shut out the sight of his smirking, victorious face and shook her head as she murmured, "I can't think right now. I need time."

"Time, my dear? That you don't have. Down there lies your dead stepmother and she can't remain there forever. You have to make your decision. It should be a very simple matter to decide. Marry me or hang. I see no great difficulty in choosing between the two. It's life or death." Brett slowly moved his finger from her chin down along her throat to rest at the curve of her collarbone where her pulse fluttered.

"Brett, for the love of God, have you no human feelings at all? Fiona is dead and all you can think of is gaining my inheritance to appease your greed."

"My dear little innocent. My feelings have nothing to do with it. Fiona was a good bed partner when she was alive, but that was all she was to me. You see, my reputation depends upon our marriage. I've acquired certain debts and if they are not paid soon then I'm ruined. I can't let that happen."

A spark of hope flared within Star as she looked up at Brett. "If that's all it is, then I'll pay your debts when I come into my inheritance. There is no reason for us to marry." Star sought desperately to extricate herself from the web he was weaving about her.

"No, Star," Brett murmured softly, bestowing his most charming smile upon her. "My debts are only one reason that I desire our marriage. You see, I've acquired a taste for a certain young virgin and I will not be satisfied until I have had her."

A shiver of revulsion raced up Star's spine and settled like a coil of squirming snakes in the pit of her stomach. The thought of Brett touching her so intimately made her want to retch. She had to find a way out of the nightmare situation, but at the present moment she could think of little else beyond the still figure at the bottom of the stairs.

"Brett, please. I feel faint. Can we not discuss this once you've seen to Fiona?" Star pleaded as she gave way to the weakness invading her limbs. She swayed and clutched at the railing for support.

Noting the white line that formed about her lips and her ashen features, Brett reluctantly gave way to her demands for the moment. His time would come after he attended to Fiona. "All right, Star. Go to your room while I see to your stepmother's body. Once that is taken care of, I'll expect your answer."

Star was too relieved by her momentary reprieve to argue. She fled to her room as if all the devils of hell were unleashed upon her heels. Slamming the door behind her, she latched it securely, though she knew her actions could hardly keep all the horrors beyond the portal at bay.

Leaning back against the door, she gulped in ragged breaths of air and fought the hysteria that was rising in her throat, threatening to overcome her. The rose silk of her night rail trembled across her breasts and her heart pounded as she sank to the floor and covered her face with her hands. The tears she had been holding in check now wet her fingers as she wept out her misery and fear.

At last, when no more tears would come, she slowly raised her head and with red, swollen eyes, stared at the moon-drenched chamber. She was weary from the emotional strain of the last hour, but her tears had seemed to cleanse the cobwebs from her mind. She could at least think coherently about all that had transpired and about what she had to do to prevent Brett from succeeding with his diabolical scheme.

Pushing herself to her feet, Star crossed to the bedside table and lit the candle. For one long moment she gazed at the blue and gold chamber as if imprinting its image upon her memory. Jasmine Hall was her home, but if Brett Tremayne had his way, it would soon belong to him. That thought spurred her into action. Crossing to the cherry-wood armoire, she opened it and rummaged through it until she found what she had been seeking: her old, battered portmanteau.

She knew there was only one thing she could do to stop Brett and that was to leave everything she loved. It was the only decision that she could make under the circumstances. She would not allow herself to be forced into marriage with such a man, nor could she stay and let herself be convicted of a murder she did not commit.

Star jerked several gowns from the armoire before she paused abruptly, a new problem arising in her mind. A tiny frown marred her smooth brow and her knuckles whitened about the fabric in her hand as she realized she had to run, but to where? There was no one to whom she could turn for help. Because of her seclusion at Jasmine Hall, she had no real friends on the nearby plantations, nor did she have any relatives nearby who would give her refuge from Brett. She had an aunt who lived in Texas, but she had never met her. By the time Star sent a message to her for help, it would be far too late. There was also no guarantee that she would receive any help from her aunt. Charles Grayson and his sister, Clarice, had been estranged since before Star's birth. She did not know what had caused the rift between them, but the years had not lessened it. Even as her father lay dying he had refused to let anyone notify Clarice of his illness.

With a resigned sigh, Star stuffed the gowns into her portmanteau and snapped it shut. As in the past, it was now left to her to care for herself. She could depend on no one else. At the present moment, her main concern was to get away from Jasmine Hall before Brett grew suspicious. Once she accomplished that, she could decide about what she would do in the future.

Star jerked upright and stiffened with trepidation at the sound of the light knock upon her door. She had hoped to avoid another confrontation with Brett, but that hope quickly faded.

Star's only chance at escape now was that she could

put him off a little longer without him guessing her intentions. Pushing her portmanteau into the shadows behind the bed, she braced herself to meet him as another tap came at the door.

"Missy, it's me, Dulcie. Let me in."

Star rushed across to the door. The wave of relief she felt at hearing Dulcie's muffled whisper was so great that her hands trembled on the latch as she fumbled with it and finally managed to slide it back. She threw the door open and let her maid enter.

"Dulcie, thank God. I thought you were Brett," Star whispered as she closed the door and relatched it.

"I know," Dulcie said, "but you don't have to worry about that man for a while. After he carried Miz Fiona into the drawing room, he went back into your papa's study and started swilling down Master Charles's best brandy."

"Then you know all that has happened?"

"I shore do. I see'd it and heard what that man aims to do."

"Then you can support my statement to the authorities that I didn't murder Fiona," Star said, her face reflecting the relief she felt at not having to leave her home.

"Missy, I would, but it wouldn't do you no good. No white man would take my word against that of another of his own kind."

Star's features fell as she realized the truth of what Dulcie had said. Her last hope of remaining at Jasmine Hall vanished.

"Dulcie, I can't stay here, or Brett will force me to marry him. Will you help me?"

"I been with you for most of your life, Missy, and I don't intend to leave you now when you need me the most," Dulcie said, and gave Star an encouraging smile.

"Thank you, Dulcie," Star murmured, hugging her. "I knew I could count on you. You've always been there to get me out of trouble."

"I just hope I can this time, Missy. What do you want me to do?"

Star pondered the maid's question, her delicately arched brows knitting across the bridge of her slender nose. She tugged at her lower lip with her teeth for a long moment before she said, "Dulcie, if I'm to get away, I'll need money, but I don't have any. Do you know where Fiona kept the money for the household expenses?" Dulcie nodded, with a secretive smile. "Then go and get it. With that and the jewelry my mother left me, I might be able to reach Aunt Clarice in Texas. It's my only hope."

"Texas?" the maid asked, her dark brown eyes widening in bewilderment. "How you a going to get all the way out there, Missy?"

"For the life of me, I don't know," Star replied honestly. "But at the moment I have nowhere else to turn. She's my only relative and my only hope."

"Obioma might help," Dulcie said, her ebony face brightening with the idea.

"The Swamp Witch?" Star asked. She well recalled her first and last meeting with the old woman known to all in the area as the Swamp Witch. A chill tingled up her spine at the memory. It had been years since the day she had gone with Dulcie to visit the old woman who lived in the swamp brewing herbs and elixirs for those who believed in her healing powers.

Though she had never been one to frighten easily, that visit had made the gooseflesh rise on her arms. Passing through the misty tendrils of fog that swirled about the trunks of the moss-shrouded cypress on the way to the tiny cabin built on stilts above the marshy ground had been enough to scare young Star, but her meeting with Obioma had terrified her.

The old woman, with her gnarled hands, deeply lined face, and mane of grizzled hair that hung in a wild, unkempt curtain to her waist, had been everything that Star's childish mind had conceived a witch to be. She had cowered near the doorway as Dulcie exchanged a ham for the elixir the cook had sent her to get for the belly cramps that had been plaguing the people at Jasmine Hall since the fresh vegetables had come into season.

"Why would she want to help us?" Star asked now as she tried to quell the eerie feeling the memory aroused.

Dulcie glanced away from Star, an uneasy expression crossing her dark face. Her words came out hesitantly, "Obioma often helps those in need."

"Dulcie, what is it you're not telling me?" Star demanded, sensing some unspoken meaning behind her maid's answer.

Dulcie's long dark fingers contrasted starkly with her white apron as she fidgeted with it at her waist. She stared down at the floor when at last she spoke, "Obioma knows how to get you 'way from Jasmine Hall 'cause she often help her own people get free of the white man's shackles."

Star gaped at her maid in astonishment, dumbfounded to learn that there was much more to the old woman's activities in the swamp than just the brewing of elixirs.

"You mean Obioma is part of the Underground Railroad?" Star asked. Even in her sheltered world at Jasmine Hall she had heard of the secret organization that helped slaves escape from their white masters.

Dulcie seemed torn between her love for her white mistress and loyalty to her own people. Slowly she nodded and then once more lowered her eyes to her hands.

For one fleeting moment Star felt the prickle of irritation toward the old woman who worked to undermine the foundations on which her life-style was built. But such feelings soon fled with her understanding. Until tonight she would not have been able to understand the reasons behind Obioma's work, but in the last hours Brett Tremayne had made her look at life differently. She now knew what it would be like to be in the position of having another human being dominate your life; giving you no choice but to obey or suffer the consequences. She didn't like that feeling at all.

With her understanding, hope flared within Star's breast. If what Dulcie said was true, then Obioma might be able to help her. As part of the Underground Railroad, the Swamp Witch would have many connections and could possibly help Star get away before Brett had time to summon the sheriff and raise a posse to look for her.

"Dulcie, I pray that you're right. Obioma may be our only chance."

"Obioma be a good woman, Missy," Dulcie whispered, and smiled as she crossed to the door and inched it open. Peering into the hallway to make certain that she would not be seen, the maid slipped quietly from the room and rapidly made her way to the master bedchamber that Fiona used on her visits to Jasmine Hall. She knew Fiona's favorite hiding place and quickly strode to the lap desk on the table. Dumping out the writing material onto the bed, Dulcie swiftly unlatched the intricate clasp at the bottom and a drawer slid open, revealing a stack of gold coins.

Dulcie smiled to herself as she scooped up the coins and hid them in her apron. In her arrogance, Fiona had not considered the maid intelligent enough to worry about keeping her hiding place a secret from her. She had often opened the lap desk in front of Dulcie to deal out the household monies that she was so miserly with to Star.

"Lucky for Missy that she thought I was too dumb." Dulcie chuckled as she closed the lap desk and made her way back into the hall. She sped quickly to Star's door and had raised her hand to tap on it when a harsh growl came from behind her.

"What are you doing, you black bitch?"

Dulcie spun about to face the man towering over her. "Master Brett, I was just checkin' on Missy," she stuttered, and clutched the gold tightly at her waist.

"Your mistress doesn't need your attention tonight. Now get back to the quarters where you belong." Grabbing her by the arm to further impress his order upon her, he shoved her roughly toward the stairs.

Under the force of his hand, Dulcie staggered and unconsciously reached out to stop herself from falling.

At the same instant she lost her hold on the money hidden in her apron and the gold coins bounced and rolled across the carpet at her feet. She froze instantly, her eyes growing round with horror at her mistake. She looked from the shining coins and back to Brett's angry face.

"You little bitch! I'll have every inch of your black hide peeled from your back for this," he swore as he drew back his hand and slapped her across the face, knocking the maid to her knees.

"Missy," Dulcie cried as she scooted backward across the carpet in an effort to get away from him. "No, Master Brett," she whimpered as he came toward her with his fist raised to strike her again.

Brett seemed to swell with rage. Star's rejection combined with the brandy he had consumed fueled his anger until he was no longer in control of himself. All he knew was that he needed to vent his fury and the maid served as a convenient object to that end. His growl was that of a maddened animal as he struck Dulcie another stunning blow to the head.

"Leave her alone, Brett," Star ordered. She had come into the hall at Dulcie's first cry, but Brett had moved too swiftly for her to stop him from striking the maid.

Brett swung about to face her, his face mottled with rage, his pale eyes holding a wild light as he glared at her. "Get back to your room, Star. This is none of your affair. I'll see to you when I'm through with this thief."

"The hell I will. Dulcie is my maid, as is Jasmine Hall my home. *You* are the interloper here, Brett."

"Not for long, my dear. I will soon own you and Jasmine Hall."

"Over my dead body," Star shouted, her control snapping. "If you think you will ever get your hands on Jasmine Hall, then you are sadly mistaken. I'd rather hang than ever let you touch me or anything else that is mine." Star faced him bravely with her head held high, her chin raised at a pugnacious angle. At that moment, she felt no fear; only rage that he had hurt someone she loved.

A feral smile lifted Brett's lips and a predatory light entered his eyes as he reached out and grabbed her by the arm, jerking her roughly against him. The fingers of his other hand curled bruisingly about her throat, choking off her air.

"It seems I shall have to deal with you first, my little high-handed bitch," he snarled down into her face. "Afterward I doubt you will be so willing to refuse to marry me."

Star gasped for air as she fought to free herself from him. The blood pounded in her temples as she struggled, beating at his chest with her fists. Her efforts only made him chuckle.

"Resist all you want, my little virgin, but it will do you no good," he said as he wrapped his other arm about her, pinning her against his hard body. "Tonight you will be mine."

With his attention centered on Star, Brett had forgotten about Dulcie. He did not see her as she moved toward the tall vase on the hall table, nor did he realize her intention until she smashed it down on the back of his head. His eyes grew round with shock before his fingers slipped away from Star's throat and he crumpled to the carpet at her feet, unconscious.

"Is he dead?" Star asked in a breathless whisper, rubbing her aching throat.

Dulcie bent over Brett's prone form and touched his chest before she shook her head. "It'd take more than one vase over the head to kill that devil, Missy." Mindful of the coins scattered on the carpet, she gathered them and then turned to Star. "We best hurry. We gotta be long gone 'fore he comes 'round."

Star hesitated only a moment as she stood gazing down at the man at her feet. Dulcie was right. They had to get away before Brett regained consciousness. She turned and fled back to her room. Taking only enough time to change from her night rail into her riding habit, Star collected her mother's jewelry and then, with Dulcie, left Jasmine Hall. Neither looked back at the two-story mansion as they took the trail that would lead them toward the swamp and Obioma.

Chapter 2

An eerie, watchful stillness settled over the swamp as the two girls made their way across the marshy ground toward the tiny cabin where Obioma lived. Their intrusion disturbed the inhabitants of the swamp. It silenced the croaking bullfrogs and the alligators that called to their mates through the curling tendrils of fog that floated above the warm, dark water. Their passage was not easy in the blackness of the night. On several occasions they veered mistakenly from the right path and found themselves up to their ankles in slimy mud. Their skirts were wet to the knees, hindering each step they took, by the time they reached their destination and climbed the rickety steps to the rough-hewn door.

"Obioma, it's me, Dulcie, and Miss Star," Dulcie called as she tapped on the door.

After what seemed an eternity to the two frightened young women, a beam of pale lantern light split the darkness as the door opened silently on well-oiled hinges. A pair of alert ebony eyes peered around the edge of the portal, taking in the two bedraggled figures before warily scanning the misty landscape beyond them. Seeing no one, Obioma stepped back and let them enter her small dwelling.

The scent of herbs, smoke, and age permeated the air of the cabin and made the atmosphere as heavy as the old woman's silence as she closed and securely latched the door behind her. Her movements were slow, her grizzled head doddering slightly upon her hunched shoulders as she turned her dark gaze on the two damp, mud-splattered girls. She assessed them for a long moment without speaking and then shuffled across to the small hearth. Placing several dry sticks of kindling on the grate, she coaxed a small flame to life before dusting her gnarled hands together as if satisfied with her work and then turning to look once more at Star and Dulcie.

"Warm yourselves and then we will talk," she ordered in a voice that was softly accented and bespoke of tropical islands far from her swampy home. It held a vitality that belied her aged appearance.

"We got no time, Obioma," Dulcie said, shifting nervously from one foot to the other. She glanced apprehensively toward the door as if expecting Brett to burst through at any moment. Her dark eyes were round and pleading as she told the Swamp Witch, "We come to ask your help."

Obioma's lined features softened as she smiled and nodded. "I suspected as much, child. Few venture into the swamp at this time of night unless they need my aid."

"Then you will help us?" Star asked. Obioma's gentle smile had conquered the last of her childhood fears of the old woman.

"First I would know why my help is needed," Obioma replied, her dark gaze resting speculatively on Star.

"Missy needs to get away from Jasmine Hall," Dulcie blurted out as she saw a look of uncertainty cross Star's face.

"Why do you want to leave your home?" Obioma asked quietly, her eyes never leaving Star's tense features.

Star correctly read the silent message in the old woman's words. She knew she had to explain her reason or they could expect no help from Obioma. Star also sensed that the Swamp Witch would know if the truth was not told. Drawing in a deep breath, she said, "I have to leave before I am accused of murdering my stepmother."

"Did you do it?" was Obioma's calm question as she bent to place the black iron kettle over the fire.

"No, Obioma. Fiona fell to her death, but it was an accident."

"Then why do you flee into the night as if you are guilty? If it was an accident, then you have nothing to fear."

"I wish that was true, but there is a witness who will swear to the sheriff that I murdered Fiona if I don't do as he orders," Star said, feeling again an impotent fury against Brett rise in her throat to choke her.

"Missy be tellin' the truth, Obioma. Master Tremayne means to force her to marry him or he'll turn her over to the law," Dulcie interjected in defense of her mistress.

Obioma's scrutinizing gaze searched both young faces before she reached up and lifted the lantern from the hook that hung from the soot-blackened ceiling. She shuffled across the room to the lone window of the cabin and threw back the wooden shutters. Setting the lantern on the sill, she turned back to the girls.

"I believe the truth of your words and I will do what I can for you. However, I fear that time may be our worst enemy and the sheriff will be called before I can get you both safely away."

Star released the breath she had not realized she had been holding as she awaited Obioma's decision. For a few tense moments she had feared that the old woman would refuse to help her. If she had, Star knew she could not really blame her. Obioma was jeopardizing all the work she did for her own people by coming to Star's aid. If anyone should ever learn of Obioma's actions tonight, her life would be in danger as well. She would be branded an accessory to murder and could be sentenced to prison or worse.

"Thank you, Obioma," Star whispered, her gratitude clogging her throat. She knew those two words were inadequate, but she could not express the extent of her feelings to the woman who courageously risked her own life to help those in need.

Obioma graciously accepted Star's thanks with a slight nod as she busied herself taking two cups from the pegs on the mantel. Digging into the leather pouch at her waist, she sprinkled her own special mixture of herbs into them before taking the kettle from the fire and filling the cups with boiling water. She let the contents steep until it had made a spicy tea and then handed each girl a cup.

"Drink this. It will make you relax and give you the strength you will need in the coming hours. If I am to get you away, we must move quickly. I've already signaled for the flatboat to be brought and when it arrives you must go. I have friends in Natchez who will help you reach your final destination.

"I hope to reach my aunt in—" Star began but found herself abruptly silenced by Obioma's raised hand and brisk shake of her head.

"Drink your tea, child. I want no more information from you. It is best to keep your secrets to yourself. That way, I cannot reveal your whereabouts if I am questioned."

"As you wish, Obioma, but I want you to know that I can never repay you for the gift you are giving me." Setting her cup aside, Star opened her portmanteau and withdrew several of the gold coins Dulcie had taken from Fiona's room. "But perhaps this will help in some small way."

The gnarled fingers closed about the coins and Obioma smiled. "I won't refuse your money because there are others less fortunate that this can help."

"Use it as you see fit. I only wish it could be more," Star said as she lifted the cup and drank its contents. It warmed her and that warmth seemed to take some of the tension out of her taut body. She was stifling a yawn with the back of her hand as the piercing cry of a screech owl broke the stillness of the night. She jumped with a start of surprise, her eyes flying wide with fear.

"It's time that you go. The hour grows late and you

must reach the safe house before dawn. God go with you, child.''

''Dulcie and I will always be grateful to you,'' Star said, and impulsively hugged the old woman about her bony shoulders.

''No, child,'' Obioma said, the lines in her aged face deepening as she shook her head. ''Dulcie cannot go with you.''

Star looked from the old woman to her friend and then back to Obioma, shaking her head. ''I won't go without her. Dulcie has risked her life to help me and to leave her behind at Jasmine Hall would mean her certain death. Brett would beat her until she died.''

''Child, you asked for my help and now you must understand that what I ask is only for your safety. You have no choice but to leave Dulcie here if you wish to escape the authorities. They will be looking for two young women traveling together.''

''No, I can't leave Dulcie,'' Star said, her young face set with stubborn determination.

''Dulcie will come to no harm. I will see that she is taken across the river to another who is in sympathy with our plight. From there she will be taken north to freedom.''

''No. Dulcie and I have been together all of our lives and we will stay together.'' Star remained adamant.

''Then neither of you will go,'' Obioma said, her voice filled with steel. She threw her hands up in the air as if dismissing the whole thought of helping Star. ''I will not be responsible for your deaths and that is what will happen if you keep insisting that Dulcie go with you. She is a slave and has no choice in what happens to her life if she is caught trying to escape. Together you will surely be caught.''

''Obioma is right, Missy,'' Dulcie said, her dark eyes bright with moisture as she gazed at her friend.

''I know,'' Star said, her voice cracking. Tears brimmed in her eyes as she looked at Dulcie, accepting

Obioma's reasoning. "But I don't want to leave you. I need you, Dulcie."

A wobbly smile played over her friend's full lips as she wiped at her eyes with the back of her hand. "Missy, you be full growed now. It's time we both be free."

"Yes, we'll both be free," Star vowed, and looked once more to Obioma. "Do you have a piece of paper so that I can give Dulcie her freedom?"

The old woman nodded as she shuffled once more to the mantel where she kept all of her valuables. She took down a yellowed scrap of paper, an old quill pen, and a precious bottle of ink. Handing them to Star, she stepped back and watched as the young mistress wrote. A smile of satisfaction played over her dark face as Star handed the paper to Dulcie.

"This is for the years of friendship you've given me. I don't know what I would have done without you, and I will never forget you, Dulcie."

New tears blurred the maid's vision and her hand trembled as she took the precious paper declaring her freedom. "I'll never forget you either, Missy."

The two girls embraced, holding each other tightly. Each knew that that moment would be their last together. They were mistress and slave, but the love they felt for each other crossed all boundaries set by their positions in society and the color of their skin. Both felt as if they were having to leave a member of their family, and it hurt.

A shaky sob escaped Star as she lifted her portmanteau and turned to the door. She hesitated at the threshold only long enough to open her bag and withdraw several coins. Rushing back, she pressed them into Dulcie's hand, and without waiting for her thanks, she turned and fled from the cabin. She did not pause again until she was at the bottom of the rickety steps.

"This way, mistress," came a deep, drawling voice from the shadows at the side of the cabin. "The boat be just down the path a ways."

Star swallowed back a new bout of tears and drew in

a deep breath. Squaring her shoulders, she turned in the direction of the voice. Before her lay the night and her future, and at the present moment both were dark.

The flatboat slipped easily along the edge of the moon-silvered waterway. The oar occasionally striking the side of the hull was the only sound to break the stillness. Against her will, Star fell into a restless slumber. She had not wanted to sleep, but she could not fight the effects of exhaustion and Obioma's tea.

As the sky grew pearly with dawn in the east, she jerked awake with a start. The flatboat scraped against the landing and rocked precariously as her nameless companion made his way toward the prow and jumped ashore. For one brief, sleep-bemused moment she wondered where she was and why the nightmare she had dreamed during the night was still so vivid in her mind in the light of day.

A shiver raced up her spine and raised gooseflesh on her arms when her thoughts began to clear and she realized that she had not imagined all that had taken place and that she was in fact fleeing from all she had ever known and loved. Questions rose to her lips, but she did not voice them to her taciturn companion, who secured the boat and turned to help her from it. She longed to ask him where he was taking her but knew it would be as useless to question him now as it had been last night. She had learned soon after departing Obioma's that he kept his own counsel, only speaking when he felt it necessary and never divulging any information that might connect him later with any other who also worked to help free those held in bondage.

Though she understood his reticence, it did little to quell her own mounting trepidation. In the light of day she realized that she had placed her life in the hands of strangers and it was only out of their generosity that she did not find herself in worse trouble than that she had escaped. The thought was sobering.

Star let the man lead her up the clay embankment and

when they reached the top, he motioned for her to follow again, turning on to a faint path that wound through thick underbrush. Briars caught at her hair and skirt on several occasions, but fearing to be left behind, she jerked herself free of them without thought of the pain and hurried to catch up with the tall, bearded man. He did not slacken his pace for her.

After a while, they reached a hard-packed road that led them through the shanty-lined streets of what Star would soon come to know as Natchez Under the Hill. She was unaware of the reputation of that section of the city, but from the few observations she made of the disreputable-looking men sleeping beneath the sagging porches of the dilapidated cabins, she sensed an underlying menace. That kept Star close to her companion's side, for she had no desire to find herself alone in that part of town.

Clutching her portmanteau in both hands, she was breathing heavily from the exertion of the fast pace he had set by the time they reached the edge of the shanty town and came to a sizable house. A wave of relief washed over her as her companion led her toward the white picket fence that surrounded the two-story dwelling. The house rose like a sentinel at the edge of the squalor, sitting like a guard at the gateway to the more prosperous section of Natchez Under the Hill. Beyond it lay Silver Street, where the rich who lived on the bluff overlooking the Mississippi River came to enjoy their vices in the saloons and gambling establishments that lined the street.

"We're here," Star's guide said, and swung open the gate. He stepped inside and paused to let her enter.

Closing the gate behind them, he led her across the well-kept lawn and along the side of the house to the rear entrance. He knocked on the whitewashed door several times before a window on the second floor slid open and a woman with a paint-smeared face and fiery red hair squinted down at them.

"Stop all that banging. You're making enough noise

to wake the dead. Go away, the place is closed," she growled before she recognized Star's companion. A pleased smile spread her thick lips and she winked at the bearded man. "So you've brought another one, huh? I'll tell Sugar."

The window slid shut and after several minutes the back door opened to reveal the red-haired woman herself wearing only a chemise and black lace pantelets. She propped herself against the door, posing to show her huge breasts to the best advantage, and grinned up at Star's companion. "Once you take her up to Sugar, why don't you stop by my room for a little rest?"

The bearded man paused only briefly, a slow smile tugging at his usually stern mouth. "Just might do that, Maud. It's been a long night."

Maud gave a deep, provocative chuckle and closed the door. She led them with an exaggerated swing to her hips up the stairs to the second floor. Star's companion knocked on the door and, hearing a soft, husky female voice bid them enter, opened it for Star and stepped aside.

He mumbled, "God speed, mistress," before ambling off down the hall in Maud's wake.

Star cast one helpless glance in his direction before stepping into the red velvet chamber. She hesitated upon the threshold, uncertain as to what to expect after the blowsy appearance of the woman who had greeted them. Her blue eyes were round with a mixture of astonishment and trepidation as she scanned the oppressively luxurious room for its occupant. She jumped with a start as the same husky voice came from the large canopied bed that sat in the far corner of the room.

"Come in, girl, and don't look so frightened. There's no one here to harm you."

Star's gaze came to rest on the woman lying amid a pile of red satin pillows. Even in the dim light that filtered through the heavy folds of the velvet drapes, she could see that Sugar was extraordinarily beautiful.

Star stared at the woman in wide-eyed wonder. She

had never before encountered anyone with such an exotic
appearance. Sugar's cheekbones were high, emphasizing
the slight tilt of her thickly fringed ebony eyes. Her narrow nose flared slightly at the nostrils above her full,
smiling lips. Like her flawless, honey-colored skin, they
were touched with rose. Her hair was jet and lay about
her bare shoulders in a curling wave of silk. All in all,
she was the most beautiful and unusual-looking woman
Star had ever seen.

Sugar Brown's smile deepened at the expression on the
girl's face. She knew the effect her appearance had on
men and women alike. The mixed blood of her heritage
served her well, providing her with the best features of
both her white sire and black mother. Yes, she knew her
own beauty and the value of it as a marketable quality.
She had used it to her advantage through the years. It had
bought her freedom and made her a good living so that
she was able to help those who had not been as blessed
as herself.

"So you've been sent to me by Obioma?" Sugar said
as she sat up and slid her long legs over the side of the
bed. Setting her feet into a pair of red-satin mules, she
stood and slipped a feather-trimmed robe over her nakedness before crossing to the windows and drawing back
the drapes to let in the morning light.

Still standing dumbfounded in the same spot, Star
could only nod in reply.

"Close the door and come over here so that I may look
at you," Sugar ordered as she settled herself on a satin
lounge.

Not knowing what else to do or say, Star obeyed. Sugar patted the seat beside her and Star sat down on the
edge, her back stiff and her knuckles white from gripping
the portmanteau so tightly.

Sugar took the bag from her hands and set it on the
floor at Star's feet before she turned to look at the new
arrival from Obioma. She studied Star's features for a
long searching moment and then shook her head.

"For the life of me, I can see no sign of your black

heritage in your face, girl. You could pass for white with no problem. True, you do have dark hair, but with those blue eyes no one would ever know the difference.''

Star jerked sharply back. Sugar's words had the power to break the trance that had held her spellbound since she'd entered the room.

''I am white,'' Star said, finally managing to find her voice.

The pleasant expression left Sugar's face and she frowned. ''I thought Obioma sent you to me. If this is some kind of ploy to get in and see me, then I'll tell you here and now that I don't need any new girls.''

''Obioma did send me. It's no trick. I need your help,'' Star blurted out in an effort to reassure the beautiful woman.

''But you're white. Why would a white girl need our help?'' Sugar asked, her suspicions not allayed by the girl's words.

Star released a long breath, dreading the thought of having to reveal all that had transpired at Jasmine Hall but knowing it was her only chance if she was to receive any help from this woman who assessed her through narrowed eyes. She needed Sugar's assistance desperately. The memory of the shanty town was still vivid and the thought of being left to fend for herself in such a place was abhorrent to her.

Drawing in a deep steadying breath, she looked Sugar Brown directly in the eyes and launched into her explanation. She fought to keep her voice calm, but as she reached the point when she had overheard Brett's and Fiona's conversation, her throat constricted with the raw pain of their betrayal. Her eyes stung with hot tears, but she blinked them away. Her voice quavered slightly, but she managed to regain some control over it as her anger reasserted itself amid her turbulent emotions. As she finished her story, she sat tight-lipped, her hands balled into fists in her lap.

''Now you know why I need your help. I must try to reach my aunt in Texas. She is my only hope.''

"Yes, I understand now why Obioma sent you to me," Sugar said. Placing a comforting hand upon Star's arm, she gave it a reassuring squeeze.

Star gazed up into the beautiful ebony eyes, trying to read the thoughts that lay behind them, but she could not. "Will you help me?" she pleaded.

"Yes, but there is one more question I would have answered first. In all you have told me, you've failed to tell me your name." Sugar smiled.

"Star Grayson," Star replied, and found herself responding in kind to the warmth the woman exuded.

"Star," Sugar murmured. "The name is as beautiful as the one who possesses it. It is a shame that Obioma could not have sent you here to work for me. Your innocent beauty would drive my customers wild."

At Star's puzzled expression, Sugar laughed aloud. Though the girl had seen Maud and herself, she still did not understand from whom she was asking help. She did not realize that she was now residing in the most exclusive brothel in Natchez Under the Hill, nor that she was speaking with the madam of that establishment.

Sugar found the irony of the situation humorous. Vice protecting virtue. It was indeed a change from her usual endeavors where beautiful girls were concerned. And if she was not careful to keep the girl well out of sight of her customers, it could become a very ugly affair. Few of her rich clients would appreciate being denied if they caught a glimpse of Star and decided that they wanted her for their night's pleasure. It would not be easy to explain the girl's presence in her house if she was unavailable to service the Red Passion's customers.

Even with the problems that could arise if Star was seen, Sugar would not change her decision to help her. She would just have to make certain that the girl understood that she was not to leave her rooms when the Red Passion was open for business.

Patting Star's hand again in a motherly fashion, Sugar said, "Star, since you will be staying here until I can find a way to get you safely to your aunt, there are a few things that you need to know about my house and the business we do.''

Chapter 3

The night sounds of the Red Passion floated up to the small room in the attic. They did little to promote sleep as Star lay tossing and turning on her narrow bed in the tiny, hot cubicle that had been her home for the past three weeks. She had closed the window and door in an effort to escape the incessant jangle of the piano in the main parlor as well as the high-pitched squeals and giggles that came from the girls as they frolicked with their customers in the rooms below. She had only managed to make herself more miserable by intensifying the heat.

The time she had spent cooped up at the top of Sugar Brown's brothel seemed more like three years than just a matter of weeks. The constant heat and confinement made her restless, but there was little she could do to remedy her dilemma since Sugar had restricted her to her room during the hours the Red Passion was open for business.

Unable to lie on her bed a moment longer, Star sat up and slid her bare feet to the floor. Padding over to the window, she threw it open and leaned back against the wooden frame with the hope of catching a breath of cool air from the river. Her gaze traveled automatically over the garden and past the white picket fence to the bright lights on Silver Street. Even from that distance she could see the activity along the much-frequented thoroughfare. Men loved their vices and were willing to pay generously for them.

With that thought, Star gave a rueful smile and shook

her head. Since she had come to Sugar's, she'd realized
the true extent of her own naiveté about the world. It was
still hard for her to believe that she, the daughter of
Charles Grayson and the owner of Jasmine Hall, was residing in one of the most notorious brothels of Natchez
Under the Hill.

The sheltered life she'd led at Jasmine Hall had kept
her ignorant of places like the Red Passion. On the plantation she had learned about the breeding of animals and
after she'd become engaged she had managed to pry some
information out of Dulcie about what men and women
did together when they were married, but Star had never
conceived the thought that women would let men make
love to them for money.

Star smiled into the darkness as she recalled that first
day when Sugar had tried to explain to her about the
business that was transacted in the Red Passion. She had
not understood Sugar's first delicate attempt to tell her
that she ran a whorehouse. It was not until Sugar had
been bluntly direct, stating exactly what transpired between her customers and the women who worked for her,
that Star had finally managed to comprehend what she
had been trying to tell her.

Her smile deepened at the thought of the picture she
must have made sitting there in front of Sugar, mouth
open in shock, staring at her as if she had suddenly grown
two heads. No, she would never forget how she had felt
upon learning that the woman who had agreed to help
her was in fact the madam of such an establishment as
the Red Passion. It had not been an easy thing for her to
accept, but having nowhere else to turn, she had been
forced to come to terms with it.

Star had grown to know and like Sugar and her girls.
They had been kind to her, and their generosity had made
her realize it was not her place to judge them. The more
she learned of them, the more she felt justified in her
decision. Each had their own reason for choosing such a
life-style. Whether it was to escape abuse or starvation,
each had fled something in her past, much as Star had

done. In many ways she saw in them what she might have become if Brett had been able to force her to marry him. If that had happened, however, she would not have been paid for the use of her body.

Star shivered though no breeze came through the window to lessen the heat in the tiny room. "But for the grace of God there goest I," she murmured aloud as she turned away from the view of Silver Street and began to pace back and forth across the uncarpeted floor.

"Had I not learned of Brett's schemes I would have been used in the same manner as Sugar's girls, but I would have been foolish enough to welcome it because I thought he loved me," Star mused aloud as all the painful memories resurfaced to haunt her. They closed in on her, making her hiding place seem to shrink in size.

Unable to flee the turmoil that possessed her, she knew she had to get out of her cramped quarters for a short while or be suffocated by her gloomy thoughts. She needed to breathe the fresh night air to clear her mind so that she could find a small measure of rest. Coming to a decision that she knew was against all of Sugar's orders, she quickly slid her feet into her slippers and opened the door. No matter what Sugar said, she could no longer endure being locked away with her memories.

Easing the door open, Star peeped into the hallway. She had to be careful so that no one discovered that she had left her room for a brief walk in the garden at the rear of the Red Passion. Moving stealthily toward the stairs the servants used, she crept down them, hoping to slip out unnoticed.

All the activity in the Red Passion centered around the parlor where Sugar provided the finest of liquors for her customers while they gambled or decided upon the girl they would have that night. Though Star had never been present during any of the transactions that occurred on the first floor, she had heard enough from Sugar's girls to know what transpired. In the afternoons when the girls gathered in the dining room for their evening meal before the house opened for business, they chatted freely about their customers, comparing notes and sometimes grumbling about the odd requests they received from some of the men.

Star often found her face burning with embarrassment at their risqué conversations, but she had also learned a great deal from listening to them. That information would now serve her well. She knew that the Red Passion's clientele would be too absorbed with Sugar's flamboyant ladies to glance twice at her in her faded muslin gown if by chance they caught a glimpse of her as she passed. They would assume that she was only a servant.

Star hesitated for only a split second at the landing to check that her flight went unobserved. In her haste, she failed to see the tall, dark-haired man who lounged in the shadows smoking a cheroot as she darted down the hallway to the rear entrance and slipped out into the still night.

Kyle Hunter choked on the pungent smoke he had drawn too quickly into his lungs as the young girl dashed past him. In the dim light provided by the lamp on the hall table, he had glimpsed her beauty for only a fraction of a second before she was gone, but it was enough to make him draw in a quick breath.

His sun-bronzed skin deepened in hue as he coughed and gasped in a breath of fresh air. His pale eyes, which were often likened to a cat's, brimmed with moisture from the burning sensation in his throat and chest. Brushing the dampness from the sooty lashes that fringed his changeable green eyes, he tossed the offending cheroot into a sand-filled spittoon. He'd had enough of that type of pleasure to last him a while and from what he had just seen there were far more interesting things here to hold his attention.

At last he managed to conquer his bout of coughing and regain his composure. Straightening his jacket and absently running his fingers through his hair, he strode in the direction the girl had taken.

Her flight had roused his curiosity and at the present

time he needed a diversion. That had been one of his reasons for coming to Sugar's tonight. He had been in Mississippi for over a month settling his uncle's estate among five greedy daughters. It would have been a simple matter and should have taken only a few days to conclude if his uncle's heirs had not come from two separate marriages. That and their greed had complicated the entire affair, taxing his patience until he wanted to wring all of their lily-white necks. After listening to them argue over every cent of the estate, he felt as if he could have tossed all of them into the river and watched their ruffled petticoats sink out of sight without a qualm.

He didn't have time for their avarice. His own affairs were suffering. He was needed back at the Bar H, his ranch in Texas. It was nearing time for the roundup. If he didn't meet the deadline to fulfill his contract to supply beef to the army, he stood to lose a great deal of money. And he couldn't let that happen. He had worked too hard to make the Bar H prosper. He had fought Mexicans, Indians, drought, and nearly everything else nature had to offer to build the ranch into what it was today, one of the largest spreads west of the Brazos.

He was also faced with another problem. When he had arrived in Natchez and had thought to have the business of his uncle's estate settled in a matter of days, he had foolishly agreed to lead a wagon train of settlers back to Sagebrush, the small town southwest of the Bar H. That had been his main reason for coming to Sugar's place. A girl that had once worked for her had been fortunate enough to marry, and she and her husband had purchased land near Sagebrush. To help the young couple get a new start, and as their belated wedding gift, since they had been married for nearly a year and had a baby several months old, Sugar had paid their share to join the wagon train.

After finishing his business discussion about the young couple with Sugar, he had fully expected to enjoy the rest of the evening with one of her girls. He had not anticipated that he would find himself bored and feeling disgusted with the entire idea of bedding one of the whores. But their painted faces and perfumed bodies held no appeal for him that night. The only reason he could find for his reaction was that in some strange way they reminded him too much of his greedy cousins. For the time being he'd had enough of women who would do anything to get their hands on money.

''Enough to last me a lifetime,'' Kyle muttered as he went out into the night. He hesitated at the bottom of the steps to let his eyes adjust to the darkness before he stepped onto the dew-dampened grass and began his quest for the young woman whose beauty had intrigued him the moment he had glimpsed it.

Spying the object of his search at the far end of the garden, he moved silently toward her. He paused in the shadow of a weeping willow and watched as she bent to pick a rose. She lifted the scarlet bud to her nose and breathed deeply of its sweet fragrance while gazing off into the distance, totally unaware of his presence.

Kyle's breath stilled in his throat when the moonlight illuminated her face. He devoured the beauty of her, standing so still and thoughtful, her dark mane of hair cascading down her back to a waist that looked small enough for him to span with his hands.

His gaze returned to her face, sweeping over her fine features from the delicately arched brows to the soft, full mouth that made him draw in another sharp breath at the sudden strong urge that arose within him to taste its sweetness.

She is a prize indeed, Kyle mused to himself from his vantage point beneath the willow. He could well understand why Sugar kept her out of sight. With her beauty and the air of innocence that seemed to surround her as she stood haloed in moonlight, he knew she would leave few clients for the other girls of the Red Passion. Sugar Brown was a businesswoman to her fingertips. She knew the treasure she had in this girl and would use it to her best advantage. Only the highest bidders would ever have the good fortune to taste the luscious body the worn muslin gown failed to hide completely. Kyle's blood began to warm in his veins as he mentally disrobed the vision before him and imagined the silken texture of her flesh beneath his hand.

Unaware that she was no longer alone with her reveries, Star absently brushed the soft petals of the rose against her cheek as she stood staring off into the distance without truly seeing the moon-silvered landscape before her. Her excursion into the garden had not had the desired effect, for she had not escaped her thoughts. Her mind's eye had once more turned inward, probing the raw wounds in her heart for the answers to questions she had repeatedly asked herself during the past lonely years. She had plumbed the innermost depths of her soul, but as in the past she could find no explanation to appease the lonely child who still dwelled within her. Her quest had only made her realize that no matter what she said or did, she still desperately needed someone to care for her; to love her.

Brett's deceit had made her wary of ever trusting anyone again, as well as having renewed the old fear that she was not the type of person anyone could love. Yet her heart still yearned for tenderness, for companionship, and for love. She could not bear the thought of a future as emotionally barren as the years that had passed since her father's death. She knew she had the strength to survive it, but why should she? The two months of her engagement, before she'd learned of Brett's low intentions, had shown her another life, one that could not easily be forgotten. Her brief glimpse of happiness had been constructed with webs of deceit, but it had made her realize how truly empty her existence had been at Jasmine Hall. Her young soul craved more out of life than just existing. She wanted a family of her own; a husband and children to fill her future. That was her dream, but at the present moment her chances of ever fulfilling it looked bleak.

With that thought, Star felt a welling of desolation within her breast. Fiona's death had severed her from the ties of her past and had thrust her toward a future of uncertainty. Her dreams would have to remain haunting images in her mind if she could not find a way to clear her name of the murder of her stepmother. She would never know the feeling of a babe suckling at her breast or of being held in the arms of a man who loved her for herself and not for her inheritance.

Growing more and more depressed, Star began to feel for the first time that if she could not be free of the black threats that Brett made, she would not want to go on living. Never before had she felt so vulnerable and afraid. Nor had she ever needed anyone as much as she did at that moment, standing alone in the garden with only her morbid thoughts for company.

The sound of twig snapping nearby, jarred her back to the present. She stiffened instantly and felt the hair at the nape of her neck rise. She jerked about, her startled gaze searching the darkness. The breeze stirred the drooping limbs of the willow, drawing her gaze to the shadows where the moonlight revealed a flash of white shirt. Every muscle in her body grew rigid as she watched the tall man step from beneath the inky bower and move toward her.

Instinct told her to flee, but the feeling that she had conjured this man into life with her thoughts kept her rooted in place. Her mind cried out for her to run, to hide, but like a small animal mesmerized by a snake, she stood and watched as he approached, unable to make her legs move. Her breath lay still in her throat and she could not draw her eyes away from the moon-silvered features of the handsomest man she had ever seen.

Unconsciously she compared this man of the night with Brett Tremayne. With his dark hair and strangely colored eyes that seemed to bore into her soul, he made Brett's looks seem insipid. Shivers of both pleasure and dread raced up her spine when he paused within a few feet of her. Never had she felt as strongly drawn to anyone as she did to this stranger. Not even when she had been completely enamored of Brett had he inspired such a feeling within her.

Star gave herself a sharp mental shake as she recalled how badly her attraction to Brett had served her. That thought alone broke the trance that possessed her and she turned to flee back to the haven of her small room. She wanted no part of that madness. She had touched the fire once and had found only pain. She would not be so foolish as to do so again. She wanted a calm and secure relationship with a man and she sensed that she would not find it with this dark stranger with his intriguing eyes.

Her instincts warned her of the danger he represented with his masculine beauty and she took to her heels before it was too late. A small cry of fright escaped her lips as his hand came down on her arm and brought her flight to an abrupt halt.

"Don't run away. The night is too lovely to be enjoyed alone," Kyle said as he drew her slowly back in front of him so that he could look down into her lovely, moon-drenched face.

"Sir, please take your hand from my arm," Star said, straining away from him.

"I would, but I have a feeling that you would disappear into the shadows and I would never find you again," Kyle said and smiled, his fingers firmly encircling her arm.

"Sir, I demand that you release me at once," Star ordered. Her voice was firm, but her insides felt as if they were turning into jelly.

"You have nothing to fear from me," Kyle murmured, feeling her tremble beneath his hand. "Surely you know that Sugar will not allow anyone to harm one of her girls."

Star gave a start of surprise at his presumption that she worked for Sugar. Offended, she raised her chin in the air and spat, "I'm not afraid of you, sir, nor, do I appreciate your high-handed manner. Now if you would release my arm, I would like to return to my room."

Kyle chuckled, enjoying the girl's spirit. He had been right. She was a prize indeed. Few whores had the fire that this girl possessed. She would be well worth the high price Sugar would demand for her and he would willingly pay it. It had been far too long since he had encountered a woman who kindled his desire to such a degree.

Victoria Prescott had been the last woman even to come close, but the fire in his blood for her had not lasted. Like all the rest, his passion for the auburn-haired woman had waned soon after he had bedded her. She'd tried to get him to marry her, but when she finally realized that he was not the marrying kind, no matter how often he shared her bed, she had quickly switched her affections to Harold Crawford, who owned the mercantile store in Sagebrush. They had married two months later, but that had not stopped Victoria's pursuit of Kyle. She was always finding some excuse to come to the Bar H, or waylaying him on the street when he went to town. He knew from her provocative looks and smiles that she would be more than willing to forget about Harold and renew their affair, but marriage and married women were not for him. Kyle had been told far too often that he was the image of his father, Buck Hunter, in appearance as well as temperament, and despite their similarity, he was determined not to make the same mistake his father had in his life.

Kyle had seen what Buck's type of man could do to a woman. He had watched his mother grow old and haggard before her time because of her roving husband. Madge Hunter, who had been considered in her youth one of the fairest belles in Mississippi, had died broken and bitter from Kyle's father's neglect. She had never mentioned the life of ease she'd left to follow Buck Hunter into the untamed land of Texas soon after their marriage, but Kyle knew from his own visits to his relatives in Mississippi after his mother's death that she must have loved his father a great deal to give up such a life to try to make a new one on the frontier. But that love had slowly withered because Buck had not had the strength to resist the wanderlust in his blood, and had left his family for months at a time to survive without him on the land now known as the Bar H.

Those years had not been easy for Kyle. While growing up he had needed both of his parents' love but most of all his mother's. Strangely he had found that his resemblance to his father had denied him that love. She had frequently reminded him that he was just like his father and would no doubt follow in Buck's footsteps when he grew up. Her predictions had hurt Kyle as a child, but as he grew older his protective instincts had made him want to guard Madge from more hurt, no matter how she felt toward him. He reasoned that her reaction was due to the hardship of a marriage in which the husband cared little about his wife or child. He had tried to ease some of her suffering by giving her his love without question, yet nothing he'd done had made her change her feelings toward him until she died. He had not blamed his mother for her lack of motherly love but had condemned his father. Without Kyle being aware of it, Madge Hunter had successfully turned him against his father and had ingrained a deep and abiding fear within him that he would turn out to be the same type of man. Because of that he had vowed never to marry.

He had built up the ranch and had made it prosper, but he would never chance making a woman suffer the same fate as his mother. He had grown to like his life the way it was without such complications. When his body required a physical release, he paid for that pleasure and then went about his own business without thought to the woman he left behind.

He had grown more and more cynical through the years. He had heard all of the stories and songs about love, but if his parents' marriage was any indication of what love led to, he felt he had no need for it. He also had come to realize that his mother had been right in her predictions about him. He suspected he had inherited his father's wanderlust in more ways than one. He had yet to find a woman who could hold his interest. Love to him was only a figment in the overactive imaginations of poets and women hunting men to take care of them. He considered marriage a cage with silken bars that would soon turn into a steel trap once the vows were spoken. To Kyle the marriage bonds had been accurately named. Once you were bound by them there was no escape.

Drawing his mind back to the girl he still held before him, he said, "I'll be more than glad to escort you back to your room."

"I have no need of your escort, nor would I accept it. The only thing I want from you is for you to release me at once. Now unhand me, sir," Star ordered, again trying to free her arm from his grasp.

"Won't you at least tell me your name?" Kyle asked as he placed his hand at her waist and drew her closer to his hard, sinewy frame.

"You have no need to know my name or anything else about me," Star said, bracing her hands against his chest to try to keep some distance between their bodies.

"Ah, but I do," he murmured, lowering his head to sniff the sweet, clean fragrance of her hair. "It would be a shame not to know the name of the beauty who will share my bed."

"I have no intention of sharing your bed. Now release me at once or I will scream for help," Star said, feeling her self-control slip precariously. Panic tinged her voice as she realized the extent of his intentions toward her. He had assumed from the first that she was one of Sugar's girls and she had foolishly done nothing to rectify that mistake. Now he fully intended to have her. The thought made her begin to struggle in earnest against him.

"Let me go," she squealed as he drew her squirming body firmly against him and captured the back of her head within the palm of his hand to stay her movements.

"Enough," he ordered, his fingers winding through the dark silk of her hair. "I see no reason for all of your maidenly protests. I know Sugar probably told you to make the game interesting for your clients, but I have little inclination toward rape. I prefer my women willing. It is much more pleasurable for both parties involved."

"You don't understand. I'm not who you think I am," Star managed to gasp out as the gentle pressure of his fingers drew her head back so that she was forced to look up into his intriguing eyes.

"Then who are you?" Kyle asked. He was growing weary of the game she was playing and would let it continue for only a few moments more. Her soft body pressed against his made him too aware of other more gratifying things they could be doing instead of this verbal sparring.

"I am . . ." Star began before realizing the mistake she had nearly made. She gaped up at him in wide-eyed horror. She couldn't tell this man that she wasn't one of Sugar's girls. That would lead to questions that she could not answer. In a quandary as to what to say, she was totally unprepared for his next move. Her lips were still slightly parted as he lowered his head and captured her mouth in a searing kiss.

She stiffened in protest but was able to do little more because his hand still held her head captive in its wide palm as his mouth moved on hers in a sensual assault. His tongue darted past the sentinel of her lips to caress hers in an intimate fashion that sent shock waves coursing through her.

Brett had been the only man who had ever kissed her, and even villain that he was, he had never used such familiarity with her as this stranger was doing. Nor had his kisses given birth to the foreign sensations that this man's touch aroused over all of the protestations conjured up by her mind. Against her will, she found the feeling and taste of him intriguing.

In her innocence of the mysteries of her own sexuality, her inherent passionate nature had lain dormant. Now Kyle's kiss was like a spark upon dry tinder. It burned away the thin veneer that had kept her sensuality hidden even from herself. Unconsciously she relaxed in his arms as he deepened the kiss and she savored the new and unbidden sensations it created within her.

Kyle felt her resistance ebb and thrilled at her first tentative response as her arms crept up about his neck and she wound her fingers into the raven hair that curled at the edge of his collar.

He was surprised at his own reaction to her first timid touch. Never at any time that he could remember had any woman had that effect upon him, especially a woman whose favors he purchased. The air of innocence about this girl intoxicated him. The taste of her, the smell of her, all combined to make him forget that she was well trained in the arts of her profession. At that moment he felt as if he would be the first man to make love to her and he gloried in the heady sensation that feeling aroused within him.

With hands of a man who had gentled many a frightened filly, he began to caress her subtly. He lightly stroked the column of her slender throat before slowly moving down to her collarbone. He felt the flutter of her heartbeat beneath the tips of his fingers as he eased them downward to the soft swell above the neckline of her gown.

He stroked the pliant flesh as his lips trailed an enticing path along the curve of her cheek to the sensitive spot beneath her ear. He felt her tense slightly as he cupped her breast in his palm and murmured soothingly, ''Don't fear me. I won't hurt you. I just want to give you pleasure.''

Star felt herself responding to the deep, rich timbre of his voice. Irresistibly, she found herself drawn to it as she once more relaxed under his gentle touch. She knew what she was doing was foolish and wrong, but as he caressed her through the fabric of her gown, she did not have the willpower to resist the sweet fire that was racing through her veins. Every inch of her seemed to burn with some unknown need that was too strong to deny. She was powerless under its assault on her senses.

Instinct reigned over all her mind's warnings as his lips traveled down her throat and along the curve of her shoulders before his head dropped to the cleft between her breasts. His lips were fire and she was the kindling that blazed beneath them as he unlaced her bodice and slipped it down to reveal the swelling mounds peaked by hardened buds of deep rose. She felt her knees giving way beneath her when his mouth captured a nipple and his tongue made enticing circles about it.

He eased her to the lush, dew-dampened grass, and at that moment in time they were no longer nameless strangers who had met by chance. They were man and woman, nature's pawns, seeking the gift given to lovers by the gods.

Kyle eased her gown down about her hips and feasted upon her breasts. His relentless assault upon her senses gave her no time to deny him even if she had the power. She moved to the music he roused in her blood with his lips and hands.

She laced her fingers in his dark hair as he stretched his lean body out beside her and sought the shadowy apex between her thighs with his fingers. She flinched at the first intrusion but soon forgot the unaccustomed sensations as new, more heady ones took their place. They magnified and grew, singing in a wild current through every sinew within her and she arched toward him, her body instinctively sensing that only he could ease its need.

Unable to control his own passion any longer, Kyle left her only long enough to disrobe. Lean and naked, he knelt at her side, his eyes traveling the length of her before he lowered his mouth once more to hers and moved between her thighs. In all of his thirty-two years he had never met a woman who could inspire him with such awe. She was perfect in face and form, and tonight she was his.

The innocent girl from Jasmine Hall died and was reborn as the woman, Star Grayson, as he thrust into her warm, pliable body. His lips absorbed her cry of shock as he breached the shield of her virginity.

Kyle froze. His passion-swollen body recoiled as the totally unforeseen reality of her innocence hit him like a bucket of ice water. He tore his mouth free of hers and stared down into her wide, glistening eyes. His face mirrored the shock he saw on hers as he rolled away from her.

"Who in hell are you and why in the hell didn't you tell me you were a virgin?" he muttered accusingly as he reached for his britches and jerked them on. "I told you I had little inclination toward rape and I have even less for breaking in virgins." Picking up her discarded gown, he tossed it to her. "Get dressed and then you're going to explain a few things."

Kyle turned away, unable to look at the stricken expression on the girl's face. Guilt was clawing at his guts with angry talons and he suddenly felt sick to his stomach. At that moment he didn't like himself at all and reacted in the only way he knew how—with anger. His fury was not directed at the girl but at himself. He felt like a rapist. He was an experienced man and should have had enough sense to recognize her innocence from her first tentative response to his kisses. Instead he had let his body control him and as a result he had taken her virginity.

"Damn," he muttered in disgust as he ran his hand over his face and through his dark hair. He sought to relieve his conscience by telling himself that the girl had been willing enough and that he had found her in a brothel, but no argument he used was able to appease the guilt gnawing at his insides.

"Now, I want to know why in hell you let me—" Kyle's words died on his lips as he turned back to find that he was alone. The girl had vanished. The only indication that he had not dreamed the whole affair was a tiny strip of torn lace lying on the flattened grass where they had lain. Retrieving it, he stuffed it into his pocket and then looked for any sign of the girl hiding in the shadows. Finding none, he released a disgusted breath. His trip to Mississippi had been one disaster after another since he'd crossed the river.

"Damn, I'll be glad to be back in Texas," he grumbled, shrugging into his jacket. Retracing the path he had taken earlier, he reached the rear entrance of the Red

Passion. He'd pay Sugar for the mistake he had made tonight and, he hoped, between now and the time the wagon train pulled out at week's end, he wouldn't make any more. Casting one last glance at the moon-drenched garden, he opened the door and went to find the madam of the house.

The pale fingers of dawn crept through the attic window to illuminate Star sitting huddled on her narrow bed. She stared blankly at the wall. Her red, tear-swollen eyes held the only color in her ashen features. Her face was as gray as the morning sky as she sat mentally reliving the events of the previous night.

She had replayed the incident in the garden over and over; hoping that all that had transpired would miraculously be altered, but each time she was faced with the same conclusion: She had given herself to a complete stranger without a word of protest. To add to her humiliation, he had taken her virginity and then had thrust her from him as if her touch soiled him.

After that degrading experience, she had not remained in the garden to let him heap more indignities upon her by making her answer his questions. She'd fled back to the safety of her small room as soon as she managed to slip her gown over her head. Fortunately, no one had seen her reenter the Red Passion so she hadn't had to explain her rumpled appearance or her tear-stained cheeks. For that small reprieve she was grateful. She didn't want to have to tell anyone of how she had demeaned herself with the man with the eyes of a cat.

During the long, dark pre-dawn hours, she had tried to rationalize the motives that had led her to act like one of Sugar's girls, but she could find no explanation for her behavior. She could place the blame on loneliness or her need to be close to someone, but she had been lonely in the past and had not acted like a strumpet. Her attraction to the stranger and the madness brought on by the full moon were the only excuses she could find and neither appeased her burning conscience. She could not find it within her heart to forgive herself for her moment of insanity, no matter how hard she tried.

"Star, may I come in?" Sugar asked as she rapped lightly on the door.

"Sugar, it's early. May we not speak later this afternoon?" Star called, cringing farther back on the bed. The thought of facing anyone made her insides writhe. She felt that her face would reflect her shameful behavior for all to see and she wanted to hide her humiliation from the world for as long as possible.

"No, Star, it can't wait," Sugar said as she slid the latch back and pushed the door open. She stood for a long moment in the doorway, her keen eyes assessing the girl cowering on the bed, before she closed the door behind her and crossed to stand in front of Star. She braced her hands on her hips and her fingers drummed lightly against the velvet that draped them as she cocked her head to one side and stared down at her guest. "You can't make your troubles disappear by keeping the door closed on them."

Made uncomfortable by Sugar's intense scrutiny, Star scrambled off the bed and crossed to the window. Turning her back on Sugar, she gazed toward Silver Street but did not see the morning activity upon it.

"I don't know what you're talking about."

"This is what I'm talking about, Star, as you well know." Sugar tossed a leather pouch full of coins onto the bed.

At the clink of the coins, Star spun about, her wide eyes going to the bed where the pouch had landed. Her features had been ashen before, but now they turned a deathly white. Her knees felt as if they were turning to jelly beneath her, and her legs refused to obey the commands of her mind. She stood frozen in place, swaying precariously.

Sugar saw her distress and moved swiftly to catch her before she could fall. She helped Star to the bed and seated her gently, before dampening a cloth in the porcelain washbowl. Placing it against Star's brow to try to prevent her fainting, Sugar breathed a sigh of relief when she saw the color returning to the girl's cheeks.

"Star, for the love of God, what ever possessed you to leave this room? I warned you not to go out when the Red Passion was open for business, and now the very thing I feared has happened," Sugar scolded. Tossing the wet cloth back into the bowl, she sat down beside Star and placed a comforting arm about her young friend's shoulders.

"I was so hot I couldn't sleep, and I kept remembering. I couldn't endure being cooped up here a moment more. I didn't mean to let anyone see me or to let—" Star's explanation came to a stumbling halt. She could not force herself to voice to Sugar what had transpired between herself and the stranger. New tears of shame and remorse brimmed in her blue eyes at the memory and she glanced down at her tightly clasped hands, unable to look at her friend.

"You don't have to say it, Star. I already know what happened. Kyle told me what transpired and left this for you. He thought you were one of my girls and I didn't disillusion him. It's better that way. At least he was generous with you and the money he left should help you reach your aunt in DryCreek."

Star stiffened. She jerked away from Sugar as if she had been struck across the face. Her eyes resembled hard sapphires as she spat, "I won't take his money. If I did, I'd *be* the whore he thought me to be." Even as the words left her lips, she regretted them. She hadn't meant to hurt this kind woman.

"Sugar, forgive me," she said hastily. "I don't know what made me say such a horrid thing. I didn't mean it the way it sounded. You've been a good friend to me and I don't condemn you for the life you've chosen, but it's not for me. I made a mistake last night, but I'll only be adding to it if I take the man's money."

"His name is Kyle Hunter," Sugar calmly interjected, unoffended by Star's rash words. She had grown to know the girl during the last weeks and knew that Star had not spoken out of malice. Sugar understood that her words came from the pain and humiliation she was still suffering. She, too, had known those feelings years ago when she was still a slave. It had been the owner of the plantation who had degraded her upon a corn-husk mattress in the slave shanty when she was twelve. Her cries of pain had been heard only by her own people and none could come to her aid against their white master. Her torment lasted until she was fifteen and her master's wife had learned of his obsession with the young slave. His wife had sold her downriver to the madam of a whorehouse in New Orleans. Fortunately for Sugar, the woman had had a kind heart and let her work with her other girls, and when Sugar finally had enough money, she'd let her buy her freedom.

"I don't care what his name is. I won't take his money. I don't want to ever think of him again for as long as I live," Star burst out angrily. She pushed herself to her feet and began to pace the floor, trying to outdistance the image of the moon-silvered visage that rose in her mind to haunt her.

"I'm afraid you're not going to get that wish, Star," Sugar said. Taking a leaflet from her pocket, she held it out to her. "Maud found this tacked up on Silver Street late yesterday afternoon. It's a poster for a reward of five hundred dollars to anyone who has knowledge of your whereabouts. The bills have been posted all over Natchez."

Star's hand trembled violently as she unfolded the paper. As Sugar had said, it was a wanted poster with her likeness sketched in perfect detail. Brett was offering a reward to anyone who had information that would lead him to her. Star let the poster fall to the floor at her feet and looked once more at Sugar.

"I should have expected this from Brett Tremayne. Nothing he does surprises me. But it's still unnerving to see your own image staring back at you from a wanted poster. He didn't waste much time in setting the dogs on my trail, did he?"

"That's why I'm afraid you're not going to get your wish about Kyle Hunter," Sugar said. "We have only one opportunity to get you out of Natchez and that is on the wagon train he'll be leading across the river at the end of the week."

"Sugar, you can't believe that I'd travel in the same wagon train as that man? He's no better than Brett. I learned that much about him last night. He's selfish, arrogant, and thinks of no one but himself. No, Sugar. I won't go anywhere with him."

"Damn it, Star, you have no choice. I've tried unsuccessfully to find a way to get you out of Natchez during the last weeks and now that I've found one, you're going to take it. You'll be traveling with friends of mine, the Ransons, and there is no reason for you to even speak with Kyle if that is your wish. He's leading the wagon train, Star. No one is suggesting that you bed him." Sugar's voice was tinged with exasperation and her dark eyes flashed with annoyance as she came to her feet.

"What you say may be true, but if I try to leave Natchez with the wagon train, I'll have to deal with the authorities. With all of the posters tacked up over the city," Star said, toeing the offending piece of paper, "how long do you think I will go unrecognized?"

Sugar frowned thoughtfully, her red lips pursing as she absently twirled a long curl about one finger and assessed Star from head to toe. The girl's appearance would create problems. She could be recognized easily from the drawing on the posters. Studying Star a moment longer a glimmer of an idea began to take root. The poster had specified a white girl, not a black one.

"I think I have a plan that will work, but you may not like it," she said and smiled.

"Recently I've learned there are quite a number of things in life that I don't like but I've lived through them all so far," Star said. She, too, smiled, the first smile Sugar had seen since entering the room. Yet her gesture held no mirth, only self-mockery.

"But how will you feel about turning yourself black?" Sugar asked, her dark eyes twinkling at the thought.

"Black?" Star asked, bemused. "How can I change the color of my skin?"

"Simple," Sugar said, laughing, "or at least I think it will be. We'll get some of the same walnut stain that we use as a rinse on our hair to hide the gray. It's a marvelous dye, though you'll have to let the stain wear off gradually."

"Do you honestly believe that no one will recognize me?"

"Yes," Sugar stated firmly. "They are searching for a white girl, a southern lady who would take a stagecoach or riverboat. They'd never suspect a black girl traveling with a young couple and a baby on a wagon train. The only problem I can foresee with your appearance will be the color of your eyes. But you can learn to act like a good and obedient slave and keep your eyes respectfully lowered when anyone's near who might suspect your ruse."

"Is the wagon train going to DryCreek?"

"No, Star, I'm afraid it is headed to a place called Sagebrush. But it is the closest I can get you to your aunt. From what I've learned from Kyle, Sagebrush is about a two- or three-day ride south of DryCreek."

"Then how will I reach my aunt's ranch from Sagebrush?" Star asked, fearing the thought of once more being stranded in a town without friends.

"I've already taken care of that for you. I spoke with Jake Ranson and he's promised to escort you to your aunt's as soon as he gets Priscilla and the baby settled."

"Sugar, I appreciate all that you've done for me, but I don't know if I can go through with this farce since that man is going to be leading the wagon train. Seeing him every day is going to be like rubbing salt into an open wound. I want to try to forget what I let happen last night. I don't want to be constantly reminded of my foolishness every time I look up over a campfire."

"Star," Sugar said as she crossed to her and hugged

her close as if she were her mother, "you can't let that one mistake destroy you. If all you've told me is true about the man who is hunting you, then he'll stop at nothing to find you. If you refuse to travel with the Ransons because of what transpired last night, then you'll surely suffer because of it. That man is out for blood if the wanted poster is any indication of his intentions.

"You have to put last night out of your mind and remember that you're still the same person today as you were yesterday. Nothing has happened to change the brave young woman who came seeking my help. You are still Star Grayson. Hold your head up and don't be ashamed. You took your destiny into your hands when you left home. You became a woman who does not have to answer to anyone except her own conscience and to God."

"That's the problem, Sugar. I have to answer to myself and I find what I did unforgiveable. I vowed never to let anyone use me again and then I fell into the arms of the next man who crossed my path. I honestly don't know what's wrong with me but something is," Star said, before giving Sugar a wry grin. "Perhaps I should stay at the Red Passion after all. My actions seem to indicate that I would be good at your profession."

Sugar laughed aloud and shook her head. "No, Star. You'd not make a good whore though if you could, I'd be much the richer for it. But that will never happen to you. A whore has to be able to distance herself from her feelings and you can't do that. You have too much love in your heart to give and you also need to be loved. Don't condemn yourself for reaching out for love, even if it was only a momentary thing. It's the natural order of life. It happens to all of us at one time or another, especially when men like Kyle Hunter are involved. There is something about men like him that draws us to them over all our protests. We can't stop how we feel, no more than we can stop breathing. Kyle . . ."

"Kyle Hunter be damned," Star swore, cutting off Sugar's words. "I'll keep my distance from that scoundrel. One mistake with that man is enough to last me a lifetime.''

''Perhaps,'' Sugar murmured and hid her smile of satisfaction. From what she'd gleaned from Star's protests and Kyle's terse explanation there was a fire between the two that could not be easily extinguished. It would be hard for either of them to resist. She'd been in the business of love far too long not to recognize the attraction the two young people had for each other, though neither would admit it at the moment.

True, what they felt was not yet love, but given a chance it might develop. Sugar chuckled as she hugged Star once more. She'd wager that the journey to Sagebrush would be interesting once Kyle learned that his mystery woman was traveling in the disguise of a black slave.

Chapter 4

A warm May breeze stirred the curtains in the open window as Star slipped the homespun cotton gown over her head and laced it down the front. Turning to the cracked cheval glass mirror, she lifted her thick mane of hair and coiled it neatly on top of her head before securing it with several pins. Retrieving the red cloth from the narrow bed, she wound it about her head in turban fashion as she had often seen Dulcie do. The red turban was an essential part of her disguise. It proclaimed her status as a slave. Freed black women wore white to separate themselves from their sisters who were still held in bondage.

Satisfied with her efforts, she stepped back and surveyed her reflection. It was unnerving to look into the mirror and not recognize her own image. The walnut stain and oil concoction Sugar had used to darken her skin had achieved the desired transformation. The skin of her face, neck, arms, and shoulders was now a deep, rich honey-brown shade. To the casual observer it would be nearly impossible to know that she was not in fact a mulatto by birth. The blue of her eyes had posed the only problem to her disguise, but Sugar had assured her that it was only a minor one. Often those born with mixed blood inherited some prominent feature from their white sires and many could easily pass for white because of it. Sugar Brown herself was a prime example. Gazing at her image, Star realized that if any of the Red Passion's customers had to decide, between herself and the madam of the brothel, who was white, Sugar would be the one ultimately chosen.

An uneasy feeling settled in the pit of Star's stomach at the thought. The full implications of the ruse she had agreed to play out disturbed her. Once she walked out of the Red Passion and joined the Ransons, she would no longer be Star Grayson, the young heiress of Jasmine Hall. In the eyes of the world she would be a slave, and as such she would be restricted to a subservient position among the whites on the wagon train. She would have to remember to act and talk like a slave. Her every move would have to be guarded when in the presence of those who believed her to be black.

Tiny lines creased her brow as she frowned at her reflection. The entire scheme went against her independent nature. She had enjoyed her freedom far too long to like the idea of giving it up for even the short time it would take to reach Texas. The only consolation she could find in Sugar's plan was the fact that Kyle Hunter would not be able to recognize her as the girl he had met at the Red Passion and she was grateful for that small blessing.

"Are you ready, Star?" Sugar asked from the doorway.

Star jumped with surprise. Lost in her reverie she had failed to hear the door open. Drawing in a deep breath to quell the queasy sensation in the pit of her stomach, she turned to Sugar and nodded. "I'm as ready as I'll ever be."

"Good. Jake and Priscilla are waiting downstairs with the baby. Little Jake is screaming his head off, so I suggest we hurry before I have a riot of angry women on my hands. My girls are usually a good-natured lot, but they do put up a row when their beauty sleep is disturbed."

Star cast one last anxious glance at her reflection before she picked up her portmanteau and followed Sugar from the room that had been both prison and haven during the last uncertain weeks. The sound of the baby's cries greeted them at the top of the stairs and Star paused, unable to go down the last few steps and set into motion the plan that would end her freedom and make her the Ransons' slave. All of the uncertainties that went with Sugar's scheme came flooding back and she turned to the older woman, her young face reflecting her feelings as she sought reassurance.

"Everything is going to work out," Sugar said, reading Star's silent plea in her eyes. Placing a comforting arm about the girl's shoulders, she drew Star down the stairs. "No one will recognize you, nor will they suspect the girl called Annie is actually the young woman described on the posters—if they've even seen any of them. I doubt they have, since they've been camped outside of town all week and have been busy readying their wagons for the journey west."

"Annie?" Star asked, wondering at Sugar's reason for changing her name.

"Yes. For your safety and the Ransons' that's how you'll be known to them. I've chosen to keep your identity a secret so that there will be no accidental slip of the tongue while you're with them. That could lead to unnecessary trouble for all concerned. After you're in safe territory you can tell them the truth if you wish, but for now you'll be Annie."

Grateful for Sugar's forethought, Star nodded. "Have you told your friends that they'll be helping someone who is wanted for murder?" she asked.

"I've explained your circumstances to Jake and Priscilla and they understand. They know what it's like to be forced into a situation that's not of your own making. They also know how it feels to need help and they are more than willing to give it. Now, let's get you downstairs before Little Jake disturbs the entire household. He's screaming loud enough to wake the dead, as well as everyone else in Natchez," Sugar said, laughing.

A petite blonde and a tall, thin man with a head of bushy red hair and an equally red beard met them at the foot of the stairs. Jake Ranson held a squalling infant on his shoulder, patting its tiny back with his wide, callused hand. He smiled apologetically at them and shook his head. "This little feller has got the colic," he said, slightly bewildered as to what he could do to quieten his son.

"So we and half the town have heard," Sugar said and smiled. She took the chubby babe from his father and cradled it lovingly in her arms, a tender expression filling her beautiful face as she gazed down into Little Jake's tiny red one. "I'm going to miss this noisy godchild of mine. I expect you to write and let me know how he's doing once you get settled, Jake."

"I will, Sugar," Jake said. "And don't you worry about us. You know I won't let anything happen to my family."

"That's my one consolation. Now take your son so I can say farewell to your wife." Sugar handed the babe back to his father and turned to Priscilla, who stood quietly at her husband's side. The madam hugged the younger woman and then pressed a bag of coins into her hand as she stepped back and smiled, her eyes bright with tears. "I'm glad you're happy, Pris. I always knew you weren't meant for the Red Passion. Your heart is too gentle. You deserve your two men. I only wish all of my girls could be half as fortunate as you've been. Remember that if you ever need anything you only have to ask."

"I know, Sugar," Priscilla said, her lips trembling with emotion and her cornflower-blue eyes misting with tears. "I'm so grateful to you for all you've done for me since the first day I came here. We're going to miss you."

Resolutely, Sugar cleared her throat and wiped at the dampness in her own eyes. "Enough of this," she said hoarsely, "or we'll all have red eyes and that's not good in my business." Turning to Star, she said, "Pris, this is Annie, the girl I told you about."

"Hello, Annie," Priscilla said as she extended her hand in welcome. A warm smile tugged at the corners of her lips, making small dimples in her cheeks deepen becomingly. "We're glad to have you with us. Now it won't be so lonely for me."

Liking the young woman instantly, Star shook Priscilla's hand. "I certainly appreciate what you're doing for me. I'll try not to be a burden to you."

"Burden? You'll be no such thing." Jake chuckled as he draped his arm about his wife's narrow shoulders. "Pris needs another woman along to keep her company. Though she denies it, she's a shy little thing when it comes to meeting people, especially other women. She still feels awkward about her past when she's around a bunch of judgmental old biddies. I've told her she's better than any of them and that she's now a respectable married lady, with a family to boot, but I can't seem to convince her."

"Jake!" Priscilla scolded before blushing a bright red to the roots of her flaxen hair.

"Well, it's true, ain't it, honey?" Jake asked. Looking to Sugar for support, he continued, "You tell her. Maybe she'll believe you, Sugar."

"Jake's right, Pris," Sugar began, but before she could say more Little Jake let out another loud howl.

Jake released a long, resigned breath and shook his head. "It was a blessing while it lasted. Annie, if you can help Pris with this little varmint, you, too, will be a blessing in disguise."

Star, Sugar, and Priscilla looked from one another and then at Jake before they burst into laughter. It took Jake a moment longer to comprehend the reason behind their mirth and then he, too, joined in the merriment, laughing at his inadvertent reference to Star's ruse.

"I'll help Priscilla all I can, but to be truthful, I've never taken care of a baby before. All I really know about them is that I like them," Star said, feeling much better about her future with the young couple.

"That's good enough for me. If you like 'em, then you've got the rest all sewn up," Jake said. "Now it's time that we got back to the wagon. Mr. Hunter said he wants us to cross the river this afternoon so that we can get an early start in the morning." Handing his son to his wife, Jake turned to Sugar. "Come here, woman."

He chuckled as he wrapped his arms about her and swung her off her feet. He planted an exuberant kiss upon her red lips before he set her down and then grinned. "That's my farewell to you, Sugar Brown. Now I'll give the women their turn while I take care of this rascal." Reclaiming his son, he strode to the door.

Priscilla's face was damp with new tears as she quickly hugged and kissed Sugar. Her throat was too tight with emotion to do or say more to the woman who had become her surrogate mother. Sniffling back a new flood of tears, she hurried in her husband's wake.

Star watched Priscilla's exit before she turned back to Sugar. For a long moment they stood looking at each other, their eyes brimming with moisture before they embraced. All Star could say was an emotion-filled thank you, but both knew those two words expressed much more. Wiping her eyes with the back of her hand, she picked up her portmanteau and quickly followed the Ransons from the Red Passion. She paused momentarily beside Jake's buckboard and looked back at the white, two-storied house. Within its walls she had learned many startling things about life and herself. She had found compassion, understanding, and friendship, and she knew she would never forget the Red Passion or its beautiful madam.

"May God bless your gentle heart, Sugar Brown," she whispered as she turned and placed her bag in the flat bed of the buckboard before climbing up beside the Ransons and their squalling infant.

The Hunter wagon train had made good time during the two weeks it had taken to cross the softly rolling landscape of Louisiana. The weather had remained fair and the road posed few problems for the oxen and wagons. It was hard-packed from much use, since it led to the center of shipping in northwestern Louisiana and the surrounding states.

Shreveport, founded by Henry Miller Shreve in 1834 on the west bank of the Red River, flourished because of the large cotton plantations in the area and its close proximity to Texas, Arkansas, and Oklahoma. Lumber, cattle, and cotton, as well as other goods, were brought to the city to be transported by flatboat down the rivers to New Orleans where they would be sold at market.

The wagon train arrived early in the afternoon at the river crossing, but the last rays of the sun were streaking through the branches of the tall pines, casting long shadows by the time the Mctaggart wagon was ferried to the opposite shore. It was the last of the fourteen wagons that had begun their journey in Natchez. Once it was safely ashore, they made camp for the night on the outskirts of Shreveport.

An air of excitement seemed to hover over the encampment as the men and women built fires and erected their sleeping tents. The smell of fresh bread and coffee filled the air as the evening meal was prepared and then eaten with hardy appetites. As had become the custom, since the first night on the trail when they had gathered to get acquainted, neighbors visited together, discussing the events of the day before their conversations turned to the main topic for one and all, the journey to Texas and what they would do once they reached their destination. Each voice and face was filled with optimism at the prospect of the new life and future they hoped awaited them once they claimed their land.

None realized the trials that lay in store. Nor did they ever imagine that when they looked back upon the jubilation they had felt during the first weeks of their journey, they would view it cynically, like an adult who reflects upon his childhood dreams and finds them tarnished beyond recognition.

Unaware of the future, and excited because only eighteen miles separated them from the Texas border, everyone in camp was in a mood to celebrate. Harry Linden retrieved his fiddle from one of the two wagons it took to move his family of ten across the country and began to play a lively jig to everyone's delight. Seth Mctaggart, in one of his rare and friendly moods, brought out a precious clay jug filled with homemade whiskey, and soon the entire populace of the wagon train was enjoying the impromptu celebration. The adults and adolescents danced, while the younger children started their own games, squealing, giggling, and chasing each other around the campfires and into the deepening shadows beyond the wagons.

No one considered it odd that the young black woman they had come to know as Annie remained at the Ransons' wagon while Jake and Priscilla, though only after much cajoling from her husband and Star, joined the festivities. Nor did Star regret the fact that she was not included in the merriment because of the color of her skin. She was content to sit by the fire, cradling Little Jake in her arms. The bundle sleeping peacefully, with one tiny, plump hand resting innocently against her breast as he snuggled closer to her warmth, brought her more pleasure than dancing a dozen times to Harry Linden's music.

Looking down into the chubby little features, she felt her heart stir with tenderness for the child who had strangely taken an instant liking to her on the first day. She brushed her lips against his down-covered head and felt humbled by his innocent trust. Little Jake Ranson had captured her heart.

Preoccupied with her musing over the new feelings the babe had awakened in her, Star failed to hear the jingle of spurs and jumped as a deep, masculine voice asked, "Don't you want to join the revelry?"

Star's heart seemed to still beneath her ribs as she recognized Kyle Hunter's voice. His sudden appearance unnerved her. During the past weeks she had successfully avoided him. Each time he came to visit Jake and Priscilla she had used the excuse of gathering firewood or caring for Little Jake inside the wagon to stay as far away from him as possible. She had thought that with the passage of time, seeing him about the camp every day, she would gradually become accustomed to his presence, but that had not happened. She'd known that she would not always be able to avoid him but had thought when the time came she would be prepared.

Now that the moment was upon her, she found that she wasn't at all ready for the encounter. Her shock made her forget to keep her eyes lowered as was expected of a slave and she stared up at him. To her regret, she found his devastating good looks did little for her peace of mind. Her heart seemed to lodge in her throat, making it impossible to speak as she gazed up at him with wide, frightened eyes.

To Star's relief, Little Jake came to her rescue. He whimpered and began to flail the air with his small arms, giving her the excuse she needed to center her attention on the child. The babe wailed loudly, sensing Star's unrest.

Ignoring Kyle's question, she stood and turned toward the wagon and safety. As she hurried past Kyle, mimicking Dulcie's speech, she murmured a quick, nearly inaudible apology. "I sorry, sir, but I gots to tend the babe."

Bemused by the girl's abrupt flight, Kyle stared at the canvas flap still swaying in the air from her swift passage. A puzzled frown creased his brow as he pushed his hat to the back of his head and rubbed his hand over the stubble of dark beard that shadowed his cheeks.

"Damn, I didn't mean to frighten the girl to death," he mused aloud. Giving an offhand shrug, he turned and strode toward the merrymakers, but his thoughts remained on the young black woman traveling with the Ransons. The look he had seen in her eyes when she gazed up at him had reminded him of a rabbit cornered by a wolf. She'd also taken flight as if she'd been one of the fleet little animals scurrying back to the safety of its den.

"I know I look rough after a day in the saddle, but this is ridiculous," he muttered under his breath as he neared the revelers. With a shake of his head, he put the girl from his mind and let the group draw him into their celebration.

Cradling the screaming infant against her breast, Star rocked back and forth on her haunches to try to quieten him while she hid in the wagon. Her heart beat furiously against her ribs as the vivid memory of her last encounter with Kyle Hunter resurfaced. All the pain and humiliation she had thought buried now came back and burned a searing path through her, opening a reservoir of tears. Until that moment she had thought she'd shed all the tears of regret that she possessed, but, this new encounter with Kyle made her realize differently and they ran unchecked down her cheeks.

After several long minutes of weeping along with Little Jake, her tears began to abate with his cries. The babe drifted off to sleep, but Star did not venture from the wagon. She knew in her present state of mind that she was not strong enough to face Kyle again that night. Spreading out the bedding, she lay down and cradled the baby in the curve of her arm. Staring vacantly up at the white canvas overhead, she mused aloud, "Why did I ever let Sugar convince me that I could travel on the same wagon train with that man and not be constantly reminded of the night in the garden of the Red Passion?"

Star covered her eyes with her hand to stay a new bout of tears as a little voice in the back of her mind argued, You didn't have any choice.

"Choice? It seems I've done nothing but make the wrong decisions since the night Fiona died. I should have stayed at Jasmine Hall and fought to prove my innocence instead of running away like a coward. By leaving, I've only succeeded in making people believe that I did kill her," she reasoned in return.

Yes, and now you have to keep running, the little voice supplied. You have no other alternative.

Star drew in a long, shuddering breath. It was true. Now her only hope rested with an aunt she had never met. If Clarice failed to help her, then she would never be free to return to her home.

"But first I have to live through the next weeks with Kyle Hunter nearby and right now I don't know if I have the strength," she whispered, her voice filling with despair as the thought overwhelmed her.

Where is Star Grayson? the little voice challenged. Where is the girl who prided herself on her independence, the girl who taught herself to shoot and ride? Has she become a coward?

Star pressed her lips into a mutinous line as the questions reverberated painfully through her mind. Since the night of Fiona's death she had lost sight of the girl she had been. She had let fear control her actions to such an extent that she had become a coward who was unwilling to face life head-on. She had let others make her decisions for her.

"That time has come to an end," she mused softly into the night. Mentally stiffening her spine, she renewed her determination. "I let Sugar plan this ruse, but now it's up to me to see it to its end and I won't let Kyle Hunter or anyone else jeopardize it." There was too much at stake. She had to reach her aunt and then find a way to set her life to rights once more.

"I'll be damned if I let one man make me a mass of quivering jelly every time I see him," Star spoke bravely, but even as the words left her lips she knew she would still try to avoid Kyle in the future. There were feelings deep within her that she didn't completely trust where he was concerned. She couldn't understand them, but she knew it was in her best interest to guard against them. The memory of his lips possessing hers and the feeling of his hands caressing her body were still able to make her breath come much too quickly for her peace of mind. The first pleasurable moments that they had shared overshadowed the last painful and humiliating ones and because of that she would stay as far away from him as possible.

Turning on her side, she cuddled Little Jake close to her body and closed her eyes. Tomorrow they would cross into Texas and she would be one day closer to her aunt and to returning to Jasmine Hall as Star Grayson.

Chapter 5

The excitement everyone felt upon reaching the Texas border soon faded. Each day seemed to bring new hardships to the members of the wagon train. Unlike Louisiana, Texas had few good roads and those were soon left behind once the wagon train passed through the more populated eastern section of the state and moved westward. After crossing the Sabine River, the roads were little more than cattle trails gouged into the dry earth. The deep ruts took their toll on the wagons, breaking axles and spokes, and slowing the train's progress to a snail's pace.

The fortunes of the Hunter party did not improve when it began to rain. The hard grayish-brown prairie clay turned into a quagmire. Mixed with the wet grass, it caked the wheels of the wagons until the teams of oxen were unable to pull the heavy vehicles. Every able-bodied member of the train trudged alongside the wagons to help keep the wheels free of the tacky substance to prevent them from being bogged down. It was a wet, exhausting chore that left everyone too tired at night to complain about the crackers and raw bacon that had become their mainstay since the rain had made it impossible to build fires to cook adequate meals.

"I never want to see another raindrop," Star muttered in disgust as a jagged streak of lightning seared the afternoon sky. An explosive boom of thunder rolled in its wake, making the earth tremble beneath her feet as she

ducked under the piece of canvas she had convinced Jake
to tack to the side of the wagon. The makeshift lean-to
provided a semidry place against the elements so that she
could make an attempt to build a fire and cook them a
warm meal.

Frowning as another rumble of thunder shook the earth
and a gust of wind drove a sheet of rain beneath the
canvas, Star dumped the wood on the ground. It was
green and wet, but she hoped to get it to burn. Wiping
the moisture from her face, she glanced up at the slate-
colored sky and shivered. It had rained every day for a
week, soaking everything and everyone. The canvas that
covered the wagons shielded them from the pelting pre-
cipitation, but it did little to protect them from the invading dampness that leaked through the thick cotton
sheeting and wet everything that was not protected by
wooded crates or trunks.

Though it was early June and the weather was not cold,
the dampness seeped through every layer of clothing and
left everyone chilled to the bone. Shivering again, she
bent and began to dig a small pit where she hoped to
build the fire. Once that was done, she carefully stacked
the wood to ensure an updraft for the blaze and then
began the task of trying to make the green branches burn.

The steady drum of the rain on the canvas overhead
blocked out all other sounds as she worked intently to
light the fire. She did not realize that she was no longer
alone until Kyle hunkered down beside her and took the
matches from her hand.

"This wood is too wet to burn without dry kindling,"
he said. Drops of rain dripped over the brim of his hat
and ran down the front of the slicker he wore as he
moved. "Maybe this will help," he said, placing a splintered pine knot beneath the wood before setting a match
to it. After several futile attempts, the resin finally burst
into flame. He smiled at his success as the blaze grew
stronger and began to consume the mesquite. Tipping his
hat to the back of his head, he held his hands out to the
flames warmth and gave Star a wry grin.

Unnerved by his sudden appearance and unable to stop herself from reacting to his nearness, she moved to the other side of the fire, putting as much distance between them as the small shelter would allow. She felt her insides turn to jelly as she looked across the fire at him, and she fought to retain her composure as she watched his affable expression fade. A prickle of apprehension raced up her spine at the intense look she saw in his piercing green eyes. It made her throat go dry and she had to swallow several times before she could murmur, "Thanks for yo' help, Master Hunter." Not knowing what else to do or say, she quickly busied herself with the task at hand and hoped if she continued to ignore him, he would leave. She picked up a stone and began to drive one of two forked sticks into the ground. They would support the rod that would hold the covered kettle of stew.

Kyle noted her agitation and frowned. For the life of him he could not understand what it was about him that frightened the girl. Every time he came near the Ransons' wagon she reacted as if the earth had opened up and spewed forth the devil. What was even more vexing was the fact that she didn't react to everyone in the same manner. His presence, it seemed, was the only one to disturb her. Since he had spoken to her only once or twice in passing, the only explanation he could find for her odd behavior was that he must resemble someone in her past who had mistreated her. Something within him rebelled at the thought and made him want to prove to Annie that he would do her no harm.

"Let me do that," Kyle volunteered. He pushed himself to his feet and moved around the fire to her side.

"No, Master Hunter. I couldn't impose on you no further," Star said, concentrating on pounding the stick into the ground.

"It's no imposition, Annie. I intend to be well paid for my efforts."

Star froze at the vivid memory his words aroused. She could nearly hear the jingle of coins he had left for her at the Red Passion for the services she had rendered. Tired from trudging through the mud all day and having had little food to nourish her strength, she thought for one wild moment that she would burst into tears from the pain the recollection brought forth. When Kyle reached for the stone she held, she jerked her hand away before he could touch her. Her wide blue eyes were shadowed as she stared up at him.

"Annie, I swear you're as skittish as an unbroken colt. I mean you no harm, so you have no reason to fear me," Kyle said softly as he gazed down into her firelight-drenched face. She regarded him warily, looking as if she was ready to bolt again if he made the wrong move.

Kyle's frown knit his dark brows across his slender nose. Until that moment he had never truly paid close attention to the Ransons' slave but now upon closer scrutiny, he realized with a start that she was truly beautiful. The golden light of the fire emphasized her delicately sculpted features and the rich honey shade of her skin. It reminded him of burnished velvet and for one brief moment he had the desire to feel its softness beneath his hand.

His thoughts were abruptly jolted away from the path they were taking by an uncanny feeling that came to him. He felt as if he had known Annie at some time or place in the past. Puzzled by the strange sensation, he searched his mind, seeking to recall the elusive memory. He knew it had not been while he was visiting his relatives in Mississippi. After his cousins had heard his views on slavery and had told him to keep them to himself or find himself tarred and feathered as an abolitionist, they had guarded their servants like a precious treasure that could be contaminated if it came into contact with him. He also knew he had not met her in Texas. It was a slave state, but the majority of the blacks there were used by the planters who grew cotton in the eastern section of the state. There were several black cowboys working on the ranches surrounding the Bar H but there were no black females.

Unable to draw the recollection from the dark recesses

of his mind, he said, "I didn't mean to frighten you. I only wanted to help. I had hoped you'd feel obligated to offer me a hot meal in exchange for my efforts."

A wave of relief washed over Star and she felt suddenly foolish for letting Kyle's presence upset her to such an extent. She had no reason to be wary of him. He didn't suspect the girl he knew as Annie to be the same one he had seduced in the garden of the Red Passion. Strangely, Star found no comfort in the thought.

It was debasing to realize how little her virginity had meant to him. He could look her directly in the face and not recognize her after only a few short weeks. He had completely forgotten her and the moments they had shared while she was constantly reminded of their intimacy each time she saw him. Humiliation and anger mingled in her as she flashed Kyle a look of loathing and silently cursed: Damn you for the cold-hearted bastard that you are, Kyle Hunter. You and Brett Tremayne were cut from the same cloth.

Kyle watched Star's expression change and wondered what he had said or done to induce the hostility he saw sparkling in her eyes. But before he could find the answer, Jake came stamping in out of the wet. Raindrops popped and sizzled in the fire as he shook the water from his hat and slicker. He grinned appreciatively at the blaze and held out his hands to its warmth.

"Damn, this feels good after being damp for so long," Jake said, glancing across the fire at Kyle and Star. Sensing the tension between them, he frowned. "Is something wrong?"

"No, sir," Star muttered as she turned her attention back to the task of driving the second stick into the ground with a vengeance. Each blow she struck, she felt as if she was striking out at Kyle Hunter and Brett Tremayne, the two men who had disrupted her life.

Bewildered by her abrupt manner, Jake looked from her furious face to Kyle and said, "Pris has prepared one of her stews and some biscuits. You're welcome to join us for supper."

"I appreciate the offer, Jake, but I'll have to forgo the invitation tonight. The rain has let up enough for me to ride out and see how high the water is in the Trinity. If we can make the crossing by tomorrow afternoon we should reach Fort Worth by the day after even in this weather."

"If you should change your mind, the offer's still open. You don't know what you'll be missing. My mouth waters just thinking about Pris's stew."

"I'll remember that," Kyle said as he pulled his hat lower on his brow and cast one last curious look at Annie before he strode out into the rain.

"Damn the man," Star cursed, still feeling the sting of her earlier thoughts.

Jake's puzzled frown drew his bushy red brows low over his eyes as he looked at her. "Did Kyle do something to make you angry, Annie?"

Star shook her head, unable to tell Jake the reason behind her ill temper.

"Then what's got your dander up? I've never seen you act like this before."

"He didn't say or do anything, Jake. I just don't like the man," Star answered, avoiding his curious gaze.

Jake did not pry. He sensed that there was more involved than mere dislike between Annie and Kyle, but he let the matter drop. He and Priscilla also had secrets that they did not want the world to know. Changing the subject, he said, "That fire looks about ready for Pris's stew. After the fare we've eaten for the last few days, I believe hot mud would probably taste good, but I'm glad that's not what we're having."

Grateful to Jake for intuitively knowing that she didn't want to discuss Kyle Hunter, Star smiled. "You're lucky I'm not doing the cooking or it *would* taste like hot mud."

"You mean you don't know how to cook?" Jake asked, his face reflecting his surprise at learning that a grown woman could not cook.

"I've never learned. I preferred to let the servants do the cooking while I spent my time fishing and riding.

Those were far more interesting pursuits to me,'' Star said, her expression growing wistful as she gazed down into the flames and recalled the halcyon days she had spent in her childhood at Jasmine Hall. She had been lonely, yet she knew now that if she could recall those peaceful times, she would gladly do so. But that could never happen. Brett Tremayne's greed had put an end to that part of her life and at the present moment she didn't know if she would ever be able to return to her home. The thought of never seeing Jasmine Hall again was so painful that tears brimmed in her eyes. She turned abruptly away to hide her misery. ''I'll go care for Little Jake while Pris cooks supper,'' she murmured before hurrying toward the end of the wagon and clambering inside.

Jake watched Star's sudden retreat and shook his head sadly as he turned back to the fire. He had heard the tears in her voice and had seen the pain that shadowed her face as she remembered her past. Watching her was like looking into a mirror at himself before he met Priscilla. Until that time he had also been hiding from his memories, afraid to let anyone know the secret that haunted his days and nights.

Jake stared thoughtfully into the flames as his mind turned once more to the past he had tried so hard to forget but could not. It had been several years since he'd turned his back on his family and their way of making a living—river piracy.

At the age of thirteen he'd begun to help his father and brothers and had thought little of the crimes they committed, running heavily loaded barges aground and then stealing their goods. It was their way of life, the only life he knew, and he'd enjoyed his share of the profits that came from reselling the goods in New Orleans. Until the deaths of the woman and little girl, he had never truly comprehended that what they did was wrong.

The memory of that night still hounded him, riddling him with guilt for not having had enough courage to go against his brothers when they forced everyone on the barge to jump overboard. In the past they had done the same thing to give themselves time to make their escape with the goods while the bargemen swam to shore, but then there had been no women or children involved. Jake could still hear the cries of the woman and the little girl as they fought against the river current before it tugged them down into their watery grave.

A shiver passed along his spine and raised gooseflesh on his arms as he again heard their terrified screams. That night had ended his career as a river pirate. He left his family, determined to try to make a better life for himself. He took none of the money from the fateful shipment with him. His cowardliness had helped kill two helpless people and he would have no part of the profits from it.

Priscilla was the only person he had ever told of that night and it had been her love and understanding that had helped him to gradually come to the point at which he could live with himself for the part he had played in the affair.

Giving himself a mental shake, he glanced once more toward the wagon and mused, "We all need someone to love, Annie. Hopefully someday you'll be as fortunate as I've been to find someone to share your past as well as your future. He might not be able to rid you of all your troubles, but his love can help you survive them."

Jake smiled as he saw his wife step down from the wagon with the two covered pots that held their supper of stew and biscuits. He hurried forward to help her with the heavy burden. Setting the kettles over the flames, he turned and wrapped his arms about his wife's small body and hugged her close. "I love you, Pris," he murmured against her hair.

Priscilla closed her slender arms about his waist and pressed her cheek against his chest, listening to the comforting sound of his heart. "I love you, too, Jake Ranson," she whispered, content with the world as long as she was in her husband's arms.

The hot midday sun bore down unmercifully, baking the moisture out of the soil and leaving the dark clay cracked and curling like unevenly laid tiles. Star squinted against its brightness as she glanced at the tense faces of the women who stood on the riverbank, watching their husbands work to get each wagon safely across the rain-swollen Trinity. Their eyes were shadowed with fear, but they stood quietly, showing no outward sign of their worry.

Star admired these women who had left all they knew and loved to follow their husbands into the wilderness of west Texas. As she had soon learned after leaving Natchez, it was not easy for anyone to travel cross country by wagon train, but it was the hardest on the women. They had to tend to their children, walk miles in the blistering sun or chilling rain, make camp for the night, cook the meals after collecting the wood for the fires, and then set up the sleeping tents. After a few short hours of rest upon the hard earth, they arose to do it all over again the following day. They worked from dawn til dusk, never sparing a thought to the back-breaking labor required of them to keep their families going onward toward their husbands' dreams. They faced each day and trial as it came, overcoming the difficulties they encountered along the way with an outward bravado that hid the fears that dwelled within them about their family's welfare.

A camaraderie had developed among the women on Hunter's wagon train. They were kindred spirits, allied by the common goal of keeping their families together and safe. Each understood the others' silent fears and instinctively sensed when her support was needed to sustain her friends during the most trying times on the trail.

Star glanced down at their tightly clasped hands and knew that they were experiencing one of those moments now. Each woman feared that she might lose a husband or son to the swift, muddy water that sucked greedily at the men as they worked with the wagons.

She was jerked away from her reflections when May

Linden broke away from the group and ran toward the edge of the riverbank.

''Sonny!'' the older woman screamed, horrified by the sight of her fifteen-year-old son being carried downriver by the strong current. He fought frantically to keep his head above the water, flailing his arms and clawing upward, seeking any hold that would save him.

Seeing that the boy could not swim and knowing that he would not last until the men could reach him, Star did not take the time to consider her own actions. She ran to the edge of the river and dove in. She surfaced a few feet downstream from where Sonny fought to stay afloat.

She struggled to reach him, but the river current tore at her. She was a strong swimmer, but her long skirts wrapped about her legs, hampering her movements; their weight threatened to drag her under the churning surface. The distance between Star and the boy lengthened and she watched, horrified, as he was swept farther downstream. She knew in that moment that she would not be able to save him and with dawning horror, she realized that she would be lucky to escape drowning herself because she, too, was now fighting to keep afloat.

She battled bravely against the current until severe cramps attacked her legs, tying the muscles into knots. The pain was excruciating and she sank beneath the muddy water. Through a haze of agony she struggled to the surface and glimpsed Kyle and Jake swimming toward her as she gasped for air. Her efforts gained her only a mouthful of water. Choking, she sank again into the reddish-brown depths. *Save Sonny* was her last valiant thought before blackness engulfed her.

Star moaned from the pressure on her back and felt her stomach heave with a sharp spasm before she vomited up the water she had swallowed. Deep shadows webbed her mind, blocking out all coherent thought as she was lifted from the ground.

''Save Sonny,'' she mumbled as her head lolled back against Kyle's strong, muscular shoulder.

"The boy's safe. He managed to grab on to the branch of a fallen tree until Jake reached him," Kyle murmured, cradling her in his arms as he strode from the riverbank to the Ransons' wagon where Priscilla had already prepared a pallet for her in the shade.

"Save him," she muttered, before slipping once more into the black void of unconsciousness.

Gently Kyle laid her upon the patchwork quilt and looked up at Priscilla, who stood hovering protectively near. Since he had dragged Annie from the river, she had remained close, fretting over her young slave, her own young face taut with worry.

"I think she'll be fine once she's rested," he said, and watched Priscilla relax visibly.

"That's good to hear," Jake said as he came around the end of the wagon with his squalling son. "May said Sonny would also be right as rain once he's dried out, but I'm not so sure about this young man if he doesn't get fed soon."

Faced with the dilemma of having to leave Annie to care for her son, Priscilla glanced uncertainly up at her husband. She didn't want to leave the girl alone in her condition, but she knew she couldn't feed Little Jake without the privacy of the wagon to protect her from prying eyes.

Understanding her distress, Kyle smiled. "Go on and see to your family. I'll stay with Annie while you feed Little Jake. Should she need you, I'll call."

"Thank you, Kyle," Priscilla said, blushing to the roots of her blond hair. She had met her husband in a brothel, yet she still possessed enough innocence to feel embarrassed at the thought of Kyle knowing why she needed privacy. It was one of the special qualities about her that Jake loved. Taking her son from her husband, she climbed into the wagon.

"I'll go round up some wood and get a fire going. Annie will need some good strong coffee when she comes round," Jake said, leaving Kyle to his vigil.

Kyle settled himself upon the ground and gazed down

at the girl at his side. Her long hair had escaped the confines of the turban during her struggle for survival and now lay about her in a dark curtain, curling damply over her neck and shoulders and clinging to the smooth curve of her cheek. Tenderly, he brushed a silken strand away from her face.

With no one to censure him, he unabashedly studied her delicate features, marveling again at her remarkable beauty. His gaze lingered on her finely arched brows and the thick fringe of lashes that cast soft shadows on her flawless complexion. He enjoyed his uninhibited exploration for a moment longer before he realized with a start that something was oddly different about the girl; something that he couldn't put his finger on.

Puzzling over his strange reaction, Kyle intensified his scrutiny, searching each of her features for the clue to explain why he felt she was different. His green eyes widened incredulously. During the past weeks her skin had grown perceptibly lighter. When he had first seen her he could have sworn the color of her skin had been much darker. Now she looked almost like the other women whose skin had been burned by the sun. Wondering momentarily if he had accidentally eaten locoweed and his mind was playing tricks on him, Kyle frowned then dismissed that theory.

Lifting a thick curl from her shoulder, he felt its fine texture between his fingers as his gaze swept over her from head to toe, searching for more evidence to prove his growing suspicions. Annie was not who she pretended. He'd bet his last cent that her skin was as white as a magnolia blossom beneath that ugly gown.

Time seemed suspended as he stared down at the girl who had bravely risked her life to try to save Sonny Linden's. Kyle found himself more and more intrigued by her. If his suspicions were correct, she had no more black blood in her veins than he did.

The thought roused his curiosity to a fever pitch. Why would the girl disguise herself as a slave? What secret was she trying to hide by such a ruse? At present, he didn't know the answer, but he was determined to solve the mystery before they reached Sagebrush.

Intent with his musing, Kyle gave a start as Jake paused at his side with his arms full of wood, and said, "After I get the fire going I think I'll go over and see if Seth will give me a little of his whiskey so that Pris can fix one of Sugar's toddies for Annie. That will warm her up much quicker than coffee."

At Jake's reference to Sugar Brown, Kyle looked sharply at Annie. The muscles across his belly contracted as the elusive memory sprang into his mind with vivid clarity. He had been right when he'd felt he'd known Annie at some earlier time. He was looking at the girl from the Red Passion.

"Damn," he muttered, astonished that he had not seen through her ruse. He had thought he would never forget the mysterious moon-maiden he'd met that night in the garden, but he had not taken into account that she might be disguised as a slave.

"Did you say something, Kyle?"

Dumbfounded by his discovery, Kyle shook his head. At the moment, he could not speak; too many thoughts were racing through his mind. He now understood Annie's avoiding him. She had feared the very thing that had just happened. She hadn't wanted him to recognize her and perhaps ruin her charade.

Her reason for fearing him did not quiet the curiosity gnawing at his guts. There were still too many questions left unanswered to suit him. The girl had gone to a great deal of trouble to perpetrate her well-played-out ruse. It must be more than just to keep him from recognizing her as the girl from the Red Passion. She might be ashamed of having worked for Sugar, but he suspected there were other reasons behind her elaborate hoax.

"What will I find when I unlock your secrets, Annie?" Kyle whispered beneath his breath as he gazed down into her ashen features. He had unraveled one part of her riddle and by doing so, he had become even more determined to solve the rest of the mystery surrounding her. Why this one girl piqued his interest to such an extent, he did not know. He just assumed his fascination stemmed from the need to appease his curiosity.

"Is something wrong?" Jake asked, puzzled by Kyle's strange expression.

"No," Kyle said at last.

"Then I'll go get the fire started," Jake said, shifting the burden in his arms to a more comfortable position before turning away.

Kyle watched Jake stride away, his eyes narrowed thoughtfully. He was curious to know what the man knew about Annie but refrained from following him to ask the questions that plagued his mind. Jake and Priscilla were part of the girl's ruse. For that reason, he knew he would learn little about her from them. All that was left for him was to watch and wait.

Star stirred. Her feathery lashes fluttered slowly open and she stared up at Kyle. Disoriented, she lay still for a long moment, trying to organize her disjointed thoughts and remember why she was lying beside the wagon with Kyle Hunter at her side. Suddenly recalling the river and Sonny Linden, she bolted upright. Tears of remorse welled in her eyes and she instinctively turned to Kyle, seeking his strength and reassuring presence as the horror of the boy's death descended upon her with brutal force.

"I tried to save him," she cried against his chest before her voice broke into a sob; in her misery she forgot to use her slave dialect.

"Sonny is safe, Annie," Kyle said, somewhat taken aback to find her clinging to him as if he was a trusted friend. He was further disturbed by his own response to the young, warm body cradled in his arms. Irritated with himself for letting her affect him in such a manner, especially since her speech confirmed his suspicions, he set her away from him.

"Sonny is alive?" Star asked, unable to believe what she had heard.

"Yes," came Kyle's brusque reply. "He drank nearly

half of the river before Jake reached him, but he's no worse for wear.''

Star sagged with relief, ''Thank God,'' she breathed.

''You and Sonny were fortunate not to have drowned. If Jake hadn't been there to help me, one of you would not have survived. What ever possessed you to jump into the river after the boy?'' Kyle asked sharply.

Star's head snapped up at the reproach she heard in his tone. ''Possessed me? The boy was drowning and I thought I could help.''

''Help? You only succeeded in nearly getting yourself drowned.''

Anger crackled through Star's veins like white-hot lightning searing across the Texas sky. It was true she had reacted without thinking, but Kyle was acting as if she had only jumped into the river to cause him trouble.

''Mr. Hunter, I apologize for your having to exert the effort to save my life, but I do not regret trying to save Sonny,'' Star said, her voice laced with ice. ''I'm grateful for your assistance today, but should it happen again in the future, you don't have to feel obligated to rescue me.''

''If that's the way you feel, then I suggest you consider your actions before the next time you go jumping head-first into danger.''

''Thank you for your sage advice,'' Star said. She pushed herself to her feet and stood unsteadily, looking down at Kyle, her eyes flashing, her jaw held at a pugnacious angle. ''I'll remember that in the event you ever need *my* help.'' With that she stalked away with as much dignity as her wobbly legs would give her.

''Damn,'' Kyle cursed as he pulled a cheroot from the pocket of his jacket and lit it. He hadn't meant to quarrel with the girl, nor had he meant to criticize the courage she'd displayed by trying to help Sonny. Being cruelly honest with himself, he had wanted nothing more than to press her back against the quilt and make love to her, and because of that, he had spoken out of his own annoyance with himself for being drawn to her while knowing everything about her was a sham.

"I don't want to become involved with any woman, much less one who is a fraud from the top of her lovely head to the tips of her toes," Kyle mused aloud. Yet even as he spoke, the memory of their encounter in the garden of the Red Passion intruded into his thoughts. His mind feasted upon the recollection of Annie lying naked in the moonlight and his wayward body responded strongly to the image.

Kyle bit down on the cheroot, disgusted with himself for remembering the feelings the girl had aroused in him that night. Picking up his hat, he clamped it down on his head and got to his feet.

"Hell!" he muttered. "I just need to bed a woman. That's all that's wrong with me." Forcing his thoughts away from Annie, he stared out across the prairie. Tomorrow they would reach Fort Worth and he'd be able to appease his body's needs with the red-haired woman who worked in the Horseshoe Saloon.

"Lil will help me get the girl out of my blood," he said, and smiled, confident in his ability not to let his life become complicated by one young girl, however beautiful. He had never let it happen in the past and he was not about to start with the Ransons' so-called slave.

Feeling once more in control of his emotions, Kyle flipped the cheroot away and strode toward the Lindens' wagon to check on Sonny.

Chapter 6

The wagon train rumbled across the last dusty miles to Fort Worth and made camp on the outskirts of the thriving little community. Since the army's desertion of the fort in 1853 it had begun to grow into a typical Texas town. Though still in its infancy, Fort Worth already boasted two saloons, a hotel, courthouse, and livery, as well as other numerous businesses that had sprung up during the past year to accommodate the settlers who were venturing west of the Brazos.

Even from the distance the town's recent growth was apparent. The wood on the newly constructed, unpainted storefronts had not had time to age. It was light in color and contrasted starkly with the weathered dark brown of those buildings that had been built when the town had been nothing more than a fort on the edge of the frontier.

Shielding her eyes with her hand against the harsh glare of the afternoon sun, Star gazed toward the town rising up on the flat prairie. Compared to Natchez and Shreveport, Fort Worth was little more than a rustic outpost, but after so many days on the trail it was a welcome sight. The board and batten buildings represented the small comforts that she had paid scant attention to while growing up in the luxury of Jasmine Hall. Just the thought of sitting in a chair and dining at a table instead of holding her plate in her lap to eat was now dear to her, as was the thought of sleeping in a bed once more. She longed to feel a soft down mattress beneath her at night

in place of the hard floorboards of the wagon. Her
thoughts drew a wistful sigh from her before she turned
resolutely away from the scene. Feeling no ill effects from
her near drowning the previous day, she longed to go into
Fort Worth, but her position in the Ransons' household
would keep her with the wagon in the likely event that
Jake and Priscilla chose to go to town themselves to re-
stock their supplies.

Ruefully accepting her fate, she turned her attention to
the task of unpacking the wagon. All of their belongings
had to be aired and dried to prevent mildew from setting
in after the past week of rain. It was an arduous chore,
but, as she had learned, there was little about traveling
across country by wagon train that was easy.

The heat of the day soon beaded her brow with perspiration as she lugged the crates from the wagon and
spread their contents in the sun to dry. When the last
trunk was removed, she paused to catch her breath before
she began to unpack it. Wiping the moisture from her
face with the hem of her soiled apron, she gazed toward
the small stand of mesquites where Priscilla and Little
Jake sat in the shade. Her friend had wanted to help her
unpack, but Star had refused her offer and insisted that
Priscilla rest. Pris had not complained, but Star knew
from her wan features and the dark circles that shadowed
the skin beneath her cornflower-blue eyes that her friend
had not been feeling well for several days.

The demands of the trail were taking their toll on Priscilla's fragile health, as well as on others in the wagon
train. Star could see it in their careworn, weatherbeaten
faces. The excitement that had glowed so brightly in their
eyes at the onset of the journey had been replaced by a
tired, resigned look. In the beginning there had been
music and laughter in the camp at night but that, too,
had faded as the grueling days wore on. Now everyone
was too exhausted to do more than seek their hard beds
when the chores of the day were done. The only sounds
to fill the nights were an occasional muttered curse,
snores, and the cries of the babies.

It's not easy for any of us, Star mused to herself as she looked about the camp and watched the other women spreading their belongings on every available space to dry. From the corner of her eye she glimpsed two men coming around the end of the wagon and turned her attention fully upon them as she realized that Kyle was having to lend Jake support to keep him on his feet.

Apprehension streaked up Star's spine at the sight. Jake's skin was the color of ashes and his hand trembled violently as he reached out to steady himself on the bed of the wagon when Kyle eased him down onto it. Star turned to call Priscilla but found her already hurrying toward her husband, leaving her infant son sleeping soundly in the shade. She and Star reached Kyle and Jake at the same time.

"Jake, what's wrong?" Priscilla asked, her own face white with worry.

"It's nothing to be concerned about, Pris," Jake murmured in an effort to reassure her. He lay back on the hard planking but was unable to hide his wince of pain as the movement antagonized his already throbbing head.

"You're burning up with fever, Jake. You need a doctor," Priscilla cried as she laid her hand against his brow and found it hot and dry.

"I don't need a doctor, Pris. There's nothing wrong with me except the bellyache. Just give me a dose of the laudanum May gave you for Little Jake and I'll be fine after I've rested a bit."

Torn between her desire to send for the doctor and her husband's wishes, Priscilla chewed at her lower lip. At last she gave way to the latter and turned to Star. "Annie, will you go into town to buy a bottle of laudanum? I used the last of what May Linden gave me when the baby had the colic."

Before Star could answer, Kyle volunteered, "Annie can ride into town with me."

"Are you sure it's no trouble, Mr. Hunter?" Priscilla asked, relieved that her friend wouldn't have to go into a strange town unescorted.

"None at all. I was on my way into Fort Worth when I saw Jake doubled over by the wagon." Assuming the matter was settled without consulting with Star, he turned and strode to where his mount was tethered at the front of the wagon.

Pompous bastard, Star fumed silently as she watched him untie the horse. She knew she owed Jake and Priscilla too much for their help and friendship to refuse their request, but she had no desire to go anywhere with Kyle Hunter. Still, she was powerless to prevent it. To all appearances she was a slave and had to do her mistress's bidding without protest.

"Annie, if you're ready I'll give you a hand up," Kyle said, bending low and clasping his hands.

At his words Star jerked her thoughts back to her present predicament. She stared first at the strong brown fingers forming an improvised stirrup for her foot and then at the tall black stallion. She shook her head. "No, I can walk."

"Yes, I know you can, but it will be much quicker if we both ride," Kyle said with a slow grin. "Now, give me your foot and I'll boost you up behind the saddle and we'll be on our way. It's getting late."

Firmly reminding herself that she was doing this for Jake, Star drew in an unsteady breath and placed her foot in Kyle's hands. With little effort, he lifted her up onto the horse's back and then climbed into the saddle in front of her.

"Annie," Pris called as she ran forward and pressed a few coins into her hand. "You'll need this to buy the laudanum."

"I be back soon, Miss Pris. Don't worry," Star said, tucking the money into the pocket of her skirt for safety.

"Put your arms around me so that you won't fall off," Kyle ordered. Gathering the reins, he nudged the horse in the side with his knee and it obeyed the gentle command instantly.

Star had silently vowed not to heed Kyle's dictates, but when the horse set into motion, she slipped precariously and had to grab him about the waist to keep from falling. Her cheeks burned with frustration and anger when she heard him chuckle.

They crossed the short distance separating the wagon train from the town in a matter of minutes, but to Star it seemed as if she had been holding on to a red-hot coal for hours. She could feel Kyle's hard muscles flex beneath his red plaid shirt as he moved with the horse. The smell of him filled her nostrils. The heat of the day had made him perspire, but his scent was not the rank, unclean odor of a man who did not bathe often. He smelled of tobacco and leather. Against her will, she found the heady fragrance stirring her senses. Her reaction to his masculine scent added to her mortification and she felt her cheeks flame once more.

With her discomfort mounting by the moment, she did not take much note of her surroundings as they rode down the wide, dusty thoroughfare. When Kyle finally reined the stallion to a halt before Harper's Mercantile and Apothecary store, she did not wait for him to dismount and help her down. She slid to the ground herself, wanting to put as much distance between them as soon as possible. With her heart pounding violently against her ribs from the mere smell of him, she had no desire to feel his hands upon her.

Trying to regain control over her wayward emotions, she turned without a word and hurried toward the store. Her hand was already on the door latch when Kyle stopped her with a firm grip upon her arm. Struggling for composure, she gaped up at him.

"I'm going over to the livery while you make your purchase. I should be back by the time you're ready to return to camp, but if I'm not, wait here for me. It'll be dark soon and it's best that you're not out wandering around Fort Worth after nightfall. I don't want anything to happen to you," Kyle said, his green gaze sweeping over Star's face. For a long moment his eyes held hers before he released her arm and turned away. His spurs jingled when his boots hit the wooden sidewalk as he strode down the street.

Star stared after him. She ignored the tender note of concern in his last words and centered her attention on his latest command. She sought the refuge of her anger in order to block the strange feelings his nearness had aroused within her.

The arrogance of the man! How dare he order me to wait for him as if I was his slave. I'll be damned if I get back on that horse with him. I'll walk back to camp if it takes me all night. Fuming silently, she strode into the mercantile and paused just beyond the threshold to give her eyes time to adjust to the dim interior.

After so many weeks in the open air, her senses were bombarded by the different scents of the store. It smelled of tobacco, unground coffee, new cloth, and the oil used in lanterns, as well as other less recognizable odors. Her gaze was drawn to the wares that crowded every inch of available space. Tools and kegs of nails were stacked along one wall to merge with the large rack of guns and ammunition that extended to the counter upon which were glass jars containing peppermint and nuts. Barrels of flour, crackers, and pickles sat before the counter, and canned goods, such as peaches and beans, were stacked on the shelves behind it. On the opposite wall, cloth, ready-made clothing, and kitchen utensils, as well as other household items, extended back to the door.

Star took it all in before she moved toward the counter where a bespectacled clerk squinted down his long, thin nose at her.

"What do you want?" he asked, but before she could answer, he sniffed disdainfully. "I ain't got all day so you'd better speak up, wench."

"Sir, I can assure you that I won't take much of your time. I came only to purchase a bottle of laudanum," Star replied sharply. The clerk's rudeness, combined with the turmoil Kyle had created within her, made her temper reach the boiling point. Her palm itched to slap the spectacles from the man's bony nose, but she suppressed the urge.

"You're a high and mighty little wench, ain't you?" the clerk sneered. He seemed to swell with self-importance as he leaned back on the balls of his heels and hooked his thumbs in his suspenders. "By the look of you, you're half white, but that don't give you no right to come in here and put on fancy airs with me. I've seen your type before and you're nothing but trouble. Cause you've got a white daddy, you get to thinking you're as good as the rest of us. Hah! If you want to do business around here, you'd better learn your place, girl."

Star felt as if she would choke on the ire that rose in her throat. Faced with the reality of true prejudice for the first time since she'd begun her ruse in Natchez, she suddenly realized how naive she had been about the slave system she had taken for granted all of her life. The clerk's open hostility gave her a small glimpse of what it was like to be on the other side of the fence, where you were judged and condemned by the color of your skin. Her insides twisted with guilt. She had lived comfortably at Jasmine Hall without ever giving thought to what Dulcie and the other servants had to endure.

Now having experienced prejudice firsthand, she realized the injustice she had blindly condoned and found it repugnant. She wanted no part of a system that thrived on hatred and made people like this clerk feel superior to other human beings just because they had been born into a different race.

Clenching her teeth and silently vowing to free every man, woman, and child slave when she returned to Jasmine Hall, Star dug into her pocket and retrieved the coins Priscilla had given her for the medicine. Placing them on the counter in front of the clerk, she lowered her eyes subserviently to hide her true feelings as well as to placate the man. It left a bitter taste in her mouth, but she knew at the present time she could do nothing else. Jake needed the laudanum. No good would come from venting her temper.

"Sir, I'm sorry. I didn't mean to speak outta line, but I worried about my master. He sick and needs the med'cine." Star thought the words would choke her as she apologized in the proper tone expected of a slave.

"That's more like it," he said. Turning to the glass-fronted cabinet to his right, he opened it and withdrew a small bottle. Setting it on the counter, he raked the coins into his hand. "There's your laudanum. The next time you're sent in here, I want you to remember your place or I'll not do business with you no matter what you need."

Star's temper flamed white-hot as she watched the man pocket the coins. She picked up the bottle and put it safely away in the pocket of her skirt before giving her anger free rein.

"You can go straight to hell," she spat. Raising her chin haughtily in the air, she turned and marched out of the store before the stunned clerk could manage to regain his speech. Devilment danced in her blue eyes as she looked back through the dust-filmed window and stuck out her tongue at the dumbfounded man.

She laughed as she heard his muffled shout of outrage, "Come back here, you black bitch." Making another face at him, she lifted her skirts and ran.

The evening twilight was giving way to night by the time Star reached the edge of town and paused in the shadows of the livery stable to rest. She drew in a deep satisfied breath as she gazed toward the campfires flickering in the distance. She smiled as she touched the fabric over the bottle of laudanum. Jake would have the medicine and she had had the pleasure of watching the obnoxious little clerk nearly strangle on his indignation.

The saucy expression on Star's face faded as the jingle of spurs alerted her to the fact that she was no longer alone. Thinking Kyle had found her she turned, determined to give him a setdown that he would long remember if he tried to make her ride back to camp with him. Her eyes widened in surprise as she looked up at three strange men.

"Well, look'ee here, boys, at what we've found hiding in the dark," one man said as he clamped his hand down on Star's arm and drew her toward them before she had time to form a protest.

"Can't see much out here, Willis. I ain't got eyes like an Indian. Let's take her into the stable where we can all get a better look at her," his companion said.

"Let me go," Star ordered, straining against the iron grip on her arm and digging her heels into the dirt to try to prevent herself from being drawn any closer to the man called Willis.

"Well, won't you listen to that, Sam." Willis chuckled. "It seems we've found us a gal with a little spunk in her."

"It's about damn time," the third man slurred. "Them gals back in the saloon shore weren't interested in anything except our money to buy them liquor."

"Charlie's right. Here we been a-hankering for a little loving before we have to take the supplies back to the ranch for old Jeb and we can't find a woman nowheres. That red-haired bitch nearly got us killed when that old man decided to protect her honor when we tried to get a little too friendly."

"Hell," Charlie grumbled. "It wasn't the old man who was the trouble. We could have easily got rid of him if it hadn't been for the younger one. Hell, I ain't never see'd nothing like it before. Them two was as much alike as peas in a pod."

"Forget the red-haired bitch, boys. We've found us another one now," Willis said. His companions chuckled in agreement.

Star's throat went dry with fear and her heart began to thump wildly against her ribs as she comprehended what the men had planned for her. They intended rape. She opened her mouth to cry out for help but found that only a hoarse whisper would come from her fear-constricted throat.

Frantic with terror, she began to struggle in earnest against Willis' hand but found that Sam had come to his aid. He grabbed her about the waist with one arm, lifting her easily off her feet while he clamped his other hand down over her mouth to stifle her cries. With little effort, he carried her into the stable and threw her down in a vacant stall filled with fresh hay.

Star kicked out at him and heard him grunt with pain, but she had no time to savor his agony. She rolled away and scrambled to her feet. Willis made to grab her but came away with only the red turban that bound her hair. Her long locks tumbled about her shoulders as she backed away from her three assailants. The deep blue of her eyes reflected the terror racing through every nerve in her body as she came up against the wall. "Keep away from me," she panted.

The light from the lantern hanging from a beam overhead illuminated the three men who stood watching her futile attempt to escape. The lustful looks she saw in their eyes sent a chill up her spine and made her stomach twist into tight knots with dread. She had seen a similar expression on Brett's face the night she had fled from her home.

"It seems we've found us a wench that's been touched by the tar brush," Willis said, and poked Sam in the ribs, smirking obscenely.

"I ain't never had me a black woman before. I wonder if they're as good as white gals?" Sam said.

"Them cotton planters must think so or this 'un wouldn't be here now. Look at them eyes and that hair. She's a white man's spawn or I ain't Willis Lundy."

"Well, I don't give a damn if she's black or white," Charlie muttered. "She'd be just as good looking to me if she was purple." He made a move toward Star, but Willis jerked him back.

"Hold on there, Charlie. I see'd her first. Ain't no man going before me."

"Damn you, Willis," Charlie growled, jerking his arm free. "You think that because you're the lead man on the cattle drives that you're the lead man all the time."

"Charlie's right," Sam said, joining the quarrel.

"You're always trying to make us step aside for you and I'm tired of it."

While the three men argued over her as if she was a bone that had been tossed to a pack of dogs, Star frantically searched for a means of escape. Her eyes raked over her three assailants, who blocked the entrance to the stall with their bulk, and came to rest on a pitchfork that had been carelessly left in a corner. She moved quickly, giving the three men no time to stop her. Grabbing the long handle, she swung the sharp-tined fork up in front of her, warding off any attempt they made to seize her weapon. Her breath came in short ragged gasps as she raised the pitchfork menacingly toward them and ordered, "Get out of my way." To emphasize her demand, she jabbed at Willis's belly.

He and his companions jumped back to avoid the sharp tines as she warily moved forward.

"Now, gal, you ain't going to get away from us that easy. There's only one of you and three of us. Why don't you put that thing down before we have to hurt you," Willis said cajolingly, though he kept his distance.

"I wouldn't be so sure of that if I were you," came a deep, masculine voice from behind them. Accompanying it was the clicking sound of a pistol being cocked.

Wide-eyed, Willis swung about to come face-to-face with Kyle Hunter, the same man who had run him and his pals out of the Horseshoe Saloon less than an hour before. He swallowed nervously as his gaze came to rest on the Walker Colt in the other man's hand. "Mister, we ain't got no quarrel with you. We settled that back in the saloon. Now we're just trying to have a little fun."

"It seems your fun always includes a woman who is not interested in it. I suggest you look for it elsewhere or find a bullet hole in your gut. My patience has about run out where the three of you are concerned." Kyle's voice was calm and deadly.

"All right, mister," Willis said, raising his hands to indicate that he was unarmed. "No black wench is worth getting shot over."

"A wise decision on your part," Kyle answered, and motioned in the direction of the stable doors. "Now get before I decide to rid Fort Worth of a few of its vermin."

The three men did not wait to be told a second time. They had seen the ease with which the man used his gun back in the saloon and wanted no part of him, nor of the Walker Colt he carried. They bolted toward the door and did not look back until they were well out of sight of the livery stable.

The pitchfork fell from Star's numb fingers and she drew in a shuddering breath. Tears of relief dampened her sooty lashes as she looked at Kyle and gave him a wobbly smile. After several long seconds, she managed to say, "Thank you."

"Keep your thanks, Annie," came Kyle's sharp answer. His voice was harsh with anger as his eyes raked her from the tips of her toes to the wild disarray of her hair before he moved to the entrance of the stall where the red cloth of her turban lay. He bent and picked it up. Deep lines furrowed his brow as he looked down at the cloth in his hand. He held it for a long thoughtful moment before handing it back to her and turning to the next stall, where a bay mare was tethered. Saddling it, he led the animal toward the stable door. He paused before he stepped out into the night. "Now if you're ready to return to camp, I'll take you back." Without a backward glance he left the stable.

Star felt the blood freeze in her veins. Questions boiled in her brain. Had he seen through her disguise? Or had he assumed that she was a mulatto? She prayed it was the latter because she didn't know what she would do if he had recognized her as the girl from the Red Passion. Coiling her hair on top of her head, she rewrapped the turban about it before she followed Kyle out into the night.

She found him by his mount. He stood with his hands folded behind his back, staring at the campfires of the wagon train. His stance and her fear of discovery made him seem unapproachable, but she knew she had no other recourse. Drawing from the depths of her courage, she crossed the last few feet to his side and paused uncertainly, seeking the right words yet fearing his response. She swallowed several times before she ventured, "I'm sorry I disobeyed your orders to wait for you. I never meant to cause you trouble." Her voice wavered as she spoke.

"Do you realize I nearly had to shoot three men because of your foolishness?" Kyle's face was set with anger as he glanced down at her. "Damn it, Annie. I warned you not to go off alone. And as for causing trouble, you seem to be prone to it if the store clerk is any indication. He was still raving mad when I came back for you."

"He—he . . ." Star began, but could find no way to explain what had transpired in the mercantile store.

"I know it all. The man wouldn't let me leave until he'd told me the entire story about the uppity wench who had cursed him."

"He didn't want to sell me the laudanum for Jake," Star said in an effort to account for her behavior though in truth there was no excuse for a slave insulting a white man.

"Did you actually tell him to go to hell?" Kyle asked. He could not suppress the twitch of a grin at the memory of the clerk's outrage. The little man had been beet red in the face as he pounded his knuckles against the counter and swore that he'd find who owned the black hussy and make her pay for cursing her betters.

Unable to say more in her defense, all Star could do was nod her answer.

"Good for you. Bastards like him deserve to be shot, but they're not worth the lead it would take to blow their heads off."

Star gaped up at Kyle, totally bewildered by his response. "You approve of what I did?" she asked, stunned to find a different side to the man she had considered so hard and arrogant, without any feelings for anyone beyond himself.

"I would have done the same thing. As for the other three, I should have shot them back in the saloon. It would have saved us all a lot of trouble," came his crisp reply as he clasped his hands to boost her up onto the stallion's back. "It's time we got back to camp."

Star hesitated. "I can ride the bay," she volunteered in an effort to avoid further close contact with Kyle. She was grateful to him for his intervention in the stable, but she was wary of being near him again. He had the power to arouse too many disturbing feelings within her for her peace of mind.

"I'm afraid she already has a passenger though he's too drunk to know it at the moment."

For the first time Star noticed the buckskin-clad figure draped over the saddle on the bay's back. His arms hung limply toward the ground and a ragged snore escaped his open mouth, blowing the long, shaggy hair that hid his features. Bemused, she looked back at Kyle to see him give a shrug of disgust.

"That, my dear Annie, is my esteemed father, Buck Hunter," Kyle said, his voice edged with sarcasm.

Not knowing what to say in reply, Star let him help her mount. When he swung into the saddle before her, she wrapped her arms once more about his lean waist. Tonight she had seen a new side to Kyle Hunter. Beneath the hard exterior lay many hidden facets. He could be kind and gentle, dangerous and unyielding, and she sensed from the way he spoke of his father that he could also be hurt.

Resting her cheek against his back, she stared up at the star-studded sky. Something within her had changed in the last few minutes but she did not understand what it was and she was too tired to explore it further. For now she was content with the warm feeling of security that surrounded her as they rode back to camp, leading the bay mare with her unconscious burden.

The laudanum had done its work. Jake slept peacefully beside his wife and son as Star slipped quietly from the tent and walked back toward the campfire where Kyle and Harry Linden were enjoying the last of the coffee.

Feeling suddenly ill at ease about interrupting their conversation, she paused in the shadows at the end of the wagon and listened as they discussed the events of the day. Her gaze was drawn to Kyle's strong profile as she watched the firelight play over his craggy features, highlighting the sculpted planes and emphasizing his masculine beauty. Tiny butterflies seemed to do a wild dance in the pit of her stomach as her eyes came to rest on his long brown fingers, now encircling the tin cup he raised to his lips. The breath caught in her throat at the rush of memories the sight aroused. Squeezing her eyes shut, she tried to block them from her mind as she silently reprimanded herself for her wayward emotions.

This can't go on, she told herself. I may have glimpsed a new side of Kyle's nature tonight, but I know the other far better. He's still the same man who used me without a thought at the Red Passion. I have to remember that and keep remembering it or I'll . . . Star could not continue the thought. It touched upon things she didn't want to examine too closely.

Her musings were interrupted when Seth Mctaggart called out to Kyle and she looked to see him approaching the campfire with Joe Wells. Not wanting her presence to be discovered, she stepped farther back into the darkness.

"Kyle, me and Joe and some of the other men have been discussing what we should do if Jake's not able to travel when we get ready to move."

Kyle raised his brows in question as he tossed the last of his coffee into the fire and looked up at Seth. His calm expression belied the tension knotting the muscles in his shoulders. He'd been afraid that something like this would eventually happen. It was rare for a wagon train to make it this far without a few quarrels or a handful of members of the party deciding they should be the ones to make the decisions for all concerned. When that happened, it wasn't unusual for a wagon train to break up.

"What did you decide?" came Kyle's cool question.

"We think it's best that the Ransons stay in Fort Worth," Seth said, glancing at Joe Wells for support.

Kyle got to his feet. His face was set with resolve as he eyed the two men. "The Ransons paid their share to travel to Sagebrush and we're not leaving them behind." His voice was firm, brooking no argument.

Seth's bravado wilted under Kyle's icy green gaze. "That's your final word on the matter?"

Kyle nodded.

"I'll tell the others, but they're not going to like it. They've heard of epidemics of cholera and camp fever killing entire wagon trains and they're afraid that's what's wrong with Jake."

"Jake's just feeling under the weather, Seth. I'm sure he'll be fine in a few days," Harry Linden interjected.

"I hope you're right, Harry, or all of us could end up paying with our lives for not leaving them behind," Seth said, and turned away.

Harry glanced at Kyle and shrugged. "I guess I'll turn in. See you in the morning."

"Night, Harry," Kyle said and watched as the three men walked back toward their wagons. He could understand their fears. Cholera was a deadly sickness feared by one and all. It could wipe out an entire community or wagon train and there was little to be done to prevent it. It moved swiftly and attacked the old and young alike, sparing neither sex. A man might be well in the morning and be dead by night.

Kyle frowned, his brows knitting above his narrowed green eyes. If he thought Jake had contracted cholera, he would have no choice but to leave him behind for the safety of the rest of the train. But at the present time, he wasn't certain what was wrong with him and he couldn't abandon Jake and his family without proof. Nor did he like the idea of leaving Annie. Everything about the girl intrigued him and he knew he would not be satisfied until he had solved the mystery surrounding her. Drawing in a deep breath, he settled the matter in his mind. He wouldn't leave Annie or the Ransons behind.

He'd grown fond of the young couple and their noisy offspring during the past weeks and he understood their dreams of building a future for their son. Jake had often discussed his plans with him. He knew the dangers he faced in a land where Comanche raiding parties still terrorized those who tried to settle it but was still determined to go on, wanting his son to have more out of life than he'd had.

Kyle understood Jake's feelings well. Someday he himself would like to have a son to inherit the Bar H, but that would entail marriage and at the present moment that did not appeal to him. There was still too much of Buck Hunter's wild, restless spirit dwelling within him. Until he managed to conquer it, he would never consider having a family. Yet despite all of his mother's predictions that he would turn out to be like his father, Kyle sensed that it might just be possible to tame that side of his nature. However, he did not know how to go about it. And until he did, he would never marry.

Kyle knew that he had land and wealth that Jake would envy, but to him, Jake was the more fortunate man. He had his wife and son and knew exactly what he wanted out of life. Kyle loved his land, yet there always seemed to be something over the next hill that beckoned him.

He had given in to the wandering urge for a short while after his mother's death. He had joined the Texas Rangers, serving his months with the hope that fighting Indians and Mexicans would appease his restless spirit, but he had failed to assuage the beast within himself. He had returned to his ranch and had thrown himself into making it into one of the most prosperous cattle ranches in Texas. Even that had not absolved him of the disquiet that he had inherited from his father. It still fermented in his blood, challenging him each day to heed its call. Yet he refused to follow, staunchly vowing never to become like the man who now lay snoring beneath the Lindens' wagon. Buck Hunter had not been strong enough to accept his responsibilities and Kyle was determined not to travel the same path.

Kyle glanced toward the buckskin-clad figure he'd come across by accident that night in the Horseshoe Saloon. He feared he might never be rid of his wanderlust if Buck was any example. The years had not mellowed or changed him. Tonight had proven that to his son. Buck Hunter was still the same reckless man who wandered where his nose led. Drinking and brawling were his life and it might well have ended on the dirty floor of the saloon in Fort Worth had Kyle not intervened when the three saddle tramps jumped Buck for interfering when they tried to force Lil to accommodate their desires.

Kyle had no doubt that his father could have taken on all three and come out the winner had he not been drunk. Buck might be all he thought him and worse, but Kyle had to admit his father was as skilled with his knife and pistol as any man he had ever encountered. The years Buck had spent living by his wits had honed his instincts and skills to a sharp edge.

Buck let out a ragged snore and muttered incoherently as he turned on his side, his back to his son. A muscle worked visibly in Kyle's cheek as he clenched his teeth and fought against the powerful sense of rejection he felt by his father's simple action. He knew Buck was in a drunken stupor and did not know what he was doing, but to Kyle it reopened old but unforgotten wounds.

Annoyed that he would let himself remember how much he had needed his father while growing up, Kyle turned away, his gaze absently moving over the line of wagons. It was time to let the past go. He was a man grown and did not need anyone but himself. With that thought in mind his eyes came to rest on the Ransons' wagon and the image of the lovely girl from the Red Passion again intruded his mind.

"No," he muttered aloud, trying to stop the memory before it could unfold. "I certainly don't need that type of trouble in my life. I've enough on my hands with Buck."

Kyle had turned away to find his own bed when he caught a glimpse of a slight movement in the shadows near the end of the wagon. Unable to discern who was lurking in the darkness beyond the realm of light, he did not pause to signal his discovery but walked toward the lead wagon where he kept his sleeping gear. When he reached it and was sure his actions could not be seen, he doubled back in the direction of the Ransons' wagon. With the stealth he had learned while hunting Comanches with the Texas Rangers, he moved silently through the darkness.

"All right, step out into the light but don't move too fast. I'd hate to put a bullet through you for no reason." His words were accompanied by the sound of the gun hammer being drawn back.

Star froze. An icy chill ran up her spine at the thought of the barrel of the Walker Colt pointed at her back. Trying desperately not to heed the urge to run, she moved into the light of the campfire.

"Annie! Damn," Kyle cursed, feeling foolish for not having recognized her before she stepped into the light. Reholstering his pistol, he let out a long breath. "I could have shot you. Why the devil were you hiding out here in the dark?"

"I wasn't hiding," Star said, turning to face him, her fear changing to anger as she glared up at him. "I sleep in the wagon."

"Then why the hell weren't you sleeping? When I saw you lurking in the shadows, I thought one of the saddle tramps had followed us back to camp to try to even up the score."

"Sleep? How could anyone sleep with all of you standing around the fire talking?" Star demanded, searching for any weak excuse to keep Kyle from knowing that she had been eavesdropping on their conversation.

"Well, it's time you were asleep now," Kyle growled, his voice laced with annoyance. He took her by the arm and drew her toward the end of the wagon.

"Let me go," Star ordered, straining against his hand

as he propelled her none too gently up the first two steps. Kyle was still standing on the ground as she reached the last step and made one final, valiant effort to free herself.

She gave a sharp jerk and felt his fingers slip free of her arm. Her victory was only momentary. The movement overbalanced her on the narrow planking and she started to fall. A cry of dismay escaped her lips as she suddenly found herself in Kyle's arms, her body pressed against his lean frame, her arms about his shoulders. His mouth was only inches from hers as she gaped up at him, wide-eyed with shock at their close contact.

A slow, mischievous grin curled one corner of his shapely mouth as he smiled down at her and tightened his arms about her waist, drawing her closer to his warmth. Before she could protest, his lips claimed hers in a searing kiss.

The feeling of his mouth combined with her earlier kind thoughts about him and his show of friendship toward the Ransons when everyone was turning against them made Star forget her bitterness toward Kyle. She responded to the subtle, heady caress. She opened her mouth to his seeking tongue and relaxed in his arms, savoring the taste of him as she wound her fingers in the dark hair curling at the nape of his strong neck. She felt his muscles tense beneath her hands, but before she could comprehend his intentions, he jerked his mouth away from hers.

For a long, nerve-rending moment he stared down into her face, his piercing gaze assessing each of her features. "Annie . . ." he began, his voice husky with the desire that coursed through his veins at the feel of her in his arms. He paused, then shook his head, regretting the fact that he could not let himself continue. Resolutely, he set her away from him. "Good night, Annie," he said curtly before he turned and left her.

Shaken by her own response to him, Star did not stay to ponder his mercurial mood but fled back to the security of the wagon. She clambered inside and huddled on her bed with her arms wrapped tightly about her legs and forehead resting on her knees. She sought to still her wildly racing heart and to rid herself of the tumultuous feelings Kyle's caress had aroused in her by telling herself that the kiss had meant nothing to him. His tone had implied as much. It had only been an impulsive gesture and once he remembered whom he held in his arms, he had thrust her away from him.

Strangely, she found no solace in her thoughts. Instead she felt only a hollow ache welling in her breast. It was so poignant that she burst into tears.

She lay back and buried her face in the pillow to stifle the sound of her sobs as she gave in to her moment of self-pity. She was surrounded by people yet she had no one to give her the comfort and love that she so desperately craved. The thought made her tears flow faster until there were no more to be shed.

Drawing in a shaky breath she rolled onto her back and wiped her burning eyes. "I don't know what's happening to me," she whispered, bewildered by her emotional upheaval over one small kiss. She had never let herself give in to self-pity in the past, even when things had seemed darkest.

Reflecting upon her strange behavior, she realized it was caused by Kyle Hunter. He had the power to bring forth the needs she kept hidden from the world and she was unable to fight against them once they surfaced.

Turning on her side, she curled into a ball. She clutched the pillow to her breast and reaffirmed her earlier resolve to stay away from Kyle. He had touched the vulnerable spot in the armor she had erected about her heart during the past years and now she knew she had to guard it well or be lost. With that thought taking firm root in her mind, Star drifted into a sleep that was haunted by dreams of the handsome, green-eyed Texan.

Chapter 7

From a cloudless sky an unmerciful sun bore down upon the Hunter wagon train as it moved slowly southwest. The wagons jolted over the uneven ground, stirring up the dry earth in a cloud of dust that hovered over the train like an ominous dark-winged bird awaiting the next victim to succumb to the sickness that held the members of the Hunter party hostage.

Since they had left Fort Worth, two adults and the youngest of the Lindens' eight children had died from the dread disease—cholera. Several others had been stricken during the past day and were now feverish and growing weaker by the hour. Among the latest victims were Priscilla and Little Jake. Fortunately, due mostly to his strong will to live because of his wife and son, Jake had managed to hold his own though he was still burning with fever.

Star fretted as she worked to make her friends more comfortable against the bumps that jarred the wagon and its occupants. Wringing out two wet cloths she placed them on Jake's and Priscilla's hot brows. There was little else she could do for them. The bottle of laudanum had been used up days earlier and now all that was left was to try to ease their discomfort and pray that they would recover.

Dark smudges of dirt streaked her face as she absently wiped away the perspiration that mingled with the dust from the trail. The fine dust infiltrated every nook and cranny of the wagon; embedding itself in hair and clothing, as well as finding its way into the food and water. It had also caused her skin to break out in a rash about her waist where her gown touched. The prickly heat itched and burned, but she ignored her own discomfort as she cared for her friends.

Turning her attention to the tiny being who had given her his love and trust, Star lifted Little Jake into her arms. Tears brimmed in her eyes and her heart felt as if it was being wrenched from her breast as she held him close. The baby lay quiet, his small face pale, his bud-shaped mouth parched and dry from the dehydration brought on by the diarrhea that would give his small body no reprieve.

Her silent tears tracked new paths down her cheeks as she looked down at the infant and listened to his shallow breathing. She knew by the sound that his tiny lungs had already begun to fill with fluid and that he would live but a few hours more.

Impotent fury welled within Star at her inability to stop Little Jake's death. She had fought against the dark angel, but he was winning the battle and there was nothing she could do to prevent it. She sensed the black-robed specter's presence hovering—eager to wrap the small life in its dark arms. She felt the need to lash out, to cry and scream in an effort to drive the death angel away, but she managed to suppress the urge. It would serve no purpose except to make Little Jake's passing harder.

Cradling the babe against her breast, she rocked back and forth. His mother was too ill to give him this final comfort, but Star would be there to let him know that he was loved until she had to release him to the forces that no man could control.

The hours sped by as she held her lonely vigil inside the canvas-covered wagon. Finally Little Jake whimpered once and looked up at her as if to say farewell, before his small body relaxed as if he had slipped into a deep sleep. His cherub face was peaceful, no longer

strained from the pain that had racked his insides from
the cramps that accompanied the disease.

Star held him close as she gave way to sobs of grief
for a child she had grown to love. She wept until there
were no more tears to be spent and then she tenderly
washed Little Jake and dressed him in his finest gown,
one Priscilla had embroidered with tiny rosebuds about
the neck and hem. She then wrapped his small body in
the patchwork quilt he had loved because of its bright
colors. Placing him gently back into the wooden cradle
Jake had made for his son with love, Star said a silent
prayer, commissioning Little Jake into the hands of God.

The babe would have a proper burial when the wagon
train made camp for the night, but until then she had no
more time to grieve over him. Her heart still ached, but
she had to care for the living. She turned her attention
back to Jake and Priscilla.

In turn she tried to force a few drops of water between
their parched lips and then remoistened the cloths and
replaced them on their fevered brows. She had had to
yield Little Jake to the angel of death, but as long as she
had a breath in her body she was determined to duel with
him for the lives of the babe's parents. She feared Death
might win again, but his victory would not come easily.

Finishing her simple ministrations, Star squatted on
the floor of the wagon and tucked a loose strand of hair
back beneath her turban. The loud crack of a bullwhip
drew her attention away from her patients to the man who
drove the oxen, Buck Hunter.

For the first two days after leaving Fort Worth, Kyle
had taken charge of the Ransons' wagon but after his
father had recovered sufficiently from his tremendous
hangover, Kyle had let Buck relieve him of the duty. Kyle
had enough problems on his hands without having the
extra chore of driving Jake's wagon. He was doing everything in his power to keep the wagon train together. Those
who had been unaffected by the disease were panic-
stricken and were threatening to try to make it on their
own. Their trepidation about crossing the frontier and

perhaps having to face a band of Indians was overshadowed by their fear of contracting cholera. The Comanches were still an unknown quantity while they could *see* their friends sicken and die of the disease.

Reflecting upon the volatile temperament of those like Seth Mctaggart and Joe Wells, Star feared that nothing Kyle could say would persuade them to remain calm. They blamed him for the predicament in which they now found themselves. She'd heard several of the men grumbling over his refusal to leave Jake and Priscilla behind. To them, Kyle was totally at fault and they did not look beyond their own self-serving motives to realize that he was doing his best to keep them all alive.

A streak of curses filled the air as Buck Hunter called the oxen every vile name under the sun. Star smiled ruefully. Buck's use of profanity had shocked her at first, but as the days passed, she had grown used to it and in some strange way found it comforting. And oddly it had become a symbol of life to her. She felt that no man would use such language if he thought he would soon be face-to-face with his maker.

Needing something at the moment to take her mind away from the sickness and death, Star thought about the man she had come to know during the past days. Buck Hunter bore little similarity to his son beyond their striking physical likeness. From what she had seen of the two Hunters, their appearance was the only thing they had in common. Unlike Kyle, she had found Buck an easy man to talk with. He always seemed to have an amusing story to relate to her when he sensed she needed something to lift her spirits. He had also been a great help to her during the times when she was too busy tending the sick to do anything else. He had made camp, built fires, and fixed their meals during the past harrowing days.

"They're as different as night and day," Star mused aloud as she remoistened the quickly drying cloths and replaced them on her patients' brows. Buck Hunter had none of the mercurial temperament his son possessed. He was carefree, taking each day as it came and looking at life as one great adventure. Buck was the type of man she understood easily, but Star doubted if she would ever truly know the depths that lay beneath his son's arrogant exterior. Kyle's moods varied from light to dark so quickly that she could only catch momentary glimpses through the hard shell he had erected about himself. She sensed from them that he was much like an uncut diamond. His outer veneer hid his deeper feelings from the world.

Star realized with a start that in that respect she and Kyle had more in common than she had thought possible. Like herself, Kyle concealed his innermost fears and passions as a means of self-defense against being hurt. Her heart fluttered within her breast. She had sensed his vulnerability that night in Fort Worth, but she had ignored it because of her own inner turmoil.

"Is that why he creates such strange feelings within me?" she whispered, trying desperately to understand her own emotions as well as Kyle's. "Perhaps I'm only responding to a kindred spirit who also has the misfortune of having an unhappy past."

Star gave herself a mental shake. At the present time she had far more important things to attend to than worrying about the strange attraction she felt for Kyle Hunter. Jake and Priscilla needed her.

Wiping their hot brows and once again replacing the cold cloths, Star gazed down at her patients. Her heart went out to the young couple who had befriended her. Without being aware of it, they had lost the most precious thing they possessed: their son. Tears again came into Star's throat and she swallowed them back as her eyes lingered on their ashen features. She didn't know what would happen to her friends when they learned of their son's death. She feared their discovery of it, instinctively sensing that it would cause them to give up their own will to live.

The wagon rumbled to a halt. Star brushed at her stinging eyes and wiped her nose. Lifting the tin washbasin she moved to the end of the wagon and pushed back the canvas flap. She tossed the dirty water onto the ground and stepped down. She stood there for a moment, stretching her tired and aching muscles before making her way to the side of the wagon where the water barrels were strapped. A commotion behind her in the distance made her pause and she glanced over her shoulder at the group of men surrounding Kyle and Buck Hunter. The tone of their voices filled her with dread as she turned and listened to them argue.

"Damn it, Kyle. We ain't going to stay. We've all discussed it and we'd rather take our chances facing the Comanches and maybe coming out alive than staying here and catching cholera," Mctaggart grumbled.

"Mctaggart, I've told you before, we're not leaving the Ransons or the Lindens behind."

"Hell, you may not leave them, but we're going to," Joe Wells growled. "I've got my own children to consider. We've been lucky so far and I'm not staying here to see if our luck holds out."

Kyle's movements revealed his annoyance as he took off his hat and ran his fingers through his sweat-dampened hair. "I say the train stays together. You hired me to guide you and that's damn well what I intend to do. I'll not have your blood and scalps on my conscience."

Mctaggart's weatherbeaten features hardened with antagonism. "As we see it, Hunter, you ain't got any choice. We hired you and we can fire you."

"Hold on now," Buck interjected, raising his hands to stay the angry comments. "I think I've got a solution to all of your problems if you'll just listen to me a damn minute."

Kyle flashed his father a hostile look. "What's on your mind, old man?"

"Hell, son. The answer is as simple as the nose on your face. There isn't another man who knows this country better than me. I'll lead the ones who want to go on and you can stay behind with the rest."

"I should have suspected you'd volunteer to be the first to run when the going gets a little tough. But since I have little choice in the matter, as Mctaggart said, it looks as if I'll have to accept your offer.'' Kyle's green gaze swept over the men surrounding him. His voice reflected his disgust with the entire situation as he said, ''You have yourselves a new guide.'' Turning, he strode toward the Lindens' wagon.

Buck frowned. His faded green eyes held a look of sadness as he watched his son stride away. He knew how Kyle felt about him and he didn't blame his son. He'd done many things in the past that he wasn't proud of where Kyle was concerned, yet he could have done nothing else without destroying the boy. There was only one person alive who knew the reason he'd deserted his family when Kyle was just a babe and if Buck had any say in the matter, no one else would ever know the ugly truth.

His shoulders sagged as he drew in a weary, resigned breath. He'd hoped by offering his help with the wagon train that he could make amends in some small way, but he had only succeeded in chalking up another black mark against him in his son's eyes. Kyle believed the worst of him, assuming he only wanted to run away from the trouble. Knowing that he could do little to change his son's opinion of him, he turned his attention back to his new duty as wagon master.

From her vantage point by the wagon, Star saw the look of futility that crossed Buck's face as he watched Kyle and her heart went out to him. She sensed his need to be close to his son but feared that would never happen if Kyle's feelings for his father did not change. She knew from the way he had spoken of Buck the night in Fort Worth that he had little respect or love for the man who had sired him.

Star turned her back on the scene and lifted the wooden lid from the water keg. She used a gourd dipper to fill the basin with fresh water and then resecured the lid to try to keep out the dust.

''Why should I worry about a little dust when they're leaving us behind to die?'' she muttered, a chill of apprehension racing up her spine as she came face-to-face with her own mortality for the first time. Buck would lead the wagon train out at dawn, but neither she nor her friends would be with them. Fear had triumphed over compassion and now they were being abandoned. There were no guarantees that any of those left behind would survive. Glancing toward the horizon where the sunset blazed across the sky in ribbons of scarlet and gold, she wondered if any of them would live to see another.

"Annie," Buck said, as he paused at her side, drawing her thoughts away from her morbid reflections, "are you all right, girl? You look as if you've just seen a ghost."

Star drew in a deep steadying breath as she looked up into Buck's concerned face. She forced the thought of her own death back into the dark recesses of her mind. She could not dwell on what might happen. Too much depended on her. At last she managed to say, "I be fine, Master Buck."

"How are your patients?"

"Little Jake died an hour ago," she choked, and could not stop the new rush of tears that brimmed in her eyes.

Buck draped a comforting arm about her shoulders and drew her against his chest. "I'm sorry to hear that. I know how much the babe meant to you. How are his parents?"

Star shook her head. "They no better."

"I was afraid of that," Buck said as he gazed solemnly down at her, his face lined with worry. "Annie, I'll be leading the wagons to Sagebrush at dawn and I want you to come with me."

Star wiped at her eyes as she gaped up at him, unable to believe that he would even think that she would leave Jake and Priscilla. "You know I can' come wit' you."

Buck caught Star by the shoulders and turned her to face him. "Listen to me, Annie. I respect how you feel about the Ransons, but if you stay, you may get sick and die as well. I've grown fond of you during the past days and I don't want to see that happen. They may own your papers, but that doesn't mean you have to give them your life."

"I knows the chances I be taking, but that don't change my mind," Star said, automatically mimicking the slave dialect after so many weeks of using it. "I won' leave Master Jake and Miz Priscilla. They been good to me and I won't desert them when they's in need."

Buck expelled a long breath and shook his head. "Can't I change your mind? You're risking your life."

"No, sir. I be grateful for your concern, but my place be here wit them."

"Hell fire, girl. You're as mule-headed as them damn ornery oxen."

"I may be that, but I could never leave Master Jake and Miz Pris to die. There's times in life when we gots to put the welfare of other people before our own, so we can live with ourselves later. I don' want to go through life with the shadow of guilt always hoverin' near me to remind me that I sacrificed my friends to save my own neck."

Buck flushed guiltily and looked away, unable to face her as his own past indiscretions rose up to haunt him. His gaze moved to the Lindens' wagon and lingered there, where his son was helping to care for the sick. He knew exactly how Annie felt when she spoke of living with shadows. He had lived with them for too many years and was now paying a dear price for leaving his son so long ago when Kyle needed his father.

"You're wise beyond your years, Annie," he said at last. "I admire your courage and loyalty. I've wished many times in the past that I had the wisdom and strength you possess. Things might be different now if I'd had the foresight to realize I was making mistakes that I couldn't rectify later. Now it's too late."

"It's never too late." Star placed her hand on his arm and squeezed it gently. "If you want somethin', you gots to fight for it."

Buck shook his head ruefully. "How can you fight a hatred that you created? I'm getting to be an old man, Annie, and I'm weary of battles. I just want to settle down and live peacefully."

"Then you don' really care enough to right the wrongs of the past. You is selfish—you want things without being willin' to work for them. I be young, but I've learnt nothin' comes easily."

Buck flinched under her reprimand. Her words stung his conscience. "Annie, I do care, but all the caring in the world won't erase the years of bitterness."

"It might not erase them, but that don' mean the future gotta be like the past."

Buck studied her serious young face for a long moment before a slow, crooked grin curled up the corners of his mouth. He shrugged. "What the hell? I guess it can't hurt to try. The situation couldn't be made any worse."

Star patted his arm reassuringly. "You may not win what you seek, but at least you know you made the effort. That be all anyone can ask of theirselves."

"You're a keen little miss, Annie. Now go see to your patients while I start building bridges."

"Bridges?" she asked, puzzled.

"Yep, bridges. You have to get over the walls somehow," Buck said, and grinned before he turned away and strode in the direction of the Lindens' wagon, leaving Star staring after him, bewildered.

"Men!" Star muttered, and shook her head. "When you think you know them, they say or do something you just don't understand." Putting Buck from her mind, she lifted the canvas flap and climbed into the wagon.

The moment the canvas fell back into place behind her, shutting off the world outside, Star heard Jake's raspy breathing and knew his lungs had begun to fill with fluid. All else was forgotten as she knelt by her friend's side. "Jake, you can't die and leave Pris," she murmured urgently. "She needs you now more than ever."

For the first time in several days, Jake opened his eyes and looked up at her. There was no sign of delirium in his gaze, only a look of calm acceptance. His parched lips cracked as he made an effort to smile. His emaciated hand trembled violently as he reached out and took hers and his voice was a hoarse whisper as he murmured,

''Thank you for being such a good friend, Annie. Take care of Pris for me.'' His hand fell away and his eyes grew glazed as his last words came, ''Tell her I love her and Little Jake.'' His body stiffened momentarily as if making one last valiant attempt to recapture life before he relaxed into death.

New tears blurred Star's vision and slipped silently down her cheeks as she closed Jake's eyes. Lifting the tiny bundle from the cradle, she placed Little Jake in his father's arms before she covered them with the sheet. Father and son were now at rest.

The morning sun blazed as Star stood on the small hillside by a freshly turned mound of earth and looked back at the stark ribs of the Ransons' wagon surrounded by all of their worldly possessions. It and the mound of earth were the only reminder of the small family who had perished within hours of each other. Priscilla had followed her husband and son into death and now they lay together beneath the dark Texas sod.

Star's gaze lingered on the sad remains of her friends' lives for a long moment before she looked toward the wagons near a clump of twisted mesquite where another desperate battle for life was in progress. The nine remaining members of the Linden family had been stricken within the past two days, so they, too, had been left behind by those fleeing the disease.

The dry, brown grass rattled in the wind that molded her worn gown against her body as she knelt and placed a small bouquet of dried wildflowers on her friends' grave. Their funeral had been simple and quick. Buck and Kyle had dug their grave before dawn without any assistance from the other members of the wagon train. After placing the Ransons in it, they had torn apart the wagon bed and had placed the boards over the bodies in an effort to prevent them from being disturbed by animals or Indians who often dug up those buried on the trail to steal their clothing. Once the grave was filled, Kyle had said a brief prayer and then returned to care for the Lindens, leaving Buck and Star to reflect upon their own mortality.

Star's cheeks burned at the scene that had followed Jake's and Priscilla's funeral. Buck had given her no time to think about anything. He had taken her firmly by the arm and, without telling her of his intentions, led her back to camp where the group awaited his return so they could be on their way. Without asking her permission, he had announced that she would be traveling with them to Sagebrush and would need to stay with one of the families on the train.

The furor that erupted following Buck's announcement had been heated. The men refused to have her ride with their families because of her close contact with the sick, as well as because she was a slave. They'd told Buck bluntly that they'd not risk their families' lives for one of her kind. Their fear had revealed the prejudice that they had managed to keep hidden so well during the past months. Buck had argued on her behalf and had begun to convince them, when she intervened with her temper flaring white-hot. She'd told them in no uncertain terms how she felt about their treatment of her friends and that she would not travel with such a cowardly, unfeeling, bigoted group of people if her life depended on it. Buck had sought to convince her that it did, but he could not change her mind. When she turned and stamped away with her head held high, she'd heard Seth Mctaggart say, "That uppity wench deserves what she gets." His words only strengthened her resolve.

Star would never forget the expression on Buck's face when he came to say good-bye. His eyes had held a mixture of emotions: concern for her and annoyance with the people he had agreed to help. There also had been a look of admiration in his eyes for the way she had stood her ground in the face of such odds. Their farewell had been tense and poignant.

"That was a brave and foolish thing you did this morning, Annie. You should have gone with Buck," Kyle said now as he placed his hand beneath her elbow and helped her to her feet.

"Perhaps it was foolish, but I couldn't have gone with them knowing how they feel about me," Star said, forgetting in her grief for her friends to use the slave dialect. She brushed a stray strand of hair from her brow as she looked back toward the Lindens' wagons. "Nor could I leave you here alone to care for the Lindens. I owe May and Harry a debt of gratitude for the compassion they showed Jake and Pris while they were ill. They're good people and they deserve better than what they've received from the rest of the wagon train."

"I'm glad you stayed, Annie," Kyle said, a slow grin curling the corners of his lips. "During the past days I've found I know little about caring for the sick. I guess I make a better cattleman than a nursemaid."

"A cattleman?" Star asked, realizing again how little she knew about this complex man.

"Yes, I own a spread north of Sagebrush," Kyle said as he took her by the arm and led her back toward camp.

There was no time for more personal conversation once they reached the two wagons in which the members of the Linden family were fighting for their lives. All their energy was focused on caring for the nine surviving cholera victims. Kyle and Star worked around the clock, sharing the nursing duties as they fought valiantly to thwart the dark angel. They ignored their own exhaustion as they bathed hot brows and bodies in an effort to make their patients as comfortable as possible. Star was grateful that Kyle had had the foresight to make camp near a stream where they could draw enough water to tend the Lindens. Bathing them to ease their suffering was all she and Kyle could do as the disease ate away their lives.

By midafternoon of the second day their death watch came to an end when Harry Linden slipped quietly from life to join the other members of his large family who now rested on the hillside with Jake, Pris, and their son.

Star was numb with exhaustion, emotionally and physically, as she followed Kyle up the slope to place Harry beside his wife. She did not cry. There were no tears left to shed. They had all been spent over the past long hours as each new mound was added to the hillside. The last of her strength faded as the final spade of earth fell onto Harry's grave.

Unable to remain standing, she sagged to the ground and stared at the line of graves. She suddenly felt old as the bitter aftermath of the vigil settled about her in an oppressive cloud. Thirteen people whom she had known and loved now lay beneath the dark loam on the lonely hillside and she was too drained to feel anything beyond the need to lie down and sleep.

Kyle tossed the shovel away and wiped the beads of sweat from his brow with the back of his hand. He felt the muscles in his legs tremble with fatigue as he gazed down at the young woman who sat with shoulders bowed from weariness. Her face was drawn and pale. Dark shadows tinted the delicate skin beneath her eyes to a deep violet as she stared blankly at the new mound of earth. He knew she had finally reached the limit of her endurance. Harry's death had broken the restraints she had used to hold her exhaustion at bay and now her tired body ruled her instead of the valiant spirit he had grown to admire during the last harrowing days.

Kyle slowly shook his head, bemused by the young woman. There were few men who possessed the inner strength that dwelled within Annie's small body. She had unconsciously shown a valor that many aspired to attain in their lives but few achieved. There weren't many people who would have jeopardized their own safety for the sake of friendship as she had done time and again.

He knew the courage it had taken for her to remain behind to nurse the Lindens. They were his responsibility, yet he'd had to look deep within himself to dredge up his own valor when the other members of the wagon train wanted to abandon them. Placing your life at risk for others was never easy, but Annie had done so, work-

ing at his side without complaint, never mentioning her
own fatigue.

Gazing down into the young, haggard face that had
once been darkly colored to disguise her identity from
the world, Kyle knew Annie was not whom she pretended, but her unselfish acts had earned her what few
men had gained from him—his respect.

Drawing in a long, tired breath, he crossed the few
feet to her side and lifted her into his arms. "I'll take
you back to camp," he said.

She did not protest as he carried her to the shade of
the mesquites where the hull of the Lindens' wagon stood
as a memorial of their passing. His limbs quivered from
the exertion as he sank to his knees and laid her upon
one of May Linden's brightly colored patchwork quilts.
Too tired to do more, he lay down beside her and cradled
her in his arms. Together they slipped into a deep, re-
cuperative sleep.

The first light of dawn was beginning to paint the sky
with deep hues of magenta when Kyle awoke to find Annie still curled at his side. Propping himself on one elbow, he lay for a long while, marveling once more at her
beauty. Well rested, he felt his body stir with desire as
he gazed down into her lovely, sleep-softened features.
Her heart-shaped mouth, parted slightly as she breathed,
seemed to beckon his kiss, but he restrained the urge to
taste its luscious sweetness.

The heat of his desire settled in his loins with an aching intensity. At that moment he wanted her as he had
never wanted another woman. Her beauty, her courage,
and the mystery surrounding her all combined to heighten
her allure. Yet Kyle did not succumb to his need.

He eased away from her and pushed himself to his feet.
Collecting his razor and soap, he quietly left the camp.
A cold bath in the stream would hopefully quell the ache
in his groin, as well as soothe his sore muscles before he
began to gather firewood to rebuild the fire.

Kyle made his way through the stand of mesquites to

the small winding stream that ribboned across the flat landscape, its water giving life and greenness to an otherwise brown and gold landscape. He stripped off his dust-covered clothing and stood naked in the tall grass that grew along the streambed. The morning sun bathed his lean body as he stretched his arms above his head, flexing the sinewy muscles in his back and shoulders. The bands that ridged his wide chest grew taut as he drew in a deep breath and stepped into the cool water. It rippled about him, flawing the image of sleek masculine beauty that was reflected in the crystaline liquid.

He rubbed a hand along his strong chin and jaw as he leaned forward and studied the image of his beard-stubbled face. Grimacing at his reflection, he lathered his shadowed cheeks and shaved off the offending growth. He smiled with satisfaction as the last stroke of the blade left his chin clean and smooth. Tossing the razor to the bank behind him, he began to scrub his body in earnest, lathering every inch of his supple skin before taking a quick dip beneath the water. He rose from the shallow pool, his hard, lean body glistening with liquid diamonds in the morning sun. Relaxed and confident that he had once more gained control over his emotions, he strode toward the edge of the stream.

Kyle froze at the sound of a twig snapping in the thick underbrush, his senses alert to any danger. When the sound came again, he moved swiftly toward the pile of clothing where his gun lay. Securing it, he grabbed his clothes and ducked behind a thick clump of tall grass. Its long blades made a dense green curtain that concealed his presence from the intruder. Sinking low, he waited, tense and ready to attack if necessary. When he saw Star step from the mesquite and pause at the water's edge, he breathed a sigh of relief but did not move from his hiding place as she began to disrobe.

Unaware of his presence, Star placed her treasured bar of castile soap on a flat rock and draped her towel over the dead limb of a fallen mesquite before she quickly unlaced her gown and stripped off the dirty garment. She had awakened to find herself alone for the first time in weeks, and assuming Kyle was collecting firewood, she had decided to use the precious time to enjoy the stream she had only glimpsed during the last frantic days. The thought of having a true bath instead of making do with a sponge bath from the tin basin had drawn her like a magnet to the meandering little stream of water.

She forgot all else as she waded out to the deepest point. Tossing her worn red turban to the bank, she unbraided her hair and let it fall down her back in a black curtain of wavy silk. Sinking down into the water, she wet the thick mass and lathered it into a froth, washing it free of the dirt and dust that had accumulated to dull her once shining locks. Dipping beneath the water, she rose laughing with pure pleasure. Her breasts and belly gleamed like soft ivory, contrasting with the slightly darker tint of her arms, face, and shoulders as she bathed her skin. She was completely unaware of her own sensuous movements as she savored the feel of the water against her clean flesh.

The varying shades of her skin emphasized her naked loveliness, making Kyle groan inwardly as he viewed her from the clump of grass. The clear sound of her laughter made the muscles across his lean belly contract sharply and he felt the heat of his desire swell once more in his loins. He muttered a low, anguished curse, but the sound did not carry to the young woman innocently playing only a short distance from him.

A tortured frown marked his brow as he fought to suppress the urge to go to her and make love to her in the crystal-clear liquid that dewed her tantalizing skin. He wanted to feel her ripe young body pressed against his burning flesh, to taste her wet skin with his tongue, to clasp her firm round buttocks in the palms of his hands as he thrust deeply within her, to glory in the moist warmth of her womanhood surrounding his hard, throbbing maleness. He knew he would not make the same mistake he had made that night in the garden of the Red Passion. When he made love to her the next time, there would be no turning back for either of them. They would both experience the ecstasy that they had only glimpsed on their first moonlit encounter.

Kyle's need seared achingly through him and he unconsciously moved toward the object of his desire. However, the sting from a cutting blade of grass jerked him abruptly back to reality. Giving himself a sharp mental shake, he eased back into the seclusion of his hiding place.

His gaze lingered a few moments longer on her naked beauty before he clenched his jaw and turned away. He moved stealthily back through the underbrush to camp. He jerked on his clothing and boots before irritably running a hand through his damp hair and clamping his hat on his head. His abrupt actions reflected his annoyance with himself for letting one young woman have such a disturbing effect upon him. He gritted his teeth and turned to the task of gathering firewood, but his thoughts were never far from the girl he had left at the stream. His body craved release, but he would not allow himself to give way to its demands, even if she should be willing. Too much had happened during the past days and there were still too many unanswered questions.

He wanted Annie, the girl he had grown to admire, and not the girl who swathed herself in a veil of lies. He knew his feelings toward her were strangely out of character for him, but something had changed within him and he didn't completely understand it. In the past he had cared little if a woman lied to him as long as he fulfilled his own needs, but with Annie it was different. He found he wanted no pretense or lies between them.

In the last days, he had glimpsed the real woman beneath her disguise and he wanted that woman and not the false identity she had built about herself. Their lovemaking would be meaningless if the barrier of her ruse still lay between them.

Kyle slammed a piece of rough, barked wood down onto the pile, hoisted it, and stamped back to camp to build the fire for breakfast. Until he met Annie he had never wanted anything from a woman except sexual release, but now he realized that other things were also important to him. He wanted to end the charade, but he knew he could not be the one to do it. He wanted Annie to come to him with the truth.

Bewildered by the new and strange feelings tumbling wildly about within him, he cursed, "Damn it, I'll have the truth if I have to choke it out of her." Yet even as the words left his lips, he knew they were a contradiction of his true desires.

Dumping the wood on the ground, he hunkered down by the blackened earth where the fire had burned the previous night but made no effort to kindle a new one. He stared down at the gray ash, his hands hanging limply between his thighs as he reflected upon what he would do if Annie continued her ruse. After a long, thoughtful moment, a mischievous twinkle glittered in his green eyes and he smiled. If she wanted to play out the game, then he would be more than willing to help her, and from what he had learned of his mysterious Annie, she would not like it.

Unaware of Kyle's plans for her, Star returned to camp, refreshed and hungry for the first time in over a week. Noting that he was busy with the fire, she stored her precious bar of soap in her portmanteau and set about making a fresh batch of biscuits for their breakfast. She was grateful she had learned much about cooking from Pris during the previous weeks on the trail. Soon her hands were coated in dough and a white smudge of flour streaked one cheek where she had absently brushed away an annoying fly.

" 'Morning, Annie," was all Kyle said as he paused at her side. Folding his arms over his chest, he watched her roll out the plump balls of dough and place them in the covered pot that would be set in the fire and heaped with coals to cook the biscuits.

"Good morning, Master Hunter," Star replied, her attention centered on her task.

"Did you sleep well?"

"Yes," she murmured, a blush suffusing her cheeks as she recalled that she had slept at his side throughout the night. The thought of him lying next to her did little for her peace of mind and she nervously plopped the last biscuit into the pot and covered it with the lid. Wiping her hands on her apron, she avoided looking at Kyle.

"Annie, I've decided that we'll rest here today and in the morning we can get an early start for the Bar H. Since Buck is now in charge of the wagon train, I see no reason for me to delay our return to the ranch any longer."

Star looked sharply up at Kyle, her eyes round in surprise at his announcement. "Master Hunter, I can't go with you to your ranch. I—" Her last words died unspoken. What reason could she give to explain her need to reach Sagebrush?

Sensing her dilemma, Kyle smiled to himself. He was satisfied that his scheme to make her reveal her ruse was already working successfully. His sudden announcement that he would take her with him to the Bar H had jolted her so much that she had completely forgotten to act the part of a slave. "Since you are now my property, I see no reason why not."

"Your property?" Star stammered, gaping up at him as if he had suddenly lost his wits.

Kyle nodded, a smug smile curling the corners of his mouth as he gazed down into her stricken face.

"That can' be," she said, vehemently shaking her head. "I was the Ransons' slave and now that they be dead, I belong to no one."

"I'm afraid you're wrong, Annie. As part of Jake's holdings, you now belong to me."

Star stared up at Kyle, her blue eyes glinting with fiery lights as white-hot rage crackled along every nerve in her body. She seethed inwardly. The greedy bastard! How dare he claim me as his property? He pretended to be Jake's friend while in truth he was nothing but a vulture awaiting his time to swoop down upon the few possessions her friends had owned.

"You have no legal right to lay claim to anything Jake and Pris owned," she spat contemptuously.

"Again you're wrong, Annie. When Jake died he still owed me money for their passage to Sagebrush and since you're the only thing left of value, your papers now revert to me."

"I don't believe you."

"It's true. Texas is a slave state, and as such, you are considered part of Jake's estate and can be turned over to his creditors as payment of his debts."

Star clenched her hands tightly at her waist in an effort to keep from succumbing to the urge to claw out his eyes. How had she ever believed that Kyle possessed a heart? He was still the same man she had met at the Red Passion. He considered no one's feelings beyond his own selfish interests. Star turned away. Hot tears of anger clogged her throat and a dull ache formed in her breast as she stared through misty eyes at the distant horizon. She was stranded in the middle of nowhere with a man who had decided that she was his property to do with as he saw fit. A wave of helpless frustration swept over her until she remembered the coins in her portmanteau and those Jake had hidden away to give his family a new start when they settled in Sagebrush.

"You'll be a welcome addition to the Bar H since I need a cook. Juan Valprez now holds that position, but he'll be of more use to me out on the range instead of in the kitchen incinerating everything he touches," Kyle said.

Star's head snapped up and she stiffened her spine. "I won't go with you," she said.

"You have no choice in the matter, Annie. You're my property now."

Star spun around to face him, her eyes flashing. Provoked beyond reason by his words, she braced her hands on her hips and spat, "I do have a choice, Kyle Hunter." She moved swiftly to the trunk where Jake's small bag of coins was hidden and retrieved them before she searched her portmanteau for the money she had taken from Jasmine Hall. She threw it all at Kyle. "You see, I do have a choice. That money clears Jake's debt to you and you now have no claim on me."

Kyle opened the bags of coins and counted the money inside. He had not foreseen Annie's ingenuity, but that did not hinder his plans. He smiled. "I'm sorry to disappoint you, but this isn't enough to settle Jake's obligations," he lied. "So you see you don't have a choice, Annie."

"Don't call me by that name," she cried in exasperation. "My name is Star Grayson and I do have a choice because I don't belong to you or anyone. For your information, you arrogant bastard, I'm not a slave, nor have I ever been one."

Kyle's eyes glinted with amusement. "I was wondering how long it would take that temper of yours to get the best of you so you'd finally tell me the truth."

"You've known all along?" she asked, gaping up at him in shock.

"Look at your skin, Star. Did you think I wouldn't notice that it has grown considerably lighter in color during the last weeks on the trail?"

Star's brows drew together over the slender bridge of her nose as she held up her hands. Her eyes widened in surprise at the sight. Only a hint of the walnut stain remained to shade her skin to a light tan. The change had been so gradual that only Kyle Hunter, the one man she didn't want to discover her secret, had noticed the difference.

Kyle smiled as he watched her expression change. "I admit your disguise was successful at first. You fooled me as well as everyone else on the wagon train."

"When did you guess the truth?" she asked, her voice no more than a hoarse whisper.

"It wasn't until you tried to save Sonny Linden that I finally saw through your ruse. I had always sensed that I had met you before, but it wasn't until then that I remembered exactly where."

Star felt her cheeks burn and glanced away from him,

unable to meet his gaze as the vivid memory of their first
encounter painfully resurfaced. "Why didn't you say
something at the time instead of waiting until now?"

"Until now it was none of my business if you chose
to pretend to be a slave," Kyle said, his smile fading.

"It's still none of your business." Star flashed Kyle a
mutinous look and turned away.

"Hold on," he growled. Locking his fingers around
her arm, he spun her about to face him. "I'm making it
my business and I'll have some answers from you before
we leave here."

"You can go to hell, Kyle Hunter. I owe you no explanation. What I do with my life is none of your concern. Now let go of my arm," she ordered, her chin
jutting out at a pugnacious angle as she strained against
his hand.

"You might as well tell me why you disguised yourself
as a slave, Star, because I intend to learn what's behind
this scheme of yours one way or the other." Kyle's handsome face was set with determination as he stared down
at her.

Star pressed her lips into a thin, defiant line as she
glared up at him, refusing to be bullied by his domi-
neering manner. She'd be damned if she'd give in to his
demands.

Kyle's fingers bit deeper into her flesh before he released her arm and let his hand fall back to his side.
"Keep your secrets for now but be forewarned. I'm a
patient man when the need arises. The days are long at
the Bar H and sooner or later you'll tell me what I want
to know."

Star rubbed her bruised arm but stood her ground.
"I've already told you that I have no intention of going
to your ranch."

"Then I suggest you either answer my questions or
start walking. Unless you tell me why you concocted such
an elaborate charade, I'm not going anywhere except the
Bar H." Kyle folded his arms over his wide chest and
regarded her with mild interest as he awaited her answer.

Filled with indecision and mounting frustration, Star avoided his gaze. She looked past him toward the flat landscape sprinkled intermittently with stands of gnarled mesquite and clumps of dry, brown grass. She knew if she was to reach Sagebrush she had no recourse but to find an explanation to appease his curiosity. Yet she could not tell him that she was fleeing the hangman's rope because of the death of her stepmother. She couldn't risk telling him the truth. He might take her back to Louisiana and turn her over to the law for the reward.

Drawing in a deep breath, she looked back to Kyle. She had to convince him to take her to Sagebrush so that she could hire someone to guide her to DryCreek. "I can't go to your ranch because I need to reach DryCreek, where my aunt lives," she said at last, deciding to tell him a portion of the truth.

Kyle arched one dark brow in question but said nothing as he waited for her to continue her explanation.

Unnerved by his close scrutiny, Star lowered her eyes to the ground at their feet, afraid that he could see that she was not telling the complete truth. "I—I ran away from my family because they were trying to force me into an unwanted marriage. If I can reach my aunt I'll be safe. She won't let my family make me marry against my will."

Kyle chuckled cynically. "Do you really expect me to believe that wild story?"

Star looked sharply up at Kyle, her eyes wide with alarm. If she couldn't convince him, she didn't know what she would do. "It's true."

"Do you seriously expect me to believe that you stained your skin black and pretended to be a slave just to escape your family? You seem to forget where we first met, Star. I seriously doubt any girl about to begin working for Sugar has a family who is interested in marrying her to anyone. Most would not even acknowledge having such a daughter," Kyle said, picking out the flaws in her story.

The blood drained from Star's face, leaving her ashen.

Lowering her eyes once more, she said, "I'm telling you the truth. It was Sugar's idea to dye my skin. My family was searching for me and the only way I could escape them was to disguise my appearance." Lifting brimming eyes to meet his skeptical gaze, her voice filled with tears as she continued. "As for Sugar—oh, never mind, you don't believe a word I've said so there is no use in trying to explain why I was at the Red Passion."

Star turned and fled before Kyle could stop her. She wouldn't stay and let him see the humiliation and pain she still suffered because of her foolish behavior that one night in the moonlit garden. She heard him call after her as she ran toward the stream but ignored him. Hot bitter tears blinded her as she pushed her way through the underbrush. The spiny limbs of the mesquite snagged and ripped at her gown as she passed but she paid no heed to the damage done to the worn material. The burden of guilt and pain she carried in her heart because of the mistake she had made that night outweighed all else.

Kyle stood rooted to the sandy loam of the west Texas prairie. He stared after her retreating form, his thoughts turning once more to their last intimate moments at the Red Passion. He remembered well his own shock at finding the girl a virgin, but he had assumed afterward that she was just beginning her profession as one of Sugar's high-priced whores.

"Could I have been wrong? Could her story be true?" he asked, unaware that he spoke aloud as he wondered if he had made a horrendous mistake that night. Kyle shook his head, bewildered, then started after Star. He had to know why she had been at the Red Passion.

He found her slumped dejectedly upon a cushion of thick grass that grew by the stream. He knelt on one knee and tipped his hat to the back of his head. Needing something to do with his hands, he picked a blade of grass and began to shred it with his long fingers as he quietly asked, "What were you doing at Sugar's?"

The muscles in Star's throat worked as she swallowed with difficulty and moistened her dry lips. She did not look at him but kept her eyes on the meandering current of water. As she spoke her voice was little more than a throaty whisper. ''When I ran away from my home, I had nowhere to go and Sugar befriended me.''

''Didn't you know that Sugar ran a brothel?''

Star shook her head and kept her eyes trained straight ahead. ''Not at first.''

''Why in hell didn't you get out when you learned what type of business Sugar ran?'' Kyle asked, trying to find any excuse to appease his own mounting guilt.

''I had no other place to hide and Sugar promised to help me reach my aunt in DryCreek. Sugar was my only hope of escaping from Natchez.''

Kyle frowned down at the grass in his hand. ''If you knew about Sugar's profession, why were you roaming about in the garden that night? Didn't you realize what could happen to you? Didn't she warn you?''

Star jerked as if he had struck her. She bowed her head and squeezed her eyes tightly shut. ''Yes,'' she murmured, her voice strained as a new wave of humiliation washed over her. ''Sugar warned me to stay in my room when the Red Passion was open for business, but it was so hot that night and I thought no one would see me.''

The muscles across Kyle's belly contracted. He felt as if he had been kicked in the gut by an iron-shod mule. He drew in a sharp breath against the guilt that twisted his insides into knots.

''Damn,'' he muttered, tossing the grass away. He felt the need to apologize, but the words stuck in his throat. In truth there were no words to make up for what he had done to her.

Getting to his feet, he bent and took Star by the elbow and helped her to rise. He looked down into her tear-bright eyes and felt as if he was the devil incarnate for having caused this young girl so much pain. Remorse welled within him as he said, ''I'll take you to Dry-Creek.''

Chapter 8

The hot Texas wind fed the dust devils that danced across the flat prairie, swirling sand into the eyes of the dark-haired man and the young woman riding pillion behind him on the black stallion. The heat from the glaring sun made perspiration bead on their brows, but it was quickly evaporated by the incessant wind, leaving their skin feeling parched.

Hiding her face against Kyle's back, Star sought to avoid the onslaught of the blinding grit that blew about them. The steady beat of his heart reached her through the rawhide jacket he wore as she pressed her cheek against the wide, muscular expanse. She did not raise her head as the spiral of wind and sand passed but lay listening to the steady rhythm as she reflected upon the strange turn of events.

To her amazement, Kyle had kept his word the morning following their encounter by the stream. While she said her farewell to the friends she had to leave behind on the lonely hillside, he broke camp. Since they had dismantled the wagon beds and used the planking to lay upon their friends' graves in an effort to keep them from being desecrated by Indians or animals, there was little to do beyond freeing the oxen and packing what they would need for their journey to DryCreek. Neither the Lindens nor the Ransons had owned a horse, so when all was complete they had both mounted Kyle's stallion and ridden west.

The past four days on the trail had been marked by the strained silence that had developed between them soon after their conversation about her reason for being at the Red Passion. Since that afternoon, they had spoken to each other only when it was necessary. Star sensed that Kyle's reticence stemmed much from the same source as her own. Each was too aware of the other to be comfortable carrying on any small talk, and both feared that anything serious they might say would lead to another argument.

Feeling his sinewy muscles flex beneath her cheek, Star again found herself musing upon the contradictions Kyle Hunter represented. He bewildered her. At one moment he could be hard and arrogant, vexing her until she thought she would explode with the fury he aroused within her, and in the next he was gentle and understanding. When she thought he had no feelings for anyone beyond himself, he would do something totally unselfish, such as remaining behind with the sick when everyone else deserted them.

He was as unpredictable as the Texas wind. His moods varied so quickly that they left her uncertain of her own feelings toward him. She found her emotions balanced precariously between love and hate, admiration and scorn. Since their first meeting there seemed to be no middle ground where she could sort through the maze of conflicting emotions he created within her.

Against her will, she found herself inexorably drawn to him when everything within her warned her that she had already made one grievous mistake where Kyle Hunter was concerned and she ought to be wary of once more making another. The logical part of her mind battled with the emotional side of her nature. It was a constant tug of war that pulled her in so many directions that she was unable to understand Kyle or herself.

Star was startled from her reverie when Kyle abruptly reined the stallion to a halt. She felt the sudden tension in the muscles beneath her hands and straightened to peer over his shoulder. She received only a view of his craggy profile as he raised his face to the wind. Sensing from his demeanor that he was aware of danger that they could not see, a prickle of fear tingled up her spine as she warily scanned their surroundings. Seeing nothing to indicate a threat to them, she asked, "What's wrong?"

"Smoke," Kyle answered before again sniffing the air like a hound on the trail of a fox.

Star frowned as she glanced about them once more. "I don't see any smoke."

"It's too far away to see, but you can smell it."

Star sniffed as Kyle had done but failed to find any evidence of smoke over the masculine odor that filled her nostrils. The heady scent of him made her feel as if she had suddenly swallowed a live hummingbird and she leaned away from him in an effort to still the wild fluttering in the pit of her belly. She scolded herself for letting him have such a disturbing effect upon her at a time when she should be alert to the danger he seemed to sense. Annoyed with herself, she again sniffed the air and found to her surprise that she could now smell the faint acrid odor of charred wood mixed with an unpleasant scent that she could not identify.

"Kyle, where is it coming from?" she asked, amazed by his keen sense of smell. Had he not mentioned it, she would never have noticed the nearly indiscernible trace of smoke.

"There's a homestead several miles west of here, but I hope to hell it's not coming from there," came Kyle's curt reply before he spurred the stallion in the side, sending the animal galloping full speed ahead.

There was no time for further questions. All of Star's attention was centered on remaining on the horse's back as its long legs stretched out across the prairie, rapidly eating up the miles. Dust clouded the air behind them as she clung to Kyle in desperation. Her bottom felt as if it was on fire as she bounced against the horse's rump and prayed that their mad race would soon come to an end.

Star breathed a sigh of relief when Kyle slowed the animal to a walk and urged him down into a gully where a thicket of scrub pine and gnarled mesquite had tenaciously taken root among the rocks and sand. She regretted the deep breath a moment later as the foul odor permeating the air invaded her nostrils. She felt her gorge rise as the rancid scent assaulted her. During all the time she had tended the sick she had not encountered a stench as repulsive as that which now accompanied the dark cloud of smoke beyond the hillside.

"My God, what is it?" Star gagged as Kyle slid from the saddle and reached up to help her down.

"Burnt flesh," he muttered, his face taut with tension as he set her on the ground and turned to his saddle bag. He withdrew an extra pistol and loaded the weapon before he handed it to Star. "I want you to stay here with the horse. If you should hear any shots or if I'm not back within thirty minutes, I want you to ride north for several miles and then cut back west. If you follow the sun you should reach DryCreek within a few hours. And don't stop for anything."

"You don't intend to leave me here alone, do you?" Star asked, glancing nervously about.

"That's exactly what I intend to do," Kyle said, tugging his hat lower on his brow to shield his eyes from the glare of the sun. He started to turn away, but Star grasped his sleeve, halting him.

"I'm coming with you."

"No, you're staying here," came Kyle's firm answer as he pried her fingers from his arm. "If what I suspect is true, there's a Comanche raiding party over that hill, Star, and I'll have enough trouble keeping my own skin whole without having to worry about you."

"I won't stay here when I might be of help to you. I can shoot as well as any man." Star raised the pistol she was carrying, her face set with resolution.

"Hell, woman! Don't you realize that you could be killed or suffer an even worse fate? You don't know what Comanches do to the women they capture. It's not pleasant, Star."

A lump of fear settled in the pit of her stomach, but

she ignored it. "I could also be killed if I stay here. I prefer to take my chances with you."

Her stubbornness exasperated Kyle, yet he knew he had no time to argue, for someone might still be alive beyond the hillside. "All right," he growled. "Keep close to me and don't make a sound, no matter what you see or hear. Our lives will depend upon it."

Having already wasted too much valuable time talking, Kyle did not wait for her reply. He turned and made his way up the grassy slope with the stealth of a mountain lion stalking its quarry. He paused intermittently to assess his surroundings, listening for any sound that would warn them of danger.

For once in her life, Star had no desire to disobey orders. She followed close upon his heels as they made their way to the summit overlooking what had once been the home of the lifeless forms now sprawled in the dirt in front of the burned-out shell of their dogtrot cabin. Every muscle in her body screamed with tension as she crouched low behind Kyle in the tall grass and watched as the Comanches gathered the horses and anything else they considered of value before riding triumphantly away from the destruction they had wrought. Their wild yells of victory floated eerily upon the afternoon breeze as they disappeared from view.

Dragging her eyes away from the scene of carnage, Star looked at the man at her side. His expression chilled her to the bone. His face was taut, his tanned complexion pale with silent rage. He held his lips compressed in a narrow line as he stared at the devastation left by the savages who sought to revenge themselves on those who encroached upon their domain. The vehemence she saw in his face unnerved her and she jumped with a start when Kyle muttered a low curse.

"Damn the red bastards to hell. Those poor people didn't have a chance against them." Kyle gave a low growl of disgust as he came to his feet and scanned the surrounding area one final time before he looked down at Star. At the thought of the grim duty ahead, a frown marked his brow and deep lines etched the sides of his mouth. "You stay here while I go down and give them a decent burial. It's all I can do for them now."

"Let me come with you, Kyle," Star said, a tingle of apprehension racing up her spine at the thought of being left alone.

Kyle's clear green eyes held a haunted look as he shook his head. "No, Star. I've seen what Comanches do to people and it's not a pretty sight. It's best that you remain here."

His expression stayed the protest that rose to her lips and she nodded her assent to his wishes. She understood that he was trying to protect her from the horror that lay below them on the valley floor and she was grateful for his concern. She didn't like the thought of being separated from him, but at the present moment she didn't know if she had enough strength left to face more death. She had seen too much of it during the last weeks.

Star watched Kyle make his way down to the smoldering ruins and pause by one of the prone figures before she turned her back on the scene. She sank to the ground, hugging her knees to her chest, and buried her face in her arms. A tremor shook her from head to toe. At that moment she vehemently wished that she had never set out to find her aunt. Her own problems now seemed small compared to the harsh realities of life on the frontier. In her naiveté she had not realized the dangers she would have to face or the strength it would take to endure each new trial. Star drew in a shuddering breath. She sought to dredge up her flagging courage. She had set her course and it was far too late to change her mind.

The report of a pistol ripped through the still afternoon, jerking her upright. Fear clamped down on her insides, twisting them into knots and her eyes were wide pools of fright as she scrambled to her feet. Without considering any danger to herself, she lifted her skirt in one hand while clutching the pistol in the other and raced down the hill. Her heart pounded against her ribs and her breath came in ragged gasps as she ran in search of Kyle.

She did not look at the still figures lying in the dirt as she passed them and rounded the side of the cabin. She came to an abrupt halt at the sight of Kyle bent double. His face was ashen and beads of sweat glistened on his brow as he wiped a hand across his mouth and turned to find her watching him.

"Kyle," she breathed, unable to say more as a wave of relief washed over her at finding him unharmed.

"What in hell are you doing here? I told you to stay put," he growled, his face taut with tension as he came forward and took her by the arm, propelling her back in the direction from which she had come. He had to get her away before she saw the charred body of the woman tied to the fence post.

"I heard the shot and thought you were in trouble," Star gasped, flinching against the pain his fingers were inflicting upon her tender flesh.

"As you can see, I'm not in any trouble, nor would you have been of any help to me by running headfirst into danger. Don't you ever stop to think before you act?" he muttered as he continued to drag her away from the grotesque scene beyond the cabin. He couldn't tell her the reason for the gunshot. People who had not lived their lives on the Texas frontier could not understand that it was sometimes necessary to perform an act of mercy by ending a life. Until a person witnessed the agony suffered by those who had been tortured by the Comanches, it was difficult to comprehend that type of compassion. It was far more merciful to end the victims' lives swiftly than to leave them to die inch by inch, the way the Comanches had left them.

He couldn't tell Star the reason he had fired the shot. If what he had done sickened him to his soul, she would never be able to understand his actions. She would no doubt consider him little better than the savages who had wreaked their vengeance upon the small family of homesteaders.

Kyle's handsome features reflected the strain of the last

gruesome minutes as he none too gently shoved Star toward the path of trampled grass.

"Go back to where I left you and stay there. I don't have time to worry about you. I need to finish here so we can ride for DryCreek to warn them that's there's a raiding party in the area so more lives won't be lost."

Star turned away but took only a few steps up the grassy slope before she swung back to face Kyle. The horror and tension of the afternoon came crushing down upon her, igniting her temper. Hot, angry tears shimmered in her eyes as she looked at him. She had come to his aid, fearing for his life, and he had the audacity to try to make her feel at fault for caring enough to risk her own life to help him. Her lower lip trembled as she glared at him and spat, "Damn you, Kyle. I just wanted to help you."

"You'll be of more help to me by staying out of my way. I don't need or want you here. Now go!" he ordered, holding a tight rein on his emotions as he saw the hurt look flash into the blue depths of her eyes. Unable to bear the feeling it caused within him, he turned away. His heart went out to her, but he couldn't let her stay and see what had been left by the Comanches. He admired the courage she had shown by coming to his aid, but the grisly duty that he now faced would be too much for her. It would test his own courage to the limit. Resigned to the fact that he had hurt her even as he sought to protect her, Kyle picked up the shovel and began to dig a common grave for those who had perished at the hands of the Indians who considered all white men their enemy.

The encroaching twilight shadowed the valley below as Kyle made his way up the grassy slope. He was exhausted. The muscles across his back and shoulders ached from his labors, yet he knew there would be no rest for him until they had warned the residents of DryCreek. There were still several hours of hard riding ahead before they would reach the small settlement.

Kyle paused as his gaze came to rest on Star lying

nearly obscured by the tall, swaying prairie grass. She slept soundly, completely unaware of his presence as he stood drinking in her beauty. He welcomed the sight of her. At that moment she represented life and he desperately needed the reaffirmation of its existence after the last macabre hours. Having grown up on the frontier, and having often witnessed the carnage left after a Comanche raid, Kyle knew he should have grown inured to such horror, but he hadn't. The senseless, brutal deaths always left him feeling sick in body and mind.

Needing to feel warm living flesh again to rid himself of the coldness of death that seemed to imbue every pore in his body, Kyle came to his knees at Star's side and gently brushed his lips against her brow. She stirred at his touch, her lashes fluttering slowly open. She stared up at him with eyes still soft with sleep. The innocent, unguarded look in their luminous depths broke the restraints he had placed on himself.

"Star, I need you," he murmured, his voice husky with emotion. He drew her into his arms before she could collect her thoughts to protest and buried his face in the curve of her neck.

Star heard the plea in Kyle's voice and lay quiescent, unable to refuse him the comfort he sought and understanding his feelings after having herself witnessed the destruction left by the Indian raid. Earlier in the afternoon she had been furious at him, but time had cooled her bout of temper and now she found her heart going out to the man in her arms. Kyle was a strong man, yet there was a vulnerable side to his nature and it touched her as nothing in the past had ever done.

Tenderly, she soothed the taut muscles in his shoulders and neck with her hand and felt him give a long, shuddering sigh before he raised himself above her. For a long moment the only sound was the wind stirring the tall grass about them as he gazed down into her eyes, searching for an answer to a yet unspoken question. At last he said, his voice soft with passion, "Let me love you, Star."

She tensed as the memory of her last experience with lovemaking resurfaced and brought a rush of hot tears to her eyes. "I can't, Kyle," she murmured helplessly before turning her face away.

Kyle saw the look of fear in her eyes before she turned from him and he groaned inwardly. He had done this to her. He had made her afraid of love because of his callous treatment of her that night at the Red Passion. He had taken her virginity and then had thrust her away from him without letting her experience the beauty of love. Her initiation into love had left her with only painful memories.

Cursing himself for every kind of heartless fool, Kyle pressed his lips to her temple and murmured softly, "I did this to you. Can you ever forgive me? I gave you only pain that night at the Red Passion without letting you know the glory of love. Let me now bring you pleasure, Star. Let me try to erase your fear by showing you that love was meant to give joy and not pain." Kyle did not wait for her assent. He captured her lips and gently tasted their sweetness with his tongue.

Star felt as if a searing streak of lightning heated her blood. Every nerve in her body seemed to awaken to the touch of the man whose lips enticed hers to open to his caress. She drew in a sharp breath, wanting desperately to deny him yet unable to find the willpower to fight the raging current he stirred to life with his touch. His stroking, probing tongue drew her over the precipice where all rational thoughts fell away, leaving only the intoxicating feelings he created. She felt her fears dissipate under his hands as they moved languidly over her, caressing her through the material of her gown. She relaxed under their gentle persuasion and her arms crept about his corded neck as she returned his kiss.

Savoring the furor building within her, she arched her body against his lean length and gave herself up to the pleasure born of the touch of his hands and lips. Her sensitive flesh burned beneath his fiery kisses as he followed the curve of her cheek to the slender column of her throat and then dipped his head to the soft skin exposed above the neckline of her gown. Star's heart pounded with anticipation and her breathing grew ragged as he unlaced her bodice to reveal the creamy, rose-tipped mounds of her breasts. She gasped with pleasure as he lowered his head and buried his face in the valley between them.

Kyle's blood flowed like molten lava, scorching every sinew of his hard body as he drew in the tantalizing smell of her before he tasted the silken flesh with his tongue. He explored the gentle ivory slope of one breast until he found the hardened bud at its crest. He nuzzled the tempting orb before capturing it with his lips and suckling her essence. With his thumb he stroked its twin and felt it respond, beckoning his lips away from the first. His body throbbed in response to the swelling mounds beneath his mouth and hand and he yearned to feel the moist, hidden glen at the junction of her thighs.

Vexed by the material separating him from his desire, he tugged the gown down about her hips and jerked it from her, leaving her naked. Then he pulled back from her only long enough to divest himself of his own clothing. For one brief moment he stood poised above her, a naked bronze giant, his hard body pulsating with desire.

Star caught her lower lip between her teeth as she gazed up at him, the sight of his arousal renewing the fear his touch had quelled. The painful memory of their first encounter chilled the warm glow of the previous moments. "I can't," she murmured, and struggled to sit up, but Kyle's hand on her shoulder stayed her movements.

He came to his knees at her side and gently framed her face in his hands. "I won't hurt you, Star," he said softly as he caressed her lower lip with his thumb. "I know you're afraid, but you have nothing to fear from me. Touch me, Star. Feel my desire for you and know I only want us to share the ultimate in pleasure." He let one hand drop to hers. His fingers curled about it and gently led it to his swollen manhood. Star tried to jerk her hand away, but he held it against him as he murmured, "Feel my passion, Star."

Star felt the satiny length of him throb against her hand and again experienced a rush of desire for him. It began in the pit of her belly and washed downward to dew the shadowy apex between her thighs. She could feel it build as she stroked the warm, male hardness with her fingers. Kyle groaned and moved away from her touch.

"Now, I will love you," he murmured huskily as he came back to her, his mouth tasting hers, nibbling enticingly at her lips as his fingers traveled over her flat abdomen to that secret part of her. She flinched only once as he delved into the dark warmth, savoring the feeling of her as she arched to his hand and moved to the same erotic music that sang through his blood. The muscles across his hard belly quivered as he fought to restrain his own passion until she was ready to receive him. His patience was rewarded a moment later when Star cried, "Kyle, love me." She clasped him about the neck and drew him down to her, her legs spreading in welcome. Kyle chuckled with pure pleasure as he lowered himself between her thighs and thrust deeply into her. She sheathed him perfectly, the honeyed walls of her womanhood caressing him tightly as they began to move in the ancient ritual of love.

The sultry Texas night cloaked them in an indigo velvet robe as hard flesh met soft. They moved in unison, their passion as untamed as the land through which they traveled. The heat of it coursed in a wild current through their veins as each thrust brought them nearer to the fulfillment they sought.

Star felt it begin as a tiny red ember that flamed higher as Kyle's passion-swollen shaft stoked it until she felt herself explode in fiery ecstasy. The glory of her release made her gasp Kyle's name in surprised wonder. She clung to him, raining kisses on his neck and shoulders as wave after wave of pleasure rippled over her entire being.

Kyle exulted in her cry of ecstasy and felt the passage

that surrounded his manhood pulsate with her release. He sought his own. His hips moved faster between her thighs as he reveled in the titillating flesh encompassing his hard member. A moan of pleasure escaped him and the muscles in his corded neck stood taut as he arched his head back and felt himself explode within her. "Star," he gasped, and collapsed over her, their bodies still intimately joined.

Star stroked his damp hair back from his brow as he lay cradled against her breast. She gloried in the ecstasy he had given her and wondered how she had ever feared something as beautiful as the love they had just shared. Her body still tingled from the enchantment of their mating. In all of her imaginings she had never dreamed that love between a man and woman could give so much pleasure.

Love. Yes, that was what she felt for the man in her arms. When it had begun, she did not know. Perhaps it had been when they nursed the sick together or even back in Fort Worth. The exact date and time was not important. What did matter was that she now understood why he had aroused so many conflicting emotions within her. She had loved Kyle without realizing it because in truth she had never loved before.

Star smiled into the night as she hugged his wide shoulders. He also loved her. Tonight had proved that. Wanting to share her newfound feelings with him, she spoke softly, "Kyle, I love you."

The muscles in Kyle's back and shoulders tensed beneath her hands and he raised himself above her. For a long moment he stared down into her night-shadowed face and then pulled away. He sat with his knees drawn up and his arms casually looped over them, staring off into the darkness without speaking.

Her heart beginning to pound with trepidation, Star sat up. Her long hair tumbled freely about her shoulders in a curtain of silk that shielded her nakedness. "Kyle, I said I loved you." Her voice wavered as a chill of uncertainty tingled up her spine.

"Don't say that, Star," Kyle muttered without looking at her.

"But I thought—" Her words trailed into silence as tears clogged her throat.

A cruel fist twisted Kyle's guts into painful knots. He drew in a sharp breath and braced himself against the agony he heard in her voice. He knew what she had thought and it was true. He loved this brave, beautiful young woman, but he couldn't let her know it. He still had too many doubts about himself to tell her of his love and then later destroy her. The thought of seeing his magnificent, passionate, loving Star turn into a bitter shrew because of him was too horrible to contemplate. As his mother had often reminded him, he was too much like his father, and Star deserved better.

"You're just like your father. I pity the woman you choose to marry." Madge Hunter's words echoed through his mind as he slowly turned his head to look at Star. The stricken expression on her beautiful face nearly ripped his heart to shreds, yet his voice reflected none of his inner turmoil when he spoke. "Star, you are a lovely young woman and I care for you, but that's as far as it goes. What we shared was desire, not love. It was a beautiful experience, but you're young and you have confused passion with love." Wanting to give her back her pride, he continued. "You don't love me, Star. Someday, when you find the right man, you'll be grateful to me for being so brutally honest with you now."

"Grateful?" Star spat venomously. Her anger was the only protection she possessed against the painful chasm that threatened to rend her heart asunder.

"Yes, grateful. When you really find love, you'll be glad that I'm not the marrying kind."

Star reached for her discarded gown and jerked it over her head. With a haughty toss of her head, she raised her chin in the air and glared at Kyle. "You're right. I am grateful to you for one thing. You've made me realize that I don't love you. I did confuse passion with love, but I'll know the difference in the future. As for you

thinking that I wanted you to marry me, you're a fool.
If you were the last man on earth I'd not suffer that fate.''

"Good," Kyle said. He got to his feet and began to
jerk on his clothing. "I'm glad we understand each other.
As long as you know that I'm not interested in the holy
state of matrimony, we should do well together."

"The hell we will," Star ground out between clenched
teeth. "Once we reach DryCreek, I hope to never lay
eyes on you again. Hopefully a Comanche will put an
arrow through that rock you call a heart and no other
young girl will have to suffer the same fate that I've endured at your hands."

Kyle's face clouded. "As I recall you purred a different tune not so long ago."

Star flinched but stood her ground. Fuming with the
need to hurt as she had been hurt, she spat, "That's the
one mistake I'll regret for the rest of my life. You've used
me like one of the whores at the Red Passion for the last
time, Kyle Hunter. I'm warning you now. The next time
you lay a hand on me, I'll kill you." With that she turned
and stamped down the hill to where the stallion was tethered.

Kyle expelled a long breath as he watched her go. Star
Grayson had more spirit than a herd of wild mustangs
and he loved her for it. Even in the shadows he had seen
the pain she experienced when he had coldly severed the
tenuous bond that had grown between them, yet she had
rebounded with claws bared.

"Damn," Kyle muttered. If he had any sense he'd go
after her and the hell with the consequences. He'd forget
the vow he'd made so long ago when he came to accept
his mother's predictions and he'd chance finding happiness. But even as the thought crossed his mind he knew
he couldn't do as his heart urged. He'd take Star to her
aunt in DryCreek and then he'd ride away alone.

He had set his course and he'd not veer from it no
matter how it hurt. He wouldn't delude himself into believing that if he married Star that he could change miraculously. The fear that the same devil that possessed

his father also claimed him had been too well ingrained in him through the years. He'd rather face a tribe of Comanches than chance putting the woman he loved through the same hell his mother had endured because of his father.

Picking up his hat, he clamped it down on his head and followed in Star's wake. In a matter of hours they would be in DryCreek and he could get on with his life. The thought did not appeal to him.

Chapter 9

Exhausted and covered with dust from the ride that should have been only a few hours long, but had taken all night because they had to detour carefully away from a Comanche campsite, Star's courage faltered as she raised her hand to knock on the door. Only a piece of wood now separated her from her Aunt Clarice, yet she hesitated. Star was filled with uncertainty at the thought of coming face-to-face with a woman whom she had never met and who might not care one way or the other about her niece's problems after her own ordeal of being wounded in a Comanche raid.

Star withdrew her raised hand and nervously wiped it against the skirt of her gown. The woman who lay beyond the door was recovering from an arrow she had received in the shoulder when she'd fought side by side with her husband to save their ranch, Toro Roca. From the doctor Star had learned that they had failed and it was a miracle that Clarice had lived when everyone else, including her husband, Joe Kendall, had been slaughtered by the Indians before they had burned Toro Roca to the ground.

Worrying her lower lip with her teeth, Star wondered again at her own naiveté. In Natchez she had been sure she was doing the right thing by coming to her aunt, but after what she had learned from the grizzled little man in the baggy black suit she doubted her decision. How could she bring her troubles to a woman who was already burdened with her own?

"Open the door and go on in. Your aunt is expecting you," Kyle said, close at her side.

Star jumped with surprise. She had been so intent on the quandary facing her that she had not heard him come down the narrow, dimly lit hallway.

"She's expecting me?" she asked, bewildered.

"Yes. Doc Simpson said he spoke with your aunt while we were having breakfast. Hè said she's anxious to see you."

"Oh," Star replied vaguely as she glanced once more at the door.

Thinking her hesitation odd after having traveled hundreds of miles and having lived through sickness and death, mud and dust, to reach her aunt, Kyle frowned as he opened the door himself and stepped aside for her to enter.

Star held back for only a fraction of a second and then resolutely crossed the threshold. Her gaze instantly came to rest on the woman sitting in the high-backed rocker, staring through the uncurtained window. Star's face reflected her surprise as she observed her Aunt Clarice for the first time. She was not what Star had expected. Even while sitting down, Star could see that Clarice Kendall was a tall woman, her slender figure rangy. Her hair was a salt-and-pepper gray, and her skin appeared to be refined leather after so much exposure to the sun and wind over the years. Star could see no resemblance to her father until Clarice turned to look at them. In that instant she knew she was looking at her father's sister. Her aunt possessed the same dark blue eyes that Star had inherited from her Grayson ancestors. Though Clarice had suffered a great loss during the last weeks, her eyes softened with a warm glow of welcome as she smiled at her niece for the first time.

"Damn me, but I would have known you to be Charlie's little girl even if no one had told me who you were," Clarice said, and eased herself carefully from the rocker.

She grimaced slightly at the ache in her shoulder but forgot it as she crossed to Star and hugged her. "It's about time I got to see my niece."

"Aunt Clarice, I'm so sorry to hear of your loss. I wish I hadn't come at such a difficult time for you." Star apologized and felt Clarice flinch for one brief second as they hugged.

"Nonsense," Clarice said, clearing her throat as she stepped back to look at Star. "You're even more beautiful than your mother. I always envied her when I was growing up. She was so small and lovely while I was tall and gawky, towering over nearly all the men who lived near Jasmine Hall. My size sure made the pickings scarce when it came to finding a young man to court."

Clarice looked past Star to the man who stood by the door. A wide smile came to her face. "And you don't have to tell me who you are. I'd know Buck Hunter's son anywhere. Ain't another soul who could resemble him that much without Buck's wild blood running in his veins."

"You know Kyle's father?" Star asked, surprised.

"Joe and I have known Buck for well over twenty years. It was Buck who persuaded us to come to Texas and begin ranching soon after we married." Clarice turned her attention back to Kyle. "So you're the one who brought my niece to see me. I hope you don't have jackrabbit feet like your father. I'd not take too kindly to you dallying with her affections and then running off after another petticoat."

"Aunt Clarice!" Star gasped, her face turning a bright crimson with embarrassment. Her aunt's outspoken manner completely disconcerted her. Clarice was certainly not what she had expected at all. She'd assumed because her mother had been gentle and quiet that her aunt would also have the same qualities, but she was quickly finding the opposite was true. To add to her discomfiture, Star glanced at Kyle to see a glint of amusement shimmering in his green eyes.

"Mrs. Kendall, that's something you'll have to discuss

with your niece, but as for the other charges, I'm guilty. I am Buck Hunter's son.''

Kyle's answer made Clarice narrow her dark blue eyes speculatively as she looked from him to her niece. "You're not pregnant, are you?''

Star paled visibly and rapidly shook her head, though in truth she could not be certain after their encounter the previous night. At last she managed to force a hoarse "No" past the tightness that constricted her throat.

"Good," Clarice said, and smiled. "I just wanted to be sure that wasn't the reason you've come to me." She gave Star a curious, assessing look. "Exactly why do I have the pleasure of this visit? And how is my brother? I've thought of him often during the past years.''

Kyle noted the slight stiffening of Star's back and he sensed the tension that seemed to fill the room at Clarice's question. Star's manner roused his curiosity, but he mentally shrugged it off. She was probably nervous about having to explain to her aunt about how she had reached DryCreek.

"I'll leave the two of you alone to talk. I know you have much to catch up on," he said.

Clarice smiled her gratitude as she draped her uninjured arm about Star's slender shoulders. "At least twenty years' worth, though my niece can only fill me in on the past . . .''—she paused and eyed Star for a moment—"I would say eighteen years. Am I right?''

Star nodded.

"That's what I thought. The last time I heard anything about Charles and his family was before your birth. It's been a long time.''

"I'll come back later to escort you to the hotel, Star," Kyle said before closing the door and leaving the two women alone.

Taking Star by the hand, Clarice led her across the small room to the bed. She slid back on the pillow and patted the mattress beside her. "Now, sit down and tell me everything. How is my brother and your mother? Are they well? How is Jasmine Hall? Does Charles still plant cotton?''

Clarice's rapid questions made Star's stomach twist into knots of dread. Her aunt had already lost her husband and now Star would have to give her even more bad news by telling her that all of her family was gone, with the exception of the niece who had come to burden her with her troubles. Swallowing back the tears that threatened to choke her, Star began to relate the tragic events that had led up to her coming to Texas.

Silent teardrops slid down Clarice's sun-browned cheeks as she wept over her brother's death. The lines in her weathered face deepened as she looked at her niece through the moisture brimming in her eyes and her voice was husky as she said, ''So many years have been wasted because of our stubbornness. The sad truth of the matter is that I was just as much at fault as Charles. For years I blamed him for not accepting my marriage to Joe, but I should have contacted him instead of waiting for him to change his mind. Now it's too late for all of us. Charles is gone, as is Joe, and nothing will bring them back.''

Seeing her aunt's obvious pain, Star took her work-roughened hand and gave it a reassuring squeeze, not knowing what more to say or do to ease her sorrow. Clarice returned the pressure and gave her a wobbly smile.

''All that's in the past. Now I want you to tell me why after all these years since Charles's death, you've finally decided to come for a visit?''

Star drew in a deep breath. She had now come to the part of her story that presented such a dilemma. She needed to tell Clarice of Brett Tremayne's threats and of Fiona's death, but her aunt had already endured too much.

Sensing Star's hesitation, Clarice sat up, her face set with determination to get at the truth. ''Young lady, we may have only met but I am your aunt. I'm all the family you have and if there's some problem, you need to tell me.''

Star looked away from Clarice's searching eyes.

"Star, look at me. We're family and as such we're supposed to help each other."

Star pressed a hand over her face for a moment before she nodded and raised her eyes to Clarice's. "I know, but you already have so many problems, it's not right that I now burden you with mine."

"Tarnation, girl! Who else should be burdened with them? You're of my blood. Now I want to know why you're here and I'll not hear anything but the truth."

"All right, I'll tell you. I've come to ask for your help," Star said as she began her tale.

Clarice did not interrupt her as she related the events of her final days at Jasmine Hall. By the time she had finished telling of her stepmother's treatment of her and Brett Tremayne's threats, Clarice was red in the face with fury. Ignoring the pain in her shoulder, she slid her long legs off the bed and stamped across the room, swearing with every step she made. She cursed the unknown and dead Fiona, as well as the man who thought to use the woman's death to his advantage against her niece.

At last having paced off much of her anger, she turned back to Star. Her face reflected something akin to defeat as she released a long, disgusted breath. "Child, I can see why you ran away, but to be honest, there is little I can do to help you. I lost everything when the Comanches burned Toro Roca. All Joe and I had was tied up in that piece of land and now all the cattle have either been stolen by the Indians or have been run off to where we'll never be able to find them. Without cattle to drive to Kansas, I've no money, and without money, I've no power to help." She shook her head sadly.

"Star, after all you've told me, I doubt that if we had all the money in the world at our disposal we could prove you innocent of what Tremayne charges. We have no one who witnessed the accident. It's only your word against his."

A bubble of hysterical laughter rose in Star's throat, but she swallowed it back. After everything she had been through, she had lost. She'd never be able to return to her home.

Seeing the look of pain that had come into Star's eyes, Clarice crossed to her niece and hugged her close. "You may have lost Jasmine Hall, but at least we've found each other. We're not alone anymore."

"I'm grateful for that," Star murmured into the almost mannishly flat bosom she was being crushed against. She let her tears flow freely, weeping for herself and for her aunt.

Clarice gently soothed Star's rich, dark curls and laid her head against them. "Yes, we have each other and that's what counts. It doesn't really matter if we have a roof over our heads or not," she murmured softly as she realized that with Toro Roca in ashes, she couldn't even guarantee her niece a place to live.

Sensing the direction of her aunt's thoughts and wanting to give her support, Star said, "Yes, we have each other and together we can try to rebuild Toro Roca." Star felt Clarice stiffen and she pulled away from her to gaze up into her aunt's taut face.

"Toro Roca is gone, child. It won't be rebuilt. Without Joe there is nothing to rebuild. It was his dream and it died with him. We'll find a way to get by, but it won't be at Toro Roca."

Seeing the pain in Clarice's eyes, Star did not argue and for the first time since she'd entered the room, she was glad that she had come. She needed her aunt and Clarice seemed to need her in return. They were both homeless, but they had inherited the strong Grayson spirit and together they would survive any obstacle placed in their paths.

There was a sharp rap at the door, but before Clarice could answer it, the doctor came bustling in. Eyeing the two women with a curious mixture of pleasure and vexation, he said, "Now it's time you rested, Clarice. Your niece can come back later."

"Doc," Clarice groaned. "I've had so much rest that I'm about to go stir-crazy from being cooped up in this room. It's been more years than I care to remember since I've taken my ease like a pampered lady and I'm out of the habit. I need to get out of here and start sorting out my life.'' Clarice gave Star a warm smile and corrected herself. "We have to start setting our lives in order.''

"We, nothing,'' the doctor said, taking Clarice firmly by the arm and escorting her back to the bed. "You're not going to do anything before that shoulder is healed properly. You've been lucky so far to avoid any inflammation getting started in that wound, but if you rip it open, I can't guarantee that you'll be *around* to set your life in order. Now get back to that bed and rest, Clarice Kendall. I'll not listen to any more of your arguments.'' Giving an exaggerated sigh, he looked at Star. "Your aunt is too stubborn for her own good. Now, miss, I'm expecting you to try to keep a tight rein on her so that we'll not be putting her six foot under. Is that understood?''

"I'll do my best, Doctor,'' Star said.

"Good. It's about time there was a woman with some sense around here. Did you hear that, Clarice?'' the doctor asked, eyeing his patient.

"I heard, but it's not going to do any good. I'll find a way to escape, you old sawbones. You wait and see if I don't.''

"Just you try it. I'll have you hog-tied to that bed if that's the only way I can keep you there. I lose enough patients as it is and I don't intend for you to be one of them because of that ornery streak you possess.'' Taking a flask from his pocket, he set it on the bedside table. "A dram of this should help you relax. Now I have to go out to the Morgan place. Emily is ready to drop that young 'un of hers and Frank is acting as if this 'un was his first instead of his sixth.''

"Doc, be careful. The Comanches would like to have that grizzled head of hair,'' Clarice said, her voice losing its bantering tone.

Dr. Simpson patted her hand reassuringly. "Don't worry. I'll make it back to keep an eye on you.'' Turning to Star, he took her arm. "Now, young lady, it's time your aunt rested." Without even giving her time to tell Clarice good-bye, he led her from the room. She cast her aunt one helpless glance before the door closed behind them.

"Will she be all right, Doctor?" Star asked.

"Your aunt has more grit than most, miss. Her shoulder is healing well and as long as we can keep her down, there should be no chance of it festering. I'm counting on you to see that she stays in bed."

Star released her breath in relief and gave him a dubious grin. "It won't be easy, but I'll try."

"If you want Clarice to recover you'll do more than try." With that parting comment he picked up his black bag and left Star staring after him.

She smiled at the doctor's outspoken manner. It reminded her of her aunt's and she wondered if it was a trait that was bred on the frontier where life was hard and often short and there wasn't time for drawing-room manners. No, she reflected as she crossed the doctor's waiting room and stepped out onto the planked sidewalk, not everyone spoke their minds so freely. Kyle Hunter was a prime example of that. He kept his feelings to himself.

As if her thoughts had conjured him into view, Kyle came striding across the dusty street. His spurs jingled as he stepped up on the sidewalk and strode purposefully toward her. "I was coming to take you over to the hotel."

"Mr. Hunter," Star said coolly, her pride still stinging from the memory of the previous night in his arms, "since we're in DryCreek, I see no reason for your continued assistance. I appreciate your help in finding my aunt, but from now on, I'd prefer to have nothing more to do with you. I told you once before that when we reached DryCreek I hoped never to lay eyes on you again and my opinion has not changed. Now good day to you." Star raised her chin at a haughty angle, lifted her skirt, and stepped down into the dusty street, the only thoroughfare the small town boasted. She walked toward the hotel without looking back at the man who stood watching her.

Kyle felt as if a tornado had brushed by him as he watched her enter the hotel. Giving a rueful shake of his head, he turned to find himself face-to-face with Clarice Kendall. She was fully clothed in boots, britches, and plaid shirt. Her salt-and-pepper hair had been carelessly tied back at the nape of her neck and her face held a pinched look from the strain of her exertions.

"Mrs. Kendall, should you be out of bed?" he asked, his voice reflecting his surprise.

"My name is Clarice and don't you start on me, too, Kyle Hunter. I've been badgered enough by Doc Simpson. And I'll tell you the same thing I told him. I have things to attend to since my niece has come to stay with me. I can't lie around when we don't even have a roof over our heads. She's my responsibility now and I have to make some sort of arrangements for her."

Kyle took Clarice by the arm and led her back into the doctor's office. He propelled her toward the rear of the building and along the narrow hallway to her room. "At the present time, your niece is safely housed at the hotel and it will do her little good if you make things worse by leaving your bed too soon."

"You don't understand," Clarice argued. She desperately wanted to free herself from his hand but found she was too weak to put up any resistance.

Kyle did not answer until he had Clarice securely tucked back into bed. Once that was done, he settled his lean frame in the high-backed rocker and said, "Perhaps if you would tell me what's troubling you, I might be of some assistance."

Clarice lay back against the pillows and eyed Kyle for a long, searching moment. He was so much like his father that it made the blood tingle through her veins to look at him. She had met Buck after she had married Joe, but that had not stopped the attraction she had felt for Kyle's father. Through the years she had fought it because of her love for her husband, but it still burned even after all this time. She did not see Buck often, but every year or so when he passed by the ranch, the fire that had been ignited when they first met still burned brightly.

Clarice had often wondered how she could love two men at the same time. Buck and Joe were entirely different in personality yet she had loved them both in different ways. She had loved Joe for his steady, hard-working nature, while it was Buck who made her blood run hot with passion—a passion that she had never allowed to be fulfilled because of her respect for her husband. No matter what heady feelings Buck Hunter stirred into life within her, she could not have betrayed Joe's faith in her. Nor would it have done her any good to have done so. Buck was also married and had a family. The evidence of that now sat across the room from her, waiting for her to tell him why she was concerned about her niece.

Drawing her thoughts away from Buck, she said, "I doubt you can help. At the present time I don't even know exactly what I can do to solve my problem."

"Let me be the judge of that."

"You can judge all you want, Kyle, but that won't put a roof over our heads or tell me how we're going to live since I've lost Toro Roca."

"Then you don't plan to rebuild?" Kyle asked as a glimmer of an idea began to form in his mind. At the prospect he felt his blood surge with anticipation.

"No. Toro Roca was Joe's. I'd have no desire to go on ranching even if I hadn't lost everything when it burned. I guess after all these years I'm tired of the hard work and worry that goes with it."

"Would you consider coming to the Bar H? I could use a cook who doesn't serve me cinders for every meal. After a while you get tired of eating charcoal."

Clarice laughed at the image his words painted. "I can imagine that wouldn't be too tasty," she said, considering his offer and growing to like it by the moment. It would solve their immediate problems, as well as bring her closer to Buck Hunter. After a long moment, she nodded. ''I think I'll accept your offer, Kyle. Star and I have nowhere else to go and at least we'd be making our own way.''

Kyle wondered briefly at Clarice's insinuation that she and her niece had no place to go. He believed from what Star had told him that they could always return to Mississippi. They had family there. Telling himself that the reason behind Clarice's choice of words was the fact that she didn't want to force her niece into an unwanted marriage, Kyle smiled. His spirits lifted at the thought of having Star at the Bar H. The idea of leaving her behind in DryCreek hadn't appealed to him and now he wouldn't have to.

''Good. We'll leave for the ranch as soon as you're recovered.''

Clarice gave Kyle a devilish grin. ''Then you'd better get your horse saddled because I'm ready to go right now. I've had all of the recuperating I can stand. Much more of this will kill me.''

Kyle chuckled and shook his head. ''That may be, but we're not going anywhere until I've talked with Doc Simpson.''

''Damn,'' Clarice muttered, wrinkling her nose in disgust. ''If you wait for that old sawbones' approval, you'd better plan on staying awhile in DryCreek.''

''We'll stay as long as necessary to ensure your health,'' Kyle said, and smiled at the look of exasperation that crossed Clarice's face.

Incredulous, Star gaped at her aunt. She couldn't believe what Clarice had just told her. Without consulting her, Clarice had agreed for them to go and work for Kyle Hunter. Star shook her head. ''I won't go,'' she muttered, unaware that she had voiced her thoughts aloud. ''I've already made too many mistakes where Kyle Hunter is concerned and I won't make any more.''

Clarice arched a curious brow. ''What mistakes are you talking about, Star?'' she asked, sensing from the vehemence in Star's voice that there was much more between Kyle and her niece than she had first assumed.

Star felt her cheeks burn and turned away quickly to hide their rosy hue from her aunt's speculative gaze. Ignoring Clarice's question, she focused her attention on the distant horizon. "I just don't like the man. He's arrogant and hateful and I won't go to live at his ranch."

"Then what do you propose that we do? Kyle has offered us a home and a way to make a living. As I see it, we have little choice in the matter. We don't have any money or even a place to lay our heads at night."

Star glanced over her shoulder at her aunt. "I could get a job here in DryCreek. They need help in the hotel's café."

"Star, I've already agreed to go to the Bar H," Clarice said, vexed at her niece's continued resistance to the idea.

"Then you go, Clarice. But don't expect me to go with you," was Star's stubborn reply. "I won't willingly live at the Bar H and become that man's mistress. That is his intention, I assure you. He thinks if we come to work for him that sooner or later I'll let down my guard and fall into his arms. He's made his feelings clear about marriage and no matter how I feel about him, I won't be his whore." Star paled as she realized too late that she had divulged more to her aunt than she had intended.

So that's the way the wind blows, Clarice mused to herself. She was beginning to understand her niece's objections. "A moment ago you said you disliked Kyle but now you speak as if you love him. What are your true feelings toward him, Star?"

Shame burned through Star and she chastised herself for her lack of discretion. But having already let her tongue run away with her, she could no longer hide her innermost emotions. Her eyes reflected the agony in her heart as she looked at her aunt and said, "I love him."

"If that's the way you truly feel about the man, then why on earth are you so determined to be separated from him?"

"I've already told you the reason. There is no future

for us. Kyle doesn't return my feelings and my pride won't let me grovel at his feet. I won't beg for the few morsels of affection he might toss my way when the mood strikes. I can't live that way. It's far better to never see him again.''

''If you come with me to the Bar H, you might be able to make him have a change of heart,'' Clarice cajoled.

Star gave a harsh laugh and shook her head. ''Kyle have a change of heart? That's impossible because the man doesn't have a heart. I've made my decision and I have no more intention of changing it than Kyle has of altering his feelings toward me.''

''I'm sorry you feel that way because I'm determined to go to the Bar H,'' Clarice said, hoping her own stubbornness would break Star's resolve. It didn't.

''Then I wish you well, Clarice, because I'm staying in DryCreek.''

Clarice threw up her hands in exasperation. Her niece had inherited her father's stubbornness and nothing she could say or do would make Star change her mind. All Clarice knew to do now was to go forward with her plan and give Star's temper time to cool. The work her niece intended to take in the hotel would soon give her a different outlook on life. After a few weeks alone and working her fingers to the bone, she might think more kindly of Kyle's offer.

Chapter 10

*T*he bedroom door trembled on its hinges as it was slammed shut, leaving Clarice and Buck staring at each other in the main room of the Bar H ranch house, bewildered as to what they had said or done to set Kyle into such a rage before he strode from the room in a huff. The sound of a loud thump against the inside of the door suggested that he had angrily thrown a boot at it to relieve his vexation as he undressed for the night.

Buck lifted one shoulder in a shrug and shook his head. "For as long as I live I'll never understand that boy. What did we do this time to set him off?"

"I don't really think it's us, Buck," Clarice said, a smug, mysterious little smile touching her lips.

Buck arched a dark brow curiously at Clarice. "All right, woman, if you know something that I don't, you'd better tell me because I sure as hell can't take much more of this. I had intended to stay awhile at the ranch this time, but if he"—Buck nodded toward the bedroom door—"keeps this up, I'll have to hightail it out of here. The way he stays on the warpath, it'd be safer taking my chances with the Comanches."

Clarice's smile deepened and her eyes twinkled as she relaxed back into the wooden rocker cushioned with handmade pillows. "I think your son is in love, Buck."

"The hell you say. That boy has ice water in his veins instead of blood. He hasn't ever been in love."

"You're wrong. Kyle is a good man and has lots of

love all locked up inside of him. His anger is the only means of venting some of the feelings that are tearing him apart.'' Clarice's smile faded with the thought.

Buck's weathered brow creased as he frowned at her. ''I wish you were right about that, but I'm afraid Madge successfully bred out any love the boy might have had in his heart.''

''I don't and won't believe that, Buck.''

''You'd better because it's true. She taught him to hate me, didn't she?''

''You could put a stop to that if you'd only tell him the truth about your marriage to Madge.''

Buck shook his head. ''We've discussed this in the past and you know I won't malign the dead. Kyle believes his mother was a saint. He thinks I've enjoyed my roving way of life. He'd never believe me if I told him the reason I stayed away was because of his mother's hatred of me. Even to my own ears, it sounds like a shabby excuse for leaving my son to survive under the care of that bitter woman.'' Again Buck gave a sad shake of his dark head. ''No, Clarice. I can't tell Kyle the truth. It would do me more harm than good.''

''But he needs you.''

''He's a man grown. He doesn't need me any more than his mother did through the years.'' Buck's voice had grown husky with emotion. ''He's made that clear to me often enough.''

''Kyle puts up a good front, but deep inside he hurts,'' Clarice said.

''For a woman who has only known my son for little over a month you seem to think you understand him better than I do.''

''I do. I've seen the look in his eyes when he lets his guard down. I also know that he has fallen in love with my niece, but there's something that keeps him from admitting it. That's the reason he's been in such a foul mood since we returned from DryCreek. He thought she'd be coming with us when he offered me the job.''

Buck eyed Clarice thoughtfully, trying to absorb what

she had told him. "I thought I was the reason for his stormy disposition. He's never liked me coming back to the ranch since his mother's death."

"This time I doubt he's even given you a second thought. It's Star he's brooding about. I'd bet my last cent on it if I had one."

Buck threw back his head and laughed. "Damn me, Clarice. You do have a way of looking at things. There are few women who could lose everything they possess and then jest about it."

"What else am I going to do? It's far better to laugh than to cry in my opinion."

"You're right and that's the reason I've always admired you. I've envied Joe through the years for his good fortune when I was stuck with a wife who hated me."

The mood in the room altered as Buck's and Clarice's eyes met. Gone were their worries over Kyle and Star. Nothing existed for them except the feelings that had fermented between them through the years. It strained the self-control they had placed on themselves to the limit. Electricity seemed to crackle in the air about them as dark blue eyes held vivid green.

"I loved Joe," Clarice said softly.

"I know you did. That's why I kept my distance. I'd stay away from Toro Roca until I knew I'd go crazy if I didn't just have a glimpse of you. Then I'd go through the hell of leaving you once more. The years haven't been easy for either of us."

"No, I'm afraid they haven't. I've been torn in two because of the way I felt for you and Joe. I've often wished the law allowed a woman more than one husband. If that could have happened I would have been the happiest woman on earth."

"That would never have worked," Buck said, giving her a wry grin. "I'm a greedy man and I would never have shared you."

"You did share me with Joe because you've known for years how I feel about you."

"We both have known how we feel, Clarice, but that

didn't change anything. We were married. I've made a lot of mistakes in my life but loving you hasn't been one of them.''

Clarice laid her head against the brightly colored pillow and closed her eyes. Her voice was soft with remorse as she said, "Buck, I feel so guilty for not being able to mourn Joe's passing as I should. He was a good man and we had a good life together.''

Hearing the anguish in her voice, Buck moved across the short space separating them and knelt before her. He took her work-roughened hand into his own and placed a kiss on the callused palm. "Joe loved you, Clarice. He wouldn't want you to grieve over him. He'd want you to be happy.''

"I know he'd want me to be happy, but I wonder how he would feel if he knew that only a few weeks after his death my only thought was to come to the Bar H to be close to you? I wasn't even sure you'd be here, but I jumped at the chance. I left my niece to fend for herself because of my desire to be with you.''

"Is that what's troubling you?''

Clarice nodded.

Buck smiled. "Then it seems that I'll have to go and get the girl to solve all the problems around here.'' He glanced toward Kyle's bedroom door. "Since my son has refused to tell me anything about what transpired since the wagon train split up, I'll have to take your word for what ails him. Maybe if I bring the girl back to the Bar H, I'll get more out of him than curses and black looks.''

"You'd do that for me?'' Clarice asked, her face glowing with love.

He squeezed her hand. "Of course. I won't have the two people I care most about in the world unhappy when I can help. Now where do you reckon I'd find your niece?''

"She works in the hotel café, and before we left Dry-Creek she rented a small room above the mercantile store.''

"Then this Miss Grayson shouldn't be too hard to find."

"She may not come with you. She has her father's stubbornness."

Buck laughed and tweaked Clarice's nose. "From what I've observed of her aunt, she didn't get it all from her father."

Feeling much like a young girl again, Clarice lowered her eyes under Buck's warm, approving gaze. "You could be right." An impish grin played at the corners of her mouth as she continued, "But I doubt it. Her aunt has too sweet and gentle a nature."

Buck chuckled as he pulled Clarice into his arms. "Sweet and gentle as a wildcat," he murmured before lowering his mouth to hers.

Weary from her day's work, Star stepped out into the clear, moonless night. Her steps were heavy with fatigue as she crossed the dusty street and made her way through the dark alley to the narrow steps that led up to her tiny room above the mercantile store. She paused at the foot of the stairs and absently rubbed at the ache in her neck. Above her, the black velvet sky was sprinkled with stars. The glory of the night was lost to her, however. She was too exhausted to appreciate its beauty.

Expelling a tired breath, she placed a hand on the railing and looked up the flight of steps. Her shoulders sagged at the thought of having to climb them to reach the small cubicle that had become her home since her aunt's departure for Kyle's ranch. For one fleeting moment she wondered if she had enough strength left to manage the steps.

Her life had not been as easy as she'd believed it would be when she had informed Clarice that she preferred taking the job in the hotel's café to going to the Bar H with her. Since that time Star had done little but work. The hours required of her were long and strenuous. She not only had to serve the cowboys the rough fare from the kitchen but she also had to help prepare the meals, as well as clean the vermin-infested hotel rooms. Her hands and arms were red and chapped from the harsh lye soap she had to use to wash the multitude of dishes and to scrub the dusty floors.

Star glanced uneasily in the direction she had just come and frowned. Along with her chores at the hotel, she had found another dilemma. To her distress, she constantly had to ward off the advances made by the men she served. It wasn't pleasant. A day did not go by without a cowhand coming in from one of the ranches in the area and deciding to enjoy himself at her expense. They would boldly pat her on the rear as she passed with a platter of food or strain their necks to try to peer down her bodice as she bent to pour them coffee. At first she had been embarrassed by their behavior, but she had quickly learned that swift retribution was the only thing that would stop their lascivious advances. Often to their dismay and discomfort they would find hot coffee dumped in their laps or their knuckles stinging from a sharp rap with the handle of a knife or fork. Her choice of weapons depended upon what was at hand at the moment.

Star's frown deepened, knitting her delicately arched brows. Though the night was warm, a chill prickled its way up her spine at the memory of the burly, red-faced man who had come into the café that afternoon. Until today, her expeditious retaliation had served to thwart any further attempts to fondle her, but this man had ignored the sharp rap she had given him across the knuckles. He had mocked her with laughter as he wrapped his meaty arms about her and pulled her down on his lap. Her struggles to free herself had only added to his merriment as he held her arms pinioned to her sides. He had grinned lewdly down at her and had boldly stated that he intended to see that they became better acquainted in the near future. Fortunately, to her great relief, the owner of the hotel had come to her rescue with a double-barreled shotgun firmly tucked under his arm. He had forced the man to release her and leave the hotel at gunpoint.

A shiver shook Star and she suddenly felt the need to

have a locked door between herself and the night. Instinct told her that the man's threat had not been spoken in vain. She glanced nervously about the dark alleyway and took the first step up the stairs. Intent on reaching her room and safety, she did not see the man step from the shadows beneath the stairway. He moved silently and swiftly and had already clamped his wide-palmed hand down over her mouth to stifle her scream for help before she realized her danger. She struggled against the bone-crushing hold as he lifted her off her feet and dragged her toward the black shadows at the rear of the building. He threw her facedown upon the ground, the impact knocking the breath from her, making it impossible for her to cry out for help. He jerked her arms behind her back and tied them securely about the wrists before he stuffed a dirty rag in her mouth to gag her. He pulled her into a sitting position and she blinked up at him, but before she could focus her gaze on his features, he pulled a large burlap bag over her head.

Star moaned and twisted in protest, but he held her still as he secured the end of the sack about her knees with a piece of rope. He then lifted her into his arms, but a moment later she found herself rudely dumped back to the ground. Unable to do more, she listened to the sounds around her and realized a scuffle was taking place. She heard a loud crack as flesh met flesh and then an agonized groan of pain before all went quiet. Her heart thumped wildly against her ribs as she lay curled in a ball, straining to hear and praying for rescue.

Her prayers went unanswered. She tensed as she again felt herself being lifted high into a pair of strong arms and laid across a saddle. She gasped for breath but gained only a nose full of dust. The sneeze that followed was excruciating in her awkward position. Her nostrils burned, bringing hot tears to her eyes. Star felt a wild rush of hysteria rise in her blood, but she fought to control it. She knew that her only chance of survival might depend on her keeping her wits instead of giving way to the fear that was eating away at her.

She felt the horse begin to move and heard a deep chuckle. "That varmint thought to steal my prize. I haven't come all this way for nothing." The voice was oddly familiar, yet she could not recognize it over the sound of her own blood pounding in her temples.

Her captor did not speak again as he led her horse out of town. The only sounds to break the stillness were the horse's hooves striking the shale. Star's awkward position made the few minutes it took to put a safe distance between them and town seem like an eternity. With the constant pressure on her stomach, and her hands and feet growing numb from lack of circulation, she was relieved when her captor drew their mounts to a halt. Once again she felt a pair of strong hands upon her as she was lifted from the horse's back and set on her feet. Her legs would not support her and she swayed precariously, but the rough hands held her upright.

"Hold on, girl, while I untie you. I don't want you to smother to death in that bag," came the muffled voice of her captor as he used his bowie knife to slice through the ropes that bound her knees and pulled the bag from her. He removed the stifling gag from her mouth before he bent to cut the rope about her wrists. "Sorry I had to keep you gagged until we were out of town, but I didn't want you hollering for help."

Star drew the crisp night air into her lungs and blinked to clear her vision. She rubbed at her raw wrists as she peered up into the night-shadowed face. Unable to distinguish his features because of the wide-brimmed hat he wore, she asked, "Who are you and what do you want with me?"

"Let's say I'm doing a favor for a friend," came the man's calm reply as he tipped his hat to the back of his head.

In that instant, Star recognized her captor. Her first reaction was relief at finding that he was not the man from the café, but it was only momentary. Anger boiled her blood as she stared up at Buck Hunter.

"How—" she stammered and drew in another breath,

"—dare you treat me in such a manner. I thought we were friends!"

Buck blinked down at Star, his brow furrowing in bewilderment as he recognized the young slave girl from the wagon train. He thumped his forehead with the ball of his hand and swore. "I'll be damned! Here I went to all the trouble to get Clarice's niece and I got the wrong dad-blasted girl."

No longer afraid, Star gave her temper free rein. She braced her hands on her hips and faced Buck, her eyes flashing blue fire. "For your information, Buck Hunter, I am Clarice Kendall's niece and you still had no right to assault me in such a manner."

"Hold on, girl," Buck muttered defensely. "I wasn't the varmint who hog-tied you. I just decided not to undo his handiwork for a little while. It seemed an easier way to go about things. And as for you being Clarice's niece, I think you need to explain a few things to me."

"I don't have to explain anything to you."

"I think you do, Annie. I've seen many things in my life, but I've never seen anyone shed black skin for white. What kind of game have you been playing?"

"My name is not Annie, it's Star Grayson, and I haven't been playing games. I used the guise of a slave to reach my aunt in DryCreek. Now I want you to take me back to town and we'll forget this unfortunate episode ever happened."

"For a girl who went to such elaborate means to reach her aunt, you don't seem to be very interested in staying with her. I suspect there are more reasons behind your pretense than you're telling me."

"My reasons are my own. Now will you take me back to DryCreek or do I have to go alone?"

Buck shook his head. "I'm taking you to the Bar H."

Stubbornly Star eyed him, her fury unabated. "I won't go with you."

"You'll go one way or the other," Buck threatened. "You can ride in the saddle or hog-tied across it, but you're going to the ranch with me."

Star was quickly learning where Kyle had gotten his arrogant, dictatorial attitude. The uncanny resemblance of father and son went deeper than physical appearance after all. "You might make me go with you, but neither you nor your son can make me stay at the Bar H," she said.

Buck's craggy features reflected his resolve as he regarded her calmly. After the years of listening to his wife's tirades, he was unaffected by her outburst. "That may be, but I promised Clarice that I'd bring you back and that's exactly what I'm going to do. Once you reach the ranch, I don't give a damn what you do after that. That's between you and your aunt."

"Clarice sent you and not Kyle?" Star asked, feeling her spirit for battle suddenly deflate.

"That's right. I'm doing a favor for your aunt, not my son. The way I see it, Kyle is man enough to handle his own affairs without my interference. He doesn't need my help with a shrew-tongued woman or with his long-horned heifers."

Left strangely bereft by Buck's answer, Star turned away. For one exciting moment she had thought Kyle had sent his father to bring her back to his ranch. The small bud of hope that Kyle's feelings had changed toward her now withered before it could come to full bloom. She felt like a fool for thinking he might have had a change of heart. He had made his feelings clear that night on the prairie and also when he had ridden away from DryCreek without a backward glance in her direction. Even as she argued with Buck about going to the Bar H, she had wanted desperately to believe Kyle had been behind her abduction.

With an effort Star suppressed the hot rush of tears that came to her eyes. During the last weeks in town she had sought to kill her love for Kyle but had failed miserably. The lonely nights in her small room had been torture. She had lain awake, wishing that she had gone to his ranch with Clarice. Now that she was to get her wish, she found the thought of being near him again bittersweet. It would be agony to live in his home and know that he cared nothing for her. The moments they had shared had not meant anything to him beyond a momentary gratification. A painful lump formed in her throat at the thought and she swallowed it back with an effort as she looked over her shoulder at Buck.

"I'll go with you peacefully, but I won't stay," she said.

Star remained morosely silent during the two-day journey to the ranch. She refused to talk with Buck except when necessary. The long hours on the trail gave her time to regroup her defenses and firm up her resolve to keep her feelings for Kyle securely locked away. No matter how she felt about him she'd never submit herself to being humiliated by him again. She also mulled over her aunt's part in having her abducted and brought against her will to the Bar H, and by the time they rode through the gates, she was furious with Clarice.

When they reached the ranch house where her aunt stood anxiously awaiting them, Star refused Buck's assistance in dismounting and slid to the ground of her own accord. She tethered her mount to the hitching post, flashed her aunt a hostile look, raised her chin in the air, and turned her back to Clarice. She had been brought to the Bar H by force and she would not act as if she was glad to be there. Consumed with ire, she did not see the warm greeting between her aunt and Buck as he strode forward and, with an exuberant hug, swung the tall woman completely off her feet.

"Put me down, Buck," Clarice ordered breathlessly, her blood racing through her veins at his touch, her voice low so that only he could hear.

Obeying, Buck set her once more on her feet and wrapped a buckskin-clad arm about her waist. He bent his head close and lowered his own voice as he said, "I brought your niece, but I'm afraid she's none too happy with the situation. I hope for all of our sakes that we haven't made things worse by bringing her to the Bar H.

I don't think either of us could take two foul tempers around here.''

"Things will eventually work out if they love each other,'' Clarice said and smiled up at him. She gave his callused hand a reassuring squeeze. ''We may have to weather a few storms, but we've lived through Comanche raids, drought, and flood, so I think we'll survive two mule-headed young 'uns.''

"I hope you're right,'' was Buck's heartfelt reply. His eyes came to rest on Star, who stood with her head held high and back stiff. Cocking his own head to one side, he grinned. ''But I think I'll weather this one between you and your niece in the barn,'' he added.

"Coward!'' Clarice said, and grinned.

"Yep,'' Buck answered without guilt. He brushed his lips against her brow and strode forward to collect the horses. He touched the brim of his hat courteously to Star as he passed and headed to the barn.

Clarice watched him stride out of sight before she drew in a deep breath and readied herself for her niece's rage. Crossing the few feet separating them, she paused at Star's side. ''I'm glad you came.''

"Did I have any choice in the matter?'' Star asked sarcastically as she cast her aunt a mutinous look.

Clarice smiled to herself. ''Knowing Buck as I do, I doubt that you did. When that man sets his mind to something, no one can change it.''

"Since you're the one who sent him to kidnap me, you didn't really expect anything else, did you?''

"I had hoped that you might be as glad to see me as I am to see you,'' Clarice said, suddenly doubting the wisdom of her decision to bring Star to the ranch. The girl had inherited the Grayson stubbornness and as the years of estrangement between herself and her brother attested, the Graysons were not a family who forgave easily.

"How could you expect that under the circumstances?''

"Star, you're all the family I have left in the world and I wanted us to be together."

Star turned to face her aunt, ready with a sharp retort, but her words died unspoken at the wounded expression on Clarice's finely lined face. She flushed guiltily and lowered her eyes. "I'm sorry. I didn't mean to hurt you. I am glad to see you, but you knew how I felt about coming here. My feelings on that subject have not changed."

Clarice placed an arm about her niece's shoulders and led her to the wide porch that spanned the front of the board and batten house. Seating Star in one of the straight-backed chairs where the men rested in the evening after a long day on the range, she said, "You're right. I knew how you felt about coming to Kyle's home, but I couldn't stand the idea of you being in DryCreek alone. There are too many things that can happen to a young woman in a frontier town when she has no one to protect her."

Star opened her mouth to protest, but the memory of the man in the café made her snap it shut. She was sure he was the one who had tried to abduct her before Buck had taken over. Suppressing the shiver the recollection aroused, she looked up at her aunt. "I can't stay here."

"I'd like to know why not?"

Star opened her mouth to answer, but Clarice waved her abruptly into silence. "I've heard your reasons before and they won't make any more sense to me now than they did when we were in DryCreek. I won't let your stubborn pride keep us apart any longer. I had hoped you'd come to your senses but since you haven't, it seems that I'm going to have to start making your decisions for you. You're too young and headstrong to know what's good for you."

Clarice paused. Her annoyance with her niece mounted by the moment. Drawing herself up, she gazed down at Star. "Since I'm you're only living relative, you're my responsibility until you're married. And I intend to do my duty. You'll stay here with me until we can earn enough money to hire a lawyer to clear up the trouble in Mississippi. When that's done, if you don't want to live with me I'll agree to stay here and you can return to Jasmine Hall. But until that time, I intend to keep you near me so I'll know you're safe and out of harm's way."

Star's lower lip jutted out as she gave Clarice a belligerent look.

"Don't look at me that way, young lady, or I'll take a switch to your backside just like your father would have done if he was still alive. You may be eighteen and full grown, but if you act like a child, then I'll treat you as one," Clarice snapped, her own temper simmering.

"Bravo!" Kyle said, hearing Clarice's last words as he stepped out on the porch and strode forward, clapping his gloved hands, a wry grin of amusement curling up the corners of his shapely lips. "Welcome to the Bar H, Star."

Star stiffened her spine and glared up at him. "I see you still haven't given up the rude habit of eavesdropping on conversations that are none of your concern."

Kyle felt the warm glow of pleasure he'd experienced upon learning of Star's arrival fade as he looked down into her set little face. "Everything that takes place on the Bar H is my business," he answered, his tone sharp.

"Well, in this matter, you're wrong. This is between Clarice and myself." Star came to her feet, her chin jutting out at a pugnacious angle as she eyed Kyle defiantly.

"As long as you're on my ranch it's my business, young lady."

"That won't be for very long because I don't intend to stay here a moment longer than necessary."

"Good," was Kyle's brusque answer. "I couldn't agree with that more." He jerked his hat lower on his brow and stormed from the porch, muttering curses beneath his breath with every step.

Clarice shook her head in exasperation. The storms she had predicted had begun much sooner than she had planned. She had hoped there would be a lull during which Star could have time to adjust to the idea of remaining with her at the ranch. That wish had not been realized. Expelling a long breath, she looked at her niece. "I'll show you to our room. I know you're tired after the ride from DryCreek."

Star gave a squeal of protest as she turned her gaze back to her aunt. "You can't mean to make me stay here after what you just witnessed. Kyle doesn't want me here. You heard what he said."

Tired of arguing, Clarice said, "Because of my age, Star, my streak of Grayson stubbornness runs much deeper than yours. I said you were going to stay and you might as well accept the fact. For now it's the best either of us can do. At least here we have a roof over our heads and we're together."

Star sighed as she accepted her momentary defeat. Her shoulders slumped and her eyes held a pained expression as she said, "Don't you realize what you're asking of me?"

"I'm only asking you to think rationally instead of with your emotions. I know how you feel about Kyle and what you believe he thinks of you, but there is no reason for all this. We can live here amicably if you will only make an effort."

"You want me to live in that man's house when he thinks I'm nothing more than a piece of baggage to be used at his convenience and then tossed aside?"

"Star, what happened between the two of you is in the past and need never happen again. I know you and Kyle are attracted to one another but if you don't want to give in to it, all you have to say is no. Kyle is not the type of man to force himself on a woman, nor does he have to if Victoria Crawford's actions are any indication. You don't have to run away like a coward."

Clarice's verbal arrow hit its mark. Star raised her chin in the air and squared her shoulders. "I'm not a coward."

"Then prove it by not running away. You might find that things are quite different from the way you believe them to be. But you'll never know until you give living here a chance.''

Star gazed thoughtfully in the direction Kyle had gone and her voice held a hint of wistfulness as she spoke. ''You don't know how much I want to believe you, Aunt Clarice.'' After a long moment she regarded her aunt curiously, arching one dark brow. ''Who is Victoria Crawford?''

Clarice smiled to herself. For a moment she had wondered if her niece had heard her mention the other woman. Satisfied that she had baited the hook, she decided she'd leave her niece dangling for a little while. It would do her good to believe that there were other women in Kyle's life. That might make her want to stay and fight for the man she loved.

''You'll soon find out. She comes out to visit Kyle often enough,'' Clarice answered, and wanted to laugh aloud at the piqued look that crossed her niece's lovely face. However, she managed to suppress her mirth. ''Now let's get you settled. I have to start supper. The men will be in soon and will be howling worse than a pack of hungry coyotes.'' She led Star into the house and along the hall to the room they would share.

''It's small, but at least it's comfortable,'' Clarice said, and smiled apologetically as she opened the door and stepped back for her niece to enter.

Star paused upon the threshold, her gaze sweeping over the austere little chamber. It wasn't much bigger than her wardrobe had been at Jasmine Hall. A large double bed and a washstand were the only pieces of furniture. A pitcher and bowl sat upon the scarred, unfinished surface of the washstand, and a small cracked mirror hung above it. An iron nail had been driven halfway into the wall to serve as a towel rack. Along the same wall several wooden pegs held Clarice's meager wardrobe. A braided rug and a patchwork quilt added touches of color to the plain surroundings, yet that did not eliminate the fact that the room had been set aside for use by the help.

Clarice sensed her niece's thoughts and shrugged. ''I'm

not a guest here, Star. I'm a hired hand, and so are you, now. The reason we're at the Bar H is to work.'' Giving her niece an encouraging smile, she continued, ''And speaking of work, I need to get busy. You rest. I'll call you when supper's ready.'' She closed the door behind her, leaving Star with her thoughts.

Star slumped down on the side of the bed, her hands falling limply into her lap. Her eyes burned with the need to cry, but she refused to give way to her tears. Her gaze traveled once more over the room. In truth it was a little better than the one she had rented above the mercantile store, but that fact did not mollify her. It galled her to think that she would have to be Kyle Hunter's paid servant until her aunt decided otherwise.

''Which might be never,'' Star muttered aloud. Lying back on the bed, she braced an arm behind her head and stared up at the ceiling, pondering the change that had come over Clarice since she'd come to the ranch. Her aunt seemed twenty years younger than when Star had last seen her in DryCreek. Her eyes sparkled with vitality and her cheeks were touched with a gentle rose. The physical change could be attributed to her recuperation, yet Star sensed something far deeper had taken place. Clarice seemed to glow with contentment.

Star yawned and turned onto her side. She didn't know what had occurred to bring about the change in her aunt, but she was happy for her.

''At least one of us can be happy here,'' Star murmured as her thoughts returned to Kyle and the woman her aunt had mentioned. Clarice had insinuated that Kyle and Victoria Crawford were lovers. Restlessly, Star raised her head and hit her pillow in an effort to get more comfortable. She failed.

''Damn,'' she muttered, and buried her face in the pillow, desperately trying to shut out the image her mind created of Kyle holding another woman in his strong, muscular arms, his mouth ravaging hers as he stroked her smooth flesh. The mental vision tortured Star and at last she gave way to the tears that had been threatening since her volatile encounter with Kyle. She wept herself into an exhausted slumber.

"Whew! What in hell's been going on?" Buck asked as he came through the back door and strode into the kitchen. Tossing his hat onto the table, he took a cup from the shelf above the black iron cookstove that his son had brought from Shreveport for his mother, and filled it with steaming coffee. Sipping the strong, dark brew, he pulled a chair out from the table and sat down across from Clarice.

"Kyle stormed into the barn as if all the furies were after him. The look on his face was as black as a thundercloud," Buck said.

Clarice grimaced. "You could say that we've just weathered our first storm."

Buck cocked one dark brow curiously at her as he leaned back in his chair. "Do you really think our meddling is going to do them any good? I seriously doubt it if Kyle's mood is any indication."

"At this moment I don't really know," Clarice answered, absently wiping several invisible crumbs from the oiled tablecloth. "All I do know for certain is that I want Star to be happy. Life is too short to be separated from the man you love. I've realized that even more during the last weeks and I don't want to see my niece do the same thing with her life that I did. I loved Joe for his goodness and I'm not sorry for staying with him, but I do regret the years that you and I could have shared together. I don't want Star or Kyle to miss a moment of their love."

Buck reached across the table and took Clarice's hand into his own, squeezing it gently, conveying through that small touch his love for her. "We couldn't change our past and no matter how much we might want to, we can't direct the future for Kyle and Star. They're both bullheaded. They may be too stubborn to ever come to terms with each other. We've really done all we can do by bringing them together. Now it's up to them to work things out."

Clarice nodded glumly. ''I know you're right, but it's hard not to meddle when I know how they feel about each other. Star has told me of her feelings for Kyle and all you have to do is to see the expression in his eyes when he looks at her to know that he cares for her. I could shake them both until their teeth rattle for being so obstinate.''

''Give it time, Clarice. Star is still upset about being hog-tied and brought here against her will.''

''Buck, you didn't?'' Clarice asked, aghast at the thought of her niece being treated in such a manner. She could well understand Star's anger if she had been forcibly abducted.

Buck gave Clarice a rakish, lopsided grin and shook his head. ''No, some other varmint had already taken it into his head to kidnap your niece before I arrived on the scene. I gave him a taste of my knuckles for his trouble and then decided he'd made my job a little easier since I hadn't figured out a way to persuade her to come with me.''

''My God,'' Clarice breathed, paling at the thought of what might have happened to Star had Buck not arrived when he did. She drew in a shuddering breath, Star's near abduction bringing home the realization that her niece was still wanted for the murder of her stepmother. Until that moment Clarice had not realized the true extent of Star's dilemma. They were so far from Mississippi that she had considered it only a minor problem to be solved once they had enough money to return and clear Star's name of the charge. It was not unusual to meet people who had moved west to avoid the law. They settled down and raised their families without any repercussions; Clarice had thought Star would be able to do the same. Now it seemed that could not happen if what she feared was true.

Her eyes reflected her worry as she looked across the table at Buck. ''Did you know the man? Or did you find out what he wanted with my niece?''

''Clarice, it was dark and I didn't stay around until he

regained consciousness to ask what his intentions were toward Star. From the way he was treating her, I doubt if they were honorable.''

''Buck, I need to go to DryCreek as soon as possible. Will you go with me?'' Clarice said as she pushed back her chair and stood.

Buck studied her for a long moment through narrowed lashes, his green eyes speculative. ''What is it, Clarice? What's worrying you?''

''I need to find out who that man was and why he wanted Star.''

Buck grinned. ''All you have to do is to look at the girl and you'll know why he wanted her.''

''I need to know for certain that he wasn't—'' Clarice's voice stumbled to a halt. She couldn't tell Buck that the man he had fought might in fact be a bounty hunter after the reward posted for bringing a murderer to trial.

Buck slid his chair back. His muscular body unfolded gracefully as he stood and moved around the table to Clarice. He pulled her into his arms and tipped up her chin to enable him to read the expression in her eyes. ''What's wrong? What kind of trouble is Star in? I've known all along that there was more to her disguising herself as a slave than just trying to reach you in Dry-Creek.''

''I can't tell you,'' Clarice whispered as she gazed up into his searching green eyes.

''Woman, I love you and you should know by now that I'd move heaven and earth to make you happy. Star is your family and I'd never do anything to hurt her or you.''

A wobbly smiled trembled on Clarice's lips as she placed a hand against his beard-shadowed cheek and stroked it lovingly. ''I know you love me and I love you, but for now all I ask is that you trust me to do the right thing. Once I'm certain of the man's identity I'll tell you everything you want to know.''

''I guess I'll have to be satisfied with that for now.'' Buck grinned. ''I'll come with you to DryCreek, but I'm warning you now, woman—I intend to enjoy every moment of it. It'll be the first time we've ever been alone together.'' Giving her a provocative smile, he winked. "We might even find a preacher in town to tie the knot.''

Clarice's eyes widened and her mouth fell open. "Is that a proposal, Buck Hunter?'' she asked, dumbfounded.

"I probably should have gone down on my knees, but I'm getting to be an old man. It's hard to get up once I'm down,'' Buck teased, his eyes twinkling with devilment.

Clarice wrinkled her nose at him. "I don't know if I want to marry an old man. I prefer my men strong and virile.''

"Men!'' Buck exclaimed in feigned anger. "I'd better be the only man in your life, woman. I've waited too many years to have you to myself and I won't share you ever again. I'd kill any man who tried to take you from me.''

"Buck, you know you're the only man I want,'' Clarice said, and threw her arms about his neck, hugging him close.

"Does that mean you'll marry me when we reach Dry-Creek?''

Clarice's bantering mood faded. The threat hanging over Star shadowed her own joy. She leaned away from him and gazed up into his expectant face. "Buck, I'll marry you, but first I have to make certain that Star is safe.''

Buck expelled a long, resigned breath. He knew Clarice would not put her own happiness before the welfare of those she loved. He had learned that through the years of her marriage to Joe. Never once would she have considered hurting her husband to find her own happiness.

"All right, I'll wait a little longer, but as soon as we've rounded up the herd, I intend to take you to DryCreek and get this thing settled.''

Clarice's face showed all the love she felt as she smiled up at him. "And I intend to see that you keep your promise, Buck Hunter, even if you are an old man.''

Buck's wry grin returned in full force. "Woman, when

you're in my arms I don't feel old. I'm as randy as a bull in a pasture full of heifers.''

''Buck Hunter!'' Clarice gasped, and slapped at him playfully. ''What would people think if they heard you talking like that?''

''They'd know that I love you,'' Buck said as he lowered his mouth to hers.

Chapter 11

A *brilliant sunset splashed the horizon with vivid yel-*
low and scarlet, drenching the land in a golden glow before the twilight chased the last light away before the
encroaching night. Relaxing after his hard day's work,
Kyle tipped his chair back on two legs and propped his
dusty boots against the porch railing. A lazy curl of blue
smoke rose from his cheroot as he sat enjoying a brief
but well-deserved reprieve from his labors. The roundup
was over and now all that was left to fulfill his contract
to the army was to drive the herd north to Fort Belnap.

Kyle drew in the pungent smoke from the square-tipped
cigar. He was well satisfied with the way things had gone.
The herd had grown considerably in size since the previous year and if his luck held, the Bar H would prosper
even more in the coming years.

He formed his lips into an O and blew several smoke
rings toward the shingled roof before he restlessly tossed
the cheroot into the dust. The peace of the moment
slipped away from him as his thoughts turned to the
young woman who now worked in the kitchen preparing
his evening meal. His dark brows knitted as he frowned.
He was satisfied with the roundup and the progress he
was making with his ranch, but that was all that had
pleased him of late.

Star had been at the ranch for several weeks, but the
tension between them had not lessened in degree with
the passage of time. Since her arrival he had seen little

of her. She had kept to herself, even refusing to take her meals at the same table with him. That in itself had done little to improve the black mood he'd been in since their confrontation on the day she'd arrived at the ranch. Recently everything had seemed to be conspiring to drive him mad. Star's enmity combined with the fact that the man who he had despised for years for his wandering ways had suddenly decided it was time to settle down at the ranch served only to vex Kyle's temper to the limit.

He knew he was responsible for Star's attitude toward him, but for the life of him he couldn't understand the change that had come over Buck since Clarice had come to the ranch. His father seemed like a different man. He'd been working hard, had not ventured into Sagebrush to drink and brawl as he commonly did after only a few days spent at the ranch, and what was even more unusual, he had not mentioned any plans for his departure. Buck seemed content to stay and work at the Bar H as if he'd always enjoyed that type of life-style. His sudden metamorphosis from wanderer to settled rancher baffled Kyle nearly as much as did his own mercurial moods where Star was concerned. He always seemed to be torn between wanting to strangle her or love her to death. And of late it seemed to be more often the latter than the former.

When she served his meals, he wanted to reach out and touch her. When he glimpsed her moving about his home, never complaining about her duties, he wanted to wrap her in his arms and feel her warm body pressed to his as he told her of his love. But he did neither and his burning need for her made him surly and short-tempered with everyone he came in contact with.

"This has to come to an end," Kyle muttered aloud as he slammed his chair down with a bang against the rough floorboards of the porch.

"What did you say, son?" Buck asked as he joined Kyle.

Kyle eyed him coldly. "Where did that come from? I've not heard you call me son in years," he ground out,

needing to vent his vexation with himself and finding
Buck the most convenient target at hand.

Buck tipped his worn felt hat to the back of his head.
A frown etched his brow as he stared down at Kyle. "You
are my son though you don't seem to like the idea that
I'm your father."

"Why should I? To me you're only the man who passed
through here every year or so when he didn't have anything better to do. I don't consider that much of a father
or a husband, do you?"

Buck's chiseled features darkened in hue as he flushed
under his son's censure. He clenched his teeth and fought
to control his own temper before he could say anything
that might further damage his relationship with Kyle.

"You're right, I wasn't much of a husband or a father.
But I'd like things to change between us, Kyle. Lately
I've come to realize what a family means and I've given
up my wandering for good."

Kyle gave a sarcastic laugh. "Don't you think it's a bit
too late to have this change of heart? The boy who wanted
and needed a father grew up a long time ago. And as for
you settling down, that's like a skunk looking to get rid
of his stench. No matter how hard he tries, he just can't
make it happen. Momma told me you'd never change and
I believe her."

"Hell, Kyle. The past is done and buried."

"You're right. I buried it when I put Momma in the
small plot of ground beneath the mesquites. But you
didn't know that, did you? As usual, you weren't here."

Pushed nearly beyond his limit by his son's antagonism, Buck ground out, "I wanted to be here more than
you'll ever know." With that he turned and stormed back
toward the barn before he told Kyle that the woman he'd
cherished had been a shrewish witch who had never for-
given him for getting her pregnant with Kyle so that she
had to marry a man she'd considered beneath her and her
high-and-mighty family in Mississippi.

He'd loved Madge when they first married and he'd
been happy about their child. She had only tolerated him,

but that had turned to hatred when he'd moved her to Texas, hoping that they could start fresh and make something of their life together. He'd started the Bar H with great hopes, but his wife's animosity had soon put an end to any such dreams. He'd managed to cling to his illusions for six years after his son's birth, but Madge had finally found a way to sever the thin thread that kept them together. He had ended up killing the drifter she had chosen as her lover to spite him for bringing her to Texas. After that Buck had not been able to stay and work the ranch. The sight of his wife sickened him to his soul. He had left the Bar H and his family behind, returning only when his need to see his son drew him back.

Buck paused in the shadows of the barn, his gaze traveling back to the weathered ranch house and the man who carried his blood. Madge had poisoned his son against him and he doubted if he would ever be able to change that. Even in death she prevailed as the martyr, the long-suffering wife who was ill-treated by the man she loved. She had been as cunning in turning Kyle against him as she had been when she had seduced him that first time beneath the magnolias of her father's plantation. He had worked for Henry Lewis and had sought to avoid becoming involved with his daughter, but she had set her cap for him, and being young and virile he had not been able to withstand her seductive charms. Her games had backfired on her when she conceived Kyle. Loving her with the foolishness of youth, he had been thrilled when he learned of her pregnancy and had boldly marched up to her father and asked for her hand in marriage. Henry Lewis had refused until he learned of Madge's condition. He had then arranged a hasty wedding and had quietly cut his daughter out of his life. Their wedding day had been the beginning and the end of their marriage. And he had paid for it ever since.

"And from the way Kyle acts I'll keep paying," he muttered aloud, and strode to the barn.

Kyle watched his father until he disappeared from view before he stood and stamped into the house, angry with himself for letting Buck reopen the wounds he'd thought were healed years ago. Striding into the kitchen, he pulled out a chair and sat down at the table, calmly regarding the two startled women.

"Is supper ready? I'm starved."

Clarice glanced toward the doorway expecting to see Buck. "It will be ready as soon as Buck comes in from the barn."

"Buck's already come and gone. If the food is ready, serve it."

Clarice glanced uneasily at the doorway, sensing from Kyle's sharp tone that he and his father had argued. Handing a plate to Star, she untied her apron. "You serve the stew. I'm going to the barn." Without waiting for her niece's reply, she tossed the apron onto the peg by the kitchen door and hurried outside.

"Well?" Kyle said, eyeing Star coolly. Clarice's exit had vexed his already short temper to the exploding point. "Are you going to serve the food or do I have to do it?"

Star cast Kyle a belligerent look as she filled the plate with the thick stew made of chunks of beef, potatoes, and onions. She plopped the plate down in front of him and then turned to pour him a cup of coffee. The hot, dark brew spilled over the sides of the cup as she set it down on the table by his hand.

"If that will be all, I'll leave you to your meal," she said, and was already turning away when Kyle's words halted her.

"Star, I want you to join me."

She glanced back over her shoulder at him. "I'm not hungry."

"Then you can keep me company while I eat," Kyle said. With the toe of his boot he slid the chair out across from him. "Sit," he ordered.

Star did not move to accept the rudely offered chair. "Kyle, I work for you, but that does not mean I have to eat with you or share your company."

"Damn it, Star," Kyle growled as he shoved his chair back and came to his feet. "Don't you think it's time that we called a truce? For the past weeks you've been avoiding me as if I had a contagious disease.''

''I haven't been avoiding you,'' Star said, her chin coming up in the air. ''I've been doing what I was brought here to do—work.''

Exasperated, Kyle ran his hand through his dark hair. It glistened with blue highlights from the light of the lantern hanging overhead. ''It wasn't my idea to have you brought here.''

''I know. You've made your feelings about me being here very clear since the day I arrived.''

Kyle frowned. ''I don't know what you're talking about. The only thing I did was to welcome you to my home.''

Star's temper flared. She swung about to face him with her hands braced on her hips, ready to do battle. ''If your actions of the last weeks are what you consider a welcome, then I'd hate to see how you'd treat a person you didn't want at the Bar H.''

Star's open animosity made Kyle's temper flame white-hot. ''Hell, woman!'' he exploded. ''How did you expect me to react when you've made it clear that you can't stand being in the same room with me? You've told me often enough that you never wanted to lay eyes on me again.''

''You're the one who didn't want me, Kyle,'' Star blurted out before she could stop herself. She blanched with the realization that she had spoken her innermost thoughts aloud.

Kyle grew still, the muscles across his flat belly contracting. His anger cooled. ''I've wanted you since the night I first saw you in the garden of the Red Passion.''

Star's heart thumped painfully against her ribs. ''Yes, you've *wanted* me, Kyle, but you also made it clear that was all it was.''

''Star,'' he breathed softly, the word a caress in itself. He moved around the table toward her, wanting at that moment to take her into his arms and erase all the mistakes he had made in the past.

Clarice and Buck came into the kitchen. Their presence destroyed the moment before it could come to fruition. The words he wanted to speak died upon his lips and he let his hand fall back to his side before he touched her. "We'll finish this conversation later," he murmured for her ears alone.

"There's nothing to finish," Star said, and turned away.

Kyle flashed Buck and Clarice an angry look and strode toward the door. He needed to give himself a good dousing in the watering trough to cool the heat in his blood.

"Kyle," Buck said before he could make good his escape.

Kyle drew in a deep breath and turned back to his father. His face was dark with annoyance as he waited for Buck to speak.

"Tomorrow morning, I'm going with Clarice to Dry-Creek. She has some business there that needs attention."

Star's face lit with surprise and delight. "What time do we leave?"

Clarice shook her head. "Buck and I are going to Dry-Creek. You're to stay here until I return."

The pleased expression faded from Star's face and her eyes snapped with blue sparks of anger. "You can't honestly mean to leave me here? I won't have it."

"I do and you will," came Clarice's firm answer. "We'll be gone only a few days at most and it's best for all concerned that you remain here."

"Damn what's best for all concerned," Star began to protest, but Clarice silenced her with a sharp shake of her head.

"I've made my decision, Star, and I won't listen to any of your arguments."

Vexed beyond endurance by her aunt's stubbornness, Star turned and stormed from the kitchen. Hot tears of rage brimmed in her eyes as she fled to the room they shared and slammed the door with all the force she could muster. The impact seemed to shake the entire house but did little to help her feelings about being abandoned at the ranch with Kyle.

Clarice grimaced as she looked from father to son. "I'll go and talk with her," she said, and followed in Star's wake.

"We'll be back before you drive the herd north," Buck said, misreading Kyle's expression as one of condemnation.

"That's up to you, old man. I've made the drive in the past without you here and I'm sure I'll do it again in the future," Kyle said, and left the kitchen.

Resigned to his son's attitude, Buck sighed as he poured himself a cup of coffee. Slumping down in a chair, he braced his elbows on the table and stared down at the steaming dark liquid. Clarice had told him it would take time to regain his son's love and trust, but he doubted if he would live that long.

Feeling a gentle, reassuring pat on his shoulder, he looked up at the woman he loved.

"Did you get everything straightened out with Star?" he asked.

"I explained why I had to go to DryCreek, but she's still furious at the thought of being left here alone with Kyle."

Buck took Clarice's hand and drew her down on to his lap. He gave her a wry, sad grin. "We're a pair, Clarice. No matter where we turn we seem to step on sore toes."

She laughed and hugged him. "Kyle and Star might not be so hard to get along with if they'd quit stamping on each *other's* toes before we get the chance. Maybe having a few days alone together will improve their dispositions."

A twinkle of amusement entered Buck's eyes as he looked at her. "Is that the reason you didn't want Star to go to DryCreek with us?"

"It was one of them," Clarice said as she hugged him close. A tiny frown of worry etched a path across her brow as she reflected upon the main reason she had not given in to her niece's pleas to come with them to DryCreek. If the man who had tried to abduct her was in fact a bounty hunter, he might still be in town. Clarice could not chance letting Star return to DryCreek for that reason alone.

Star stood fuming silently with her arms folded over her chest and her foot tapping out her vexation against the rough-cut boards of the porch. Clarice had abandoned her here in the wilderness with the man who was the bane of her life. None of her aunt's explanations could change that fact. She knew Clarice was thinking of her welfare, but blast it, it was her life and she should have some say in it. She also suspected her aunt of having other motives for leaving her at the ranch alone with Kyle. That thought galled her. She resented being manipulated like a puppet on a string.

Glancing at Kyle, who stood nearby, thoughtfully regarding the two riders in the distance, she turned her resentment on him. This was all his fault. He was the force that had knocked her world out of kilter. Had he not offered Clarice work at his ranch, she and her aunt would now be together, trying to make a new life for themselves.

"This is all your fault, Kyle Hunter," she muttered, unaware that she had spoken aloud until he looked at her, one dark brow arched in question.

"Would you mind telling me what crimes you're now laying at my door?"

"This," Star said in exasperation, and, with a wave of her hand, encompassed them as well as their surroundings.

Kyle nodded as if he understood. "The Bar H? Yes, I'm responsible for making it into one of the more prosperous holdings west of the Brazos."

"No, blast it! I'm not talking about your infernal ranch."

"Then would you be good enough to tell me what you're talking about? I can read a little Indian sign language, but I'm afraid yours has me completely baffled."

"Damn it, you know exactly what I mean. You're responsible for us being here."

Kyle shook his head in bewilderment. "Star, you continue to amaze me. I swear that one day you're going to accuse me of making the sun rise and then also blame me when it sets. I had nothing to do with Clarice and Buck going back to DryCreek. I thought your aunt explained her reasons to you."

Star flushed guiltily. "She did."

"Then why are you accusing me of being behind her leaving when you know that I didn't have anything to do with it?"

Feeling slightly foolish for her outburst, Star admitted, "I know you're not to blame for her riding back there, but I should be with her."

"Did you ever consider the fact that she might not want you with her? She might want to be alone with Buck."

"Why would she want to be alone with Buck?" Star asked, perplexed.

"If you haven't noticed, Buck and Clarice are a man and a woman."

Star felt her cheeks burn at Kyle's insinuation. "My aunt and your father, together?"

Kyle nodded sagely and smiled. "If what I suspect is true, Buck and Clarice are in love," Kyle said, voicing the suspicion that had been growing in him since the previous night. It was the only reason he could find for the sudden change that had come over his father. Love made people act in strange ways, as Kyle himself was finding out considering his own actions of late.

Strangely, he hadn't suspected there was anything between them until he'd passed the kitchen door on his way to bed after bathing in the cool water of the animal trough. He'd seen Clarice sitting on Buck's lap while they talked with their heads close together. The expressions on their faces had been those of two people who were deeply in love. He hadn't interrupted them but had gone on to his bed, surprised at himself for not being angry about the scene he had witnessed.

"That's impossible." Star shook her head, rejecting

the idea. "Aunt Clarice has only been a widow for a matter of weeks. Anyway, they're too old to have such feelings."

Kyle's grin deepened at her naiveté. Star was a woman grown, yet she was innocent of so many things in life. She had seen and experienced much in the past months, but there was still a child dwelling in her passionate woman's body and he cherished her for it.

Unable to resist the urge, he pulled her into his arms. Her skin felt warm against his own as he murmured, "Star, it's never too late for love." He claimed her lips with his own as he had wanted to do so many times in the past weeks.

Star felt her senses reel at the touch of his mouth upon hers. She sought to deny his tongue entrance but found it was only a halfhearted gesture. She wanted his kiss. She had craved the silken caress of his lips too long to refuse him now. For one fleeting moment she recalled her aunt's words. "You can say no. Kyle won't force himself on you," but she didn't want to say no. She wanted Kyle. She had wanted him since their last moments together on the lonely grassy hillside. She had sought to kill her feelings for him by telling herself that there was no future for them because of the way he felt toward her. She had not succeeded. His touch made her achingly aware of that fact. With the heady sensations his kiss aroused coursing through her blood, she did not care if Kyle was her bane or her blessing. All she knew at that moment was that she loved him.

Molding her body against his lean, masculine form, she returned his kiss, treasuring the moment no matter how fleeting it might be. She moved her hands up his hard chest, savoring the feeling of his flesh and the crisp mat of hair in the V opening of his shirt before wrapping her arms about his neck to draw his head down to hers. She entwined her fingers in his hair, letting the dark strands curl naturally about then, relishing the rich texture.

Her blood turned to white-hot lava in her veins. The

past did not matter and the future did not exist. She eagerly grasped the moment. She was a miser hoarding away each sensation to cherish when she no longer had Kyle to hold in her arms. She would store all the memories of their tender moments together because after she left the Bar H, that would be all she would have of the man she loved. These precious moments would have to last her a lifetime because she knew she would never love again.

Star's response surprised and delighted Kyle. Since their last time together, he had yearned to feel her warm, young body pressed against his throbbing flesh. He had found little rest during the past weeks, knowing that she was so near yet so far away from him. The nights had been long and tortured as he lay awake, hard with desire, needing her beside him in his lonely bed. He had sought oblivion in sleep, but his dreams had been haunted with visions of her lying beneath him in the throes of ecstasy. Not even his nightly dousing in the watering trough had managed to quench the burning need the thought of her aroused in him.

The warmth of the Texas morning was cool in comparison to the fire that coursed through Kyle's body as he lifted Star into his arms and strode into the house. He held her possessively against him, afraid that reality might encroach upon this dream at any moment and she would vanish from his arms. He kicked open the door to his bedroom and crossed to the large spindle bed. Laying her gently upon the down-filled mattress, he turned to the windows and threw open the gingham curtains to let the sun stream across the bed. Eagerly he turned back to her, but the sight that met his eyes held him transfixed.

Star sat in the middle of the fluffy mattress, her fingers working at the fastenings at the front of her gown. The breath stilled in his throat as he stood mesmerized, unable to move as he watched each inch of her creamy skin being exposed to his view. He felt his heart would burst through his chest from its violent pounding and his mouth went dry as she slipped the gown from her shoulders and down over her hips. She lay back, her lithe body bathed in golden sunlight. She raised her arms to him, beckoning him to her side with a shy, provocative smile.

His trance was broken. With a haste that made him forget the buttons on his shirt, he ripped it from him and then, with equal speed, tossed the rest of his clothing into a pile in the corner of the room. The muscles in his arms rippled as he lowered himself to the bed. He moaned with pleasure as Star wrapped her arms once more about his neck and drew his head down to hers.

Greedily, he devoured the sweetness she offered as her tongue enticed his, stroking and gently sucking until he moaned from the pleasure of it. Her skin was warm beneath his hand as he stroked the soft mounds of her breasts and then moved down to her narrow waist. From there he followed the gentle swell of her hip, massaging her satiny flesh with fingers and palm before moving to the flat plane above the mat of curling silk.

Yearning in his excitement to see and taste all of her, Kyle began his erotic exploration with his lips and hands. He found the sensitive spot beneath her ear and felt her shiver with delight as he lapped at it with his tongue before he trailed a moist, languid path down the sleek line of her throat to the small concave pulse beat at its base. He teased her flesh, flicking it with the tip of his tongue as he lowered his head to her breasts.

In the valley between the swelling mounds, he drew in the heady scent of her before taking one hardened rose tip into his mouth. He nipped at it gently with his teeth before suckling it until his need rose to know its mate as intimately. He feasted there and felt Star roll her hips against his, but he did not heed their sensual, beckoning call. With a sigh of half regret and half excitement for the quest to come, he left the creamy rose-tipped breasts and moved enticingly along the downy trail to the dark junction of her thighs.

With reverence he moved his hands across her flesh, kneading her hips and buttocks as he raised them to him and lowered his mouth to her essence. He breathed in

the musky, woman's smell of her and felt his body throb
in answer. Her thighs quivered and she moaned with
pleasure as he flicked the tiny bud that had swollen in
welcome. The taste and smell of her was intoxicating and
he probed deeply into the moist depths, savoring the pri-
mordial instincts that drove him to know her as he had
known no other woman. He worshipped at the shrine of
her womanhood, that secret, mysterious place where life
was nourished and brought forth, where man was given
pleasure and renewed his own spirit with the seed that
would carry his blood.

Star arched her hips, giving all of herself to the man
who held her heart and soul. She moved to the primitive
music in her blood, hearing its wild drumbeats and following where his caresses led. Tingling sparks of pleasure shimmered through her, exploding over and over
again until she felt she would faint from the tiny bursts
of rapture showering each sinew of her body.

At last, knowing that she could stand no more of the
exquisite torture and needing to feel his hard length buried deep within her, she moaned his name.

Her voice held her plea and he answered, unable to
prolong his foreplay. His tanned body contrasted starkly
against her creamy flesh as he covered her and took her
lips once more. She met his thrust and he slipped easily
into the moist sheath of love. She pulsated about him,
welcoming his swollen manhood with the caress. Their
bodies moved together in a passionate sonata of love. Its
sweet melody flowed through their blood, carrying them
swiftly to the ultimate fulfillment.

Star cried Kyle's name again, her hips arching against
his as she clung to his wide shoulders and trembled into
ecstasy. She felt his shuddering release as he moaned his
pleasure into her parted lips. Together, with limbs entwined and bodies still intimately joined, they lay savoring their heady moment of rapture.

At last Kyle raised himself on one elbow at her side
and peered down at her, a contented smile playing about
his shapely lips. The expression in her eyes mirrored his

as he gently caressed the line of her cheek with the pad of his thumb. He felt as if he had been reborn.

Twenty-four hours ago the future had looked bleak, but now it seemed much brighter with Star curled in his arms like a tiny, satiated kitten. And he knew at that moment that if he ever lost her again he would not want to live. She was as much a part of him as the air he breathed.

"Star, I—" Kyle's vow of love came to a halt as she pressed one finger against his lips and shook her tousled head.

"Don't say anything. I know how you feel and I don't want to ruin what time we have together by rehashing the past or worrying about the future."

A chill rippled down Kyle's spine and he frowned down at her. "You don't still intend to leave, do you?"

Star gently brushed a stray curl from his brow as she looked up into his searching green eyes and silently mused, I don't want to leave you, Kyle. I would remain here for the rest of my life if I thought you could ever come to love me as I love you. But aloud she said, "You already know my answer."

Kyle moved away from her and sat up on the side of the bed. His hands fell limply between his strong, corded thighs as he painfully digested the fact that he had found love at last and would soon lose it. His voice held a hint of wistfulness as he spoke. "I thought that had all changed after this morning."

Star sat up and pulled the handworked counterpane over her to shield her nakedness. "I promised Clarice that I would stay for a while, but I can't remain here forever."

"Damn it, Star," Kyle ground out, as he swung about to face her. "I don't want you to leave."

The expression in his eyes caused Star's heart to thump against her ribs and her throat went dry with expectation. Could Clarice have been right? Could Kyle's feelings be changing toward her? If they were, she'd stay at the Bar H for as long as necessary to win the man she loved. Yet even as the thought crossed her mind, the memory of her reason for coming to Texas intruded, shattering any hope she had for the future.

In the lie she was living there was no guarantee that she *had* a future. If she couldn't clear herself of the murder charge, and if the man Clarice had gone to DryCreek to find turned out to be a bounty hunter as her aunt suspected, Star knew that eventually she'd be torn away from Kyle and perhaps even hanged.

Star's gaze moved lovingly over Kyle's handsome face. She realized for the first time that all of her qualms about coming to his ranch and letting herself love him had been foolish. She had wanted more than a few minutes of happiness in his arms, but in her present position, she had no right to expect marriage or any type of commitment.

Her heart constricted. Kyle had been honest with her from the first and she had done nothing but build a wall of lies about herself to keep him from learning that she was a wanted criminal. If he ever learned of her duplicity, he would despise her. That fact alone made her realize the need to treasure every moment they had together.

''I'll stay for as long as possible,'' she murmured, and tenderly reached out to him. Laying her head against his bare shoulder, she said softly, ''Let us be happy with what we have now.''

Her strange mood confused Kyle and left him with an overwhelming need to keep and protect her. Turning to her, he took her in his arms and held her against his bare chest, crushing her to him. For now and forever, he vowed silently as his mouth came down on hers.

Chapter 12

It was a hot and humid day. The waxy magnolia leaves lay still and dusty in the calm afternoon air as the burly man rode up the winding drive to the large white mansion known as Jasmine Hall. His appearance had improved somewhat since the night he had ridden out of DryCreek. His broken nose was no longer swollen and he had managed to control the lisp created by the new gap that had been formed when two of his teeth had been knocked out. That gap and the black and purple half-circle beneath his right eye were the only visible signs of the beating he had received while trying to earn the reward Mr. Tremayne had promised him.

Reining his mount to a halt, he slid to the ground and draped the reins through the ring of the hitching post that was shaped out of wrought iron in the form of a horse's head. Hitching up his britches and straightening his leather vest, he strode up the steps to the veranda and knocked on the wide double doors. After his second knock the door swung open to reveal the man he had come to see. Holding his hat in his hands, he said, "Mr. Tremayne, I've come to give you the report on the girl. You'll have to pardon the way I look, but I was in an accident a few weeks back."

Brett eyed the man distastefully, his nostrils flaring from the smell of sweat that emanated from his bulky unwashed body, but stepped back to let him enter the foyer. "I hope you have news about my missing fiancée.

If you expect to collect any more money it had better be good.''

Reed Jarvis shifted nervously. ''I—I found her like I said I would. I followed the trail to her aunt in DryCreek and sure enough there she was, just as pretty as you please, working in the hotel café.''

Brett's face lit with jubilation. At last he had Star and soon he'd own Jasmine Hall. ''Where is she? Did you bring her with you or did you leave her in town?''

''Mr. Tremayne,'' Jarvis said, catching his lisp before it could form. ''I—I had the girl in my hands, but some cowpoke stole her away from me. He hit me from behind.''

Brett grabbed Jarvis by the lapels of his prized leather vest and hauled him off his feet as he jerked him forward. Brett's pale blue eyes resembled cold shards of glass and his face was flushed with rage as he glared down into Jarvis's coarse features. ''You had her and you let her escape! Damn you, Jarvis. I could kill you for this.''

''I didn't do it on purpose. I was hit from behind,'' Jarvis whined.

''Do you expect me to believe that when you still bear a black eye and are missing several teeth?''

''Ah, hell, Mr. Tremayne,'' Jarvis said, prying Brett's hands away from his vest. ''I found the girl once and I can do it again. At least we know more about her whereabouts now than we did when we first started looking. Texas is a big place, but there ain't many people in it. Someone will know where the girl is, you can bet your last dollar on that.''

''I may *be* betting my last dollar if she isn't found soon,'' Brett muttered under his breath. To Jarvis he said, ''We will find her this time. I intend to go with you to ensure that she comes back with us. Be ready to leave in the morning.''

Jarvis nodded and smiled, revealing his snaggled teeth. ''I'll be ready.''

''Brett, is that man gone?'' a soft feminine voice asked

from the drawing room as he closed the door behind Jarvis.

"Yes, darling," Brett said, casting one last glance at the door before turning to enter the drawing room. He smiled down at the woman who sat gowned in pink satin, lazily waving a handpainted silk fan back and forth in front of her.

"Did he find her?" she asked, giving Brett one of her most enticing smiles as she flipped the fan shut and tapped it on the striped satin settee at her side.

"Yes, he found her," Brett said, accepting her invitation. He relaxed back against the curved backrest and frowned. "But the fool let her get away."

Blond curls bounced about her white shoulders as Fiona came to her feet with a squeal of dismay. "He let her get away! Damn the lout. I knew he was too much of a bumbling idiot to do the job. I told you from the first that he didn't have enough brains to get rid of the chit."

The time Brett had been dreading had finally arrived. "I didn't send him to kill her, Fiona. I sent him to bring her back here."

"You what?" Fiona asked, outraged. Her blue eyes flashed fire as she braced her hands on her hips and stood towering over Brett on the settee. "I thought the plan was to find Star and get rid of her before she could come back here and ruin everything for us."

"I know what you thought, Fiona, but I decided otherwise. I need to own Jasmine Hall legally and the only way I can achieve that is by marrying the girl. Her death wouldn't do us any good. The land would go to her aunt, Clarice Kendall. And being your lover, even if you are the one to manage the absentee owner's property, does little to improve my standing with my creditors. I now have a little over a month to find and marry Star if I'm to keep myself from ruin. I've managed to put them off this long, but they've only given me until the tenth of next month to pay my debts or they'll turn me over to the law. So, my dear, my only hope is to find Star, bring her back here, and marry her. And I intend to do exactly that. I'm leaving the first thing in the morning. Jarvis said it should be easy to track her down from Dry-Creek.''

''Then I'm coming with you.''

''Don't be a little fool. At the moment the girl believes you dead. That's the only leverage besides the black bitch upstairs that I have over her.''

''It didn't work before,'' Fiona spat, still resentful of the way she had been treated after her fall. It had taken several weeks for the headache to disappear and all Brett could do was worry about finding her stepdaughter. He hadn't thought of her welfare once during his frantic search.

''It'll work this time because Jarvis is going to pretend to be a federal marshal with an arrest warrant. Once I get her here and she learns that you're alive, I'll use the black hussy chained in the attic to make her do as I want.''

''Wasn't it fortunate that you found Dulcie before she could make her escape?'' Fiona said, her voice laced with sarcasm.

''It was fortunate for us, Fiona, that I found her or we'd have no hold on Star. She loves her maid and she'll do my bidding to keep me from having Dulcie whipped to death or sold down the river.''

''After you marry the little bitch, what do you intend to do?'' Fiona asked, her suspicions mounting by the moment.

Brett smiled, but the gesture held only malice. ''I intend to make her pay for all she's put me through during the last months. That sweet little virgin will never cross me again once I'm through with her.''

Jealousy ripped through Fiona with searing force. ''It's not only Jasmine Hall that you want, is it? You want Star. You've always wanted her, haven't you?''

Brett regarded his lover for a long indecisive minute and wondered for what seemed the hundredth time during the last months what he had ever seen in her. The beauty she had once possessed now seemed tawdry when compared to the memory that had become an obsession with him. Star was the woman he wanted and he would have her. However, for the moment, he had to appease Fiona to keep her from ruining his chances of gaining his desire.

"Fiona," he said, his voice dropping seductively low as he reached out and captured her about the waist. Drawing her down into his lap, he dropped a light kiss on the tip of her nose. "You know you're the only woman that I've ever wanted. Once I've married Star and we have Jasmine Hall, I don't really care what happens to the girl."

"Oh, Brett," Fiona whimpered as she wrapped her arms about his neck and pressed her powdered face into the fine brocade that covered his shoulder. "Promise me that you'll not take her to your bed. I couldn't bear it."

"Darling, you know that I have to consummate the marriage to make it legal and binding. But I'll only have you in my thoughts when I do. Trust me, Fiona. There's only one woman for me and I intend to have her as soon as all of this is settled." Brett's words were a soft caress against Fiona's blond locks, but in his mind he was seeing black velvet curls and indigo eyes.

"Take me to bed, Brett," Fiona whispered. "I want you to make love to me until you have to leave."

With her face still pressed against his shoulder, Fiona did not see the flicker of disgust that passed over Brett's face as he murmured, "With pleasure, love."

Weary and travel-stained, Clarice sat staring down at the cup of coffee before her. She absently drummed her fingers against the checkered tablecloth. Tiny lines of worry fanned her eyes and etched new paths at the sides of her mouth as she pondered the lack of information she had gleaned from the sheriff and the owner of the hotel. Neither knew anything about the man Buck had stopped from abducting her niece.

"Well, it looks as if we've come to DryCreek for nothing. Do you want to start back to the ranch today or take a room here for the night?'' Buck asked, leaning back in his chair and arching a dark brow at the woman who sat across the table from him.

Clarice expelled a long, tired breath and shook her head as she looked up at him. ''Someone in this town should know something about the man. In a place as small as DryCreek a stranger that causes trouble is news.''

''The man probably decided it was in his best interest to get out of town before someone alerted the sheriff to what he was up to.''

''You may be right, but there's one last place I want to check before I'll be satisfied. If Doc Simpson doesn't know anything about him, then I guess all we can do is to go back to the ranch.''

Buck pushed his chair back from the table and stood. He clamped his dust- and sweat-stained hat down onto his head. ''Then let's go see the doc. I know that until we get this thing settled about Star you won't even consider looking for a preacher.''

''I wish I could, Buck, but until I know that Star is safe, I can't put my own happiness first. We've waited nearly a lifetime to be together and a few more days won't hurt.''

''That may be easy for you to say, woman,'' Buck said, and grinned down at her as he opened the door and they stepped out onto the sidewalk. ''I'll just be glad when you tell me what this is all about.'' Taking her arm, he escorted Clarice across the street to the doctor's office.

Doc Simpson looked up from his paper-strewn desk and smiled as they entered. ''I hope this is a social call and you've not been tangling with any more Comanches, Clarice.'' Scrutinizing Buck from the tip of his dusty boots to his battered hat, he continued. ''I could have sworn that you were much younger the last time I saw you. Either my memory or my eyesight is failing me.''

''You old sawbones.'' Clarice laughed. ''Your eyes and your memory are as keen as ever. This is Buck Hunter, Kyle's father.''

"You could have fooled me. They're as much alike as two peas in a pod." Doc Simpson chuckled. "Except this 'un's older." Turning his attention back to Clarice, he asked, "How have you been feeling? Has your wound completely healed?"

"I'm fine, Doc."

"Then to what do I owe the pleasure of this visit? Usually I don't get to see you unless something ails you, Clarice."

"I've come to ask if you know anything about a man who was in town a few weeks ago. He might have come to you for help after his encounter with Buck."

Buck grinned and rubbed his knuckles with satisfaction.

Doc Simpson nodded, his smile fading. "I know the man you're talking about. He had a broken nose and two missing teeth."

"That's him." Buck chuckled.

Clarice flashed Buck a quelling look. "Doc, did he tell you his name or what business he had in DryCreek?"

The doctor shook his grizzled head. "He didn't tell me anything. At the time he could only mumble because his mouth was too swollen." Turning to the paper cluttered desk, he opened the top drawer and withdrew a folded piece of paper. He handed it to Clarice. "I found this on the floor after he'd left. I thought you might find it of interest. I haven't told anyone about it."

Clarice unfolded the grimy paper. Her face paled as she looked down at the wanted poster in her hand. Star's image stared back at her and beneath it read: $500 reward for information leading to the whereabouts of one Star Grayson, late of Jasmine Hall Plantation, Mississippi. Brett Tremayne's address in Natchez was printed at the bottom.

"What is it, Clarice?" Buck asked, and took the paper from her trembling hand. He read it twice before looking once more at the woman who stood quietly watching him, her face pinched with worry. "Now I think it's high time you told me what this is all about.'' He handed the paper back to her.

Clarice nodded and crumpled up the poster.

Sensing their need for privacy, Doc Simpson collected his black bag and picked up his hat. ''I've a patient to see,'' he said, and turned to the door.

''Doc, you've been a good friend. I appreciate what you've done. This,'' Clarice said, lifting the ball of paper, ''is a mistake.''

Doc Simpson smiled. ''I figured as much. That's why I didn't turn it over to the sheriff. I'm a pretty good judge of character and your niece didn't seem to me like the type who would be running from the law.'' With that he put on his hat and left the office.

''Well?'' Buck asked when Clarice did not offer an explanation for the wanted poster in her hand.

''It's a long story, Buck.''

''I have plenty of time.''

''This really all began years ago when my brother died,'' Clarice said, then she began to relate everything Star had told her upon her arrival in DryCreek. At last her story came to an end and she waited for Buck's reaction.

The long, silent minutes seemed to stretch into hours, grating against her taut nerves as he mulled over all she had told him about Star. She could not read the expression on his chiseled features or the distant look in his eyes. All she knew was that she would scream with vexation if he didn't say something soon.

At last his speculative gaze came to rest upon her. ''There's something peculiar in all this.''

''You don't believe Star is guilty of murder, do you?'' Clarice said, instantly coming to her niece's defense.

Buck shook his head in denial. ''That's not what I'm talking about. I believe what Star told you is true. That's why I feel there's something wrong. The poster didn't mention anything about her being wanted for murder. If the law was involved in all this, Tremayne wouldn't have been mentioned. It would be the sheriff who should be notified.''

"Buck, do you think all of this could have been a mistake, as I told Doc?" Clarice asked, her face suddenly brightening with hope.

"I wouldn't go as far as to say that. You're forgetting about Star's stepmother's death and the bounty hunter who managed to track her as far as DryCreek. For him to go to that much trouble, someone had a strong reason for wanting her back in Mississippi.''

"I suspect from what Star told me that Brett Tremayne would go to any length to get Jasmine Hall and the riches that come with it. If Star had not fled, he would have forced her to marry him by using her stepmother's accident as leverage against her.''

"That's what I find strange about this entire situation. Why doesn't the poster mention the murder?''

Clarice's face screwed up thoughtfully. "He might still have hopes of controlling Star with his threats once he finds her.''

A wily light entered Buck's piercing green gaze. "How would you like a honeymoon trip to Natchez?" He grinned down at her as he wrapped her in his strong arms and drew her against him.

Clarice was bewildered by Buck's unexpected suggestion until comprehension dawned, and her face lit with all the love she felt for him. "You intend to clear Star's name, don't you?"

"That and other things," he murmured, and dropped a quick kiss onto her smiling lips. "I still say that there's something not quite right in all this and I intend to get to the bottom of it. I don't want my grandchildren to have an outlaw for a momma."

"Buck Hunter, I love you." Clarice threw her arms about his neck and hugged him close. "I think a honeymoon in Natchez sounds wonderful.''

Buck held her at arm's length and peered down into her shining eyes. "Then I suggest that we find a preacher.

We can't have a honeymoon without getting married, or so I've been told.''

Within the hour, Buck and Clarice stood before a scandalized Baptist preacher. His thin face was pinched with distaste as he eyed Clarice's choice of wedding garments. She had taken only enough time to wash and change into the extra pair of britches and shirt that she had brought with her. However, the preacher did not voice his disapproval. He'd known Clarice since he'd come to Dry-Creek and though he'd not come to accept her odd behavior, he would not complain about it. She'd always been more than generous with her gifts to his church and if she chose to dress like a man, that was her business, as long as she kept filling the offering plate.

Regarding the man at her side who looked to him to be little more than a saddle tramp, he wondered briefly if the ordeal she had suffered at the hands of the Comanches had finally pushed her over the brink of sanity, deranging what little wits she possessed. Feeling that it was his Christian duty to pity the poor, mad woman instead of condemning her, he read the marriage vows uniting Clarice Kendall and Buck Hunter in the holy state of matrimony.

Buck let out a loud yippee when the last vow was spoken and tossed the preacher a shining twenty-dollar gold piece before he swung his new bride up into his arms. She giggled like a young girl and buried her flushed face against his shoulder as he strode from the church and down the street to the hotel.

He ignored the curious glances cast in their direction as he ordered the hotel's best room and meal. Rejuvenated by the thought of what was to come, he happily carried Clarice up the flight of narrow, thin-carpeted stairs for their wedding night, a night that he had awaited for nearly twenty years.

Buck kicked the door closed behind them and crossed the few feet to the wide bed. He laid his precious burden down upon the lumpy mattress and knelt by the bed, suddenly shy. Taking her hand into his, he pressed his lips to the callused palm but didn't notice her work-roughened skin. To him it felt like silk. Nor did he note the fine lines of age that etched her features as he gazed lovingly down at her. He saw only the woman he had met when they were both young. The years dropped away like a cocoon from a butterfly and made Buck feel much like a callow youth who was unsure of his own prowess in the arts of love.

Clarice sensed Buck's hesitation and understood. At the moment she felt like a shy bride of eighteen instead of a widow of forty. She gave him a timid smile and placed her hand against his cheek, gently stroking it. "Buck, I love you," she whispered softly.

"And I love you," he murmured as he lowered his mouth to hers for a searing kiss. His moment of timidity evaporated under the heat wave that washed over him at the touch of her lips. He came to her, his strong hands disrobing her with a gentle urgency, caressing and titilating the flesh he exposed to his hungry gaze.

Clarice, possessed with a need equal to that she saw in Buck's eyes, responded in kind. Her fingers sought the buttons at the front of his shirt and then moved to the belt buckle at his lean waist. Her own shyness vanished as his clothes were discarded and she boldly caressed him, enjoying the feel of his hard masculine body beneath her hands.

With an eagerness that made Buck gasp with pleasure, she took his swollen length into her hand, stroking the satiny flesh enticingly as she drew him to her, her thighs spreading in welcome.

"Oh, Buck!" she breathed. "I've wanted you for so long." She gasped with pleasure as he plunged into her moist warmth.

"And I've wanted you," he murmured huskily as he began to move within her.

Their reason for coming to DryCreek was banished before the torrid winds of their passion. The years of denial and waiting were over and now it was their turn to savor love to its fullest.

Chapter 13

Motes *of dust floated lazily in the golden morning sun-*
light that streamed through the window and across the bed
where Star slept curled against Kyle. Unlike the woman
at his side, he lay awake, propped on one elbow, feasting
upon her beauty. A contented smile curled up the corners
of his lips and his eyes were soft and unguarded as he
gently brushed a dark skein of hair away from her face
to give him an unobstructed view of her lovely features.

At his touch, she stirred but did not awaken. She snuggled closer to his lean warmth and folded her gracefully
shaped hands as if in prayer beneath her cheek. The small
gesture made Kyle's heart well with tenderness for Star.
He was still amazed by the depth of feeling that she had
inspired within him in such a short span of time. In a
matter of a few short weeks she had altered everything
that he'd believed of love and had made him realize that
it was not a figment of his imagination as he had once
thought. Its existence was a real and viable thing that
now filled the restless void within him.

Kyle eased back on the pillow so as not to disturb her
and folded one arm beneath his sleep-tousled head. He
stared up at the ceiling, reflecting upon the changes that
had occurred inside him since he had found Star. Until
she had come into his life, the only person he had ever
loved had been his mother, and those feelings were entirely different from the intense emotions that this girl-
woman created in his heart. Star had made him come

alive; she'd forced him to look at his life and see that he
was not satisfied with the path he had chosen as much as
he had thought he was at one time. Being with her had
made him face his fear of committing himself to a woman
and realize that the vow he had made so many years ago
because of his parents' marriage had been foolish.

His feelings for Star had made him reexamine all the
things he had believed of himself because of his mother's
predictions, and by taking a closer look, he'd found them
to be untrue. He now understood that faithlessness was
not something he'd inherited from his father that would
rule his life. His life was his own and he alone was responsible for how he lived it. It had not been easy to
readjust his thinking. Through the years his mother had
successfully convinced him that he was so much like Buck
that he had little choice in what he did, but now he knew
that was not true.

Glancing down into Star's sleeping face, he felt as if
he had finally grown up. He was no longer cowering behind his mother's skirts, guarding his heart against an
unseen, unreal enemy that had made him fear himself
and the blood that flowed through his veins. He was free
at last to let himself love and be loved in return.

The look of contentment faded from Kyle's face as he
once more traced each of Star's lovely features with his
gaze. He had finally come to the conclusion that he had
nothing to fear where love was concerned and now he
was afraid that it might be too late. Painfully, he recalled
his words to Star that night on the prairie when she had
voiced her love for him. She had been honest with her
feelings, but he had rejected them and now he might have
to pay for that mistake for the rest of his life.

Pensively Kyle returned his gaze to the beamed ceiling. It had been two weeks since Buck and Clarice left
for DryCreek, yet in that time Star had never again spoken of her feelings for him. They had spent the nights
and several afternoons making love and she had come to
him eager and responsive, but he sensed that she still
withheld part of herself from him. Guiltily he turned on

his side and drew her into his arms. He had carelessly created this barrier between them and it was left to him to tear it down.

Star awoke as she was drawn into Kyle's embrace. Her lashes fluttered and she smiled dreamily up at him before laying her cheek against his furred chest. She stretched sensuously, then let her arm fall across his waist.

"Isn't it time to get up?" she murmured, and yawned lazily.

Kyle curled a long, dark strand of hair about his finger and held it up in the light, enjoying the way the sun brought out the blue highlights. Its color reminded him of a black and shining raven's wing.

"I can think of far more interesting pursuits this morning," he murmured huskily as he raised himself on one elbow and propped his cheek in the flat of his hand. He gave her a seductive smile, his emerald eyes flickering with wicked lights.

Star made an impish face at him and rolled to the side of the bed. Her hair cascaded down her back, shielding her bare bottom from view as she sat up and looked over her shoulder at Kyle. "You're paying me to work, Mr. Hunter. I can't get the bread baked by staying in bed all day."

"Then consider this your work, woman." Kyle chuckled. Not realizing his blunder, he reached out and wrapped his arm about her waist to draw her back to bed with him.

Star's stomach lurched. His words hit her in the gut like a solid, rock-hard fist, and she gasped with indignation as a wave of blinding fury swept over her. With a squeal of rage, she jerked herself free of his hold and scrambled off the bed. She looked at him through narrowed eyes gleaming with pinpoints of blue fire. Standing naked with her hands braced on the gentle swell of her hips, her breasts rising and falling with each angry breath, she spat, "So that's how you feel about me, you son of a bitch! I should have known that you really hadn't changed from the arrogant bastard I first met at the Red Passion.''

Incensed by her choice of words, Kyle rose naked from the bed, his lean body uncoiling like a lithe mountain lion in search of its quarry.

''I would suggest you calm down and watch your tongue. I don't know what I said or did to set you off on this tangent, but I won't tolerate being called a son of a bitch.''

''Well, you are a—'' Star's words came to an abrupt halt as Kyle's hands snaked out and clasped her by the upper arms, jerking her against him. His fingers bit into her flesh and his face was black with fury as he glared down at her and growled, ''Don't say it, Star.''

Defiantly she stared up at him, her eyes brimming with angry tears, her small chin thrust forward at a pugnacious angle. ''I hate you, Kyle Hunter, for what you've done to me.''

''Damn it, Star,'' Kyle ground out between clenched teeth, fighting the urge to shake some sense into her lovely head until her teeth rattled. ''I thought we'd settled that long ago.''

''We've settled nothing it seems except the fact that you consider me nothing more than your paid whore.''

''Hell and damnation,'' Kyle cursed. He shoved her away from him and grabbed his britches from the back of the chair. Jerking them on, he then shrugged into his shirt, and then pulled on his boots. His eyes sparkled like the gems they resembled as he turned to look at Star.

''I can't understand you and I've given up trying. You wax from hot to cold so fast that I never know what to expect from you. One minute you're a cuddly little kitten and in the next you're a spitting wildcat. When you can decide exactly what you want from me, let me know.''

''I don't want anything from you. I just want to do an honest day's work and be left alone. You may have met me in a brothel, but I'm not a whore to be used by you when the mood strikes. I'm paid to cook and clean, not to share your bed.''

"Hell and damnation," Kyle muttered again. Hurt and anger mingled within him, clouding his face as he said, "If that's all you think you've meant to me, then perhaps you'd better take a long, hard look at yourself. You came to my bed of your own free will, I didn't force you."

Unable to look at him, Star turned away. Her cheeks burned with guilt as Clarice's words came back to haunt her. She couldn't lay all the blame on Kyle. She had ignored the fact that he had made his feelings about her clear that night on the prairie, and if he thought her a whore, she had willingly acted the part because of her own desire and love for him.

"Just get out and leave me alone, Kyle," she said tonelessly.

Kyle took one step toward her, his heart urging him to end the hostility between them, but his anger stayed him and he swung toward the door. "If that's what you want, then you'll damn well get it. I'm sure I can find a woman who doesn't think my attentions are as distasteful as you seem to find them."

He slammed the door loudly behind him, grabbed up his hat and stalked out of the house. He paused on the porch to button his shirt and to run his fingers through his hair before clamping his hat down onto his head. Expelling an exasperated breath, he wondered again what he had said or done to make Star start ranting about him considering her his whore. All he had wanted was to make love to her and she had exploded like a keg of powder with the fuse lit.

"I'll be damned if I'll apologize for something when I don't even know what I'm apologizing for," he growled as he stamped off the porch and toward the barn.

Kyle's threat had effectively squelched any feelings of guilt that Star felt. Hot, angry tears burned her eyes, but she dashed them away with the back of her hand. Retrieving her gown from where she had eagerly discarded it the previous night, she jerked it on and turned to the mirror above the porcelain pitcher and bowl on the washstand. She eyed her reflection belligerently through glistening lashes and ordered, "You're not going to let yourself be jealous." But even as the words left her lips, the green-eyed monster was chewing away at her insides.

The name Victoria Crawford rose up to taunt her. She had as yet to meet the woman, but she remembered well Clarice's reference to her on the day of Star's arrival at the Bar H. Disgruntled for letting herself be disturbed at the thought of Kyle with another woman, she picked up the hairbrush and began to pull it through her long tresses. To add to her annoyance, the bristles of the brush became tangled in the thick, dark strands. Aggravated nearly beyond endurance, she jerked it free and cursed, "Damn you, Kyle. You can have Victoria Crawford for all I care."

Tossing the offending brush onto the bed where she had found so much happiness in Kyle's arms, she turned resolutely away and strode from the room. She closed the bedroom door firmly behind her as if the action could also shut out the pain from her heart.

The sweet aroma of fresh bread filled the kitchen as Star pulled the crisp, brown loaves from the oven and dumped them out onto the clean, checkered tablecloth to cool. Heat from the cast-iron stove combined with that of the afternoon sun beaded her brow with perspiration and she wiped it away with her sleeve as she turned back to the task of peeling potatoes for the stew she was preparing for the evening meal.

She was grateful for the few weeks she had spent helping her aunt in the kitchen. She had learned a little about cooking from Priscilla and then later by watching the cook at the hotel, but she had learned the most from Clarice during the short time they had spent working together at the Bar H. It was fortunate for all concerned that she had acquired the basic skills required to prepare a simple meal. If she had been forced to count on Clarice's return they would have starved to death by now.

Picking up the knife, she cut away the dark outer skin and tossed the last white orb into the broth with the chunks of beef and onions. Placing the lid on the black pot, she gathered up the peelings and dumped them into the bucket that held the scraps for the pigs. Satisfied with her morning's labors, she dusted her hands against her apron and turned to the open doorway. The kitchen was stifling and she hoped to find a breath of cool air, though she had learned during the last hot weeks that little could be found on a summer's day in Texas.

A gust of hot wind spun a dust devil across the dry, powdery yard as she relaxed back against the door frame. She watched the swirl of wind and grit until it dissipated in the stand of mesquites that grew by the small stream beyond the paddocks. That stream, she had learned from Clarice, was the life of the Bar H. It provided the water for the cattle that Kyle raised for the army.

Absently fanning herself with the hem of her apron, Star let her gaze wander from the mesquites, past the well-kept paddocks and weathered barn to the land that Kyle loved. During the past weeks she had also come to love this land, almost as much as she loved the man who owned it. Compared with the verdant landscape of Mississippi, this land appeared barren, yet there was a harsh, intense beauty about it that called to her heart and made her understand why people had fought Mexicans, Indians, and nature to claim it.

Staring out across the flat, grassy range, Star realized that it reminded her much of Kyle. He too was blessed with a rugged beauty in face and form. At times he could be as hard and unyielding as the drought-baked Texas soil, yet he could also be as startlingly gentle as the bluebonnets that sprang into bloom after a spring shower. He was a man of contrasts as much as the land he claimed as his own.

With her thoughts on Kyle, she squinted in the direction he had ridden early that morning not long after their quarrel. His mood had not improved when he had come back to the house to tell her that he was going into Sagebrush to buy supplies and that he wouldn't be back at the ranch until late afternoon. After his threat that morning she suspected he had other motives for going into town, mainly to see Victoria Crawford.

Star frowned, her pleasant daydream dissolving like the dust devil against the mesquites. The green-eyed monster that she had thought to put to rest stretched and yawned and then clamped down on her insides with its vicious talons as she thought of Kyle with another woman. She tried to tell herself that she'd brought on much of her own misery by believing that she could be satisfied with living for the moment and not expecting a future. But that did not appease the angry beast that chewed unmercifully at her heart and again blackened her mood.

The sound of galloping horses drew Star's attention, and as if conjured by her thoughts of him, she looked through the doorway to see Kyle mounted on his black stallion, racing through the gates of the Bar H. Her heart leapt at the sight and a smile of welcome touched her lips before she saw the sleek bay mare behind him, its rider a vision of loveliness in a turquoise riding habit. Star's smile vanished. She gaped at the woman who leaned low across the animal's neck, urging it to a greater speed as she tried to win the race. The wind whipped her auburn hair back from her face and shoulders and it lay in a mass of gold-streaked curls down her back. The curves of her lithe body were emphasized to perfection as she stretched forward and moved with the animal as if rider and mount were one.

Every muscle in Star's body grew taut. Instinct told her that the woman who drew her mare to a skidding halt beside Kyle's mount was the woman her aunt had told her about and until now, her unseen rival, Victoria Crawford.

Unconsciously Star balled her hands into tight fists at her sides as she watched Kyle reach up to help her nemesis dismount, his strong, tanned hands nearly spanning her narrow waist. She heard her own teeth clash and grate together as Victoria bestowed a provocative smile upon Kyle and placed her hands on his wide shoulders.

Star did not miss the advantage she took of the situation by letting their bodies come into intimate contact as she slipped to the ground. Star's blood seemed to catch fire at the sight of Kyle touching Victoria. The reality of it was far worse than anything she had imagined.

"Damn," she swore, and spun on her heel. She stamped back into the kitchen. She'd not stay and witness their tender moments. If she did, she wouldn't be responsible for her own actions. Stalking back to the stove, she jerked the lid from the pot and banged it loudly against the cast-iron surface, angrily wishing that it was Kyle's head that she had hit. She took up the ladle and stirred the stew in earnest, her jealousy provoking thoughts of poisoning it for Kyle and his lover.

"It would serve him right," she muttered, and banged the lid back down on the kettle.

"I beg your pardon," came a seductively soft feminine voice from the doorway behind her.

Startled, Star swung about to come face-to-face with her enemy. The knuckles of the hand that gripped the ladle were white with tension as she stared at the woman who appraised her in turn.

"I didn't mean to startle you, but I thought I might ask for a glass of cool water. The ride from town was quite hot." Victoria smiled sweetly at Star as she fanned herself with a lace-edged handkerchief and dabbed at her brow for effect.

Giving herself a sharp mental shake, Star gathered her befuddled wits. "Of course. I'll get you one." Taking a glass from the breakfront where Madge Hunter's precious china was stored and never used, Star filled it with water and turned back to find Victoria ensconced at the table as if she was a member of the family.

"Thank you—, I'm sorry I don't know your name," Victoria said as Star set the glass on the table in front of her.

"It's Star—Star Grayson."

"Oh, yes. I do seem to remember that Kyle mentioned your name when he told me he had hired a new cook and helper." Victoria's gaze swept condescendingly over Star. "Which one are you, the cook or the helper?"

"Right now, I'm both," Star said, further annoyed by the woman's superior attitude. It reminded her too much of the way her stepmother had treated the slaves, and she had to control the urge to slap Victoria's lovely face. "Now, if you will excuse me I've supper to prepare." Star turned back to the stove, which seemed to have cooled in the last minutes because of the heat in her own blood.

The amiable expression slipped from Victoria's face when Star turned away. Her eyes glittered with malice and her full lips curled contemptuously at the corners as she assessed Kyle's new cook. Like a mongrel sensing another encroaching upon its territory, she bristled. Star Grayson was too beautiful for her peace of mind. She could well pose a problem where Kyle was concerned.

Victoria sipped the glass of water as she speculated on how it would be best to deal with this new threat to her plans of renewing her affair with Kyle. Until that afternoon she had been sure that her endeavors would eventually succeed with him. Now that she had met Star, she was experiencing the first qualms of uncertainty.

That in itself annoyed Victoria. She had always been a self-assured woman who had no doubts about her own charms. She was also a woman with a strong sense of determination who did not take no for an answer. When she wanted something, she did not stop until she had it. And she wanted Kyle Hunter. She had wanted him since their first meeting two years earlier at the church social. She had used all of her feminine charms to lure him to her but, to her dismay, he had not succumbed to her wiles as easily as all the other men in her past. He had flatly refused to marry her. That had been a shattering blow to her vanity and she had quickly married Harold Crawford out of spite. It had not taken her long after her marriage to realize that she would not be satisfied until she had Kyle as well. He had become a challenge, a symbol to her injured pride that she had to conquer in order to prove to herself and the world that she was a woman to be reckoned with.

Now this new and unforeseen dilemma of Star Grayson had arisen to put a kink into her plans. Instinct told her that there was more between Kyle and his new cook than he had indicated when he'd come into the mercantile store to order supplies. She had immediately sensed a difference about him but had not been able to pinpoint it until he had ordered several bolts of cloth, telling Harold that his new cook and helper were in need of a few gowns since all their possessions had been lost when the Comanches burned out their ranch near DryCreek. Kyle's face and voice when he mentioned Star had told her more than his words. She had hurriedly excused herself from helping her husband with the stock and had rushed home to change into her riding habit so that she could accidentally meet Kyle on his way back to the Bar H and have an excuse to inspect her new rival for his affections.

Her ploy had worked and now that she had met Star, she knew her suspicions were true. The girl was too lovely for Kyle to ignore. From her own experience with him, she knew that he was a man who enjoyed women and he would not deny himself this young morsel because she worked for him. Yet that was not what truly worried Victoria. She suspected that this girl had touched Kyle's heart and that was something much harder to fight. She had to find a way to get her out of Kyle's life before it was too late. However, she was faced with one major problem. At the present moment, she had no idea how she could go about gaining that end. "But I'll find a way," she murmured beneath her breath as she eyed the slender, ramrod-straight back turned to her.

"I see the two of you have already met," Kyle said as he came through the doorway. Sniffing the air, he smiled. "Something smells good, Star." When she did not respond to his compliment, he helped himself to a drink of water with the gourd dipper that hung above the wooden bucket. Hanging the dipper back on the peg by the rawhide strip through the handle, he turned his attention to Victoria. "I had wondered where you'd gotten off to while I was watering the horses."

"Our race made me thirsty so I came in for a drink of water. Has Gilly cooled down?"

"Yes, she'll be ready to ride when you are." Kyle pulled a chair out from the table and sat down. He cast a curious glance in Star's direction but did not comment on the fact that if she didn't quit stirring the stew soon, it would be little more than soup by suppertime.

Victoria felt her bristles rise once more as she watched the direction of his gaze. Damn you, Kyle. She'll not have you if I have anything to say about it, she raged silently. Yet when he looked back at her, she gave him one of her warmest smiles. "I'd forgotten until today how much I used to enjoy our races. I hope you'll give me another chance to recoup my reputation as a horse-woman."

"You know you're an excellent rider, Vicky, but Gilly can never win against Lightning."

Victoria arched one russet brow and gave Kyle a sultry look through half-closed lids. "You should know me well enough to know that I don't accept defeat easily. When I want something, I don't stop until I get it."

Kyle read the innuendo in her words. He eyed her coolly. "You'll have to accept it. Your mare is neither as strong nor as fast as my stallion. I doubt Harold would approve of your riding Gilly to death because you refuse to admit defeat."

Victoria drew herself up, incensed by his blatant reminder of her husband. "I don't really care what Harold approves or disapproves of. Why should I, when his only love is that blasted store? We haven't ridden together in months because he can't get his nose out of the coffee and flour long enough to see me."

"I'm sure you could persuade him to take some time off. As you've just said, you have a way of getting what you want."

Victoria flicked the white lace at her wrist in disgust. The conversation was not going as she had hoped and she knew it was time for her to retreat and form a new strategy. "I'm sure you're right," she said as she rose from the chair. "Now it's time that I get back to town. Harold will be worried about me if I'm too late."

Kyle pushed his chair back and stood. "And we can't have that can we, Vicky?" He chuckled as he took her arm to escort her back to her horse.

Ignoring his glib comment, Victoria said, "Thank you for the water, Miss Grayson. It's been so nice meeting you. When you come to town, please stop in and say hello." Her hollow invitation and thanks only received a curt nod from Star, who stood silently fuming over the woman's obvious attempt to seduce Kyle.

Victoria felt she would explode with exasperation as they walked across the yard to where her mare was tethered by the paddock. Kyle had rebuffed her once more and had taken no pity on her where her husband was concerned. Damn you, Kyle. I won't be that easily dissuaded, she mused stubbornly to herself as they reached the mare. Turning to him, she ran one manicured finger along the buttons on his shirt as she gazed up into his catlike eyes. "Kyle, ride with me back to town. Harold is working late tonight as usual and it would only be the two of us for dinner."

Kyle's fingers curled about her hand, stilling its movement. He shook his head. "Vicky, it's over. You know I won't sneak into another man's house and bed his wife. I've made my feelings clear to you about that for over a year."

Victoria's eyes flashed with fire and her face contorted with the fury that had been building within her since she had met Star. She balled her hand into a fist and hit Kyle on the chest as she spat, "Oh, how high and mightily moral you've become. But I bet your morals don't extend to your little cook, do they?"

"Leave Star out of this," Kyle growled, his face darkening with anger. "I've never given you any reason to think there could ever be anything more between us. So let it die, Vicky. Go back to your husband. You may not love him, but he loves you. You've been fortunate that his love has blinded him for so long to your antics. Few men would tolerate their wives visiting an ex-lover the way Harold has put up with you constantly finding some excuse to come out here.''

''Damn you,'' Victoria ground out as she swung about and climbed into the saddle. She looked down at Kyle, her eyes sparkling with rage. ''I'll see that you pay dearly for rejecting my love. You and that little hussy you call a cook will rue this day. That I promise you.'' Giving the mare a vicious kick in the side, she galloped back toward Sagebrush.

The muscles across Kyle's wide shoulders drew his red plaid shirt taut as he stood with arms akimbo and feet spread, a thoughtful expression playing over his ruggedly handsome face as he watched the cloud of dust roil from beneath the mare's hooves. He hoped he'd finally settled the matter between himself and Victoria Crawford once and for all. He was tired of her games. At one time he had thought them amusing but now he only found them exceedingly annoying. The only reason he'd put up with her constant visits to the ranch and her waylaying him on the street in Sagebrush was because until now he hadn't cared about anyone enough to stop her little schemes to get back into his life. His feelings for Star had finally made him realize that Victoria could only cause problems.

He'd seen the expression on Victoria's face when he'd entered the kitchen. It had boded no good for Star. The woman's jealousy had been plainly visible until she had discovered his presence and had plastered that too-sweet smile back onto her face. At that moment he had decided to put an end to her plan before she had a chance to hurt the woman he loved.

Kyle grinned at the memory of Star standing by the stove, stirring the stew as if her life depended upon it. Her back had been as stiff as a board and though he couldn't see her face, he could well imagine the dour expression that had been on it. The tension in the room had been much thicker than the stew that Star was pureeing with her ladle. He chuckled as he turned back toward the house.

Unaware that Kyle stood quietly watching her from the doorway, Star stood simmering much hotter than the mush she was still making of what had once been a fine beef stew. When Kyle and Victoria had left the kitchen she had been unable to stop herself from sneaking to the door and watching them. What she had seen had made the green-eyed monster grow in size within her until she thought she would choke on her fury. She had watched Victoria turn to Kyle and intimately run her finger down his chest while giving him one of her seductive smiles. She had also seen Kyle take her hand and hold it tenderly to his chest. She hadn't been able to see his face, but she had seen enough of Victoria's to know what was transpiring between them. Star had not waited to see more. She had stalked back to the stove to wreak her vengeance upon the pulpy stew.

Leaning one shoulder against the door frame, Kyle folded his arms across his chest and with one knee bent, the tip of his boot braced on the floor, he said, "Don't you think it's time you quit stirring that blasted stew before we have to drink it?"

Startled, Star spun about, the ladle splattering brown gravy across the floor. Her face was flushed from the heat of the stove as well as her anger. Her eyes glittered with fiery blue lights as she raised her chin belligerently in the air. "If you're such an expert, why don't you do the cooking?" she spat and tossed the dripping ladle onto the table, soiling the clean checkered cloth.

Kyle suppressed his grin. Knowing the answer to his question before it was asked, he said, "What's got your dander up? Are you still angry about this morning?"

Star thought her eyes would bulge from her head at the burst of fury that exploded in her brain. "What's got my dander up? You know damn well what it is, you son—conceited, arrogant, good-for-nothing." She managed to stop herself before she called him a son of a bitch again, well remembering his reaction to it that morning.

Kyle's brows creased as he screwed up his face in a thoughtful frown, enjoying Star's jealousy. To him it was a sign that she still cared. "No, I don't know what has set your temper off. Is it the stew? You certainly seem to be taking out your anger on it."

"Damn you, Kyle. Don't play with me. I'm in no mood for your games after you've flaunted your lover in my face this afternoon."

"My lover?" Kyle asked, unable to stop himself from teasing her.

"Yes, your lover—Victoria Crawford. How dare you leave my bed and then go to meet her?" Star stormed. Her fury gathered force and she strode to the table. Grabbing up the ladle again, she sailed it at his head before he realized her intention.

He managed to duck in the nick of time but couldn't avoid being splattered with the excess stew that clung to Star's weapon. He made a disgusted face as he wiped the sticky mush from his cheek.

"Calm down, Star. It's not what you think," he said, deciding it was time to call a truce before he found the entire pot thrown at him.

"Calm down!" she squealed. "I've only just begun." Picking up one of the fresh loaves of bread that still rested on the table, she threw it at him as well.

Kyle caught it in midflight. "Star, if you keep this up we won't have anything left to eat at the ranch."

"Don't make fun of me," she growled, and grabbed the large frying pan from the hook on the wall. She raised it threateningly.

Kyle held up both hands in surrender. "Truce?"

Star did not relinquish her weapon. "You want a truce? Then I'll give you a truce the only way you understand anything and that's by being hit over the head with it." As the words left her mouth she hurled the cast-iron pan at him.

He sidestepped it easily. "Star, for the love of God, stop this before someone gets hurt."

"Someone is going to get hurt and that someone is you," she snarled, her eyes already searching the kitchen for another weapon. Spying the wood box behind the stove, she headed for it, ready to use one of the pieces of dry mesquite against him. But before she reached her destination, Kyle decided it was time to put a stop to her attempt to do him injury. He moved swiftly. Wrapping one strong arm about her waist, he lifted her off her feet. Star kicked at him and squealed in fury as he carried her from the kitchen. He considered it much safer if he removed her from her stock of kitchen utensils.

"Calm down, you little hellion. You've no reason to be jealous of Victoria," Kyle ordered as he set her on her feet. However he was not foolish enough to release her, until he was sure she had altered her plans to do him damage.

"Jealous! How dare you think I'm jealous of the likes of her. For all I care Victoria Crawford can have you."

Kyle again suppressed his grin. The workings of a woman's mind bewildered him at times. Here she was raving about him bringing Victoria to the ranch and then she denied feeling any jealousy.

"If you're not jealous, then what in the devil has gotten you all fired up to try to kill me?" He turned Star to face him but kept a firm hold on her.

She glared up at him, her anger unabated. "You know damned well what it is."

"Is this a riddle that I'm supposed to solve, Star? How am I to know what has upset you if you won't tell me?" he asked, the bantering tone now gone from his voice.

Star felt tears sting the backs of her eyelids and she blinked rapidly to stay them. She'd be damned before she gave way to them in front of Kyle. Her eyes were glistening pools as she stared up at him, stubbornly refusing to answer.

"Star, talk to me," he said, his voice softly cajoling.

He rested his hands on her shoulders and slowly kneaded them, soothing away her tension with voice and touch.

Star sought desperately to keep her anger alive but found it evaporating under his gentle attentions. Sighing, she gave up the effort and leaned against him, her face pressed to his chest.

"Talk to me, Star," he murmured against her hair as he wound his fingers in her thick, dark curls.

Star drew in a deep breath and with it came the scent of him. It teased her senses and made it difficult for her to speak, yet she forced herself to ignore her hammering heart and venture into an area that could only bring her more pain.

"Kyle, I've no right to be angry with you because of Victoria, but it hurts when I . . ." Her words trailed off into silence as she lost her courage. At that moment she did not know if she could withstand another rejection from him.

Kyle's breath stilled in his throat and his heart began to pump hard and fast as he sensed she had come close to voicing her love for him before she faltered. "Tell me, Star. We can work out anything if we're honest with each other. The only thing I could not abide would be if you lied to me."

Star flinched at his simple request. Guilt raised its mocking head, chastising her for her deceit. She tried to block out all of the lies she had woven about herself in the last months as she wrapped her arms about his waist and clung to him. Squeezing her eyes tightly shut, she pressed her cheek to his chest until she could hear the rapid beat of his heart. Kyle wanted honesty between them, but the only truth she could voice was that which lay in her heart. Softly she murmured, "Kyle, I love you."

Kyle's senses soared. At last she had said aloud the three small words that he had been longing to hear. He threw back his head and laughed from the pure joy the words created within him. "Star, my glorious Star. You'll never know how much I feared that I'd never hear those precious words from your sweet lips again.''

Star gaped up a him with wide, bewildered eyes. His reaction was far from what she had expected. ''But—but I thought,'' she stumbled to a halt and then after swallowing several times began again. ''You mean you really wanted me to tell you that I love you?''

''More than anything else in the world,'' Kyle said, grinning down at her as if he had won a grand prize, and to him he had.

''But you told me—,'' Star began, but Kyle pressed a finger against her lips.

''Yes, I know what I told you and I now know what a fool I was for saying it.''

Star's heart trembled within her breast. Uncertainty and hope mingled as one in her as she looked up into his much-beloved face. ''Why, Kyle? Why now when you have Victoria?''

''Do you really have to ask that question, my beautiful little hellion?'' Kyle chuckled.

''Yes, I have to know,'' she replied softly, and waited for his answer with bated breath. Every muscle in her body grew tense with expectancy.

Kyle's face softened. His expression reflected all of his feelings as he looked down into Star's upturned face. ''You little fool, it's because *I* love *you*.''

A flicker of incredulity passed over her face before it lit with joy and wonder. Her eyes misted with happiness and her lower lip trembled as she smiled radiantly up at him and threw her arms about his neck. ''Oh, Kyle,'' she breathed before burying her face in his shoulder and bursting into tears.

Kyle held her as she wept, bewildered by her bout of crying. He had expected her to be happy when he told her of his love. Now as she wet his shirt through to the skin, he wasn't certain. Nor did he know what to say or do. He felt suddenly like a pubescent youth, inexperienced in dealing with women and their emotions.

He held her close and awkwardly patted her back,

murmuring, "Don't cry, my love. I didn't mean to make you unhappy."

Sniffling and feeling slightly foolish for her outburst, she leaned back and looked up at him. Her face glistened with moisture and again her lips trembled as she gave him a wobbly smile. "You've not made me unhappy. My tears come from joy."

Bemused again by the mercurial moods of females, Kyle shook his head and smiled. "My unpredictable Star," he said as he drew her tightly against his lean frame and lowered his mouth to hers.

No doubts or insecurities intruded to hinder Star's response. She gave herself up to the kiss with fervor. The knowledge of Kyle's love shattered all of the barriers she had erected to defend herself against being hurt again. Eagerly, she became the aggressor, her tongue seeking his enticingly as she wound her fingers in the softly curling hair at the nape of his neck and drew his head closer.

A low growl of pure animal pleasure came from deep within Kyle's throat and a tremor of desire shook his sinewy body as her small tongue darted sensually over his, teasing him provocatively with each stroke. He crushed her to him and felt the soft mounds of her breasts flatten against his chest, their hardened, aroused nipples leaving pinpoints of fire on his flesh even through the clothing that separated them. Unable to endure more of the exquisite torture, he swept her up into his arms and carried her to the bedroom.

Kicking the door open, he strode to the bed and they fell together upon its downy softness. Hungrily he disrobed her, his hands exploring each inch of flesh before he discarded his own clothing with equal haste. There was no need for foreplay to arouse them. When hard, masculine sinew touched soft, pliable flesh the furor it created left them breathless with desire. Their passion set their bodies aflame like lightning against dry prairie grass. It exploded into a wildfire that burned through their veins, searing them with its intensity.

Star moved her hips against Kyle's, beckoning him to

her. He heeded her call and thrust into the dewed warmth of her young body. Savoring the heated flesh that caressed his swollen length, he lay still for a long moment, gazing down into her lovely, desire-flushed face. Her eyes were soft blue velvet as she gazed up at him, their shimmering depths reflecting a hunger to equal that which raged through him in a torrid current of desire that only she could quench. Giving way to his need he began to move in slow, even strokes. His leisurely lovemaking aroused them both until they could no longer contain the sweet storm in their blood. They moved to the drumbeat of their hearts and all else faded into oblivion except the exquisite sensations they shared. Nothing existed beyond their love for each other as they trembled into ecstasy.

Star smiled up at Kyle as he lay above her, supporting his weight on his elbows, his lean body still intimately joined with hers. "I love you," she whispered, and reached up to caress his cheek.

"And I love you," he murmured before turning his face into her hand and pressing his lips to her palm in a gentle kiss. "I'm going to miss you during the next weeks."

"Why should you miss me? I'll be here with you."

"Yes, you'll be here, but I won't be," Kyle said, and smiled before he dropped a light kiss on the tip of her nose and rolled away from her. He sat up on the side of the bed. "We begin the trail drive tomorrow."

Kyle reached for his britches and withdrew a folded envelope from the back pocket. He handed it to Star. "I had meant to give you this earlier, but I got a little sidetracked by a beautiful, hot-blooded woman."

Star blushed at the compliment as she looked down at her name scribbled across the front of the wrinkled letter. She recognized Clarice's handwriting and tore it open, eager for any word of her aunt's intended return, as well as what she had learned while in DryCreek. Now more than ever Star wanted to clear her name. She had finally found the love that she had craved for so many years, but until she could prove herself innocent of murdering her stepmother, she had no right to embrace it.

The glow of happiness left by Kyle's lovemaking slowly faded as she read her aunt's cryptic note. It said little beyond the fact that what they had feared had turned out to be true and that she and Buck would not be returning to the ranch for several weeks.

Despair welled within Star's breast as she slowly folded the letter and tucked it back into the envelope. Clarice had written nothing that might be misconstrued by anyone reading the note but Star had been able to read between the lines of her short message. The man Clarice had gone to find had been a bounty hunter as they had feared. That meant that someone had been wise enough to guess that she would come to Texas to find her aunt. After all she had gone through to hide her destination and to disguise herself, she had been tracked down.

A dark, foreboding cloud seemed to hover about her as she looked up at Kyle. She had gained his love but their future together now looked bleak. If the bounty hunter had been able to locate her whereabouts, then the law would also be able to find her. She would be arrested and taken back to Mississippi to hang for a crime she had not committed. The thought was agonizing, yet her greatest fear was of Kyle realizing that she had lied to him. When he learned of her deceit, it would destroy any love he had for her. Even if she managed to prove that Fiona's death had been an accident, the fragile bond between herself and Kyle would be shattered beyond repair. He had asked for honesty between them and he would not be able to forgive her deception.

Kyle eyed Star curiously as he pulled on his britches and shrugged into his shirt. It was still early and there was work to be done if everything was to be ready for him to leave the following morning.

"What is it, Star? Is there bad news from Clarice?" he asked as he sat down on the side of the bed to pull on his boots.

Star longed to throw herself into his arms and tell him

the truth, but her fear held her back. The courage that had always come to her aid in the past now failed her. She wasn't brave enough to chance destroying his love for her after just finding it. Instead she shook her head. "There's nothing wrong."

"Did Clarice say when they'd be returning to the ranch?" Kyle asked as he thrust his foot into his boot.

"She said it would be several weeks." Star crumpled the letter in her hand.

"Damn," Kyle muttered. He ran his fingers through his tousled hair and looked over his shoulder at Star. "I had hoped I wouldn't have to leave you here alone."

"Then let me come with you," she said, scrambling to her knees at his side. Her long, dark hair fell in a curtain about her, shielding her nudity as she anxiously awaited his answer.

"I wish that I could," Kyle said, lifting an ebony curl away from the creamy mound it concealed from his gaze. He wound it about his fingers until his hand rested on her bare shoulder. "But a cattle drive is no place for a woman."

"Kyle, please don't leave me here," Star pleaded, suddenly sensing that if he left her behind, she might never see him again.

Kyle frowned at the underlying note of fear he heard in her voice. Turning to her, he framed her small face in his hands, his gaze holding hers. "What is it, Star? Why are you afraid?"

The truth arose achingly in her throat, but she swallowed it back and threw her arms about his strong, corded neck. She hugged him tightly. "I'm afraid of being left alone."

"My precious Star," Kyle murmured, holding her in the comforting warmth of his arms. "You'll be safe here. When I said you'd be alone, I didn't mean that you'd be the only person at the Bar H. I'm leaving my foreman, Lucas Brown, and several other men here to see to things in my absence."

"I know I'll be safe, but I don't want to be separated

from you. I've just found your love and I don't want to lose it.''

''You'll never lose it, Star. I've waited too long to discover true love and now that I have, I won't let anything come between us.''

Star squeezed her eyes tightly closed and clung to him. In silent anguish she thought, Oh, God, if only I could believe that was true I would tell him everything. Yet she remained quiet. The fates had not been kind to her in the past and she could not depend upon their benevolence in the future. All she could do was to cherish what time they had left together.

''Love me, Kyle,'' she whispered softly against his ear, and felt his arm tighten about her as she moved her breast sensually against his bare chest. She began to kiss him, raining his throat and the line of his jaw with tiny kisses until she came to his shapely lips. She flicked their smooth surface with the tip of her tongue and felt a tremor shake him before he tumbled her back on the bed. His mouth hungrily captured hers, his tongue devouring the sweetness of the velvet cavern he plundered.

Their kiss deepened as she worked to free Kyle of his clothing. She eased the loose shirt from his shoulders and tossed it over their heads. It landed against the wall as she turned her attention to the buttons on his britches. After several fumbling attempts she managed to unfasten them. Freeing her mouth, she pushed Kyle onto his back and then with his help removed his britches and boots. Naked, his sinewy body hard and aroused, he unabashedly lay back on the pillows and smiled up at her.

Star knelt at his side, savoring the splendor of his masculine beauty. Her bold gaze swept from his strong shoulders to his wide furred chest and then moved down along the dark trail of hair to his swollen manhood, standing proud with his desire. A thrill of excitement tingled up her spine as she realized that she had the power to bring forth such a response from him.

Shyly she placed her hand on that hard part of him and heard him moan with pleasure. She slowly explored the

warm, satiny length of his arousal. She felt it respond to
her touch and curled her fingers about it. Slowly she
moved her hand up and down. Kyle's hips arched upward
with her caress and he again expressed his pleasure with
a soft moan. Recalling the fire he had built within her
with his mouth and wanting to give him the same pleasure, she lowered her lips to him, her tongue teasing the
silky smoothness while her hands kneaded his flat belly
and corded thighs.

She was surprised to find her own blood simmering
from the erotic caress. Her breathing grew heavier as
Kyle's hands moved up her thighs to find the dark entrance to her womanhood. She felt her own moist desire
sweep down in a trembling wave to welcome his explo-
rations. Her heart pounded against her ribs and her thighs
spread to give him full access. His probing fingers worked
their magic and her hips moved against his hand as she
continued to caress him with her mouth.

A hunger that only Kyle could satisfy began to grow
deep within the core of her femininity and she rained
small kisses across his belly and up his wide chest as she
moved to straddle him impaling herself. A gasp of pure
pleasure escaped her lips as he captured her hips and
began to move her with him toward the pinnacle of ecstasy. Her head arched back as she savored the rising tide
of rapture, yet before it crested, he grasped her hips,
stilling her movements. Dismayed at being denied the
ultimate fulfillment, she stared down at him, her passion-
swollen lips pouting like those of a small child refused a
treat. She moved her hips against him temptingly, but he
shook his head.

"No, my love. You will not have all your pleasure at
once. I, too, am greedy to know more of you." With
those words he rolled her onto her back and raised himself between her thighs. Green fire danced in his eyes as
he leaned forward and spread her dark mane of hair
across the pillow, fanning it about her in a silken halo.
A tender smile played over his lips as he touched her
face, caressing her cheek. He stroked the slender line of

her throat with the tips of his fingers, and then moved along the smooth curve of her shoulders. Her skin burned from his touch and she arched upward as he filled his palms with her breasts. Gently he kneaded them before lowering his head to receive a pert, hardened nipple into his mouth. He flicked it with his tongue, arousing it further before nibbling and suckling at it. Greedily he moved to its mate as he slid his hands along her torso to the swell of her hips. There his fingers again worked their magic, playing lightly over her skin before he left her breasts. He leaned back, the muscles in his thighs straining against his supple flesh as he knelt between her thighs and gently caressed their softness with the palms of his hands.

Star's hips arched toward him, beckoning him into the moist warmth, yet he ignored their call. She gasped as his hands went beneath her and turned her onto her stomach. She lay expectantly, wondering at his intentions, but she soon learned them. Kyle brushed her hair away from her neck and began his downward exploration. His lips left a trail of fire across her shoulder and along her spine to her rounded buttocks. He moved ever downward, his tongue gliding over her flesh, creating a furor within her as he lapped at the sensitive spot behind her knee. He played her body like a musician playing a fine violin, stroking it until he brought forth the responses he desired. Star moaned and tossed her head restlessly from side to side, unable to bear his fervent caresses, needing to feel him deep within her.

"Not yet, my love," he murmured huskily, prolonging his foreplay. Again his hands and tongue were on her, moving upward along the inside of her thighs toward the dark valley as he kneaded the soft mounds of her bottom. Star moaned and twisted until she lay on her back. She arched to his seeking mouth, glorying in the feel of the dizzying caress. She opened to him, savoring the heady sensation his probing tongue aroused. Forgetting all else except the burning need building within her, she moved against his mouth and felt herself explode with rapture.

Kyle tasted her ecstasy and knew he could no longer delay his own. He covered her with his hard body, the muscles in his shoulders and back rippling beneath his tanned flesh as he grasped her hips and thrust into her moist, pulsating passage.

Star gasped at the onslaught of renewed passion his throbbing manhood created as he moved within her. She had thought that she had experienced the heights of ecstasy, but they paled compared to the feelings that Kyle was now building within her. She moved with him, riding the wind across a flaming sky filled with shooting stars of ecstasy to the land of enchantment.

The power of her release was so intense that she arched away from Kyle, a cry of rapture upon her lips. She pressed her hips to his as the force of it made her tremble from head to toe. Then, when the tremor passed, she collapsed, her hair spreading in a silken wave about them.

"My beautiful Star," Kyle breathed, his voice husky with emotion. He rolled to his side, carrying her with him, and raised himself on one elbow. He gazed down at her, a contented smile playing about his lips. "I love you," he murmured as he bent to nuzzle the smooth curve of her cheek.

Star snuggled closer to his lean body. She savored the warm glow left by their lovemaking. She would not let the past or the future intrude upon the peace she had found in his arms.

"And I love you, Kyle," she whispered softly before her lashes fluttered down over her eyes and she slept with a satisfied little smile curling her lips.

Kyle wrapped her in his arms and held her close as the sun sank below the horizon and the shadows of twilight slipped stealthily into the room, cradling them in its velvet mantle. He pushed the thought of the work he had neglected from his mind. Now was the time to be with the woman he loved. Resting his cheek against her silken hair, his sated body relaxed and a peaceful smile also touched his well-molded lips as sleep claimed him.

Chapter 14

The chill left from a rain shower the previous night ruled the morning as Buck tossed a piece of wood on the smoldering campfire and hunkered down beside it to place the coffeepot in position to brew when the wood caught fire. Patches of fog swirled about the base of the trees as if hiding from the first rays of the sun that climbed over the treetops, seeking to vanquish the misty shroud from the warm day to come. The golden light spread across the campsite to touch Clarice, sleeping with her head cushioned on her saddle and a blanket wrapped snugly about her to ward off the damp air.

Buck smiled as he looked toward his wife of two weeks. Though the mission they had set for themselves was a serious one, he had never been happier in his life and the reason for his happiness lay only a few feet away.

It was still hard for him to believe that after so long he had finally married the woman who had held his heart for twenty years and he wondered at his good fortune as well as the changes that had occurred within him during the last weeks.

He felt twenty years old instead of fifty-two. Clarice had been the catalyst that had wrought the changes and had finally helped him to find an inner peace that he had been seeking through all his years of wandering the frontier. The man who had always looked for a fight, who could outcurse and outdrink most men, and who was never satisfied to stay in one place for very long had disappeared. In his place was a man who could look back on his past and realize that everything he had done had been because he'd been unhappy. And he loved the woman responsible for turning his life around more each day for that.

Buck's eyes twinkled with devilment as he moved to her side and picked a blade of grass. He drew it slowly across her upper lip, tickling her until she screwed up her face and batted away the annoying pest. Thoroughly enjoying his teasing, he waited until she relaxed once more before tickling her again with the grass. Again she wrinkled her nose and blew through her lips to rid herself of the nuisance that kept disturbing her rest. At last when she could tolerate it no longer, she peeped from beneath her lashes, ready to swat her persecutor. Seeing Buck grinning down at her, she pretended to sleep again, awaiting his next move. When it came, she bolted upright, threw her arms about his neck, and tumbled him over backwards.

"Tickle me, will you, Buck Hunter?" she growled in feigned anger as she straddled him. Sitting astride his hard middle, she did not wait for his answer but began tormenting him in kind, running her fingers up his ribs and tickling him unmercifully under his arms.

Buck burst into agonized laughter as he squirmed to rid himself of the wiggling fingers in his armpits. When he found that he could not, he gasped, "I surrender. You win, woman!"

Clarice ceased her torture and grinned down at him. She folded her arms across his chest and propped her chin on them as she lay forward, arching a provocative brow. She mused aloud, "I know you have a better way to awaken me, but since you can't seem to remember it, I guess I'll have to show you." With that she wiggled her hips against his middle and lowered her mouth to his in a searing kiss.

Buck growled as he wrapped his arms about her and tumbled her to the ground beneath him. When he released her mouth, he grinned down at her, his eyes glowing with desire. "Woman, I may be old, but I haven't forgotten the proper way to awaken a hot-blooded female."

"Hot-blooded female? You're the one who stays as randy as a horned toad." Clarice laughed up at him, her arms still looped about his neck.

"Where you're concerned, you could be right." Buck chuckled as he nuzzled her neck. "Hell, I know you're right," he murmured huskily, his bantering tone fading with his rising desire.

"Then show me," Clarice challenged, winding her fingers in his hair and drawing his head up so that she could taste his lips. He took up the gauntlet with passion.

The morning sun drenched their bodies with golden light as they sought and reached the paradise reserved only for lovers. Blissful and content, they then lay savoring their love beneath the moss-draped limbs of the tall Louisiana live oaks.

When their heartbeats slowed to normal, Buck raised himself on his elbows above Clarice and gave her a wry, mischievous grin. "Did that wake you up, woman?"

"I've no complaints about your methods." Clarice laughed. She wiggled from beneath him and reached for her clothing.

"I'm glad to hear it. I'd hate to have to go and practice on someone else until I learned to please you."

Clarice swatted him on the shoulder. "You know damned well that you please me, Buck Hunter. And I'd better not catch you ever looking at another woman. Once I was through with you you'd feel like you'd been hit by a Texas tornado."

"I'm not that brave," Buck said, and feigned a shiver of fear.

Clarice slipped on her clothing and knelt by him. She wrapped her arms about his neck and pressed a kiss on his stubbled cheek. "As long as I can keep you afraid of me, I guess we'll get along."

Buck chuckled and grabbed her about the waist to pull

her down into his lap, his body instantly responding once more to her nearness.

"Oh, no you don't. We have other things to do today." Clarice squirmed free of his arms and straightened her shirt. "Or have you forgotten why we've come this far?"

Buck buttoned his own shirt and cocked his head to one side, eyeing his wife wickedly. "I was just trying to keep in practice for our honeymoon."

"If it was left to you, all we'd do is practice." Clarice laughed as she pulled on her boots.

"You can't blame a man for trying," Buck said, and tweaked her nose before getting to his feet. "But I guess we'd better get this mess cleared up so we can concentrate on that honeymoon I promised you."

Her smile faded. "What will we do if we find that we can't clear Star of murdering her stepmother?"

Buck ran his hand through his hair and shook his head. "I don't know. Until we know all the facts about how things stand, all we can do is hope for the best."

Clarice stood and wrapped her arms about his lean waist. She rested her cheek against his chest. "I keep telling myself that everything will be all right, but I can't stop myself from worrying. If Tremayne has concocted enough evidence to make Star look guilty, I don't know how we will disprove it."

"We'll worry about that when the time comes, love," Buck said soothingly. "For now we need to break camp and reach Natchez before nightfall. Then we'll start unraveling this mess. If we don't learn anything from the local marshal, we'll ride to Planter's Landing tomorrow. Someone there will know all the gossip from Jasmine Hall. A murder isn't something that you can keep quiet, especially when it involves the owner of one of the richest plantations in the area."

"Buck, I love you so much. Few bridegrooms would be as understanding about this affair as you've been. I don't know what I would do without you."

"I want you to be as happy as I am, Clarice. Once we've settled this matter about your niece, then we can put the past behind us and look to our future. I hope Kyle and Star will do the same. I'd like to have some little 'uns to bounce on my knee. I missed too much of Kyle's youth and I don't intend to miss my grandchildren's."

"Grandpa Buck and Grandma Clarice," she mused aloud, and smiled. "It does have a nice ring to it, but it won't happen if those two stubborn mules we left at the ranch don't get together."

Buck grinned. "I think they're probably already together. My son takes after me in more than his looks. He won't be able to resist Star any more than I could resist her aunt."

"And if that niece of mine has any sense in that beautiful head of hers, she won't be foolish enough to waste twenty years like I did to grab him."

"I was well worth the wait, wasn't I?" Buck chuckled, holding her close.

"Like I said, I've no complaints. No complaints at all."

Buck dropped a light kiss on the top of her head and put her at arm's length from him. "Woman, we'll never make it to Natchez if you keep talking that way. Now get busy and fix your man some breakfast."

Clarice placed her hands on his shoulders and raised herself on tiptoes to brush her lips against his. She dodged his strong arms before he could recapture her and gave him a saucy smile as she strolled toward the campfire. "Remember, you want your breakfast and it doesn't come with dessert." She laughed, feeling young at heart and much lighter in spirit from having Buck's support in helping her niece.

The whistle of the paddleboat sounded in the distance to notify the residents of Planter's Landing of its arrival. Along the riverfront it signaled an end to the lazy afternoon for those who had merchandise to be shipped downriver to New Orleans. Bales of cotton and barrels of molasses were hauled by slaves from the warehouses to the docks to await the vessel's arrival.

Clarice took note of the activity on the docks as she and Buck rode into Planter's Landing. That much had not changed since the last time she had seen the land of her birth. Every year it was the same; during planting and harvesting season the docks were always a hive of activity.

Reining her mount to a halt in front of the mercantile store where a large sign proudly proclaimed "Smith's General Mercantile, prop. Jesse Evans Smith, Esq.," she glanced about her surroundings. The docks and warehouses were the only thing that had remained the same in Planter's Landing. When she'd left it over twenty years before, it had only been a stopping place for the paddlewheelers to pick up the planters' harvests or drop off the seeds and supplies for the plantations in the area. Now it boasted a hotel, a saloon, several haberdashers, and dress shops, as well as the mercantile store and livery. To her surprise there was even a small tea shop where the ladies in the area could refresh themselves while in town to shop.

Yes, much had changed since the independent, headstrong girl of eighteen had left everything she had ever known behind to follow Joe Kendall to the wilds of Texas. She remembered how she had held her head high when they boarded the paddlewheeler that would take them to Natchez where they would join the wagon train to Texas. She had been determined to show the world that she didn't care if they thought she was making a horrendous mistake by marrying a man they considered beneath her. She had loved Joe Kendall at that time almost as much as she loved Buck today. And she would not trade one of her experiences in Texas for a dozen Planter's Landings and the snobbery that existed in such places, where people judged others by what they had rather than by what they were.

The town had grown, but Clarice doubted that the minds of its inhabitants had grown with it. The elite plantation owners who controlled the economy also held sway over the politics. If they recognized the average ma~

their equal, they would be lessening the power of supremacy that they had built about themselves over the years. Those beliefs and her love for Joe had separated her completely from her family.

"You're wearing your thoughts on your sleeve," Buck said as he reached up to help Clarice dismount. "Are your memories painful?"

"Not really. Too many years have passed and so much has changed," Clarice said, and smiled as she slipped to the ground beside her husband.

"Well, I hope we learn more here than we did in Natchez," Buck said as he took her arm and they stepped upon planked sidewalk.

"Do you think we should question the sheriff?"

Buck shook his head. "I don't want to bring the authorities into this unless it's necessary. If Tremayne is playing a game, as I suspect, the sheriff might not even have been notified of the woman's death. From what we gleaned from the marshal in Natchez, my suspicions are proving true. There's something funny about all of this and I want to hear what the local gossips have to say before we contact the law. If we stir this thing up before we know all the facts, it might well go against Star. For now let's just act like we're looking for work."

"All right, we'll start by asking"—Clarice paused and looked up at the sign swaying over the door—"Mr. Jesse Evans Smith, Esq., if he knows where we might be able to find work."

"That a girl." Buck grinned, his face beaming with pride for his wife. She had more strength in her slim body than many men he had met. She was an intelligent woman who understood when to use discretion.

A brass bell over the door jingled as they entered. It alerted the clerk who was stocking the shelves behind the wide counter of their presence and he paused in his labors as they came forward. He wiped his hands on the white apron about his waist and smiled his greeting. "Good day to you. Is there something I can help you with?'' he asked as Buck left Clarice by the bolts of cloth stacked neatly on the shelves along one wall.

"I believe you might be able to help me and the little woman," Buck drawled.

"I'd be glad to. I can show you some of this material. It's just arrived all the way from New York and it's in the latest patterns," the clerk said, glancing at the woman clothed in britches and shirt. "I'm sure your wife would love a gown made from it."

"Naw, I'm afraid that's not the kind of help I'm a-needing. Me and the little woman just rode in from N'Orleans and we're looking for work. We'd heard that there was a plantation here called Jasmine Hall that had a new owner who was looking for an overseer who could manage his slaves," Buck drawled.

The clerk frowned and shook his head. "I'm sorry, I don't know anything about that. As far as I know, Mrs. Grayson hasn't sold Jasmine Hall."

"That's strange. We were told that the owner had died and the place had been sold."

The clerk screwed up his face thoughtfully and tapped at his chin with one finger. "Mr. Grayson did die some years ago, but his widow still has control of the place as far as I know. She was in here not too long ago and she didn't mention needing a new overseer." Glancing once more toward Clarice, he continued, "She bought several yards of that cream-colored lace and said it was as fine as any she'd found in Natchez or New Orleans."

"Then we've made the trip for nothing. I appreciate your help, but I guess all that's left for us to do is to head on up toward Natchez. Maybe we'll be lucky and find work there."

"Sorry I couldn't do more for you," the clerk said, turning back to the cans of peaches and putting the dust-stained travelers from his mind, since they weren't interested in purchasing any merchandise from him.

Buck sensed all of the questions brewing in Clarice's mind as he took her arm and led her from the store.

"We'll talk once we're out of town," he said as he un-tethered their horses and helped her to mount.

Clarice felt as if she would explode with curiosity as they rode out of Planter's Landing and headed north along the road to Natchez. When the town was several miles behind them, she jerked her horse to a halt. "You don't really intend to go back to Natchez, do you?"

Buck reined in his mount and folded his arms over the pommel of his saddle. A devilish grin touched his lips as he shook his head. "You didn't actually believe I would, did you? I only wanted to make sure everyone *thought* that was where we were going in the event that someone from Jasmine Hall came into town before we can find out what's going on out there. At this point I don't want anyone to know who we are or what we're doing in the area. There's too many things that don't fit with Star's story and the wanted poster."

"Then let's go to Jasmine Hall and see exactly what is going on."

"That was my intention all along, woman, but we can't go busting in like we own the place."

"I can and will. Jasmine Hall is my home and I'll be damned if I sneak around as if I have no right to be there."

"Hold on a minute, Clarice," Buck ordered, his voice stern. "We've come too far to ruin things now. If Tre-mayne is out there we have to go easy. The man could be dangerous."

"Buck, I've faced raiding Comanches, so I'm sure as hell not afraid of the likes of Brett Tremayne. Jasmine Hall belonged to my brother and is now my niece's in-heritance, and I won't stand by while she's convicted of a crime she didn't commit."

"I'm not asking you to do that, Clarice. All I want is to find out if anyone has died, in the first place. From what the clerk said, Star's stepmother came to his store recently. All of this could be a hoax to get Star back to Mississippi so Tremayne and her stepmother can force her to relinquish her claim to Jasmine Hall."

Clarice gaped at her husband, her eyes wide with surprise. "I hadn't thought of that." Her face lit with hope and she smiled. "I pray that you're right."

"It would certainly explain a few things," Buck said. "Now which way to Jasmine Hall?"

Memories of her childhood flooded Clarice's mind as she stood obscured by the thick foliage at the edge of the gardens, staring at Jasmine Hall. Each place her eyes rested elicited images she had not recalled since leaving this land. The years fled before the tide of recollections and she was again a young girl playing chase with her brother upon the neatly trimmed lawn while her mother rested on the veranda in a high-backed rocker, a gentle, loving smile curling her lips as she fanned herself with her favorite painted-silk fan and watched her children at play.

Clarice's gaze swept over the expanse of the two-storied mansion as she recalled the day she had been sent to her room for arguing with Charles over who was to ride their pony. A small smile briefly touched her lips. Charles, being the elder, had been allowed to have the ride while she had been reprimanded and sent to her room for her unladylike behavior. However, she had wreaked her vengeance on her brother. When he had returned from his ride, she had dumped the contents of her chamber pot over his head as he started up the steps to the veranda. She had been soundly spanked for her actions, but it had been worth it to see the look on Charles's face before he ran screaming to their parents to tattle.

Her gaze passed over the house to the gazebo where the honeysuckle vines made it a secluded arbor. There she had clandestinely met with Joe when he could find the time to slip away from his father's small farm to visit her. It had been there that she had learned how to love beyond the sweet, innocent kisses that she had received from her proper, boring yet acceptable gentlemen callers.

Her eyes moved over the hedges that edged the garden to the small plot of ground surrounded by a wrought-iron-spiked fence. A gentle ache formed in her breast as she looked at the grave markers where her family lay buried. None were left to call this land their home except one young woman. Those who rested beneath the sandy Mississippi loam had fought and worked too hard to pass the heritage of Jasmine Hall down to their heirs for her to let anyone steal it from her family.

Clarice frowned and turned to look at the tall man at her side. This land was no longer her home; her future lay with him on the Texas frontier, yet she owed it to those who had passed before her to do everything within her power to protect Jasmine Hall from people like Brett Tremayne.

Buck saw her frown and placed a comforting hand on her shoulder, giving it a gentle squeeze. He understood what she was feeling. This was the home of her youth and though her life was now in Texas, she was still bound to it with invisible ties. You could sever yourself from the land but not from the blood that flooded in your veins.

"Has it changed much?" he asked quietly.

Clarice shook her head. "No, Jasmine Hall is still as beautiful as I remembered."

"Do you think you'd ever want to come back?" Buck asked, already knowing her answer but wanting to let her know that his love for her would not change if she asked him to leave all that he knew behind to return to Jasmine Hall.

"No, my home is with you. I'm much more of a Texan now than a plantation belle. I could never be happy living this type of life again."

"Then it's time we got to the bottom of this and got back home," Buck said, and smiled widely.

"I couldn't agree with you more," Clarice answered as she slapped at a mosquito that had landed on her arm for a feast. "At least we don't have to put up with these pests at the ranch."

"You're right about that and I'm glad. I'd forgotten how much they enjoy my blood." Buck chuckled. He turned his gaze back to the white mansion sitting majestically amid the flowering gardens. "I think it's time we paid a visit to those living at Jasmine Hall."

Clarice and Buck stealthily made their way back through the woods to the road where they had tethered their horses. Mounting, they rode up the sandy drive as if they had been invited for tea. They left their horses with a small black stableboy and marched boldly up to the front door and knocked.

"I'm here to see Mr. Tremayne," Buck announced to the young black woman who answered the door.

"Master Tremayne ain't here, sir," she said, her dark gaze sweeping over the two dusty travelers. Taking in their attire and knowing from it that they were not local gentry, she did not invite them inside.

"When will Mr. Tremayne be back? He told me to come to Jasmine Hall as soon as we arrived in Planter's Landing," Buck lied, and watched as the young woman frowned.

"I don't rightly know when Master Tremayne will be back. He be gone now going on two weeks."

"Then who should I see about the position as overseer?"

"That be Miz Fiona, but she's resting now, so you'll have to come back later," the maid said, and started to close the door.

Buck braced his hand against it, impeding her efforts. "Mrs. Fiona Grayson?"

"That's right, sir. She the one you'll have to see. She the one who runs Jasmine Hall and not Master Tremayne," she answered, and again tried to close the door on Buck as an irritated female voice came from the drawing room.

"Who is it, Elsie?"

"It's some man who says Master Tremayne asked him to come here to see 'bout the job of overseer."

"Tell him there's been a mistake. We already have an overseer at Jasmine Hall and I have no time to waste speaking with him since the position is already filled."

"You heard Miz Fiona, sir. Now good day to you."

The maid closed the door, leaving Buck and Clarice on the veranda.

"That hussy," Clarice growled, and made for the door. Her hand was already on the brass knocker when Buck captured it with his own, thwarting her efforts.

"That's enough, Clarice. We've learned what we wanted to know."

"Enough? Not by a long shot. I intend to march in there and pull every hair from that witch's head for the hell she's put Star through. My niece fled from her home, lived through a cholera epidemic, and chanced being killed by Comanches to reach me and it was all because of the greed of that bitch and her lover. I have a good mind to forget about pulling her hair out and just blow her head off. That would rid the world of at least one varmint."

"Calm down, woman!" Buck ordered. "For now you're not going to do a damned thing. We're going back to the ranch and tell Star what we've learned and let her decide what to do about her stepmother. She's the only one who has any rights here. If we interfere we'll end up in jail ourselves. We've done what we set out to do. We've cleared Star of murder and now it's up to her." Buck took Clarice's arm and propelled her back down the veranda steps and across the drive toward the horses.

"Hellfire, Buck! We should at least try to find Tremayne. Star can handle Fiona, but that man is a different matter altogether. He's the one who set the bounty hunter on Star." Clarice came to an abrupt halt, her lined face draining of color as her heart began to pound with fear. "My God. The man knows Star was in DryCreek and he can easily find out that she's at the Bar H. If he's been gone for two weeks, he may have already found her. We have to get back to the ranch and warn Star before he uses the fake murder charge to force her to come back to Mississippi with him. If that happens, I don't know what he'll do to her to force her to give him Jasmine Hall."

"Then we'll have to make sure that doesn't happen," Buck said as he untethered the horses and helped Clarice to mount. He gave her leg a reassuring pat. "Don't worry. Star is with Kyle and he won't let that scoundrel harm her even if Tremayne shows up at the ranch. If he tries, he'll wish he had been turned over to the Comanches before my son gets through with him."

"I'm grateful for that at least. I know how Kyle feels about Star and she'll be safe as long as she's with him."

"It's going to be fine, Clarice. Now that we know that there is no murder charge hanging over Star's head, we shouldn't have any trouble dealing with Tremayne and Miz Grayson," Buck drawled, imitating the maid's southern accent.

"I know you're right, but I won't be satisfied until we're back at the ranch and I see that no harm has come to Star."

"Then what are we waiting for? We're never going to get down to the serious business of our honeymoon if we don't finally end this thing with your niece."

Clarice's face softened as she looked at her husband. "You'll never know how much I love you, Buck Hunter."

"Then you'll have to try to show me, won't you?" Buck said. He gave her a rakish grin as he spurred his horse and they set off back in the direction of Planter's Landing, where they would take a ferry across the river to Louisiana.

Brett lounged in the straight-backed saloon chair and sipped at his glass of whiskey. His appearance little resembled the Natchez dandy who was so finicky with his attire. His once immaculate white shirt was drab with sweat and dust. His expensive boots were no longer polished to a high shine but were scuffed from the days he'd spent on the trail. A reddish stubble of beard contrasted sharply with his blond hair yet blended with his sunburned complexion. Unused to the heat, his lips were parched and cracked and he winced slightly at the sting from the alcohol when the whiskey touched them. Wiping his mouth with the back of his hand, he set the glass down and eyed the man across from him.

"Now that you've dragged me to this godforsaken place, I hope you've come up with a few answers, Jarvis," he ground out, his mood black from his rumpled state as well as his irritation with the bounty hunter.

Reed Jarvis downed the whiskey in his glass as if it were water and poured himself another drink from the bottle on the table before him. Downing it, he belched and smiled. "I think we've hit the jackpot."

"What did you learn?" Brett asked, leaning forward, his eyes lighting with interest.

"She's here," Jarvis replied calmly. Refilling his glass, he leaned back in his chair.

"I'm in no mood for guessing games, Jarvis," Brett growled. "Where in the hell is she?"

Jarvis took a long, slow sip of whiskey. "I don't rightly know at the moment."

"What in the hell do you mean, you don't rightly know? I'm paying you to know."

"Don't get yourself all fired up, Tremayne. I ain't wasting your money. We're supposed to meet a Mrs. Victoria Crawford outside of town at three this afternoon and she said she'd take us out to where your girl is staying."

"Who in hell is this Crawford woman and why would she want to help us?" Brett asked suspiciously.

"All I know about her is that she's married to the man who owns the mercantile store. When I started asking if anyone knew of Star Grayson's whereabouts, she was the only one who seemed to know anything about her. From what I gathered, she don't like your girl any more than you do, but she wouldn't say much with her husband around. She said she'd meet us this afternoon but only if we agreed to let her go with us when I arrested Star."

Brett relaxed back in his chair and took out his pocket watch. He flipped open the gold cover and eyed the delicately wrought hands that pointed to the Roman numerals. "We have thirty minutes till it's time to meet her."

"Yep. Just enough time for a few more drinks," Jarvis

said. He downed the whiskey in his glass and then re-filled it.

"You've had enough, Jarvis. I don't want you reeling drunk when we ride out to get Star. If you'll remember, you're supposed to be the marshal from Fort Worth."

"I ain't forgot nothing, so get off my back, Tremayne. I'll do the job you're paying me to do."

"Jarvis, I'm warning you. You've nearly ruined everything for me twice already and I won't stand any more of your blunders. Because of your drinking, you nearly killed the hotel clerk in DryCreek."

"Listen, Tremayne. I got the information you wanted, didn't I?" Jarvis said. He patted the gun at his side. "Me and old Betsy here know our job and we do it. The man didn't know where the girl had up and gone to, but he did tell us that her aunt had moved on to Sagebrush."

"You got the information, but you damned well could have gotten us thrown into jail. If we hadn't ridden out of DryCreek before the old man could contact the sheriff, we'd be behind bars for the beating you gave him in your drunken fit of temper."

Jarvis cast Brett a surly look as he raised the glass to his lips once more. He belched loudly and leaned back in his chair, his hand resting on the pistol at his side. "Tremayne, I'm about damned tired of your high-falutin' manner. If you don't like the way I do things, then pay me what you owe me and we'll call it quits. You can go and get the girl on your own."

Brett's sunburned face flushed a deeper hue of red as he eyed Reed Jarvis angrily. The man knew that he was an invaluable part of Brett's plans and if he didn't masquerade as the marshal from Fort Worth they would not succeed. It galled Brett to have to back down to the bounty hunter. However, if that's what it would take to get his hands on Star's fortune, then he would do it.

"Jarvis, I don't give a damn how you do your job. I just don't want the law to get involved. There's too much at stake."

Jarvis hitched up the waist of his britches and smiled

triumphantly. "Then keep your damned mouth shut in the future. Now if you want to get that little gal you're all fired up about, we'd better get a move on."

Brett thought he would choke on his rage. His pale eyes glittered with malice as he came to his feet, silently vowing to see Reed Jarvis dead once he had his hands on Star. No man talked to Brett Tremayne in that manner and got away with it. Jarvis would be no exception. With eyes narrowed, Brett glared at the bounty hunter's back as he walked through the swinging saloon doors. It will be a pleasure to put an end to that swine's life, he mused as he followed in Jarvis's wake.

Chapter 15

The afternoon was golden. It was one of those rare afternoons that was hot but not uncomfortable. A gentle, cooling breeze caressed the landscape and relieved the intense summer heat. It stirred the tawny prairie grass and the feathery dark green leaves of the mesquites that shaded Star as she sat enjoying the quiet that had settled over the ranch since Kyle and his men had driven the cattle north to Fort Belnap.

Relaxing back against the bole of the tree, she rested her head against its grayish-brown bark and closed her eyes to savor the languid euphoria she still felt from the time she had spent with the man she loved. She hugged herself and gave a contented sigh. The warm glow of their lovemaking surrounded her with its radiant veil even now, and she treasured the feeling.

It was still hard for her to believe the happiness she had found. The past two days and nights had been filled with enchantment. Kyle had postponed the drive until he could no longer avoid it if he wanted to make the delivery date for the army. During that time they had spent every moment together, enjoying the glory of their newfound love and sating themselves with their lovemaking.

Star peered through her lashes at the ranch house, remembering the sweet kiss Kyle had given her before he joined his men. It had held a promise of their future together, a promise that he had spoken aloud in the early morning hours as they lay with naked bodies pressed together. He had asked her to marry him as soon as he returned from Fort Belnap and without a thought for her past or what might lie in her future, she had accepted his proposal. At that moment nothing had mattered to her beyond the love they shared.

Her smile of contentment faded and the tranquil feeling she had experienced the moment before dimmed as she considered the commitment she had made to Kyle. She had been so wrapped up in joy that she had recklessly made him a promise that she could not keep until she was honest with him about her past. She knew the chance she would be taking when she told him the truth, but she realized that she loved him too much to let any barrier stand between them and the happiness they could share. Lies had a way of spawning more deceit, and no love, no matter how strong, could withstand such a burden for long. It was best to confess her duplicity and pray that his love for her would allow him to forgive her.

"I'll tell him as soon as he returns," Star murmured to the quiet afternoon, feeling suddenly as if a great weight had been lifted from her shoulders with her decision. Getting to her feet, she squared her shoulders and raised her chin in the air, defying the fates to deny her the happiness she sought. She drew in a deep breath and smiled, her spirits buoyed by her resolution to put an end to all of the lies that lay between herself and Kyle. Feeling as if she had finally grown up, she held her head high as she strode back to the ranch house and stepped up onto the planked porch.

"I'm guilty of no crime except foolishly becoming infatuated with the wrong man and then lying to protect myself from him," she said. She raised her face to the golden sun streaming in across the porch. "And I'm tired of being a coward," she murmured, her voice firm as she relinquished the last of her fear of destroying Kyle's love by revealing the truth. She was no longer a young frightened girl but a woman, and it was time she faced life again instead of running away from it. If she was to continue to have Kyle's love, she had to be willing to fight for it. And she was.

The sound of approaching horses interrupted Star's introspection and she looked up to see three riders approaching the gates of the Bar H. Her heart seemed to stop within her breast as she recognized two of them, Brett Tremayne and Victoria Crawford. The first thought to cross her mind was to flee, but her new resolve stayed her. She would not run away again.

Standing straight and proud, she watched as the three riders reined in their mounts before the house. She did not speak as they dismounted and tethered their horses to the hitching post. When Brett turned and started to come forward, she ordered, "That's far enough, Brett Tremayne. You and your friends are not welcome here."

"Is that any way to welcome your betrothed, Star?" Brett asked as he strode toward her.

"As you damned well know, you're not my betrothed. I made that clear to you at Jasmine Hall."

"I suspected that you'd feel that way. That's why I brought Mr. Jarvis along."

"I don't really give a damn whom you brought with you. I won't be forced into a marriage with a man that I loathe. If that was your plan, then you've made a long journey for nothing."

"My dear Star," Brett drawled sweetly. "I have no intention of trying to force you to marry me. That's not the reason I've come all this way."

"Then what do you want, Brett?"

"Me?" Brett said, placing one hand against his chest. "I want nothing more than to see justice done. That's the only reason I'm here. I'm sure that's also the reason Mrs. Crawford accompanied us today. Being a good, upstanding, law-abiding citizen, she thought it her duty to rid her town of a murderess."

Star paled as her gaze swept past Brett to Victoria and to the man Brett had called Jarvis. "Then all of you have come here for nothing. You know as well as I do that I'm innocent of Fiona's death."

"I'm not the one you have to convince, Star. The courts will have to decide about your innocence. That's why Mr. Jarvis, or should I say, Marshal Jarvis, is here."

"Marshal Jarvis," Star breathed, unaware that she spoke aloud as she looked at the man who walked toward her. A memory niggled at the back of her mind as she took in his beefy frame, but before she could call it forth, he stopped at the foot of the steps leading up to the porch.

"Yes, Miss Grayson. I'm the marshal from Fort Worth," Jarvis said as he reached into his pocket and withdrew a sheet of paper. He unfolded it. "This is a warrant for your arrest for the murder of Fiona Grayson of Jasmine Hall plantation, in Mississippi. I'm here to take you back to stand trial."

"But I'm innocent. Fiona's death was an accident. Brett knows the truth. He saw it happen. She fell down the stairs; I didn't push her," Star said as her heart began to beat frantically against her ribs.

"I'm sorry, Miss Grayson, but that's not what we've been told. Now if you will come along peaceably, there will be no reason to tie you to your horse."

"I won't go with you. I've done nothing wrong," Star said, shaking her head.

"You'll only be making it hard on yourself, my dear," Brett said, smiling his satisfaction. "The marshal is here to do his duty and nothing you can say or do will stop him." Brett could hardly suppress his glee at Jarvis's performance. If he hadn't known better, the man would have convinced *him* that he was in fact a marshal.

"Tell him, Brett. Tell him the truth. You know I didn't murder Fiona," Star demanded, turning to Brett, her eyes flashing with ire.

"I don't know what you're talking about, Star. I only came here to identify you, not to plead your innocence to the marshal."

"Damn you to hell, you lying bastard," Star spat. She raised her hand and struck Brett across the face with all the force she could muster.

Brett's head snapped back from the blow and he

grabbed his cheek. His eyes glittered with malice as he rubbed his stinging flesh. "Bitch, you'll pay for that once I get you away from here," he growled in a low voice that only Star could hear.

"Here now, Miss Grayson. Control yourself," Jarvis ordered as he withdrew the pistol from the holster at his side and aimed it at her. "I had hoped you'd see reason so this wouldn't be necessary to get you to come along peaceably but I see now that it will be."

Star glanced from Brett to the evil-looking gun pointed directly at her and then to Victoria, who stood watching the scene with a smug smile playing about her red lips. "Victoria, are you going to let them take me when I'm innocent of what they claim?"

"Of course," came her calm reply. "I certainly have no intention of interfering with justice. And I'll be glad to see you gone from here. When Kyle learns of your arrest, he'll thank me for helping the marshal and Mr. Tremayne get you out of his life." She licked her lips.

"You're wrong, Victoria. Kyle will never thank you for letting the woman he loves die for a crime she didn't commit."

"Kyle doesn't love you, you little fool. He's only been playing with you," Victoria snarled, jealousy ripping away her composure. She wanted to hurt Star as much as her pride had been hurt by Kyle's rejection. "But don't feel too bad for believing he loved you. You're not the first one to be taken in by his lies. I also believed him when he told me he loved me. Fortunately, I found a man who loves me enough to accept the fact that I was deceived out of my innocence by a heartless rogue who cares for no one but himself."

"I don't believe you," Star said. Her voice was firm, but Victoria's words had shaken her. She had also had similar thoughts about Kyle in the past. It had only been during the last two days that she had spent in his arms that had convinced her that he could love.

"Believe what you want. It doesn't matter to me one way or the other. But if you think Kyle will come rushing to your rescue, then you're sadly mistaken. He'll consider you another notch on his belt and move on to his next gullible little virgin.''

Brett's face hardened as he listened to the exchange between the two women. His pale eyes glittered with rage. Star had been meant for him and he would not forgive her for giving herself to another man. Once she was his wife, she would pay dearly for her wanton behavior. Yet when he spoke his voice was pleasantly soft, revealing none of his ire. "So, my dear little Star, you're no longer the innocent I thought you."

"That's none of your damned business," Star spat, her eyes flashing him a look of contempt.

"You may change your mind about that in the near future," Brett said smoothly as he reached out and took her arm. "You may need my help to keep the hangman's noose from around your lovely neck."

Star shot him a look of disgust as she strained against his grasp but found she could not free herself. "I'd rather die first."

"You may get your wish if the marshal has his way," Brett growled, and gave her arm a brutal squeeze before he thrust her down the steps before him.

"I won't go with you," Star squealed in protest as she dug her heels into the ground.

"What's going on here?" Lucas Brown said as he strode around the corner of the house and came to an abrupt halt at the sight of Star struggling against the blond-haired man, while another trained his pistol on her.

"Lucas, don't let them take me," Star cried as she again tried to twist free of Brett's hold.

"Let her go," the foreman ordered, "and get the hell off the Bar H before I have you shot for trespassing." Unarmed, there was little more that he could do or say.

"Stay out of this, mister," Jarvis ordered. "I'm the law and this here woman is under arrest for murder."

"I don't believe you."

"Then look at this," Jarvis said, and handed the foreman the wanted poster with Star's likeness.

Lucas scanned the paper, able to make out but a few words written on it. He had never learned to read but for a few simple words and his name.

However, he did recognize Star's image.

From the foreman's puzzled frown, Jarvis guessed his secret and thrust a forged document at him. "And this is a warrant for her arrest."

Bewildered as to what he should do, Lucas tipped his hat back and scratched his head. He looked from the paper in his hand to Star. "Miss, I can't interfere with the law."

"For the love of God, Lucas. You can't let them take me," Star pleaded.

"I wouldn't listen to her if I was you, unless you want to wind up an accessory to murder. You'd find yourself in jail along with her," Jarvis threatened. "The thing for you to do is to saddle her a horse so we can be on our way."

"It don't look like I have much choice," the foreman said as he gave a sad shake of his head. He looked at Star and tried to give her an encouraging smile. "When Kyle comes back from Fort Belnap, he'll see that this mess is straightened out, miss. You can count on that."

I wish I could believe that, Star mused sadly to herself as she watched the foreman walk resignedly toward the barn to saddle her a horse. Victoria's words gnawed away at her confidence in Kyle's love for her. He might have stood by her if she had told him the truth, but when he returned and found her gone and Lucas told him the reason, he would not come after her. In that Victoria had been right.

A few minutes later, Lucas returned with her mount and helped her into the saddle. She had no personal possessions to take with her except the gown on her back. She had shared her aunt's meager wardrobe since Buck had brought her to the ranch so precipitously, leaving all of her clothing in DryCreek.

"Good luck, miss," Lucas said as he looked apologetically up at her. "Don't worry. Everything will work out."

"Lucas, please tell Kyle that I'm innocent of any crimes and that I love him."

Lucas nodded and turned away.

"We ain't got all day. We've wasted enough time already. I want to get a good start back to Mississippi," Jarvis said as he swung up into the saddle and glanced over his shoulder at Star. "Now if you know what's good for you, you won't cause any more trouble." He bent and grabbed the reins of her mount and with a jerk, led it forward behind his own mount.

Tears clogged Star's throat as they passed under the swinging sign branded with the symbol Bar H. She glanced up at it before looking back at the weathered ranch house where she had found such love and happiness with Kyle. Their time together had been brief, but she would treasure every moment and memory of it for as long as she lived.

Brett's temper simmered anew at Star's forlorn expression. It galled him to know that she grieved not because she was being arrested for murder but for another man. Giving the reins a sharp jerk, he urged his horse alongside Star's mount.

"You might as well accept the fact that your little dalliance is over. If I were you, I'd start contemplating a way to try to save my neck. You heard what Victoria said about your lover. You're only one among many and he'll have forgotten all about you by the time we reach Mississippi. I'm the only person who can help you now."

Star's eyes were cold with hatred as she turned them on Brett and gave a harsh little laugh. "Did you ever stop to think that if what she said is true, I might not want to be saved?"

"You'll change your mind when you feel the rope about your neck. Your love of life will be much stronger than your love for the Texan. I can guarantee that, Star. No one wants to die."

"Don't be so certain. In all of your scheming, did you

consider the fact that to thwart your plans I might prefer
the hangman's noose if it was the only way I could be
sure that you'd not get your hands on Jasmine Hall? At
my death, the property will go to my nearest living relative and that is my aunt.''

"At least I'll have had my revenge.''

"True, but that's all you'll have. For such a greedy
man, you've gone to a great deal of trouble for a little
revenge.''

"You can be assured that I'll have much more, Star,"
Brett said. He gave her an enigmatic smile and turned
his attention to the woman who rode on his other side.

Star kept her eyes trained straight ahead and tried to
ignore Brett and Victoria as they chatted together like
old friends out for a leisurely ride instead of two people
who had been drawn together because of their vendettas
against her. They discussed the latest fashions that had
arrived in Natchez before Brett had left, as well as other
trival matters that Victoria, like most women living on
the frontier, was starved to hear. By the time they reached
the fork in the road that would take them east toward the
Brazos and Victoria south to Sagebrush, Star felt as if
she would scream. Her entire world was crumbling about
her and to add to her torment she had to listen to their
mindless chitchat. She wanted to be left alone to try to
sort out everything that had happened. She needed time
to think. It would take all of her ingenuity to find a way
to thwart Brett's scheme to see her married or hanged.

She was relieved when Brett and Victoria exchanged
pleasant farewells and the woman turned her mount south
toward Sagebrush. However, Victoria rode only a short
distance before reining her horse in and turning in the
saddle to look back at Star. She smiled sweetly.

"I'll ride out to the Bar H to give Kyle my condolences
after you're hanged. I'm sure Mr. Tremayne will be kind
enough to write and tell me that he has seen to it that
justice has been served.''

"I'm sure Mr. Tremayne would gladly do so if he had
money enough to post a letter when his creditors are

through with him," Star returned sweetly. "But if I were
you, Victoria, I wouldn't expect it. As for your condolences to Kyle, I'd advise you to stay as far away from his
ranch as possible when he learns of the part you played
in this day's farce. It would be in your best interest."
Star spoke calmly, her voice reflecting none of the ire
that twisted her insides into knots. She'd not give Victoria the satisfaction of knowing that her catty remarks had
any effect on her.

"Bitch, it will be a cold day in a hot place before I
heed your advice," Victoria spat. She spurred the bay
mare in the side and set it galloping toward Sagebrush.

"From now on, keep your mouth shut or I'll shut it
for you," Brett growled, infuriated by her references to
his financial status. He wanted no one, especially Jarvis,
to know that he didn't have a cent to his name beyond
the meager amount Fiona had given him to finance bringing Star back to Mississippi.

Star turned her icy gaze on him. "I'm not afraid of
you, Brett. The only thing I've left to lose is my life and
you've already made it clear to me that you intend to see
me hanged. You're also too much of a coward to kill me
with Marshal Jarvis nearby. You'd be putting the noose
about your own neck if you harmed me."

Brett's eyes glittered with malice as he leaned across
the space separating them and gripped her hand with
bruising force. "I wouldn't be so sure if I were you, Star.
I can make you wish you were dead many times before
we reach Mississippi and Jarvis won't say a word to stop
me."

The streak of Grayson stubbornness Star had inherited
from her father came to her aid, refusing to let her cringe
under the bone-crushing pressure of his hand. A whim-
per of pain rose in her throat, but she swallowed it back,
determined not to show any sign of weakness in front of
Brett. She might not have long to live if he succeeded
with his plans but while there was a breath in her body,
she'd never cower again. She'd endured too much because of him and she'd not give him the satisfaction of

watching her suffer. Staring at him through narrowed lashes, she impaled him with her cold gaze until he grew uncomfortable and released her hand.

"You'll come round before I'm through with you," he muttered before spurring his mount and galloping ahead of Jarvis, who sat smirking at her.

"Little lady, I'd suggest you mind your manners where Tremayne is concerned. He has an ornery temper that won't stand much defiance."

"It's your job to see that I get safely back to Mississippi to stand trial," Star said, hiding her aching hand beneath the folds of her skirt and wiggling her fingers to regain the circulation that Brett's harsh grip had cut off.

Jarvis untied the strings on his saddlebag and raised the leather flap. He withdrew a bottle of whiskey and uncorked it. He eyed Star indifferently as he took a long swallow of the fiery liquid. Giving a loud belch, he wiped his mouth with the back of his hand.

"Little lady, I do the job I'm paid to do and that's all. What happens between you and Tree-mayne ain't none of my affair."

"What do you mean?" Star asked, an uneasy feeling creeping up her spine.

"Just what I said," Jarvis replied as he raised the bottle to his lips again. His beefy features flushed a darker hue as the whiskey burned down his throat.

Star watched Jarvis replace the bottle in his saddlebag. She'd had no experience with the law in the past, but she sensed by the way he casually guzzled down whiskey that he was not whom he claimed to be. Her gaze passed over the beet-faced Jarvis to the man riding ahead of them. Brett Tremayne was a devious man and it wouldn't be beyond him to pay Jarvis to pose as a lawman to get her back to Mississippi where he could try to force her to relinquish her rights to Jasmine Hall. Star's suspicious gaze shifted back to Jarvis. She'd been too shaken by Brett's sudden appearance at the ranch to take time to read the warrant for her arrest and had foolishly believed everything they had told her without question.

"Marshal, can I see my arrest warrant?" Star asked, and watched Jarvis shift uncomfortably in the saddle.

"There ain't no need of that, Little lady," he stuttered, glancing nervously in Brett's direction.

"It's my right to know what crime I'm being charged with."

"Just take my word on it. You're under arrest for the murder of your stepmama."

Star jerked her horse to a halt. "Until I see the warrant I'm not going any farther."

Jarvis's puffy features hardened as he swung about to face her. "You'll do exactly as you're told," he growled as he withdrew his pistol from its holster and aimed it at her. "I ain't never shot a woman before, but there's always a first time for everything. Now get moving."

Star's throat went dry as she looked down the barrel of the gun, but she made no effort to obey. "You don't have a warrant for my arrest, do you?"

"As I see it, that don't make a bit of difference now. You're going to do what I tell you or you won't live to regret it. I'm being paid to take you back to Mississippi and that's what I intend to do."

"You're not a marshal, are you? You're working for Brett, aren't you?" Star asked, once more experiencing the sensation that there was something of importance that she should remember.

Jarvis grinned, revealing the gap between his teeth. "So you've finally figured that out, have you? Tremayne didn't think you'd be smart enough to see through his little plan."

Jarvis had confirmed her suspicions, but before she could grasp the full significance of what she had learned, Brett reined his mount in beside her.

"What in hell is the hold-up, Jarvis? You know I want to put as many miles between us and Sagebrush as possible before we have to make camp for the night," he growled, anger flushing his sunburned face scarlet.

"It seems your little lady here has come to the conclusion that I'm not a real lawman."

"I hope you convinced her that you are, Marshal."

"I'm not the gullible young girl that I was when I thought you loved me, Brett. During the last months I've been forced to grow up," Star said before Jarvis could reply.

"You might have matured a bit, but that doesn't change the situation," Brett said, a muscle working in his stubbled cheek.

"I think it does, Brett, because I'm not going with you."

"You're going with me, Star, because you're still wanted for murder."

Star felt suddenly light-headed as the truth behind Brett's scheme dawned on her. If she was wanted for murder, he would not have had to go to such extreme measures. She smiled and shook her head. "I see through all of your lies. I'm not now, nor have I ever been, wanted for murder, or you would not have had to pay Jarvis to pose as a lawman to get me back to Mississippi."

Jarvis chuckled as he reholstered his pistol and reached for the bottle of whiskey in his saddlebag. "It seems she'd got more brains in that pretty head than you gave her credit for, Tree-mayne. She's already figured out that her stepmama is still alive and kicking."

Stunned, Star gaped at Brett. "Fiona is alive?"

Brett ignored her question and turned furiously to Jarvis. "Shut your drunken mouth."

"I ain't taking anymore of your orders," Jarvis growled as he tossed the reins of Star's horse to Brett and uncorked the bottle with his snaggled teeth. He spat the cork on the ground before downing the last of the whiskey. Licking his lips, he tossed the bottle away and eyed Brett hostilely. "As far as I'm concerned it's your problem now. Pay me what you owe me and we'll call it quits, Tree-mayne."

"I'll give you what you've deserved ever since you fouled up your first attempt to bring Star back to Mississippi." Brett reached inside his coat and withdrew a small derringer. He aimed it between Jarvis's eyes and pulled the trigger before the other man realized his intentions. The impact shattered the bounty hunter's skull and knocked him from the saddle to land facedown in the dirt.

Shaken, Star squeezed her eyes tightly shut against the grisly sight. Nausea churned her stomach and she drew in a trembling breath to try to quell it.

"Now I suggest you don't give me any more trouble or you'll end up like Jarvis. I don't let anyone cross me and get away with it," Brett said calmly as he reloaded the derringer and dropped it back into his pocket.

Star kept her gaze averted from the grisly form on the ground as she raised her eyes to Brett's. Tension twisted her insides, yet she knew if she showed any sign of weakness it would only add to her dilemma. Like all madmen, Brett drew his strength from those who were not strong enough to fight against him. Her only chance to save herself was to make him believe that she was not afraid of him. "You've no hold over me, Brett."

For a long, nerve-rending moment, Brett appraised her coolly. Then he relaxed back in the saddle, a confident smirk playing over his lips. "Jarvis forgot one thing, Star. I'm a gambler and I always have an extra card to play. I wouldn't have survived this long if I didn't keep an ace up my sleeve to use when things are going against me."

"Your gambler's luck has finally deserted you. My stepmother's death was the only thing you had to use against me. I know you can kill me as easily as you murdered Jarvis, but if you do, you'll still lose."

"I have no intention of killing you, Star. However, if you don't come with me, poor Dulcie's fate will not be pleasant."

"You're bluffing, Brett."

"Believe what you will, my dear, but you're risking your maid's life if you think to call my hand."

Star's heart began to thump uncomfortably against her ribs at the confidence she heard in his voice. The blood slowly drained from her face and she had to swallow several times before she could speak over the lump of fear that constricted her throat. "What do you mean?"

Brett gave her a calculating look. "Exactly what I said. Your beloved maid did not make her escape the night you fled from Jasmine Hall. The hounds tracked her to the hut in the swamp where the old witch lived."

"Lived?" Star asked.

"Unlike your maid, the old woman didn't survive my questioning. If her heart hadn't given out on her, she could have kept Dulcie company."

Obioma, I didn't mean for you to be harmed, Star grieved silently as she looked at Brett and felt an urge to kill the beast who had ended the life of an old woman who had only lived to help others. However, Star suppressed the urge. She had to think of the living. "Where is Dulcie?"

"Safely out of harm's way unless you decide her life means nothing to you. If that is your choice, then I can assure you that her demise will be slow and painful."

Unable to look into his malicious face any longer, Star closed her eyes. Now she again had to make a choice, when in fact there was none to be made. It was Dulcie's life or her own happiness and she knew she could not let her friend die, as Obioma had, because of her own selfish needs. Brett would not hesitate to carry out his threat if she refused to go with him.

Anger and frustration flushed Star's cheeks. She had no recourse but to give in to his demands. "You win. You can have it all. When we arrive at Jasmine Hall and I see that Dulcie is unharmed, I'll sign it over to you and then I pray to God that I'll never see your vile face again for as long as I live."

"Your prayers will go unanswered, my dear. We were betrothed before you chose to run away and take up with the blasted Texan. You may be soiled, but I intend to see that our marriage takes place. As I told you, I don't like to be crossed."

"You can have Jasmine Hall, but I won't marry you, Brett. I loathe you."

"I think you will if you care about that black hussy's life."

Bitter tears brimmed in Star's eyes as a wave of futility washed over her. She had come full circle. She was again faced with the same threat that had made her flee everything she loved, but now it was not only her life and future at stake but Dulcie's as well.

Impotent fury welled in Star's breast at her own inability to stop Brett from using her and those she loved to gain his evil desires. She knew at the present moment she had no alternative but to do as he demanded, yet she vowed she would not accept defeat meekly. To save Dulcie she would pretend to submit to his wishes, but she would never stop searching for a means to extricate herself from the web he had woven about her. She would seek it for as long as she lived. She suspected that would not be long once they were married. He would kill her when she refused to be his wife in every way.

Unless I kill him first, Star mused vindictively as she glared at him through narrowed eyes. Until today she had never considered taking another human life, but now she discovered she would feel no guilt at ending his vile existence if she was given the opportunity. He was an animal who thought nothing of destroying people's lives to appease his own greed. He was far worse than the savages who had raided the Kendall homestead. The Comanches fought for the land they had claimed as their own for centuries, not out of avarice. She could understand their reasons though she didn't condone their brutality toward those they thought encroached upon their domain. In comparison to Brett Tremayne, the Indians seemed noble.

Star's heart filled with a deadly, cold rancor. In the past she had thought she'd felt hatred but until now she had not truly known what the word meant. Now she knew in full measure. She hated Brett Tremayne with every fiber in her body.

"Star, I'm waiting for your answer," Brett said, shifting uneasily in his saddle under her direct, piercing stare.

"I'll do as you ask," Star replied, a mutinous light glowing in the blue depths of her eyes.

"I thought you would finally see reason." Brett smiled. "We'll do well together, Star," he murmured as he reached out to run a caressing finger along the smooth line of her cheek.

Star jerked away from his hand. "Don't touch me, Brett. I'm warning you. If you lay as much as a finger on me before we're married, I promise that you'll regret it."

Brett's face tightened with annoyance. "If you think your paltry threats will stop me from having you, then you are mistaken, Star. I can do with you as I want."

"But you have to remember that you'll get nothing if I die," Star said, her face set with resolution. "And I will die before I'll submit to you. I've agreed to your terms to save Dulcie, but not even my love for my friend will make me submit to your touch before we're married. I will die fighting before I'll let you degrade me."

Brett considered her thoughtfully for a long moment before he smiled coldly. "I can wait until our vows are said, but I promise you that on our wedding night you'll regret it. You'll also rue the fact that you've acted the slut with that Texan instead of coming to my bed as the virgin to whom I was betrothed."

"I'll never regret my love for Kyle, no matter what you do to me."

A sneer curled Brett's lips. "I think you will by the time I'm through with you, my haughty bitch," he growled. Gathering the reins to Jarvis's mount, he wheeled back around and gave Star's horse a sharp kick in the side. The actions startled the animal and it shied, nearly unseating her. Brett laughed over his shoulder at her distress and urged the horses into a fast gallop.

Regaining her balance, Star glanced back at the figure sprawled behind them in the dirt. Vultures were already circling overhead, waiting to swoop down and devour the unfortunate remains. Star felt ill at the thought. She hadn't liked Jarvis, but he had not deserved such a fate.

"Brett, you can't leave him like that," she shouted over the sound of the pounding hooves.

Without slackening their pace, he glanced back at her. "I can and will. I don't have time to waste burying the bastard because of his bungling the job I paid him to do in the first place. If he'd brought you back when he tracked you down to DryCreek, I wouldn't be so pressed for time. Everything would have already been settled with my creditors."

The memory that had been suppressed by all that had transpired since Brett's arrival at the Bar H now came blindingly to light in Star's mind. Jarvis had been the man who had accosted her in the café in DryCreek and who had tried to kidnap her before Buck had stepped in. If she had only recognized him at the ranch, she might not be on her way back to Mississippi.

No, Star reflected sadly. That was not true. She would still be with Brett because he held Dulcie's fate in the palm of his hand.

Her heart might cry out for Kyle and the love they had shared for such a brief and beautiful time, but she knew she would remain with Brett until Dulcie was safe. Once she was assured of that, she would do everything within her power to escape the trap Brett had so cleverly set for her.

Star glanced one last time at the vee-shaped shadows gliding smoothly over the flat prairie toward the lifeless form below them before she resolutely turned her back on the scene. Jarvis was dead and she could do nothing more for him, but Dulcie still lived and she had to concentrate on finding a way to save them both.

Chapter 16

Star's image stared back at Kyle from the poster Lucas had given him when he returned from Fort Belnap three days ago. Rereading it for the hundredth time, he wadded it up and tossed it into the flames that popped and sizzled from the drops of rain splattering down the chimney. The weather matched his mood as he morosely watched the ball of paper blacken and crumple into ash, much as all of his hopes and dreams had done when he'd arrived back at the ranch to find Star gone.

Kyle's green eyes were shadowed by introspection as he leaned his head against the back of the chair and stared into the fire. After two weeks away from the Bar H he had been so eager to return to Star that he had stayed only long enough at the fort to collect the money due upon delivery of his cattle. Knowing that Star was waiting for him, he had foregone the pleasures the busy army post offered and had ridden straight back to the ranch. When he arrived and found her missing, he had momentarily gone mad and would have throttled his foreman had Lucas not shown him the poster.

Kyle's knuckles whitened as he curled his fingers about the chair arms and gripped them tightly in an effort to ward off the raw ache that formed about his heart when he thought of Star. Until he met her, he had never loved another soul beyond his mother. Star had managed to break down the barriers he had built about himself and she had wormed her way into the very depths of his soul.

Like any love-smitten fool he had let himself be duped into believing that she was different from the other women he had met and now he was paying dearly for that mistake. He was sick in his heart and soul. His faith in Star had been destroyed when he realized that everything about her had been nothing but a lie. He had believed in her; he'd given her his love, only to find that he had been deceived. Lucas had given him her message, but after all of the lies, he could not believe anything she said, including her vow of love for him.

Kyle's shapely lips thinned into a straight line as he pressed them firmly together and gave a rueful shake of his head, mentally mocking himself for entrusting his heart to her when he had known from the beginning what she was like. Her charade as the Ransons' slave proved her guileful nature and her cleverness at deception.

Kyle's expression grew flinty. His eyes resembled hard green crystals that glowed with the fierce light of suppressed anger. He had been a fool where Star was concerned, but it did not help to realize that he had to share the blame for his own misery. He had ignored the fact that she was capable of such deceit. Because of the emotions she aroused within him, he had wanted to believe in the virtues he had seen her display when they were stranded with the sick on the wagon train.

"Damn it to hell," he cursed, infuriated for letting himself remember how valiantly she had nursed the cholera victims without thought of jeopardy to her own life.

Kyle shifted in his chair and leaned forward to brace his elbows on his knees. Covering his face with his hands, he tried to block out the bittersweet memories that rose hauntingly to his mind. Yet he could not stop himself from recalling how she had wept at the graves of the friends she had battled so bravely to save, how she had come running to help him with pistol gripped in her hand when she thought him in danger at the homestead, and the most painful recollection of all—how she looked when she lay beneath him in the throes of passion.

He didn't want to remember their time together. It

served only to deepen his hurt and resentment toward her. He had found paradise and her lies had destroyed it. He wanted to wipe every thought of her from his mind to try to rid himself of the constant gnawing pain in his heart.

"Stop it, damn you," Kyle growled as he splayed his fingers through his hair and pressed down on his skull to try to eradicate the encroaching memories and the anguish they brought with them. It was a futile effort.

He rubbed at his stinging eyes and let his hands fall limply between his strong, corded thighs. Everywhere he looked he was reminded of her. Star cleaning the fireplace, Star preparing his meals, Star sitting on the porch, and Star bathed in sunlight, lying naked in his bed.

A distant rumble of thunder rolled across the land. Kyle came to his feet, his face set with resolution. He had to free himself of the hold Star had upon him and the only way he knew to do that was to cleanse his mind of the taste and feel of her with another willing body.

A fierce light entered Kyle's eyes as he narrowed them speculatively. A cynical little smile curled the corner of his lips. He knew of no one who would fill that position better than Victoria Crawford. She had been eager to help the law take Star from him and she owed him a debt for her part in breaking his heart. Tonight he would collect the debt by using her body to purge himself of Star.

Strapping his gun belt about his lean hips and tying the holster to his thigh, he took his rain slicker from the peg by the door and pulled it on. The night was wet but nothing would dampen his determination to rid himself of the anger and misery churning his insides.

A steady stream of water ran from the brim of Kyle's hat as he reined his horse to a halt in front of the Sagebrush mercantile and peered through the misty window at the man who worked at the small desk by lantern light. Harold Crawford sat hunched over the thick ledger, the tip of his pencil moving steadily as he added the figures in the columns.

For a long, soul-searching moment Kyle watched the younger man as he diligently worked at his bookkeeping. Victoria had been right about her husband in one respect. He did love his business. The store had been closed for several hours and the man was still at work. That left his wife at home alone, as Kyle had suspected when he set out to pay Victoria a visit.

His mood as black as the rain-drenched night, Kyle urged his horse in the direction of the small board and batten house at the edge of town. Guilt pricked at his conscience, but he firmly ignored it. Tonight his needs were all that mattered. To appease his feelings of culpability he told himself that Victoria was more than willing to have him in her bed. She had made that obvious all too often in the past, and if her husband was fool enough to prefer his books to his wife then he'd have to suffer the consequences.

Kyle rode into the dry warmth of the Crawford stable and dismounted. He shook the rain from his hat and slicker and wiped the moisture from his face as he stood gazing at the small frame house. His entire body was taunt with tension. Rage, frustration, and pain mingled within him as he released a long breath and strode toward the pool of light that spilled through the front window onto the porch. He hated Victoria; he wanted to hurt her as he had been hurt, yet he needed her to help release the pent-up emotions within him before he went mad.

His water-soaked boots made little noise as he stepped upon the porch and peered through the window to see Victoria sitting primly in front of the fireplace, knitting. She made the perfect picture of a proper wife darning her husband's socks yet, he was not fooled or dissuaded from the purpose that brought him out on such a miserable night. He knocked firmly upon the door.

"Kyle, what on earth are you doing here?" Victoria asked as she opened the door.

"Vicky, you should know why I'm here," Kyle said, and gave her an enigmatic grin. "You've invited me here often enough in the past."

"Are you drunk or mad, Kyle?" she asked anxiously, scanning the rain-drenched night for any sign of her husband.

"Does a man have to be mad or drunk to accept your invitation?" Kyle asked as he stepped into the parlor. His wet rain slicker dripped water in a pool about his feet. "Aren't you glad to see me?"

Victoria cast one last apprehensive glance outside and then quickly closed the door behind him. She was torn between joy that Kyle had finally come to her and the fear that Harold might return and find him. "Of course I'm glad to see you, but you shouldn't have come here," she told him. "It's too dangerous. Harold may come home any minute. I've been expecting him for the last hour."

"Your devoted husband is still busy at the store, so we have nothing to worry about, Vicky," Kyle said as he reached out and pulled her against his wet body.

"Kyle, you're wetting my gown through," Victoria cried, and tried to push away from him.

"Then take it off. It only hinders what I came here to do," Kyle growled as he took hold of the front of her bodice and began to unfasten the tiny false pearl buttons.

A tingle of something akin to fear crept up Victoria's spine as she looked up into the green eyes staring dispassionately down at her. They held a cold, tormented expression that made her suddenly wary of the man she had coveted for so long. In the past she had seen his eyes flame with rage as well as passion, but she had never seen the wintry, resolute light that now held her spellbound and chilled her to the bone. Drawing in a steadying breath, she managed to say, "Stop it, Kyle. I want you to leave here this minute."

"I'm not going to leave after all of the trouble you've gone through to have me to yourself, Vicky. You've wanted this for a long time and now I intend to see that you get your wish."

Panic rose in Victoria's throat as she braced her hands

against his chest and strained away from him. "Are you trying to punish me for caring about you?"

"I hadn't realized you thought my lovemaking was punishment." Kyle calmly gripped the front of her gown and jerked her to him. "Until tonight I thought you enjoyed it. Or did you just pretend, like all the other whores in this world?" he growled, his rage surfacing as his icy green gaze swept over her pale features.

"You know that I love you. I've never lied to you about my feelings," Victoria whimpered.

A cruel, cynical smile curled his lips up at the corners as he used his free hand to tip up her chin. "You lie as well as all the other bitches in this world."

"Kyle, you're hurting me," Victoria cried, her eyes brimming with tears.

"Hurt you? I'd like to throttle you for what you did." Kyle's voice was dangerously low. "But since I don't want to hang for murder like Star, I think I can find other ways to make you pay for your part in ripping my heart to shreds."

"I only helped the marshal because of my love for you. I didn't want to see you hurt. I knew you were falling in love with the girl and I wanted to protect you."

A violent tremor shook Kyle from head to toe. He shoved her away before he lost control of himself and did her harm. His face reflected his disgust with her as well as with himself for coming to her to purge himself of Star. He had only succeeded in cleansing his mind of that mad idea. The truth glared at him with frightening clarity and he was sickened by what he had come here to do. He hadn't come to rid himself of Star but to make Victoria suffer as he suffered. He'd wanted revenge.

His face was a granite mask of fury as he glared at her. "A black widow spider knows more about love than you do, Victoria. She devours her mate completely and doesn't leave him torn into pieces to die a slow death." Kyle turned to the door and opened it.

"Kyle, why are you blaming me for hurting you? I'm not the one who lied to you. I've never hidden my love for you, yet you turned away from me and chose to love a woman who is guilty of murder,'' Victoria cried as she ran forward and gripped his arm.

Kyle's expression was frosty as he looked down at the hand on his arm. A sneer of contempt curled his lips as he shook it from him and growled, ''Can't you get it through that head of yours that I want nothing to do with you? I made my feelings clear about that long ago, yet you persist in saying you love me when in truth you've never loved anyone but yourself.''

''I do love you,'' came Victoria's frantic cry as she followed him through the doorway and onto the porch.

Kyle paused and looked back at her. ''Good-bye, Victoria,'' he said, and stepped out into the rainy night.

Victoria heard the death knell to all of her hopes in his final words. The only man she had truly loved was gone from her life. She had gambled and lost. She stifled the sob that broke from her throat as she stared into the darkness. She finally accepted the fact that it was over between them.

Drawing in a ragged breath, she sought to compose herself before Harold came home from the store. She was grateful that she still had him to depend on and that he was ignorant of her feelings for Kyle Hunter. She loved Kyle in a way she would love no other man, but she was resourceful and could make do with her marriage and her standing in the community. That was the one positive aspect of her life with Harold. As the wife of the owner of the mercantile, she merited a certain measure of respect from those who had to trade with her husband and since he owned the only store within two days' ride, that was everyone in Sagebrush.

Feeling somewhat better, she turned back to the door but before her hand touched the latch, her eyes widened in shock as they met her husband's angry gaze. The blood slowly drained from her face, leaving her ashen.

''Harold,'' she breathed, and forced a smile to her lips. ''I'm so glad you're home. I've kept your dinner warm.''

Harold Crawford's face was white with rage as he came forward and took Victoria by the arm. His fingers bit deeply into her flesh as he forcibly propelled her into the house and slammed the door behind them. His thin mustache quivered violently and a muscle twitched beneath his right eye as he swung his wife about to face him.

"You slut," he growled as he brought his hand up and slapped her across the face. "I'd heard rumors of your visits to Kyle Hunter's ranch, but I believed in you and look what I've gained from my trust. You've betrayed me in my own house."

"No, Harold! It's not what you think. I've never been with Kyle since we married."

"If you haven't, then it's not from lack of trying." Harold shoved her toward the stairs. "Get your bags packed, hussy. I'll not have you under my roof another night."

"You can't throw me out of my own home. You have to believe me," Victoria pleaded.

"I believe what I heard when you told Hunter that you loved him, but I'll not believe anything else you have to say. I overlooked the fact that you'd slept with him before we were married, but I'll not do so again. I want you gone from my house, Victoria. As far as I'm concerned you're no longer my wife and I intend to start legal proceedings to that effect as soon as the circuit judge arrives in Sagebrush next week. Until that time, where you go or stay is your business. Now get out of my sight. You sicken me."

Tears blinded Victoria as she stumbled up the stairs to the bedroom she had shared with her husband. A flash of lightning illuminated the expensive furnishings that Harold had proudly ordered from back east for her. Now that it was too late, she could finally appreciate everything he had given her, as well as the man himself.

A ragged sob escaped her as she fell facedown upon the bed and covered her head with her arms. Until tonight she had not really considered Harold a man. She had thought him weak because he had been generous with her in every way, overlooking her faults and pampering her to try to make her happy. Now she knew he was much stronger than she had dreamed possible. Beneath that quiet, gentle exterior he showed to the world, lay a will of iron that would not let him forgive her, no matter what she said or did.

Victoria's tears wet the crocheted counterpane beneath her cheek as she wept over her own foolishness. Kyle's rejection had injured her vanity and to appease it, she had been determined to prove to him that he could not resist her. That arrogance had cost her her entire future.

With his hat in hand, Kyle wiped his face with the back of his sleeve as he strode from the barn, intent upon giving himself a good dousing in the watering trough. The afternoon was hot and humid after the rain and it required little exertion from him to be drenched with perspiration. His shirt was deeply stained with sweat down the front and back, as well as under the arms.

Hanging his hat on the fence post, he pumped water into the trough before shedding his shirt. The muscles in his shoulders and back flexed beneath his supple, tanned skin as he put his head under the spout and pumped cool water over himself. A shower of crystal droplets sprayed around him as he shook his dark head and bent to splash his arms and chest with the refreshing liquid. Savoring the momentary relief from the heat, he wiped his face free of water and stood rubbing the fine mat of crisp curls on his chest as he gazed up at the overcast sky.

He hoped the rain had ended. The deluge the previous day had made it risky for the cattle to come to the watering holes. He'd been up since dawn helping Lucas and the other hired hands check on the herd. Fortunately they'd only found two cows and a calf bogged down in the mud by the creek. However, if it continued to rain, more would get trapped and he'd end up losing some of them.

Kyle massaged the dull ache in his shoulder. He was tired from his morning's labors, as well as his insomnia.

He hadn't slept a night through since he'd returned from Fort Belnap and it was beginning to take its toll on him. He'd thought last night when he'd returned from his visit to Victoria that he'd be able to rest but he'd ended up pacing the floor nearly all night trying to come to terms with his feelings. By dawn he was beginning to doubt that he ever would. Nothing he said or did changed anything. The silken threads Star had woven about his heart were stronger than bands of steel and it was not easy to escape them.

The sound of approaching riders interrupted Kyle's musings and he looked to see Clarice and Buck galloping through the gates. He frowned. At the present time he had no desire to see his father, much less Star's aunt. His life was in enough turmoil without them adding to it with their questions when they learned that Star had been arrested for murder. Running a hand through his damp hair, he stood watching as they reined their horses to a halt in front of the house and dismounted without a glance in his direction. They hurried inside, but a few moments later they came back out again, striding purposefully toward him.

"Where's Star?" Clarice asked, coming directly to the point without any preliminary greetings, even after their long absence. Her finely lined face was pinched from the strain of worrying about her niece since the day they had learned that Fiona Grayson was still alive.

Kyle shrugged as he took his hat from the fence post and set it on his head. "As far as I know she's on her way back to Mississippi to stand trial."

"What the hell do you mean?" Buck growled, his green eyes narrowing menacingly.

"Just what I said, old man," Kyle answered as he picked up his soiled shirt and wadded it into a ball.

An angry rumble emanated from low in Buck's throat and he took a step toward his son, but Clarice stayed him with a firm hand on his arm.

"Kyle, please," she said. "You have to tell us everything you know."

"I have," Kyle answered coolly. He didn't want to talk about Star with anyone. It was too painful and he had no desire to let the world know how she had made him suffer. Turning his back on Clarice and Buck, he strode toward the house.

"Damn that boy," Buck muttered. "It's about damned time I made him realize who his father is. Through the years I've put up with his disrespect toward me, but I won't tolerate it when it comes to you. I'll beat the insolence out of him. He may be a grown man, but he ain't never too big for me to give a good thrashing when he deserves it."

"No, Buck," Clarice said, her voice frantic with worry. "Now is not the time to settle things between you and your son. We have to find Star. That's the most important thing at the moment."

"All right, woman. I'll hold off beating the hell out of him for a little while, but if he keeps acting like a jackass, you can't expect me to ignore it for very long."

Giving Buck's arm a grateful squeeze, Clarice hurried in Kyle's wake. She found him in the kitchen pouring himself a cup of day-old coffee that looked strong enough to eat through the porcelain. Resolve made her voice firm as she said, "Kyle, I want to know what happened to my niece." It was not a question but a demand.

Kyle glanced at her as he pulled a chair out from the table and sat down. He braced his elbows on the checkered tablecloth as he blew on the steaming cup of coffee he held between his palms. Taking a small sip, he wrinkled his nose in disgust at the taste and set the cup aside. "I've told you all I know. I was in Fort Belnap when the marshal came and arrested your niece for murder. Beyond that I know nothing more."

Clarice sank down into the chair across the table from Kyle. She drew in several long breaths in an effort to try to keep her temper under control. A fierce light glowed in the depths of her blue eyes as she looked at him, her face set.

"I left her in your care. You had no right to go off and leave her here unprotected."

Kyle's face hardened with anger under her censure. "Your niece would still be here if she had not been wanted for murder. I saw to it that there were enough men left at the ranch to protect her while I was away, but because of all the lies I was told, I didn't foresee the fact that they'd have to deal with a federal marshal."

"Damn it," Clarice spat, slamming her fist down on the table to vent her mounting fury, "my niece isn't wanted for murder, you young fool. If you had any sense in that head of yours you'd know that Star couldn't kill anyone. The man who pretended to be the marshal may kill her. That's why I have to know everything that happened."

Kyle's heart seemed to stop in his chest. "What are you talking about? Lucas said the man had a warrant for her arrest. I saw the poster he left with my foreman."

"Did you read it, Kyle?" Buck asked from the doorway.

"Read it, old man?" Kyle growled as he came to his feet, feeling suddenly on the defensive. "I read the blasted thing a hundred times."

"Then you know it said nothing about murder. The paper you saw was only Brett Tremayne's way of locating Star."

Kyle ran his hand through his hair in exasperation. He didn't know what in hell was going on, but he was determined to find out. "Don't you think it's damned time you explained to me what all this is about? You're acting as if I'm at fault, when in truth I know even less about this situation than you seem to."

"Sit down, Kyle," Clarice said. Her shoulders sagged and her eyes were shadowed with fear for her niece's life as she looked up at him. "It's a long story."

Kyle eyed Clarice curiously for a moment and then obeyed. He listened, dumbfounded, as she told him of the events that had led up to Star's arrest. The cup of coffee in front of him sat untouched and was cold by the time her tale reached the point at which she and Buck learned that Fiona Grayson still lived and began to suspect that Brett Tremayne's absence from Jasmine Hall boded ill for Star.

The silence in the room lengthened as Kyle stared at the woman sitting across the table from him. He was unable to fully grasp all she had told him, but he wanted to believe every word of it. Hope leaped within his tormented soul, yet the last few days of misery made him cautious. He was wary of letting down his guard again where Star was concerned. He knew if he let himself believe that she loved him and then learned once again that he had played the fool, his ravaged heart would not survive.

"If all you say is true, then why didn't Star tell me?" he asked, desperately wanting to hear an explanation that would appease his battered pride.

"Why should she have told you anything?" Buck asked. He eyed his son critically as he lounged in the doorway with one shoulder braced against the frame. "From what I gathered before we left for DryCreek, there was little love lost between the two of you."

Kyle flashed his father a contemptuous look. "Stay out of this, old man. This is none of your affair."

"I'd say it is, since Star is my wife's niece."

"Your wife?" Kyle asked, glancing at Clarice for confirmation. Seeing her nod, he felt his blood begin to pound in his temples. The old, deep-seated anger against his father resurfaced. How dare the old bastard go off and marry another woman so he could put her through the same hell that his mother had endured?

"Yes, Clarice and I were married in DryCreek before we went to Natchez to see exactly what charges were being brought against Star."

"I guess congratulations, or should I say condolences, are in order, Clarice. I hope Buck doesn't make your life as miserable as he made my mother's," Kyle said, his voice laced with sarcasm.

"Damn it, Kyle. I've had about all I'm going to take

from you on that subject,'' Buck growled, his body tensing with anger.

Kyle came out of his chair as if hit by lightning. His eyes glittered with rage as he faced his father with his hands balled into fists, ready to do battle. "Old man, if you think you can take me on, then you're welcome to try it. I've waited many a year to give you the beating you deserve."

"Stop it, both of you!" Clarice said as she came to her feet between the two men who stood glaring at each other. "Kyle, Buck is your father."

Kyle gave a harsh, mocking laugh. "Father? He's never been a father to me. A father is someone who's there when you need him, not a man who passes through when he has nothing better to fill his time with between barroom brawls and visits to whores."

The animosity Buck saw in the eyes that were so much like his own made his insides feel as if they had been put through a meat grinder. He loved this man who was the image of himself twenty years earlier, but there was nothing he could say or do to change his son's feelings toward him.

"Son, I didn't come here to argue with you," he said, his anger leaving him as swiftly as it had come.

"Don't call me son. You may have sired me, but you gave up your rights as my father long ago when you ran out on my mother."

Buck released a long breath and glanced at his wife. "I'll leave you to talk with him." With that he turned and left the house.

Clarice saw the look of anguish in Buck's eyes before he turned away and her heart went out to her husband even as her fury mounted against his arrogant, unfeeling son. She turned on Kyle, her eyes shooting sparks of blue fire as she glared up at him. "You stupid, ungrateful, unfeeling little whelp. I have a good mind to take a switch to you and treat you like the spoiled brat that you've been acting. Don't you realize what you've done to that man? He loves you, you idiot. You blame him when in fact you should be blaming your mother for driving him away from the both of you."

"Don't say anything against my mother, Clarice, if you want to remain in this house," Kyle growled as he glared down at her.

"I'll say what I damned well please, Kyle Hunter. It's about damned time someone said something around here. That's been the problem all along. Nobody wanted to tell the truth and it's caused nothing but trouble."

"Clarice, I'm warning you. You and Buck are pushing me and I won't tolerate much more."

"Like hell you won't. You'll listen to me, Kyle Hunter or you'll find your ears boxed resoundingly if you don't. Your father—" Clarice began and then raised her hand as Kyle opened his mouth once more. "Don't say it because he *is* your father. He loves you whether you want to admit it or not. And he didn't stay away from you all these years because it was something he wanted. Madge drove him away with her hatred."

"Shut up, Clarice. You've said enough!"

"Not by a long shot! I haven't even begun to tell you everything that happened in the past that your father never wanted you to know because of his love for you."

"I won't listen to any more slander against my mother. Especially from a woman who has taken her place in my father's bed!"

"Don't try that with me, young man," Clarice ordered, her eyes flashing with ire. "You should know you can't intimidate me so easily. And as for me taking your mother's place in your father's bed, Madge has been dead for ten years but their marriage ended years before she died. You already know that, but what you don't know is why."

Kyle's heart began to pound against his ribs and his breathing grew short as he sensed that Clarice was determined to touch upon things he did not want to hear, things that he feared were true and he was afraid to face.

Clarice narrowed her eyes speculatively as she gazed

up at Kyle and watched his expression grow wary. "You already suspect; don't you? But you're afraid to admit it because it would mean that you've hated your father all of these years for nothing."

"Get out of my house, Clarice, and take your husband with you," he ordered, and turned his back to her.

Clarice would not let him off so easily. She grabbed Kyle by the arm and jerked him back around to face her. "Not until you understand that Buck has always loved you. I've known him for nearly twenty years and I've seen the agony he has suffered because he left his family."

Kyle eyed Clarice coldly and shook his head. "You don't lie as well as your niece."

Before she could stop herself, Clarice gave Kyle a resounding blow across the face. "Don't you dare say anything against Star. You don't understand her any more than you do your father. They both did what they had to do. Can't you get that through your thick skull?"

Kyle rubbed at the angry red marks on his cheek but gave no other sign that he felt the blow. "No. I don't understand that lies and desertion are necessary."

"Then it's time you grew up and realized that people often have to make a choice in their lives that might not seem right to others when in fact it is the only decision they could make for the good of all concerned. Would it have been better for your father to have stayed here with Madge and let you live in the hell that two people can put their children through when there's only hatred left between them? And would you have believed Star if she had told you the truth in the beginning? I seriously doubt it because you're too hypocritical in your judgments. You've proven that by not ever giving your father a chance to show his love for you. There are always two sides to every story, but you've chosen to see only one—your mother's. You're *still* letting Madge's bitterness blind you."

A nearly unbearable ache welled within Kyle's chest at the truth of Clarice's accusations. He remembered all too well his mother's hatred for his father and the condemnation he had suffered from her because of his resemblance to Buck. That had made him afraid to give his love to Star. Kyle felt his anger evaporate like the heat of the day under a cool shower of rain. His eyes reflected his anguish as he looked at Clarice and asked, "What is it you want of me?"

"All I want is for you to forget the past and give your father a chance to make amends for all of the years you've lost. He wants that desperately."

"I can't make any promises that my feelings toward Buck will change, but I will make an effort."

"That's all anyone can ask of either of you," Clarice said, and smiled tenderly at the young man with the haunted green eyes. She placed her hand on his arm and gave it a reassuring squeeze before she turned away, her mind already returning to the problem of her niece.

"Clarice," Kyle said, and watched as she paused at the door to look back at him. "You never answered my question earlier. Why didn't Star tell me the truth?"

"She was afraid, Kyle. She was innocent of the crime she was being accused of, but she had no way to prove it."

"You know that I love her."

"Yes. I've known that longer than you have. I also know that Star loves you."

Clarice's confirmation made Kyle's spirits soar and he grinned. "Then why in hell are we standing around here arguing when we should be on our way to Mississippi to bring her back home?"

"That's what I've been wondering since we arrived," Clarice said. "Since Star's stepmother is still alive, Tremayne can only hold that threat over her head until they reach Mississippi and she learns the truth. I fear he's found another devious scheme to use against her then. I pray that he doesn't intend to harm her to get his hands on Jasmine Hall."

Kyle's face darkened with fury at the thought. His eyes

glittered with a cold, deadly light and his voice was laced with steel as he said, "If he touches one hair on her head, he's a dead man."

Chapter 17

Weary to the bone, Star drooped in the saddle as they rode up the winding drive toward her home. Jasmine Hall stood magnificently in the center of the gardens, its white columns and wrought-iron balcony as majestic as she remembered, but she felt no elation at the sight. The land that she had loved with an intensity that had made her heart ache with the memory as the wagon train took her away across the flat prairie now brought forth none of that emotion. Looking at the two-storied mansion the only thing she could feel was apprehension as to what awaited her within its walls.

Casting a furtive glance at the man who rode at her side, she wondered at her lack of feeling at returning to the land of her birth. At one time she would have fought tooth and nail to hold on to every inch of the rich, dark loam, but now she would willingly give it all up just to be free of Brett Tremayne so that she could return to the flat, grassy Texas prairie and the man she loved. Compared to the open spaces of the ranch, Jasmine Hall's lush greenness seemed oppressively confining, reminding her only that this was to be her prison.

During the past weeks of hard riding, she had tried to find a way to extricate herself from Brett's plans for her but every time she thought she had found an answer, she would remember that Dulcie's life was at stake. That would thwart any thought of creeping away while he slept or bashing in his head with a rock. She could do nothing until she made certain that Dulcie was safe. Once that was accomplished, she was determined to let nothing stand in her way of breaking the hold Brett had on her. She had already accepted the fact that she might die, but that was far better than what he had planned for her after he'd forced her to marry him.

Each night while they sat by the campfire, he had enjoyed himself by telling her each heinous thing that he intended to do to her when she became his wife. He had spared no detail of each act of perversion or torture. The nightly mental torment had taken its toll on her and on several occasions she had awakened screaming only to find Brett grinning at her malevolently, well knowing he was at the root of her distress. The lack of sleep, the hard pace he'd set, and his harassment had worn down her strength, testing her courage and endurance to the limit.

Drawing her eyes away from Brett, she glanced up at the two small windows beneath the gabled roof. Behind them Dulcie was imprisoned and it was left to her to find a way to help her friend.

"Admiring the beauty of our home, my dear?" Brett asked as he reined his mount to a halt and tossed the reins to the stableboy who came rushing forward to assist them. Brett slipped to the ground and then reached up to help Star from her horse. She tried to avoid his hands, but he gripped her firmly about the waist and drew her down from the saddle. "I'm sure you're glad to be at Jasmine Hall instead of in that Texan's hovel where I found you."

"If I have to live here with you, then I'd prefer an Indian's tepee."

Brett's pale eyes hardened as he cast a quick glance at the stableboy. Slaves spread gossip quicker than wildfire and he wanted nothing said to indicate that his marriage to Star was anything but a love match.

"Our journey has tired you and made your temper testy. Once you've had time to rest, you'll feel better," he said as he gripped her arm, squeezing it painfully. "I'm sure your maid, Dulcie, will be glad to see that you've returned home after your visit to your aunt. She has missed you.''

Star's eyes flashed with loathing as she glared up at Brett. ''And I'm sure my stepmother will be glad that you've returned.''

Brett's fingers bruised the flesh of her upper arm as he led her up the steps to the veranda and into the foyer of Jasmine Hall. A young house servant that Star did not recognize came hurrying forward, but Brett waved her away. ''Get out. I'll call you when you're needed.'' Her head bobbed up and down twice and then she turned and fled.

''What have you done with my servants?'' Star asked as she tried to jerk free of his brutal grip.

''They've been sold or sent to the fields. I thought it best that we start our marriage off with everything new including ridding ourselves of slaves who were too nosy for their own good.''

''You mean the ones who were loyal to me, don't you?''

Brett shrugged. ''I saw no reason to keep people near me who might not obey my orders. As you will learn, my dear, I'm thorough when it comes to carrying out my plans. So if you have any schemes to try to prevent our marriage, I would suggest you forget them before you cause your poor maid to have an accident that might be detrimental to her health.'' Brett gave Star's arm a sharp jerk. ''Come along now. I'm sure you want to see your stepmother.''

''I don't want to see Fiona. I want to see Dulcie.''

''Your maid is fine for the time being and if you want to keep her that way, I wouldn't argue,'' Brett said as he led Star toward the drawing room.

Fiona looked up from the brightly colored threads of her embroidery as Brett and Star entered the room. Her icy gaze swept over her stepdaughter to the man at her side. ''I see you found our wandering Star.''

''And what a pleasure it is to see you looking so alive and well again, Stepmother, dear.'' Star's words dripped with sarcasm. "I only wish . . ." The pressure of Brett's fingers cut off her words as he forced her into a chair and crossed to the Queen Anne table where the brandy decanter sat.

"You knew my intention was to find her," Brett said as he poured himself a drink. He downed the fiery liquid in one gulp and turned back to the two women who sat glaring at each other. "Fiona, you should know by now that once I set my mind to something, I'm not easily dissuaded from my course. I have too much at stake to let anything stand in the way of my owning Jasmine Hall."

Fiona's eyes flashed with irritation as she looked up at him. "Then I suppose that means I should begin preparing for your nuptials to my dear stepdaughter," she spat venomously, unable to hide the jealousy that had been eating away at her since Brett set out to find Star.

"The sooner the better. I have only a short time left before my creditors close in on me."

Fiona eyed Brett sullenly, her face pinched with annoyance. "Isn't there another way to deal with this situation without your having to marry the bitch?"

"He doesn't have to marry me, Fiona," Star said, her voice icy with contempt. "I told Brett I would sign Jasmine Hall over to him if he would release Dulcie unharmed and let me go back to Texas to my aunt."

Fiona's eyes widened with surprise and her face lit with hope as she looked to Brett for confirmation. "Is that true?"

"Yes, she said I could have Jasmine Hall," Brett said without elaborating. He knew he was standing on shaky ground where Fiona was concerned.

"Oh, Brett. We couldn't have asked for anything more. You'll have the plantation and then we can be married," Fiona breathed with excitement.

"Don't be a fool, Fiona. Star would say anything to be free of me and to save her maid. How long do you think we would keep Jasmine Hall after she went to the authorities and told them we had coerced her into signing away her home? She also saw me, uh, injure Jarvis and would be eager to tell the sheriff. However, as my wife she can't testify against me in a court of law," Brett said, seeking any excuse to keep Fiona appeased until his marriage to Star took place. After that he didn't care if Fiona knew exactly how he felt about her. He'd be more than happy to tell her himself to get her out of his life. He was tired of her jealousy and her constant harping and whining.

Fiona's features fell as her hopes for a future with Brett dissolved. She flashed Star a look of hatred through narrowed lashes. "You may have to marry the little bitch, but that doesn't mean that I have to have her in the same room with me. Get her out of my sight. Take her up and chain her with the slave she loves so much. They are fit company for each other."

Star came to her feet, her fists braced on her hips. "This is my home, Fiona."

"*Was* your home," Brett calmly interjected as he came forward. "It is now my home and I'll not have the two of you caterwauling at each other in my presence like two cats fighting over a fishbone. From now on you will both act like ladies or you'll answer to me."

Star eyed him contemptuously. "Like hell I will," she snapped, her rage making her forget her tenuous position.

"Your spirit is one of the things I admire about you, Star. However, it may cause Dulcie to suffer unduly unless you learn to control it." Brett spoke softly, yet his words held a menace that Star couldn't ignore.

"I want to see Dulcie and assure myself that you haven't already harmed her," Star said, struggling to regain control over herself. Venting her temper would do neither Dulcie nor herself any good at the present time.

"That can easily be arranged," Brett said as he took her elbow to escort her from the room.

"Brett, I want Star locked away," Fiona ordered as she came to her feet, her face livid with rage. "She's a cunning little bitch and she'll do everything within her power to bring us to ruin.''

Brett gave Fiona a look full of scorn. "You do take me for a fool, don't you, my dear? I've brought her back and I'll take no chances on losing her again. Of that you can be assured. I'm too close to having it all to risk letting her roam free.''

"Leave her in the attic with the maid. She doesn't deserve more after all the trouble she had caused us." A smug smile curled up the corners of Fiona's red lips at the thought of Star's discomfort.

"I don't take orders from you, Fiona. Star will remain in her own room until our wedding night. Then she will share the master suite with me as is her right as my wife.''

Fiona's face flamed, but she did not argue. She shot Star a look laced with malice and then turned away. Her jealousy choked her as she raised her chin in the air and walked out of the room and into the gardens beyond the french doors.

Brett chuckled at Fiona's discomfiture as he escorted Star up the carpeted stairs and to the end of the hallway, where a narrow flight of steps led up to the attic. He let her precede him to the locked door of Dulcie's prison. Taking a ring of keys from his pocket, he unlocked the door and stepped back for her to enter as it swung open.

Star gasped at the sight of her friend lying in a pool of afternoon sunlight, her restraints making it impossible to find any shade from the hot rays that filtered into the room through the windows. Dulcie's face glistened with perspiration and her ragged gown was drenched through with sweat caused by the stifling heat of the unventilated room.

"Dulcie," Star breathed as she hurried forward and knelt at her side. Gently she wiped the dark brow free of moisture as she said again, "Dulcie, can you hear me?"

Dulcie's ebony eyes slowly opened and she gazed up at Star, disoriented from the heat and lack of water. It took her several moments to focus her eyes on Star's face. "Missy, is it really you?"

"Yes, Dulcie. I'm here to take care of you," Star comforted her as she reached for the pitcher that had been left several inches beyond the maid's reach. She poured a glass of water and lifted it to her friend's parched lips. "Drink and you'll feel better," she urged as she looked back at the man standing in the doorway. "Is this what you mean when you said she had not been harmed? She would have died of thirst in this oven before long."

Unperturbed, Brett said, "My dear Star, as you well know I've been with you during the last weeks and have had nothing to do with the care of your maid. When I left Jasmine Hall, she was in fit condition. I'm not to blame for what happens in my absence."

"I want her released at once, Brett, or our deal is off. Dulcie will die if she's kept chained up here like an animal."

A glacial light entered Brett's eyes. He'd had enough of women's demands for one day. "Star, I'll tell you the same thing I told Fiona earlier. I don't take orders from you. Your maid will stay as she is until after our marriage has been consummated and she'll be released no sooner. If you want her freed, then I suggest you start preparing for our wedding."

"Brett, please," Star pleaded. "Don't leave her like this. At least unchain her so that she can get out of the sun. She can't escape through a locked door and the windows have been nailed shut for years."

For a long moment Brett considered Star's request. The maid did look near the point of death and for the moment he could not chance that. Dulcie was his trump card; the only thing that he had to use to get his hands on Star as well as the wealth she controlled. "All right. I'll unchain her, but if she gives me any trouble, you'll both regret it."

"Look at her, Brett. She's not able to cause trouble. Fiona has starved her until she's too weak to move."

Brett came forward and unlocked the manacle about

Dulcie's raw wrist. He wrinkled his nose in disgust at the scent of excrement that rose to his nostrils. Damn Fiona, he silently raged as he gazed down into the grayed ebony face. Fiona had nearly killed the maid with her neglect and that could have cost him dearly. His eyes glittered with ire as he took Star by the arm and led her forcibly from the attic, leaving Dulcie lying in the same position.

"Let me stay with her until I know she's better," Star pleaded, but to no avail.

"No," Brett growled as he propelled her toward the top of the narrow steps. "You'll stay in your room while I attend to some business I've been neglecting too long." After relocking the attic door, he led Star back down the stairs and along the hallway to her bedchamber. He shoved her inside and locked the door behind her.

Star felt she would scream with frustration. Dulcie lay semiconscious in the sweltering heat of the attic and she was unable to help her. Balling her hands into fists, Star pressed them to her temples as she stood in the middle of the room, agonizing over her friend and her inability to do more than wait until she could find a way to help them both escape the madman.

"Damn you to hell, Brett Tremayne. I promise you that you and my dear stepmother are going to pay dearly for your evil scheme. If it's the last thing I do in this world, I'll see you receive the retribution due you for this," Star swore aloud, her face a mask of hatred.

The muscles in her legs quivered from exhaustion as she crossed to the bed and sank down across it. Her eyes burned with the need to cry but she refused to shed any tears. She wanted to hold all of her bitterness inside to ferment against Brett and Fiona. She would use her hate to give her strength to fight them.

Through narrowed eyes she stared at the french doors that led out onto the balcony and knew without checking them that they were also locked. Brett was confident that his plan would succeed, but she was equally determined to see that it failed.

A shrewd little smile curled up the corners of her delicately molded lips. Brett thought he had sealed all avenues of escape, but he had failed to realize that she had one thing to her advantage—Fiona's jealousy. She had seen it in her stepmother's face and had heard it in her voice before she'd stalked from the drawing room. Without realizing it, Fiona had given her a weapon to use to defeat Brett.

In this game Star knew the stakes would be high. She was gambling with her life, as well as Dulcie's, but she had to use any means at her disposal to stop Brett. He had bragged about being a gambler and she prayed that when all was said and done she would come out the winner. If not, she would forfeit all.

Rolling onto her back, she covered her eyes with her arm as she contemplated her course of action. By using Fiona's jealousy as the catalyst, it should not be difficult to alienate the two allies. However, she had to use caution or she would find herself in a far worse dilemma. She had to move slowly to keep Brett and Fiona from suspecting her actions. Satisfied that she had finally found a chink in Brett's plan, she closed her eyes and drifted into sleep.

Brett regarded the woman standing with her back to him at the far end of the garden. A sneer of disgust lifted his upper lip and his nostrils flared as he drew in an angry breath. The self-serving bitch, he cursed silently as he made his way along the flagged path toward Fiona. If that black hussy had died, I would have had to kill Star or end up on the gallows myself.

Fiona was unaware of Brett's presence until she felt his hand come to rest on her shoulder. Thinking he had come to apologize for the way he had treated her in front of her stepdaughter, she glanced up at him, a forgiving smile already forming on her lips. However, at the look in his eyes, she swallowed convulsively and the smile died before it was fully born.

"Fiona, we need to get a few things straight," he said

softly, his voice reflecting none of the ire burning in the depths of his pale eyes.

"I don't know what you mean, Brett," Fiona answered guardedly.

"You know exactly what I'm talking about. Because of your careless neglect, you've damned near killed the only thing we have to keep Star in our control. If that had happened I swear you would have paid with your own life for ruining my chances of getting Jasmine Hall."

Fiona gave a disdainful toss of her head, her jealousy overshadowing any fear she might have of Brett. "The maid isn't what has you concerned. It's Star. You know that without Dulcie to use as leverage she'd never consent to marry you."

"I've suffered enough of your jealous tirades, Fiona. They serve no purpose. You know as well as I that your stepdaughter means nothing to me, but you keep acting as if I'm betraying you by completing the plan we set into motion months ago."

"You don't have to marry the little bitch. She's agreed to sign Jasmine Hall over to you, but you're still determined to make her your wife even though there would be no reason for you to do so once her signature was on the papers. Your actions are enough to show me that there's more between the two of you than you're telling me."

"I've already explained my reasons to you once today, or has your jealousy made you forget everything else?"

"I know what you told me, but there's a simple solution to the problem of Star going to the sheriff once we have the deed to Jasmine Hall. You know that as well as I do. She could have a fatal accident while out riding or she could drown while taking her morning swim in the river. No one would ever be the wiser."

Brett suppressed the urge to place his hands about Fiona's slender neck and squeeze until he strangled the life from her. For the time being he didn't want to alienate her to the point of exposing him to the authorities herself. Until his marriage to Star was secure, he'd have to coddle her, but once he was sure that he had the plantation and Star, Fiona would get what she so richly deserved.

"My dear, you forget that Star still has an aunt who probably knows everything that has happened to her niece in the past months. She could arrive here at any time. It would do neither of us any good should she find that Star is not well and happily married," Brett cajoled. Tracing the smooth line of Fiona's cheek with his knuckles, he tipped up her chin. "Don't you understand that we can't let anything happen to Star until I'm married to her? Trust me, Fiona, I'm doing this for us."

Unable to resist Brett's coaxing manner, Fiona drew in a resigned breath. "I'm afraid that something will happen to ruin all we've worked to gain."

"Don't worry, love. As long as we have Dulcie, we have Star exactly where we want her. That's why I was so upset when I saw the maid. If she dies, then all of our plans will come to nothing."

"Brett, I know I've been foolish," Fiona said as she wrapped her arms about his waist and pressed her face to his chest. "I took out my spite on Dulcie when you wouldn't let me go with you to find Star. Please forgive me. I'll try to keep my jealousy under control in the future."

Brett curled his fingers in the hair at the back of her neck. They itched to slip farther down, to tighten about the white column of her throat and put an end to the trouble she'd caused him but he controlled them. The time will come, he told himself as he held her and murmured, "I understand what you've gone through, my love, but you have nothing to fear. Soon it will all be over."

Her jealousy momentarily allayed, Fiona snuggled against Brett's lean frame, almost secure in his love for her.

A tall black man stood with his arms folded across his wide chest, seemingly impervious to the hot sun that

beaded his face with perspiration as Star gathered fresh
flowers for her room. To her great frustration, he had
become her constant companion when she was released
from the confinement of her bedchamber. He guarded
her well for his master who'd had the foresight to make
sure that she had no chance to escape again.

Star cast a furtive glance at Zebulon, wondering fu-
tilely what he would do if she threw down her basket of
flowers and made a dash for the thick underbrush beyond
the carefully tended gardens. It was only a wistful, fleeting thought. She knew she would not flee Jasmine Hall
without Dulcie even if she was given the chance.

Snipping a long-stemmed red rose, she placed it in the
woven basket she carried and glanced up at the attic windows. Thankfully, Dulcie's health had improved greatly
during the past days, but she was still weak.

Star glanced once more toward her guard. A new
surge of frustration filled her breast. She had planned
to use Fiona's jealousy against Brett but he had successfully thwarted her without realizing what he was
doing. He had managed to keep her away from her stepmother.

As Obioma had once told her that time was her worst
enemy. It was slipping away too quickly and if she did
not find a way to extricate herself, she would find herself
married to Brett at the end of the week.

Star turned her attention back to the roses. Obioma,
she mused, if only you were here to help me solve my
problems as easily as you did the last time. But the last
time caused her death, Star silently reminded herself,
and felt the sting of tears before she pricked her finger
on a thorn.

"Damn," she cursed, and stuck the injured digit into
her mouth to nurse it. Obioma's death was one more
score she had to settle with Brett and Fiona. Her fury
rising once more, Star tossed the basket to her stoic companion and stalked into the house.

The thorn prick had done more than wound her, it
had also goaded her into action. It was time to set her

plan into motion if she was to succeed. Resolutely she decided that if the mountain wouldn't come to her, she would have to go to the mountain. She could wait no longer or she would end up married to Brett Tremayne. With Zebulon following in her footsteps, she went in search of Fiona and found her curled in a chair in the study, reading a book of poetry. Star's guard remained respectfully at the door.

Fiona glanced up at her entrance, a look of disdain flickering over her powdered and rouged face. Closing the book, she laid it on the highly polished Queen Anne table at her side. Her eyes flashed with hostility as she asked, "What do you want?"

Feigning an air of confidence, Star strolled across the study with her head held high. She seated herself in the chair opposite her stepmother and absently smoothed the soft voile fabric of her skirt before folding her hands gracefully in her lap. "I've come to tell you that I've made a decision, Fiona."

"And what, pray tell, is that?" Fiona remarked sarcastically.

Giving her stepmother a haughty look, Star said, "Since I'm to become Brett's wife at the end of the week, I've decided it's best for me to accept the fact and try to make my marriage work."

"You do have grand illusions, don't you? If you believe your marriage to Brett will succeed, then you're a bigger fool than I imagined."

Star ignored Fiona's remark. "You've never given me any reason to show you my beneficence, but I thought I would give you a chance to save your pride by letting you pack your bags and leave Jasmine Hall before Brett asks you to leave."

Fiona's red lips spread wide and her harsh laughter filled the study. "You little fool. I have no intention of leaving Jasmine Hall or Brett. Nor will he ask me to go. Brett loves me."

"I know you believe that, Fiona, but your belief changes nothing," Star said, giving her stepmother a pitying look before she lowered her eyes to her hands. "Once Brett and I are married, I will be mistress once more of my home and as such I will have certain rights. He will no longer have need of you to fill his bed."

"Rights?" Fiona spat, stiffening with anger at the thought of Star and Brett together. "Where Brett is concerned you have no rights."

Star raised her eyes and looked directly into the flashing, hate-filled eyes glaring at her. She calmly said, "I will be Brett's wife, not his mistress. I will also someday be the mother of his children. That will certainly give me the privilege of asking him to order you from my home."

Fiona bolted to her feet, her face livid with anger. "You'll be nothing to Brett but an encumbrance that he'll soon rid himself of once he owns Jasmine Hall."

"Brett won't kill me, Fiona. That would raise too many questions. My aunt knows the entire story behind my visit to her in Texas. My sudden demise would be too suspicious for him to take that chance."

Star's words had the desired effect upon Fiona. They voiced nearly the same excuse Brett had given her when she had last suggested her stepdaughter's accidental death. Her insides twisted with jealousy as she stared down at the younger woman whose skin was not yet flawed by the tiny lines of age and whose body was still youthful and firm. She was too beautiful to remain long as Brett's wife without his succumbing to her charms. Fiona suddenly realized that if the marriage took place as he planned, that would mean that she would never have him again. He would gain Jasmine Hall and a luscious young body to share his bed while she would be left with nothing except her empty dreams. Fiona clenched her jaw against the agony the thought brought with it.

A shrewd light entered her eyes as she gazed at Star. She had to put a stop to the wedding. It would be her last chance to have the only man she had ever loved. Fighting to regain control over her temper, she sat down once more. "Star, you surprise me. I wouldn't have thought you would give way so easily to the demands of others. Your lack of spirit in accepting your marriage does not resemble the girl I knew."

"I admit that I don't want this marriage, but since there is little else I can do but accept it, I see no reason to keep fighting the inevitable."

Fiona smiled triumphantly. "Would you even take the chance to escape your nuptials if given it?"

Feigning a martyred expression, Star nodded. "I would gladly take it if not for Dulcie. She will lose her life if I refuse to marry Brett. I can't risk that, so you see such ideas are useless," Star said, and watched Fiona closely. She could nearly read her stepmother's calculating mind as she sought a way to rid herself of the rival for Brett's affections.

Perceiving a plan that might solve all her problems, Fiona's face lit with astonishment for not having thought of it before. It was so simple and in the end she would have Brett as well as Jasmine Hall.

"Would you be willing to sign Jasmine Hall over to me if I were to help you and Dulcie escape?"

Star felt like bursting into tears with relief, but she managed at the last moment to control them. She had carefully manipulated Fiona to this point and could not ruin it now by showing her feelings. "If I thought I could trust you, Fiona, I would gladly do as you ask."

"It's either trust me to help you or find yourself married to Brett," Fiona said with assurance. "I'm your only hope now, Star."

"Why would you help me? You've never done anything for me in all the years since my father's death," Star asked, trying to ascertain her stepmother's sincerity. Fiona could easily say that she would help them escape and then place them in a worse position by telling Brett, in order to get back into his good graces.

"Don't you have any brains in that fool head of yours, Star? You should know why I would be willing to risk everything to be rid of you. I love Brett, but as long as you're here, I can never have him to myself. If I own Jasmine Hall *I* will be the one he chooses to marry.''

Star's heart leapt with hope within her breast. It pounded against her ribs as she asked, ''But how could you help us? Dulcie is locked away in the attic and I'm guarded by that great giant in the foyer.''

Fiona smiled smuggly. ''The Texas heat did addle what few wits you had, Star. If you will recall, I am the one who masterminded Brett's wooing of you in the first place. He is not the only person here who can devise ways to get what he wants out of life.''

How true, Fiona, Star mused silently to herself. But if I have my way, neither of you will succeed with your diabolical schemes. However, she said aloud, ''You can have the plantation. All I want is to go back to Texas.'' She added silently, to be with Kyle, if he will have me.

''Then we have a deal. I will start making the arrangements today. I'll bring the deed to the plantation to you and you can sign it over to me and then I'll be ready to help you.''

''I won't sign over my home to you until Dulcie and I are free. I might have agreed to trust you this time, but I'm not the simpleminded fool you'd like to believe. Once we're safely away from here, then and only then will I relinquish my rights to Jasmine Hall.''

Fiona pursed her lips and her eyes again held a sparkle of anger. ''I'll give way to your demands, but if you try to cheat me out of Jasmine Hall, then you'll rue the day you ever set eyes on me. I promise you that, Star.''

I rued that day long ago, Star mused, but said aloud, ''I will keep my word, Fiona. You make sure you don't go back on yours. Brett would not be too happy if he was to learn of your plans to thwart our marriage,'' Star said, and smiled with satisfaction at the uncertain look that flashed across Fiona's face before she managed to conceal it.

''Don't threaten me, Star,'' Fiona hissed.

''I make no threats. I make only promises that I will keep if you think of tricking me,'' Star said as she stood and calmly walked from the room. Zebulon awaited her and escorted her upstairs.

The sound of the lock clicking after she'd shut her bedroom door did not have the usual depressing effect upon Star. She had succeeded. Fiona had gullibly let her jealousy rule her and that had been Star's intention from the onset. Now all that was left to do was to wait until her stepmother devised a way to help them escape. Star smiled with satisfaction as she twirled around and around. Soon she would be free. Soon she would be once more with Kyle at the Bar H.

Her moment of joy faded with the thought. She wanted desperately to be with the man she loved, yet she feared after everything that had happened and all the lies she had told, he might never forgive her.

Clasping her hands tightly to her breast, she squeezed her eyes shut and prayed, "Please, dear Lord, let him still love me because I don't think I could endure losing him a second time."

Chapter 18

Forty-eight hours had passed since her encounter with Fiona and Star had received no word from her stepmother. She was beginning to grow anxious. Fiona was a fickle person who might have reconsidered her offer to help and was now merely enjoying the thought of Star fretting over her lack of action.

"No," Star muttered vehemently, startling Dulcie awake.

"Missy, you say something?" the maid asked as she raised herself on one elbow and looked up at Star with wide, searching eyes.

"I was only thinking aloud," Star answered, busying herself with the tray of food she had brought for Dulcie. "Do you think you feel well enough to eat? Do you want me to feed you?"

Dulcie smiled. "I feel like my old self again thanks to you. I hungry enough to eat a hoss, hooves and all."

"I'm glad to hear it," Star said, relieved to know that her friend would at least be able to travel if Fiona provided them with the help she promised.

"Then what got your pretty young face all screwed up in a frown?" Dulcie asked as she took the bowl of soup from Star.

Star leaned back against an old trunk and drew her knees up against her chest. Draping her arms over them, she looked at her friend. She knew it was time to explain her plans. "Dulcie, Fiona has promised to aid us in escaping Jasmine Hall."

Deep lines etched the maid's dark brow as she looked at Star. "You ain' gonna trust that woman after all she done to you, are you, Missy?"

"I have no other choice. At the moment she's our only hope. If I don't get away from Jasmine Hall before tomorrow, I'll have to marry Brett."

Dulcie set the soup bowl aside, leaving the rest of the nourishing broth to grow cold. "It's 'cause of me that you came back, ain't it, Missy?"

Not wanting to put such a burden on her friend's shoulders, Star lied, "Brett forced me to come back with a warrant for my arrest for the murder of my stepmother."

Dulcie regarded Star speculatively for a long moment. She had known her mistress since birth and knew when she wasn't telling the truth. "If that be the case, then you could have left Jasmine Hall after learning that Miz Fiona was still alive. You stayed 'cause of me."

Star looked away from the keen black eyes. "It doesn't matter why I stayed. All that's important now is that we get away from the plantation before I have to marry."

"Then you go without me, Missy. I don't want to drag you down."

"Dulcie, I'll hear no more of such talk. I won't leave without you."

"Missy, you have to, and fast. That Master Brett be a mean devil. He'll kill you once he gets his hands on your property. He's a snake who ain' got no feelings for anyone but hisself."

"I know what Brett is and that's the reason I won't leave you behind when I do escape him. You will come with me or we'll both stay here. There's no need to argue with me, Dulcie. My mind is made up, and you know from long experience how stubborn I can be when I've come to a decision," Star said, and smiled affectionately at her friend.

Dulcie released a long, resigned breath and shook her head. "Missy, I've knowed you since we were wearing nappies, but that still don' change anything. Your stubbornness could get you killed.''

"If Fiona does as she has promised, we'll have nothing to worry about.''

Again Dulcie shook her head. "That woman won' do nothing unless it's to her advantage.''

"That's exactly what I'm depending upon. Fiona doesn't want my marriage to Brett any more than I do. She's afraid that once we're married he will have nothing more to do with her and because of that she's willing to help us.''

"I still don' like it, Missy. That woman is rotten to the core.''

"I agree, but she's our only means of getting away. There is no other way. You're locked away up here, and I'm held prisoner in my room, and without her assistance we have no hope of outwitting Brett.''

"I only hope you don't pay with your life for trusting that viper.''

"I'm willing to risk anything to escape Brett Tremayne, Dulcie, even my life.''

"Since your mind is set, I guess there ain' no use in arguin'. I've always been at your side when you was up to mischief and I'll be with you this time.''

Star moved to her friend's side and hugged her. "Dulcie, I love you,'' she said, and laughed with relief. Had Dulcie refused to come with her, Star would have had no choice but to abandon her plan. Otherwise it would have cost her friend's life. Now her only worry was Fiona's capriciousness.

With her elbows resting on her knees and chin braced upon her hands, Star sat on the foot of her bed. The sapphire depths of her eyes flashed with loathing as she stared at the ivory satin symbol of her wedding the next day. The beautiful creation represented everything she despised and she longed to take a razor to the shimmering fabric and slash it to ribbons. She needed to vent all her pent-up frustrations and her mounting anxieties, but she knew it would serve no positive purpose to destroy the wedding gown. If Fiona did not come to her rescue within the next few hours, she would need the gown for the mockery that was to take place at noon the following day.

The sound of a lock clicking drew Star away from her depressing thoughts and she looked up to see her step-mother quietly open the balcony doors and motion to her impatiently.

"We haven't much time. Brett has ridden into Planter's Landing to gamble with some of the local planters. We have to get you away before he returns," Fiona whispered, warily glancing behind her on the dark balcony.

Star came to her feet in an instant. "Have you freed Dulcie?"

Fiona's face tighted with irritation. "I haven't had time to even think of your maid. I've been at my wits' end trying to find a way to free you. I would have been here much sooner if Brett hadn't stayed constantly at my side during the last two days. Until tonight I had begun to think that he suspected I planned to help you. Now we must go."

"I won't leave without Dulcie. That was part of our agreement, Fiona. If you want me to sign Jasmine Hall over to you, you'll have to help her as well."

"Damn you, Star. If so much wasn't at stake, I'd let you rot in here."

"That's your choice, Fiona, but I will not go anywhere without Dulcie. Brett would kill her when he found me gone."

Fiona's face flushed an angry red. "All right, damn you. We'll try to reach your precious maid, but I'm warning you, Star, I'll kill her myself if you give me any more trouble. I've already risked too much to help you."

"You'll gain more than you've risked, Fiona. Remember you'll get Jasmine Hall and Brett once I'm free," Star said. Stepping past her stepmother onto the balcony, she moved along it toward the french doors that led into the master bedchamber. She paused at the threshold and glanced at the nervous Fiona. "Do you have the keys for the attic?"

Without a word, Fiona handed her the ring of keys.

"Good," Star said, clasping them tightly. "You keep watch here while I go and release Dulcie. It will be much quicker if I go alone."

"For the love of God, do hurry, Star. If Brett should return and learn of our intentions, he'll kill all of us," Fiona said as she glanced anxiously about them.

Star moved swiftly through the bedchamber where she had been born eighteen years earlier and eased open the door to peer into the hallway beyond. Seeing no one, she slipped quietly from the room and sped toward the flight of stairs that led to the attic. Her slippered feet made no sound on the thick carpet, yet her breathing seemed loud in her ears as she took the steps two at time. The tension building within her seemed to magnify the grating of the key in the lock as she twisted it and swung the attic door open. She peered into the darkness, searching for her friend, "Dulcie," she whispered. "We've little time. Are you ready?"

Dulcie stepped out of the shadows into the pool of light that spilled through the doorway from the small sconce at the top of the stair landing. "I'm ready, Missy."

"Then we must hurry before Brett returns from Planter's Landing." Star carefully relocked the attic door. She hoped that would prevent anyone learning of Dulcie's absence before morning. They needed time to make good their escape and if the alarm was raised too soon, they would not succeed. Placing a supportive arm about Dulcie's waist, Star helped her down the narrow flight of steps and along the hallway to the master bedchamber. She breathed a sigh of relief once she closed the door behind them.

"Fiona?" she called in a loud whisper, but received no answer. A prickle of apprehension tingled its way along her spine as she helped Dulcie toward the french doors that still stood ajar. "Fiona?" she said again, but once more received no answer from her stepmother. "Damn that woman. Where has she gone?" Star muttered, her voice strained.

"Star, I'm here," Fiona said quietly as she stepped out through the french doors that led into Star's bedchamber.

"Missy, something ain' right. I can feel it," Dulcie warned as they moved toward Fiona.

"Everything will be fine," Star reassured her friend, though she, too, had a similar premonition. She forced herself to ignore it as they hurried toward her stepmother, anxious to be away from Jasmine Hall.

"Why in the devil didn't you stay to keep watch?" Star demanded when they reached Fiona's side.

"Star, I—" Fiona began, her eyes wide in her pale face. She glanced fearfully back into the bedchamber behind her.

Star followed her frightened gaze and the blood slowly drained from her face. Inside the doorway stood Brett with pistol in hand, the menacing-looking barrel aimed directly at her.

"The game is over, Star, and I've won." Brett spoke softly, yet each word was laced with venom. "Did you really believe I was so naive as to think that you wouldn't attempt to escape me?" Brett motioned the three women into the room with his pistol. "If you truly thought that, then you should not have made your plans where Zebulon could hear them." A predatory smile touched his lips as he glanced toward the tall black man standing by the door. "Zebulon has served me well and will be justly rewarded."

Star felt like the world's greatest fool. She had been so careful to plan everything down to the last detail, but her scheme had failed because of one thoughtless moment when she had forgotten to close a door. That minuscule detail might well cost them their lives.

Brett's cold gaze came back to rest on the women, centering intently upon Fiona. "My dear Fiona, your duplicity will also be rewarded," he said, a diabolical light glowing in the depths of his pale eyes. A cruel little smile tugged up the corners of his mouth as his gaze shifted once more to Zebulon and then back to his lover, who stood trembling in fright. "I've decided that since you're always so hot to have a man in your bed, I think Zebulon will fill that position nicely. He was hated and feared by the other slaves at the plantation where I found him because of his perverted tastes."

"You can't mean that, Brett," Fiona gasped as she took a step backwards, her hand spreading protectively over the bare flesh exposed by the low neckline of her gown. "I won't let you do this to me."

Brett glared at her malevolently through narrowed eyes. "I meant every word I said and you have no choice in the matter, my dear. One man is as good as another to you and if you're worried about the color of his skin, all you have to do is to blow out the lamp." Brett chuckled at his own evil humor. "However, don't become too attached to him. I've promised him his freedom for his loyalty."

"My God," Fiona breathed as she sagged to her knees at his feet. Pleadingly she looked up at him. "Brett, you can't do this to me. I love you and you love me." She held up her hand, beseeching his beneficence.

"Get away from me, bitch. I've never loved you. I only needed you to get close to Star so I could get my hands on Jasmine Hall."

"I don't believe you. You're only angry with me for trying to rid myself of my rival. We've shared too much for it to all have been lies."

"If you don't believe me, look at your stepdaughter. Do you think any man in his right mind would choose an old crow like you over this young, beautiful raven? Accept the fact, Fiona, and go with Zebulon. He can keep you warm enough."

Tears streamed down Fiona's face and she shook her head. "No, no," she cried frantically, scooting backward across the carpeted floor as the tall black man came forward and gripped her arm.

"Let her go," Star demanded, forgetting in her shock that Brett still held the pistol trained on her. She ran forward and grabbed Zebulon's sleeve in an effort to stop him.

To a man of Zebulon's strength and size, she was little more than a hummingbird tackling a hawk. He shoved her aside easily and then dragged Fiona to her feet. Star's stepmother swayed unsteadily for a moment and then her eyes rolled up in her head and she fainted into the tall black man's arms. He lifted her and started toward the door.

"Stop!" Star squealed, and made for him, but Brett's hand brought her to an abrupt halt. His fingers bit into her flesh with bruising pressure and she flinched under the pain but did not cry out as he jerked her about to face him.

"Stay out of this, Star. Fiona is only getting what she deserves for betraying me. As you will recall, I also owe you for deceiving me on the eve of our wedding."

"You've gone completely mad," Star gasped, straining away from him. She winced with renewed agony as his hand tightened cruelly on her arm and drew her against his hard body.

"My dear, sweet Star. You will learn that I don't have to be a madman to reward those who are loyal to me and to punish those who try to trick me." He thrust Star abruptly away from him and she stumbled backwards onto the bed. His gaze raked scathingly over her before he turned his attention to Dulcie, who cowered by the french doors, her ebony eyes wide, glistening pools of fright.

"We made a bargain, Star, and you have forfeited your maid's life by reneging on your part of the deal." He spoke calmly as he raised the pistol and aimed at Dulcie.

"No!" Star screamed in terror as she bolted from the bed and knocked Brett's arm to throw off his aim. The pistol exploded, the bullet shattering the wall plaster near Dulcie's head.

"Run, Dulcie," Star cried as she wrestled with Brett in an attempt to thwart him from firing again. From the corner of her eye she saw the maid dash through the french doors and into the night, but she did not cease her struggles. She knew now that her own life was in jeopardy. With Dulcie free, Brett would have to kill her to keep her silent about his crimes. Star fought with all of her strength, but she was no match for her much larger foe. He drew back his fist and clipped her soundly on the tip of the chin.

Her head jerked back from the blow. Blinding flashes of light exploded in her brain, disorienting her and she tasted her blood where her teeth had cut her lip on impact. She swayed and then slumped to her knees on the carpet at Brett's feet. A moan of pain escaped her lips and she doubled over as her stomach reacted to the excruciating agony. Her insides heaved with nausea and bile rose in her throat to choke her.

"You little bitch," Brett snarled as he knelt at her side and rolled her roughly onto her back. He grabbed the front of her gown and with one wrenching jerk, he bared her breasts to his burning gaze. "You're going to pay dearly for all of the trouble you've caused me."

"No!" Star mumbled. She flailed at him and tried to squirm away, but he thwarted her easily. He grabbed her hands and forced them over her head as he glared down at her, an insane light glowing in his eyes.

"If you keep fighting me, you're going to end up like Fiona. I'm sure Zebulon would enjoy your young body when he's finished with that whore. However, if you'll give yourself to me as freely as you did to that Texan, I might go easy on you."

"You can go to hell," Star muttered through her swelling lips, renewing her struggles. She knew Brett intended to kill her regardless and she'd be damned if she would soil herself and what she had shared with Kyle by giving herself to him freely. He had the strength to force her to his will but she would fight until her death to prevent it.

"Ah, Star. The game has been interesting, but now it's time to end it. I've waited too long to have you." Brett said, and chuckled at her futile efforts to free herself. He straddled her, pinning her legs to the floor with his weight. He held her wrists in one hand while he used his free hand to stroke the slender line of her throat down to the creamy, rose-tipped mounds. He tweaked one nipple and chuckled again as she flinched in pain.

"That, my dear, is only a sample of what I intend to do to you. When I'm through with you, you'll be groveling at my feet, pleading for mercy. I've learned all sorts of delicious little tortures in the whorehouses in New Orleans. And I intend to teach you every one. You'll soon learn that pain is pleasure and pleasure is pain," Brett murmured huskily as he covered her breast with his hand and squeezed.

Star cried out, unable to bear the fiery tentacles of agony that shot through her. She thrashed but could not budge his weight. Tears of pain, humiliation, and anger trailed down her cheeks as she gasped in a ragged breath, and drawing from the depths of her courage, she spat in his face.

Cold fury hardened Brett's face into a demonic mask as he grabbed her about the throat. His pale eyes were wild as he glared down at her, his mouth contorted in a snarl of rage. "You should not have done that, Star," he growled menacingly as his fingers tightened slowly about her throat.

Star gasped for breath and felt her blood begin to pound in her temples under Brett's stranglehold. At that moment she accepted her death. Fate had decreed it long ago, but she had managed to delay the inevitable through a cholera epidemic, Indian raid, and near drowning. Now fate had grown tired of waiting for its due and Brett Tremayne would be its instrument by killing her.

Dark shadows danced before her eyes as she slowly felt her body giving up life. Her limbs twitched convulsively as she began to slip over the precipice where darkness reined. Her only regret as she floated near the edge of the black void was that she would never see Kyle again.

A high-pitched curse pierced her semiconscious state and she recognized Fiona's voice screaming, "You bastard!'' Star felt the constricting fingers about her throat grow limp and fall away before a rush of life-giving air swept into her lungs. It was crushed from her as a heavy weight descended upon her chest. She arched upward, her body instinctively fighting for life. She clawed for air, flailing with her arms at the imprisoning form that lay over her. Dragging several deep breaths into her raw throat, she managed to focus her gaze enough to see Fiona standing over her with a pair of dripping scarlet seamstress scissors in her hand.

Star felt a scream build in her throat, but no sound issued past her lips as she twisted and squirmed out from beneath Brett's lifeless body. Her eyes were wild with horror and her breasts heaved with the exertion as she scooted across the floor to the edge of the bed. Pressing her back against it, she trembled as she gazed up at her stepmother.

Fiona stood, blood-splattered, her hair a mass of tangles, her face bruised and battered as she stared blankly down at Brett and wiped the bloody scissors against the skirt of her gown. Her vacant expression chilled Star to the bone as she knelt and tenderly ran her fingers through Brett's blond hair.

''Fiona,'' Star managed to croak, but regretted it a moment later as her stepmother raised her eyes to her. The vacant look was replaced by a savage expression.

''You killed him, Star. You killed the only man I've ever loved,'' Fiona said, her voice dangerously low, her eyes glittering with madness.

''No,'' Star gasped, the word torn from her bruised throat.

''Yes, you killed him. You made him send me with Zebulon so you could have him all to yourself. But you didn't expect me to defend my honor, did you? Zebulon will not obey any more of your orders. I saw to that,'' Fiona said, and lifted the bloody scissors. She smiled at Star. ''Now, you're going to pay for all you've done.'' Her voice had a singsong lilt to it as she spoke.

Star moistened her dry, swollen lips as she realized

that her stepmother's mind had snapped under the pressure of Brett's cruelty. Frantically she scanned the room for a weapon to use to protect herself against the madwoman. Her gaze came to rest on the pistol that Brett had laid aside when he attacked her. Drawing in a deep breath, she lunged across the floor, her fingers reaching for the gun, but Fiona reacted more swiftly, grabbing the pistol out of her grasp before her hand could close about it.

Fiona smiled malevolently at her as she raised the pistol and aimed it at Star. "You're a clever little bitch, but you can't outwit me as you did Brett. I'm not susceptible to your charms. Get to your feet and move slowly across the room," she ordered as she, too, came to her feet and motioned with the pistol in the direction of the wardrobe. "You wanted to take everything from me and now I'm determined to see that you have it all."

Star regarded her stepmother warily as she moved in the direction she pointed. "Fiona, you can have it all. I don't want Jasmine Hall."

The sound of Fiona's high-pitched, insane laughter filled the room. She shook her head, her tangled mass of hair swaying wildly about her shoulders. "There's no use trying to trick me with your lies. I'm no fool. I know exactly what you've wanted all the time."

When Star reached the wardrobe, Fiona continued, "Now take out your wedding gown and put it on. I want you dressed to perfection when you go into Brett's arms."

"You have to believe me, Fiona. I'll sign Jasmine Hall over to you as we agreed."

Fiona's lower lip trembled and her eyes grew glassy. "I've no need for this blasted place now. When you're dead I intend to burn it to the ground. I've never found anything here but misery."

She wiped her face with the back of her hand as she eyed Star venomously. A semblance of a smile touched her lips as she continued. "I've decided you're going to get a taste of the hell you've put me through with all of

your scheming to take Brett away from me. Now get out
of that gown.''

Unnerved by her stepmother's demented state and not
wanting to push her too far, Star obeyed. She let her torn
garments fall to the floor at her feet and slipped on the
ivory satin gown. Her hands trembled violently, making
it impossible for her to fasten the tiny row of pearl buttons down the front.

"Leave it like that," Fiona ordered. "A whore should
show her wares."

"Fiona, please, you've no need to threaten me with
the gun. I'll do as you ask," Star cajoled in an effort to
appease her.

"You can't talk your way out of this, Star," Fiona
said, cocking the pistol. "Now, I want you to walk slowly
to the door and down the hall to the stairs that lead to
the attic. If you make one rash move I promise to put a
bullet in your back. Is that understood?"

Star nodded as Fiona bent and retrieved the ring of
keys from the floor where Star had dropped them earlier.

"All right, move," she ordered, and followed close
upon Star's heels as they left her bedchamber and walked
down the hall. At the narrow flight of steps, Star paused,
but the pressure of the gun barrel at the small of her back
urged her upward. When they reached the attic, Fiona
unlocked the door and pushed Star inside. She slammed
and locked the door behind her.

Star spun around and banged on the closed portal.
"Fiona, let me out! I'll do anything you want. I promise
I won't tell anyone you killed Brett."

"You lying little bitch," came Fiona's muffled reply
through the door. "I didn't kill him, you did. You're the
reason he's dead. I may have put the scissors between his
ribs, but you're the one who's responsible for his death.
You enticed him away from me. Your lies turned him
against me—the woman who loved him more than life
itself. Now I intend to see you pay for your evil ways.
You're going to feel the flames of hell even before you
die.''

''Fiona, for the love of God, you can't mean this. Please let me out,'' Star pleaded, but the only answer she received was the sound of her stepmother's mad laughter.

A chill of terror raced down Star's spine. Fiona intended to set the house on fire and let her burn to death. Star pressed her forehead against the door and rolled it back and forth as she prayed, ''Dear God, please let me die before the flames reach me.''

Heavy beard shadowed the faces of the two men who led their horses down the ramp and off the barge when it docked at Planter's Landing. They had wasted no time on such niceties as shaving. Their mission was too urgent. They had ridden hard, eaten in the saddle, and slept little during the past anxious days.

Clarice looked little better than Kyle and Buck. Her hair was matted with sweat and dust from the trail and her face was haggard with fatigue, yet she did not complain about the hard pace Kyle had set for them since they'd left the ranch. Fear for Star's safety had driven them across the hundreds of miles that separated Texas from Mississippi. It had given them the strength to endure the hardship of traveling nearly nonstop, slowing their pace only when it was necessary to give their horses time to rest. Their gaunt faces reflected the strain they were under as they climbed back into their saddles and rode toward Jasmine Hall.

They were all too tired to carry on any conversation. The only sounds to disturb the stillness of the night were the clippity-clops of the horses' hooves and the lonely cry of an owl searching for his evening meal. Kyle's mount suddenly snorted and shook its head, alerting him to the lone figure running down the road toward them. He reined Lightning to a halt and waited till the young black woman reached them.

''Please, oh, please, you gotta help my mistress,'' she cried as she grabbed Lightning's bridle, swaying with exhaustion. "He be going to kill her for sure if you don't help."

A prickle of apprehension tingled its way up Kyle's spine as he bent forward and clasped her firmly by the arm. "Who is your mistress and who is going to harm her?"

"It's Miss Star. He'll kill her if you don' help."

Star's name had barely passed the maid's lips before Kyle had released her and kicked his mount in the side, sending the stallion galloping at full speed down the sandy road. Buck lifted Dulcie up in front of him and then he and Clarice followed in hot pursuit. As they neared Jasmine Hall the smell of smoke permeated the air and a bright orange glow showed through the trees.

"My God! The house is on fire," Clarice screamed as they raced up the winding drive in Kyle's wake.

He was already on the ground, running toward the burning mansion, before Lightning came to a complete halt. Flames licked the interior walls, shattering the glass with their heat as they devoured everything within their path. Suffocating plumes of smoke seeped from beneath the double doors of Jasmine Hall as Kyle kicked at them and found to his horror that they would not budge. Frantically, he sought another entrance, but every portal and window on the first floor was engulfed in flames. A piercing scream rent the air, chilling him to the bone as he ran from the veranda to see Clarice staring in horror.

"Kyle," she cried, her voice filled with terror as she pointed to one of the small attic windows. They could see Star beating wildly against the panes.

"Is there another way in?" Kyle asked, his eyes scanning every inch of the mansion.

"There are steps that lead up to the balcony from the garden," Clarice said. The words had barely passed her lips before Kyle was running in the direction she had indicated. Clarice and Buck followed quickly upon his heels and stood anxiously waiting as he bolted up the winding steps, taking them two at a time, and entered the house through the french doors that led into Star's bedchamber. Their faces were pinched with worry as they held each other, sharing their anxiety over the fate of the two young people they loved so deeply.

"He'll get her out, Clarice," Buck murmured against her salt-and-pepper gray hair. He spoke to reassure her as well as himself as he watched his son dash into the blazing inferno.

The cloud of smoke was blinding as Kyle entered the bedroom and nearly stumbled over Brett's body. With his entire being focused on reaching the woman he loved, he paid no heed to the lifeless form.

Another scream rent the air and he instinctively followed the sound into the hallway and along it to the steps that led up to the attic. He took the first stair, but a soft feminine voice behind him caused him to pause.

"I wouldn't go any farther if I were you."

Kyle swung about and came face-to-face with Fiona Grayson. She stood smut-blackened, with pistol in hand and aimed directly at his chest.

"Woman, I don't know who in hell you are, but you'll have to use that gun if you think to stop me from reaching Star."

Fiona's mad laughter rose above the sound of the flames in the foyer below. "I intend to do exactly that. I won't let you save that hussy. She's going to die for what she's done to Brett."

Life on the frontier had honed Kyle's reflexes to a keen edge. They were finely tuned when faced with danger and he reacted instinctively as Fiona pulled the trigger. He jumped to one side, managing only to avoid the full impact of the bullet. It grazed his arm before lodging itself into the wall at his side. Heedless of his pain and knowing he had no time to waste if he was to save Star from being burned alive, he launched himself at Fiona, knocking her backwards before she had time to pull the trigger again. The gun flew from her hand and slid to the edge of the landing.

Maddened beyond reason, Fiona gave a wild cry and broke away from him. With her demented mind intent only upon her revenge, she ran to retrieve the weapon. Her legs became entangled in her skirts, overbalancing her as she frantically reached for the gun and she tumbled down the stairs into the inferno below. One agonized scream rose and then all was silent except for the popping and cracking of the fire that was consuming Jasmine Hall.

Knowing there was no help for the poor madwoman, Kyle spared no further thought to her as he bolted up the steps to the attic. His lungs burned and he coughed from the blue haze that filled the air. Bracing his hands against the door frame for leverage, he put all of his power into the kick that shattered the lock and splintered the door, sending it crashing back against the wall.

"Star," Kyle called, but received no answer. Terror ran rampant through him as he began his frantic search of the smoke-filled room. His eyes watered and each breath he took was agony. Fear made his heart thump against his ribs when he found her slumped near the windows.

"God let her be alive," he prayed as he lifted her limp body into his arms and made his way back down the stairs through the smothering haze. Hungry flames ate at the hall carpet and walls. The floorboards were hot underfoot as he paused to ascertain the safest route of escape. The fire licked out of the doorways along the corridor leading back toward Star's room. Feeling as if his lungs would burst, Kyle at last spied a small space between the flames in the entrance to the master bedchamber. He dashed toward it and was relieved to find that the room had not yet been consumed. Without hesitating, he carried Star through the chamber and out onto the balcony. One swift glance in the direction of the stairs leading to the garden told him that avenue of escape was already blocked by the fire. Fiery tentacles leapt through the windows and doors of the ground floor as he peered into the garden below, seeking a means to safety.

Buck saw him first and rushed forward. "Let her down to me. I'll catch her," he shouted over the roar of the flames.

Knowing that he had no other choice, Kyle eased Star over the wrought-iron railing. The balcony trembled as the supports beneath it were eaten away. He brushed his lips against her soot-blackened brow and murmured, "I love you," before he released her.

Buck caught Star easily, but her weight made him stagger backwards to land with a thump upon the grass. Clarice hurried to his aid and together they carried Star a safe distance from the burning house.

Seeing that she was safe, Kyle made to swing himself down from the balcony, but as he put his weight on the railing, the structure squealed in protest and began to collapse beneath him. He dove through the air and landed with a crash into the tall hedge below before tumbling to the ground, scratched and bruised, and bleeding from the bullet wound in his arm. His eyes burned and his lungs ached as he pushed himself to his feet and staggered away from Jasmine Hall. He collapsed beside Star, coughing and gagging as he drew in deep breaths of cleansing air. "Is she—" he began, but could not finish the question.

Clarice smiled and patted him on the shoulder, "You reached her in time."

"She'll be fine once she regains consciousness, son," Buck said, placing a wide, comforting hand on Kyle's shoulder.

Tears brimmed in Kyle's smoke-reddened eyes as he placed his hand over his father's and looked up at him. "Thank you," he murmured before another bout of coughing overtook him. The two words seemed meager in proportion to everything his father had done for him during the last days but he knew that Buck understood them. With those two words, he had laid the past to rest. Buck had come to his aid at a time when Kyle needed him more than he had ever needed him in the past. Buck had stood by his side during the worst trial his son had faced in his entire life.

Star coughed and stirred. She began to beat the air wildly with her arms before she bolted upright with a cry that resembled a frog's croak. Slowly she became aware of the three people who knelt on the ground around her, their faces taut with concern. As her gaze cleared, she peered up at Kyle, an incredulous look crossing her soot-smudged features.

"Kyle?" she asked hoarsely, unable to believe what she saw.

"Yes, my darling, I'm here," Kyle murmured tenderly as he placed his hand against her cheek and caressed it lovingly.

Still dazed, she glanced up at Clarice and Buck. "When I saw you riding up the drive, I thought you were only an illusion created by my imagination because I wanted to see you again before I died." Star's eyes widened with the memory of her ordeal and she jerked about to see the once-beautiful mansion engulfed completely in fire. She made to rise, but Kyle held her back.

"No, Star. Jasmine Hall is gone. There is nothing you can do for it or anyone left inside."

"Fiona?" Star questioned.

"She died in the fire."

"The poor madwoman," Star murmured as she gripped his arm about her waist. A loud crack drew her gaze back to what had once been her home. A wave of anguish washed over her. She could not tear her eyes away from the blue and orange flames shooting toward the sky. She felt as if she was losing her father again. A part of him had remained with her as long as Jasmine Hall existed and now in a shower of smoke, cinders, and ash, he was being ripped away from her once more. The flames were devouring much more than a wooden structure. They were destroying the heritage left her by her father and the generations before him.

Clarice sensed her niece's feelings. She too was experiencing a great sense of loss. She had not lived at Jasmine Hall for over twenty years, yet it also represented the lives of her ancestors who had worked and fought to claim this land. Her throat clogged with emotion as the roof gave way, sending glowing sparks toward heaven as if in some pagan offering to appease the angry gods.

"My home," Star cried as the walls collapsed inward.

Hearing the anguish in her voice, Kyle came to his feet and lifted her into his arms. "You've seen enough. Jasmine Hall and the past are gone. We're going home," he said. His voice was filled with determination as he held her close to his heart.

"Jasmine Hall is my home," Star murmured as tears welled in her eyes and ran down her cheeks.

"Jasmine Hall *was* your home. Your home is with me now. I intend to take you back to the ranch and never let you out of my sight again. And I'll hear no arguments on the subject. I've gone through hell to get you back and I'd fight the devil himself if he tries to stop me from keeping you."

Star glanced over Kyle's shoulder at the flames. He *had* gone through hell to reach her. Resolutely she turned her back on the scene. This place was of the past. Her future now rested with Kyle. Together they would build a new life and heritage for their children in the wilds of the Texas frontier. She could now understand why Jake and Priscilla had risked their lives for such a dream. It wasn't what someone else had done in the past that counted in life but what *you* did. Heritage and ancestry were fine to look back upon, but it was the future and your own achievements that mattered. And the most important thing was the love you shared with another whose dreams were the same as yours. That person in her life was Kyle Hunter.

Her arms tightened about Kyle's neck as she hugged him close and smiled. "You'll get no arguments from me."

"Good, I like my women meek and agreeable." He grinned down at her, his white teeth flashing in his soot-blackened face.

Star's eyes widened and her spirit returned in full force. "You arrogant, conceited, jack—" Kyle silenced her with a kiss that left them both breathless.

"I said I liked women who were meek and agreeable, but I love a certain little hellcat beyond life itself." Kyle crushed her to him, thinking how close he had come to losing her.

"And I love a certain arrogant, stubborn, hot-headed Texan," Star said, and smiled up at him.

"Star, I hope you mean me. I'd hate to have to go gunning after another man. I'd prefer to find a preacher so we can begin our honeymoon like Buck and Clarice."

Kyle grinned at her surprised expression. He glanced back to where his father and Clarice stood arm and arm. "They were married in DryCreek, but I certainly don't intend to wait till we get back there for us to tie the knot."

Elated by the news, Star placed a kiss on his bearded cheek and then whispered in his ear, "The minister in Planter's Landing will do nicely, I think."

Kyle's teeth flashed whitely again as he threw back his head and laughed. "I think he will at that, and as soon as possible." He went up to his father and stepmother. "You're invited to a wedding as soon as we can get into town," he said, and strode toward his mount.

Buck draped a strong arm over Clarice's shoulders and grinned down at her. "It's about time them two tied the knot. Since we're now respectable old married people, we can't have any shenanigans going on unless they're all legal like ours." He chuckled.

"You rogue." Clarice laughed as she put her arm about his lean waist. "To keep the peace, I hope the minister in Planter's Landing will perform the ceremony on such short notice. I'd hate to see the fight that would take place when you tried to act the proper guardian for my niece. I suspect that Kyle and Star would be too much for you to handle."

"I hadn't thought of that," Buck said as he screwed up his face thoughtfully. "I guess I'd better let Kyle handle his own affairs and tend to my own. As I recall I'm due one honeymoon myself." He winked at Clarice, who smiled happily back at him.

Star went to the young black woman who stood silently watching them. She hugged her and smiled warmly. "You're part of our family, Dulcie, and we'd like for you to come with us back to the Bar H. Will you come?"

Tears came into Dulcie's eyes as she hugged her friend in return. She nodded. "I'd be pleased to come."

"Then it's settled." Star laughed. "We're going to have a wedding and then we're all going home."

ABOUT THE AUTHOR

Cordia Byers was born in the small north Georgia community of Jasper and lives there still, with her husband, James, and their two children, Michelle and Michael. Cordia likes to think of her husband as being like one of the heroes in her novels. James swept her off her feet after their first meeting, and they were married three weeks later.

From the age of six, Cordia's creative talents had been directed toward painting. It was not until late 1975, when the ending of a book displeased her, that she considered writing. That led to her first novel, HEATHER, which was followed by CALLISTA, NICOLE LA BELLE, SILK AND STEEL, LOVE STORM, PIRATE ROYALE (Winner of a *Romantic Times* Reviewer's Choice Award), and STAR OF THE WEST. Finding more satisfaction in the world of her romantic novels, Cordia has given up painting and now devotes herself to writing, researching her material at the local library, and then doing the major part of her work from 11:30 P.M. to 3:00 A.M.

Cordia enjoys hearing from her readers. Her address is Route 1, Box 63E, Jasper, GA 30143.